PAW

THIS SPELL WAS not only the most intricate that Gavalon had ever attempted, but the most intricate that any sorcerer had attempted since humans first arrived on the world that the Imperium's star-maps had called Sigmatus.

The beastmen took their places. Gavalon held a dagger with a wavy blade in his right hand and a lighted torch in his left, both of which would have to be introduced to his flesh at the appointed moments. He was no stranger to constructive self-mutilation, and it would not be the first time that he had put out an eye or cut off a designated appendage.

When the appropriate points of the ritual arrived, therefore, Gavalon the Great did not hesitate or tremble. Nor did he begrudge the god he was proud to serve the last and least of the many sacrifices he had offered in pursuit of this particular end.

Oh to be a Lord of Change! he thought. *Oh to be a master of metamorphosis, defiant of common decay! What bliss it is to serve the true god, and to be free!*

A WARHAMMER 40,000 NOVEL

PAWNS OF CHAOS

Brian Craig

A BLACK LIBRARY PUBLICATION

First published in Great Britain in 2001 by
Games Workshop Publishing
Willow Road, Lenton,
Nottingham, NG7 2WS, UK

10 9 8 7 6 5 4 3 2 1

Cover illustration by Adrian Smith

A CIP record for this book
is available from the British Library

ISBN 1 84154 141 9

Set in ITC Giovanni

Printed and bound in Great Britain by
Omnia Books Ltd., Glasgow, UK

See the Black Library on the Internet at
www.blacklibrary.co.uk

Find out more about Games Workshop
and the world of Warhammer 40,000 at
www.games-workshop.com

PROLOGUE

IT WAS NOT until he saw the wall dissolve that Zarcon realised how stupid he had been to imagine that men like him could possibly make a stand against the invaders. The man to his left was blown apart by a shot that went clean through the stones, and then through him. The billowing grey dust seemed, absurdly, to be mopping up the blood and shredded flesh in mid-air.

The man to his right died barely a second later, having raised his head above the parapet to measure his throw. A searing flash of light drilled a hole through his right eye a moment before bits of his brain sprayed through an improbably neat exit-wound above the nape of his neck. The snapping sound which might or might not have been the discharge of the weapon responsible had arrived a split second later. By then the dead body had already begun to fall back, its lifeless limbs crumpling.

The firepot which the defender had been intending to hurl down at the enemy truck went the wrong way, but the arm holding it had lost its strength so abruptly that the primitive bomb dropped to the sandy ground with a dull thud. The stone jar cracked. The wick set fire to the oil that leaked out. It looked more like a broken lamp than a weapon of war.

That's all we are! Zarcon thought, his mind in a panicked whirl. *Not fighting men – just pathetic broken lamps, matching our light against the blaze of the noonday sun.*

The ugly cloud that had been blasted out of the first dying man's shattered body stretched as far as a dozen feet behind him before beginning to settle and dissipate. Zarcon could make out two severed legs, and an unsightly lump that might once have been a head, but the arms had been catapulted out of sight, while the torso and abdomen had both been ripped into ridiculously tiny shreds.

The men further away to Zarcon's left and right were faring no better. Those who had not been blasted apart by bolters or holed by lasguns were in the process of being crushed and maimed by falling stones. Some of them were screaming, but not many. No one was running away. It had all happened too fast.

Zarcon realised, far too late, that the only reason he was still standing, still able to see what was happening to either side of him for a few moments longer, was that a section of wall in front of him, no more than four or five feet wide, had been haphazardly spared by the first careless sweep of the heavy bolter.

He knew that the respite was momentary, and that the second sweep would slash him down as easily as the first had cut down his companions.

He had never, even in his wildest nightmares, imagined such destructive force. He had been told that there were such things as bolters and lasguns – and he had been told what they could do – but his imagination had been unable to turn the words into accurate images.

He knew now how foolish he had been to think of the wall as a real defence. It had seemed a protected vantage point, from which he and his fellows could rain down missiles upon the invaders' vehicles, but it was not. There was not a wall in Gulzacandra that could provide adequate cover against massed Imperial firepower.

This was not a skirmish; it was a massacre. If it were to be conducted on these terms, the defence of Gulzacandra would not be a war but a mere folly: an endless series of savage sacrifices offered to the hungry war-machines of Kalazendra.

Zarcon had known all along, of course, that the missiles the defenders possessed – arrows, rocks, javelins and firepots – were pitiful by comparison with the guns the enemy possessed. While the enemy were numbered in their thousands, though – tens of thousands at the most – and the defenders of Gulzacandra in their hundreds of thousands, he had clung naively to the opinion that no matter how many battles the defenders lost, the invaders could not possibly win the war.

Now he knew different.

He had been told that the invaders had only a few bolters, and only a few lasguns, and that the vast majority of their troops would be armed with cruder weapons churned out by the factories of Kalazendra. But he knew now that even a handful of bolters and lasguns would be more than enough to take the invaders into the deepest heart of Gulzacandra.

Once they had taken the city of Rintrah and the port of Chemosh, it would be impossible to be rid of them. Even if they exhausted every last bolt shell and every last power pack in attaining that primary objective, they would be impossible to dislodge once they had the heartland. What could possibly stop them? Not men like him, that was certain. Not even magic, of any kind to which he had ever been a witness.

Determined to make one last effort before he fell, Zarcon hurled his own javelin with all his strength – but even though he knew that he would die within seconds, he could not quite bring himself to expose his head long enough to take proper aim. He heard the head of the javelin strike solid metal, and knew that it had bounced harmlessly from the vehicle's armour.

Even if he had taken the risk of raising his head, it was unlikely in the extreme that he could have done better, but as he saw the last section of the wall implode, and knew that he was about to be torn to pieces by the blast, he cursed himself for his failure.

Once he was dead, of course, it did not matter at all what the last thought to cross his mind had been, or the last emotion to stir his heart. It would not have served Gulzacandra or Gulzacandra's god any better had he died with a prayer on his lips, or with the futile hope in his heart that the invaders' intentions were not as violent as the Wisdom of the Dreamers had prophesied.

It did not matter, as Zarcon's own severed head bounced on the ground, haloed with bloodstained dust, whether his fate were his alone or far more, a symbol of the fate of an entire continent. There was no one left to see it fall but the implacably advancing gunners, who had seen such things happen far too often to read more than the slightest significance into any single death.

Had they had a better idea of what they were, or what they were supposed to stand for, the invaders might have thought Zarcon's death even less significant still. For what could the death of one mere man on one mere world possibly mean, in the context of a battleground that extended across four hundred billion stars, and a war that might last a billion years and never be won?

ONE

DATHAN WAS SITTING under a domberry tree on Metalion Hill when he noticed the great plumes of dust way out in the Amber Waste. As soon as he saw them he knew that there was something odd about them. He had often seen riders approaching the village from that direction, usually horsemen moving in small groups at a trot or the gallop, or sedate pack-trains of camules. Twice he had seen camule-trains moving much faster, pursued by brigands, but even they had not stirred up as much dust as whatever was approaching now.

It must, he told himself uneasily, be some kind of freak wind. Perhaps it was the beginning of a violent but localised storm, or even an earthquake.

Dathan had only lived fifteen years, and had never experienced an earthquake, but he had heard of them. He had lived through a hundred dust-storms without ever seeing one like this, but he had never actually seen the start of a storm, so he could not be certain that they did not begin in this fashion.

Either way, the phenomenon was new and deserved close attention, so he stood up and stepped out of the shadow of the domberry's crown, shading his eyes against the mid-morning sun as he peered into the distance.

The Amber Waste was awkward territory for travellers. The crystalline sand-particles that rendered the land incapable of growing crops were often sharp as well as hard, and if a particularly nasty specimen became trapped between a horse's shoe and hoof it could pierce the horny part of the hoof and prick the living flesh within. The seemingly soft-footed camules, which had always lived in the wastelands rather than sharing the territories occupied by the human colonists, were better equipped by nature to resist such penetration, but even they preferred the higher and harder ground that was regularly – if rather ineptly – swept by the wind. For this reason, there were trails across the Amber Waste that every experienced traveller followed. The plumes of dust that Dathan was watching were fanned out broadly and indiscriminately, so they had to be some kind of weather formation.

Or had they?

Dathan began to feel a peculiar sick feeling deep in his stomach, and he couldn't help wondering whether it might be a kind of premonition. He had never had a premonition before – and not for want of trying – so he didn't know what they should feel like. He had often asked Hycilla, who had them all the time, but she had never been able to give him a clear answer. Hycilla had so many premonitions that Pater Saltana, the local priest, had declared her a sensitive and marked her out for early initiation into the Mysteries – but that had come as no surprise to anyone, given that her family was said to be distantly related to that of Gavalon, the most powerful coven-master in all Gulzacandra.

Dathan and Hycilla had been close friends when they were children, but that was because they had been born within days of one another. Now they were almost adults they were bound to grow apart, and would have been directed towards different goals even if Hycilla had never shown the least talent for wise-dreaming.

The ochre dust-clouds continued to rise higher and higher, billowing and spiralling in such an uncanny fashion that they seemed almost alive. Occasionally Dathan caught a glimpse of a half-formed shape suggestive of a leering face, but such semblances of order flattered only to deceive, dissolving into confusion as soon as he tried to make sense of them.

Long ago, so legend had it, the Amber Waste had been a very different place – not a desert at all but a fabulous land so full of life that the very rock had been animate. The 'amber', shards of which gave the waste its name, was said to be the remnant of some exotic life-form, half-plant and half-animal, which had dominated the landscape before the human colonists arrived. It fed on multitudinous creatures too tiny to be seen by human eyes and provided food in its turn for all kinds of exotic walkers and flyers, of which only a handful that were useful to man – including camules – had been allowed to survive. Perhaps it was true and perhaps it wasn't; there was no way to know, even though wise-dreamers sometimes claimed to have returned to that magical time while they slept, to see the world as the first humans had seen it – except, of course, that according to those same wise-dreamers, the first humans in the world were not the very first, but only new arrivals from some other world, which had in turn been seeded by humans from elsewhere.

According to the Wisdom of the Dreamers, the stars in the Great Cluster were suns, with worlds of their own. Dathan doubted this. Given that the stars moved like coloured fireflies in the night sky, how could they be suns? If they really were distant suns, similar to the great light that stood above him in the sky, why was there so much strange colour and confusion in the shades of night? The Wisdom of the Dreamers undoubtedly had much wisdom in it, but Dathan had begun to wonder of late whether his ancestors had contrived to sift out all that was merely dreaming, of the kind that anyone might do.

He had, of course, kept such thoughts entirely to himself; it was direly unwise to challenge Wisdom that even coven-masters revered.

As he realised at last what he was looking at, the hand that had been shading Dathan's eyes began to tremble. Premonition or not, the sick feeling in his stomach had been right to give him warning.

The plumes of smoke were not the result of some freakish limited storm, nor were they the produce of an earthquake. They were like any other plumes of dust, raised by the passage of travellers – but these newcomers weren't riding horses or camules. They had vehicles.

The travellers' tales that told of the wondrous vehicles of Kalazendra had never seemed to Dathan to belong to the same class as those legends which spoke of the time before there were men on this world or in these distant reaches of the Great Cluster. Tales of wondrous vehicles that could cross deserts were only a few generations old at most, and whether or not the men who had arrived on the world to fuel such stories were its second wave of invaders or its first, there was little doubt that they were invaders. These men had never crossed the Amber Waste in force before, but they were crossing it now, and one thing upon which every rumour that spoke of them agreed was that when invaders like these arrived, they would not come as traders, let alone as friends.

Dathan was terrified, but he knew that he had to fight his terror. He was fifteen years old, and the one thing that frightened him more than any other was the possibility that he might seem childish to others. He was an adult now, and he had to act and react like an adult. Yes, he could let his fear show – but only if it seemed like mature concern, born of a dutiful worry for others rather than a paralysing and crippling dread of what might happen to him. Yes, he could run, but he must not simply run away, screaming and sobbing. He must run to the village, waving his arms so that no one would know that his hands were trembling, and he must shout a warning in a voice that was clear and loud and forceful.

So he turned and ran westwards, back towards the village, waving his arms and calling the alarm in a voice that was clamorous without ever quite falling into hysteria. The fact that he was moving helped him, channelling the energy of his fear into appropriate action and away from merely childish expression.

Although travellers who were passing through it sometimes called the village Odienne, to Dathan and everyone else who lived there it was merely 'the village', just as the world was merely 'the world'. It was where he and everyone else he knew had always lived. He had expected that he always would live there, as a journeyman of some sort: a carpenter, perhaps, a roofer or even a baker. His own father was long-dead so could provide him with no craft to follow, so he had become everybody's helper and nobody's apprentice, but the village looked after its own and a firmer place would have been found for him soon enough. Now, all of a sudden, he had to face the possibility that the map of his life would have to be torn up, and that the village might be reduced to rubble before the sun set.

He was surely entitled to be terrified. Was this not the most terrifying possibility imaginable?

'The Imperium!' he cried, as he ran pell-mell down the slope towards the gap between the Negram farm and the forge. 'The Imperium is coming!'

Dathan had little idea what 'the Imperium' was, but he had been taught from infancy that the Imperium was the ultimate enemy, and that the worst thing in the world that could ever happen to his village or to the entire land of Gulzacandra was that the Imperium would come. He had been taught, too, that he would know the Imperium when it came, because the Imperial forces would come in vehicles. So large had the bugbear loomed in his imagination that he had always conceived of the vehicles in question arriving in thousands, manned by giants twice as tall as ordinary men, but the fact that they were far less in number did not matter.

Just speaking the ominous words 'the Imperium' aloud seemed to make the threat fully real, and the sound of the syllables made tears rise into Dathan's eyes.

'The Imperium!' he howled, trying with all his might to convert all of his ravening fear into furious anger. 'Imperial vehicles are coming across the wastes! They'll be here within the hour!'

His shouts provoked an instantaneous response as he ran past the forge and the blacksmith's cottage towards the thatched houses on the road to the village square. The smith must have been in the stables behind the forge, because his brazier had not been lit – nor had the fires beneath the kilns which the village wives used to harden their pots. Most of the people who came running from the smaller houses were women and children, because their menfolk were at work in the fields, but when Dathan came closer to the square, where the houses were made of wood instead of earth, with sealed log roofs, the craftsmen left their tools and followed their wives. Caborn the carpenter and Relf the baker ran past Dathan, obviously intent on making sure that what he had seen really was an Imperial force, but neither challenged him as they went. They allowed him to continue on his course, shouting his chilling warning.

Dathan knew that if anyone who heard his shouts doubted the truth of them, that doubt would not be allowed to stand in the way of quick action. The mere possibility that it was true would be enough to set all everyday matters aside. Every man who had a weapon would run to fetch it, and every man who had never had money with which to buy a machete or a craftsman's bow would go to fetch a club or a pitchfork. There was little enough money in the village – the resident craftsmen had to make almost everything that was needed by its people – but the harvest had been good enough in five out of the last eight years to allow the bigger landholders to sell their surpluses over in Mancip and Elvenor, so the village's stocks of keen blades were by no means restricted to its spades and kitchen-knives.

The Imperium, it was rumoured among menfolk whose conversations Dathan had occasionally overheard, had guns that shot forth lightning and liquid fire. It was also said, however, that the Imperial masters had sunk mines in Kalazendra and built factories there to turn out guns of much simpler design which fired metal bullets, and mechanical bows that fired darts like shortened arrows.

Every child in Gulzacandra was told that the Imperium's wheeled metal vehicles could move faster than a galloping horse, but it was also said that the Imperium was training cavalry to use lances, and conscripting sucars from the far south to turn the loxodonts they used as massive beasts of burden into living engines of war. From which it seemed to follow, so far as Dathan could deduce, that the Imperium could not have very many guns that shot forth lightning and liquid fire, nor very many wheeled vehicles, nor the means of easily making more.

In which case, Dathan had to suppose, there was a possibility that the Imperium could be fought, even with the crude kinds of weapons that hunters and farmers kept. Perhaps there was even a possibility that the Imperium might be beaten, if only there were enough hunters and farmers in Gulzacandra to force the invaders to use up their best resources and make them fall back on makeshift reinforcements.

'The Imperium!' Dathan yelled again and again, as he ran through the square into the lane between two other rows of relatively mean dwellings, heading for the huts whose inhabitants were said to keep cleaner straw for their animals than they did for themselves. Even the disreputable were entitled to be warned, and even men who were said to be too fond of the ale their wives brewed to be good labourers would fight with all the ferocity they could muster to defend their homes.

By this time, Dathan had delightedly discovered that his fear really was turning to anger, and that the excitement pumping through his blood as he ran was three parts fighting instinct and only one part impulse to keep on running. 'Take arms against the Imperium!' he cried – and others were crying the same, now that Caborn and Relf had seen what he had seen.

Alas, Dathan's instincts could not keep that brave balance once he came in sight of his own petty hovel and saw his mother hurrying to meet him. Other people called his mother Ora, but to him she was simply his mother, and in her presence no words were enough to stir aggression. In her presence, he would always be a child, even if he grew to the ripe old age of forty and she somehow clung on to life long enough to reach a venerable fifty-five.

'Dathan!' she shrieked. She had made no effort at all to hold back her tears and negotiate her terror into wrath. She did not ask him whether it was true, because she trusted him. She had heard him coming while he was still at the forge, and she was already thinking of the next move – but her mind was on flight, not fight.

'I need a blade!' Dathan shouted, but he knew as he spoke that it was useless to hope that his mother might find one for him.

'Run!' she said. 'Run to Pater Saltana. You must help him with the children. He knows where to hide them.' At least she had the sense, or the courtesy, to commission him to help with the children rather than to be one, but it was still no job for a real man.

'I must find a weapon,' he gasped, as he came panting to a halt. 'The village must be defended.'

'The men will defend what they can,' she told him. 'But what must be defended above all else is the children. That is the most important duty. Go to Pater Saltana – he too has need of men. Go!'

He had no time to answer, because Kanak the headman was now at his shoulder, demanding to know exactly what Dathan had seen. Kanak already had a blade in his hand – perhaps the only blade in the village that really qualified as a sword,

although there were a dozen men who claimed to be swords-
men and took a very generous view of the nature of their
machetes. Many villagers carried knives far bigger than was necessary for the simple task of cutting bread and meat, but
Dathan's own eating-knife was a miserable thing with a blade
no bigger than his little finger, fit only for a child.

'I saw six clearly,' Dathan said, although 'clearly' was a slight
exaggeration, 'but there must have been many others obscured
by the dust. There was so much dust there must have been at
least twenty, perhaps more than thirty. They were coming faster
than the fastest horse. An hour away, I thought – not much
more, and possibly a little less. These hills slow tired horses,
but they won't slow these things.'

Kanak didn't need to know any more, and he didn't have
time to thank Dathan for the information. He was already
turning away, shouting orders – but he did pause long enough,
after barking three or four instructions to his fellow elders, to
bark one at Dathan. 'Help Saltana!' he said. 'Get the children
into the cave!'

'I need a weapon,' Dathan said, again.

'There's none to spare,' was the headman's abrupt response.

'You heard him,' Ora said. 'Now go!'

'What about you?' Dathan protested, his voice sudden small
again.

'I have work to do,' she said.

It was something she had said a thousand times or more, but
in the past she had always meant everyday work: the work that
every village woman did as a matter of routine, over and over
and over again; the work that maintained the uniformity and
continuity of life. Today, she meant that she had to do what she
could to preserve what she could, to make provision for life
after disaster – if there were, indeed, to be life after the disaster.
Like everyone else, she had to assume that there would be –
what other assumption could she possibly act on? – but she
had to know that there might not.

Dathan ran off, towards Pater Saltana's house. The children
of the village were already running behind and ahead of him.
Like everyone else in the village, Dathan knew exactly how
many there were: twenty-seven. It was a figure that did not
include babes-in-arms, although it did include a handful who
had learned to walk so recently that they hardly knew how to

run and could not possibly keep pace with their elders. They would have to be carried, some by the eleven- and twelve-year-olds, some by men – men like Pater Saltana, and Dathan – and some by unwed women.

By the time Dathan drew up at the priest's house, Hycilla was already there, counting and organising. She didn't waste time with a greeting before thrusting a two-year-old boy into Dathan's arms. It was Houlme, Kanak's son: a responsibility and a half.

What was the point of Hycilla's supposed talent for premonition, Dathan wondered, if it couldn't give adequate warning of a life-threatening event like an Imperium attack? Where was the virtue of wise-dreaming if the Wisdom of the Dreamers could not provide for the end of the world? Where was the much-vaunted generosity of Gulzacandra's almighty god, if all the sacrifices offered to him in the past had served merely to maintain the harsh and difficult life that all villagers led, while their worst enemies lived in great cities like legendary Sostenuto, possessed of all manner of miraculous machines?

Such thoughts were, of course, treasonous and terrible, but Dathan had never been able to believe that they were unusual. Surely they were questions that every man must ask himself. Surely they were questions that many a man had even dared to voice, at one time or another, to his most trusted confidants. Papa Saltana, who was supposed to be every villager's most trusted confidant, must have heard their like a hundred times over, though not from Dathan – who had only ever voiced his more trivial doubts, and then only to Hycilla, having sworn her to a secrecy she had presumably respected.

Little Houlme began crying as Saltana led the party out of the village on the westward side. He was not alone, and all of the other sobbing children were older than he was, but Houlme was old enough to know that he was the headman's son and old enough to know the meaning of shame, and he tried so valiantly to stem his sobs that Dathan was almost ashamed to comfort him. Dathan had a vague notion that his duty was to tell the child that everything would be all right, but he had a much sharper conviction that such words would be a lie, and he did not want to be a liar, even for the sake of the headman's boy.

While they moved through the orchard towards the edge of the judeye forest, Hycilla asked him how large the Imperial force was. Dathan repeated what he had told Kanak.

'That many!' she gasped. 'That's an army!'

What she meant was that a force of twenty vehicles might be carrying as many as a hundred and fifty fighting men. The village could just about muster a hundred and thirty men, if the labourers from the outlying farms could respond to the summons in time – but any significant difference in weaponry, Dathan knew, would make a mockery of a near-equality of numbers. If the invaders had guns of any of the kinds that featured in the tales he had heard, they would not need to be giants to slaughter villagers armed with clubs and pitchforks.

'Twenty trucks isn't an army,' Pater Saltana said, glancing back over his shoulder at them. 'It's just a raiding party. A far bigger force is said to be making rapid inroads in the north, and I suspect even that's but a fraction of the whole. I fear that this is the invasion of which our wise-dreamers have been warning us for many years. If so, the great bulk of the Imperial forces will follow the shock-troops at their own pace – the pace of marching men, not even that of horses and camules. What the invaders will want to begin with is a series of beachheads and supply-points, but their ultimate aim is to destroy us all. We have to prevent them from establishing a secure base here. If Kanak can empty the granary and torch the fields…'

Dathan could complete Pater Saltana's unfinished sentence as easily as he had been able to finish Hycilla's. If Kanak could destroy the village's reserves of food, the headman could prevent the marauders from getting the supplies that they needed to feed themselves in the coming weeks and months – for they couldn't have carried very much cargo across the foodless and waterless expanse of the Amber Waste – but if Kanak succeeded in that, the invaders would make the village pay in blood.

If the villagers put their fields to the torch, the Imperium would put them to the torch – although, if what he had always been told was really true, they would do that anyway.

Pater Saltana was quoting the Wisdom of the Dreamers when he said that the ultimate aim of the invaders was to kill everyone in Gulzacandra. The Imperium, it seemed, did not like worshippers of the god of Gulzacandra, who was supposedly a deadly enemy of their own great deity, and of everything the Imperium stood for.

Dathan had not the slightest idea of what the Imperium 'stood for', or why the gods were enemies one of another, but he did understand that thieves and murderers always liked to justify their actions. He had never heard of a man who wanted to be thought of as evil, no matter how violent and destructive his actions might be. To justify their slaughter, the Imperium had to claim that the god of Gulzacandra was a bad god, utterly undeserving of their worship.

'If there's nothing left for them here,' Dathan said, grimly, 'at least they'll go away – and we'll be free to pray that they won't come back for a lifetime and more.'

'If only it were that simple,' Pater Saltana said. 'If they're crossing the Amber Waste in force as well as sending truckloads of soldiers into the northlands and the southlands, they'll need a base hereabouts. If they decide that Odienne's well-placed to serve as a way-station, they might be here for a lifetime... and more.'

'And what shall we do then?' Hycilla wanted to know. 'If any of us is still alive?'

TWO

EVEN THOUGH GAVALON'S makeshift army had barely begun to come together, let alone seen any action, the noise and the stink of the encampment were becoming unbearable. There were too many beastmen in it, and too many men who were almost as careless in their hygiene.

Had the profession of sorcery been kinder to its followers, a man like Gavalon would have been immune to all offensive odours, and if it had been kinder still the reek of beastmen might have seemed a delicate perfume, but the world was not a kind place, even to the most faithful servant of the truest god. In the end, Gavalon had to step out of his tent in search of fresher air, but he did not find it.

In order to take his mind off the noisome quality of the air, Gavalon looked up – with a great deal of pride and a little trepidation – at the banner fluttering above his multicoloured tent, which stood out bright and clear even against the cloudless violet sky. The image painted upon it was that of a huge eye rimmed in red, with a thin purple iris surrounding a huge black pupil. A cataract of white fire jetted from the centre of the pupil, extending into a beam as wide as the banner's hem.

23

The fluttering device was not magically active at present, but it was menacing even as a mere image.

The eye on the banner was the all-seeing eye, the withering eye, whose gaze could blast minds and scorch them clean of any vestige of rational thought when the banner came to life. The banner that bore such an eye was more than a weapon: it was the potent symbol of Gavalon's power and authority. It was the badge of the most powerful sorcerer in Gulzacandra, which meant the most powerful in all the world nowadays.

Gavalon was known to everyone who knew his name as Gavalon the Great, although his enemies had applied less flattering epithets to him in the days before their extermination.

Five lifetimes ago, if the intelligence of lore and legend could be trusted, the most powerful sorcerer in Gulzacandra would have been the smallest digit on a hand of five fingers, each finger symbolizing one of the five civilizations which shared the world's three continents. But four lifetimes ago the stars had slowed their ceaseless movement in the night-sky and the Imperium had fallen from the sky in a shower of slow meteors.

Within ten years, Gavalon had been told, the Imperium had taken absolute control of Kalazendra, and within a further twenty-five years three other civilizations – Zendamora, Bulzavara and Yevelkana – had become mere puppets, slaves to imported law. Only Zendamora had been joined to Kalazendra but the seas that divided the world had not been barrier enough to protect Bulzavara and Yevelkana, or the island of Melmayaka that lay half-way between the westernmost cape of Kalazendra and the easternmost extremity of Gulzacandra. Only the girth of the world, and the wastelands and high mountains that divided the landmass shared by Yevelkana and Gulzacandra, had kept Gavalon's homeland safe from invasion… until now.

Now, the time had finally come. Yevelkanan mercenaries were pouring through the coastal lands in the far west and Zendamoran warfleets supplied from Melmayaka were blockading the eastern ports, while what remained of the once all-powerful Imperial forces were striking westwards across the wastelands to drive deep into the heart of Gulzacandra.

The strategy was sound enough. For centuries before the Imperium came, if not millennia, the men of Gulzacandra had organised their defences to withstand the raids of Melmayakan pirates and Yevelkanan adventurers. The heartland, buffered by the wastelands, had never needed significant fortification. Caravans of camules could cross the wastes, and men on hardy horses could carry water enough to get them across provided they carried little else, but no ordinary army weighed down by its equipment could hope to arrive in any condition to fight. Only the Imperial army itself could do that, and for two hundred years the Imperium had had more important things to do.

Now, with the exception of a handful of islands inhabited by savages, Gulzacandra was the last territory to resist Imperial law: the last territory where the true faith was openly and gladly professed, and its customs publicly followed. There were sorcerers still in Yevelkana, Zendamora and Bulzavara – and more than a few even in Kalazendra – but they had perforce to operate in the strictest secrecy. Not one of them ever achieve the kind of pre-eminence over his fellows that entitled Gavalon the Great to the tribute of his surname.

Banners and standards fluttered over a dozen other tents pitched on the so-called headland, but they all displayed open hands rather than eyes. Some of the hands carried flaming skulls, while others bore serpentine symbols, but Gavalon had reserved the withering eye for himself. His thrall-wizards and his beastmen wore various versions of it, to mark them out as officers of his personal retinue, although his lesser servants made do with the same annular insignia as any other gun-fodder.

Gavalon had already begun thinking of the bulk of his forces as 'gun-fodder', even though they had never faced guns before. The incredibly powerful weapons that the Imperial forces had brought with them to their epoch-making landing were rumoured to be almost out of ammunition now, but their owners had made the most of their temporary advantage. The guns produced in their Kalazendran factories were by no means as powerful as those their forebears had brought from the star-worlds, but they were guns nevertheless. There was nothing in Gulzacandra that could compete with them – except, of course, magic.

If the Imperium was to be stopped, magic would be the force that would do it.

Gavalon had every respect for and every faith in magic –
how could it be otherwise, given that he was the greatest sorcerer in Gulzacandra? – but he also had every respect for
history, and he knew that magic had not saved the sorcerers
of Kalazendra from Imperial firepower, and that magic had
not prevented the series of treasons that had brought
Zendamora, Bulzavara and Yevelkana into the Imperial fold
one by one.

For whatever reason, the god who had once been the god
of all five great nations had decided, after his impenetrably
mysterious fashion, to let his children suffer defeat after
defeat after defeat, even though the stars had begun to swim
in the night-sky like so many multicoloured fish almost as
soon as the Imperial ships had landed. No more ships had
come to reinforce the first wave of immigrants – and if the
god of Gulzacandra chose to be merciful, no more ships
would ever come – but those which had come had done
damage aplenty.

Only now was the tide to turn, if it were to turn at all – but
if and when it turned, it would surely turn with all the savage
fury of which the vengeful god of Gulzacandra was capable.

Perhaps, Gavalon thought, that was the way his lord preferred to play out the game – for what was life to the gods, and
everything else in the universe besides, but a game? The
world's misfortune might, if seen in the right light, be nothing
but a stage for his own glory. Gulzacandra had been the least
of the five civilizations, the smallest finger on the mighty
hand, but it was now the pulsing heart of the true god's
worldly kingdom, and its sorcerer-in-chief was Gavalon the
Great, Gavalon the Summoner and Gavalon the Keeper of the
Vessel: in brief, Gavalon the Midwife of the Future.

Almost as though he had summoned him up, the Vessel –
whose name was Nimian – came out of the tent behind his
keeper, looking nervously from side to side at the beastmen
which stood guard at its entrance. They were extraordinarily
ugly, even for beastmen – they had great, horned, shaggy
heads like yaks and feet like ostriches – but there was no reason in the world why the Vessel should fear them.

Perhaps it was another of the god's little jests that had made
Nimian nervous of so many things, or perhaps there was
some purpose in it which Gavalon could not yet comprehend.

Even Gavalon the Great was merely a mortal, at least for the time being – but who could know what a favourite servant of the true god might one day become, in the right circumstances?

'It has begun,' Nimian said. The boy had obviously slept late again, as all wise-dreamers tended to do, but now he was awake there was something about him that would have discomfited any ordinary man. Even the most innocuous of wise-dreamers grew to intimidate their fellows, and for all his seeming feebleness and obvious trepidation Nimian was not the most innocuous of wise-dreamers.

'Of course it has begun,' Gavalon told him. 'Why would I take the trouble to gather an army, if the final phase had not already begun? This is not the sort of enterprise one undertakes for idle amusement. You can have no idea of the planning that is required to maintain an army, even if its members are merely sitting around, waiting for orders as to how to dispose themselves when they march to meet the enemy.'

In fact, he thought, it was more difficult to maintain an army that was resting than an army on the move, because of the inevitable problems of supply and sanitation, but there was no point in trying to explain that to Nimian. The Vessel was thirteen years old and not destined to get much more than a day older – although he was not destined to die, either, in any ordinary sense of the word.

As for the one who would come to occupy the Vessel... that one, hopefully if not presumably, would need no explanations of anything mundane.

Hopefully.

Presumably...

Gavalon furrowed his brow as he realised that this was an inconvenient point of ignorance. He had no idea what explanations the being he was to summon would require. But the shadow passed quickly enough. A loyal servant of the Changer of the Ways had to do a great deal of hopeful presumption, and had to put up with a great deal more inconvenient ignorance.

What was faith but mortar to hold the bricks of certainty together, and what was hope but the plan of the edifice to be built?

'We should not be here,' Nimian told Gavalon petulantly. 'This is not the place, and the time will soon be upon us.'

'When the time comes,' Gavalon said, 'we shall be exactly where we are supposed to be. Today, I am supposed to be here. I am the commander of this gathering host and I must be seen. My banner must be seen, and I must be seen standing beneath it. I am the living symbol of the withering eye, and the ritual is not my only duty, for all that it may be the first and foremost.'

Nimian looked around at the humans and beastmen hurrying in every direction. Gavalon guessed that the boy was thinking that hardly one in ten of them had time to look up at his banner or sideways at his face – and that even those who had time would prefer not to do either. Ideally, the withering eye ought to have been a flesh banner, its design inscribed on magically-animated skin flayed from a dead enemy, but the opportunity to make such a device had not yet presented itself. In any case, tanned camule-skin was much more resilient than the hide of any of the species which, if legend could be trusted, humans had brought with them when they first arrived on this world, thousands of years before the Imperial ships had proved to the sceptics that there really were other worlds orbiting other, distant suns, and that there really might be a million colonised worlds inhabited by men.

Camule-skin or not, however, the withering eye banner was a potent weapon, and an intimidating sight even in its rest-state. It was not surprising that few men or beastmen cared to look up at it for long. When the time came to pack up the gaudy tents and put on armour, everyone drafted to this force would remember that fell banner well enough. They would march as if the gaze of that terrible eye were still upon them – and as if the gaze of Gavalon's eyes were upon them too.

Gavalon was well aware that the years had transformed him into a sight almost as unsettling as his banner. The channelling of his lord's dark magic had exacted its heavy penalties upon his flesh, but he did not mind that in the least. In the days before he had been Gavalon the Great he might have been reckoned merely ugly, but no one would ever again think of him as 'merely' anything. His ugliness was now spectacular, if not sublime. People who did not know him occasionally took him for a beastman, even though his feet still required boots and none could put a name to the twisted beast whose head he now wore.

'One does not need to be stared at in order to be seen,' Gavalon assured the Vessel. 'A man to be reckoned with is a man who impresses himself upon the mind even if he is glimpsed for a quarter-second out of the corner of one eye. A man fit to be more than a man impresses himself even on those who do not know that they have seen him, to whom he appears only as the figment of a nightmare: a shape sensed in a shadow, or a cloud of dust but never clearly seen at all. Don't doubt that my presence here is known and felt – and will still be known and felt when I must withdraw my person in order to complete the ritual that will seal the fate of this world.'

'In order, in order,' Nimian muttered, as though the phrase harboured some obscenity. The boy was hopping up and down on his feet, as if he needed to urinate – but the force that animated him was far more primal. He was, in truth, an unexpectedly miserable specimen: short, thin and ugly. Gavalon knew, however, that it was always the ugliest grubs that metamorphosed into the most powerful ogreflies and the most beautiful daymoths. Even megascarabs began life as mere wireworms – and what was the metamorphosis of such humble beings but a living testament to the sacred whimsy of the almighty Changer of the Ways?

Gavalon signalled to a group of beastmen who were sitting in a circle, painstakingly but not very skilfully sharpening their spears. The one who first responded to the summons was only slightly less stupid than the rest, but he could be trusted to transmit a command. 'Make ready,' Gavalon said to him. 'The Vessel departs for the rock within the hour.'

The beastman only growled, its bovine throat being ill-equipped for any other kind of reply, but Gavalon was confident that his will would be done. The great advantage of stupidity was that it was so easily transformed into loyalty. A beastman might be far less capable of conversation than a human fool like Nimian, but any in his retinue would be prepared to hurl itself in front of its master in order to intercept a deadly missile, or to charge a battle-tank armed only with a spear if ever there was a tactical situation that demanded such futility. Had Nimian not been the Vessel, the foolish boy could not have been trusted to fetch a cup of water from a well.

A human captain strode up, carrying a parchment map, to say that two beacon-fires had been sighted in the north-east, signalling that the enemy had been sighted. Gavalon cursed. Ierius Fulbra's assault force was moving faster than anyone had anticipated; it was already too close for comfort. His wise-dreamers had revealed that a second contingent was skirting the southern edge of the Amber Waste, and – more disturbingly – that a third appeared to be cutting straight across. If a part of that third force were somehow to reach the place where the ritual was scheduled to take place before Nimian's metamorphosis had been completed…

Was it possible, Gavalon wondered, that the Imperium still had psykers powerful enough to have obtained intelligence of his plans, and so-called inquisitors clever enough to take proper note of such intelligence? It was far more probable, though, that the Imperial soldiers crossing the Amber Waste merely intended to establish a base. Even so, they might prove troublesome.

The captain laid out his map for Gavalon's inspection, showing him the positions of Fulbra's advance party and the larger force plodding in its train – but Gavalon was more interested in the route taken by the third force

'What village is this?' he asked. The map had few names on it, apart from Rintrah and Chemosh.

'It is Odienne, my lord' the captain said. 'I was there once. It's tiny, and its fields are poor, but it does have a good well.'

'Does the headman know what to do if he's attacked?'

'Of course. But asking villagers to poison their own well is like asking a common soldier to fall on his sword. No matter how thoroughly he's been drilled–'

'Very well,' Gavalon said brusquely. 'You'll have to move your men north and make ready to meet Fulbra – at least fifteen miles, perhaps twenty.'

The captain's eyes clouded, but he made no protest. No doubt the man thought that it would be folly to go to meet Fulbra, and that the wisest course was not to fight a pitched battle at all – but the captain knew nothing of the Vessel and the ritual.

'You'd better leave a reserve here, though,' Gavalon added. 'A couple of hundred men. We'll almost certainly have to use them as reinforcements against Fulbra, but we might have to react to the presence of this third contingent before then.' He wished that he knew how many vehicles the third contingent had, and what kind of firepower they were carrying, but his wise-dreamers had been unable to go into detail.

'Yes, lord,' the captain said. 'It will be done as you wish.' He sounded slightly resentful, as soldiers led by sorcerers often did, Gavalon knew. He would be grateful enough for magical aid once the fighting actually started, though – he knew full well that his ragamuffin militia wouldn't last ten minutes against even a single Imperial platoon without it.

'Don't worry, captain,' Gavalon said, making no particular effort to sound confident, or even sincere. 'No one will be asking you to fall on your sword, even if things go wrong when the first clash comes. No one is expendable now, not even for honour's sake – and the final settlement will depend on forces far beyond your control.'

'That I know,' the captain said glumly, glancing sideways at the Vessel. The glance almost turned into a stare, but there was something in Nimian's seemingly-innocent appearance that prevented it. When the captain dropped his eyes it was to the floor. He had not even attempted to meet Gavalon's eye, or the banner's.

'We are the destined victors!' Gavalon said, coldly. 'Gulzacandra will save the world. We are the favoured children of the Changer of the Ways, and we shall be his instrument of vengeance against the invaders.'

'My lord,' the captain said as he turned away. If he doubted what Gavalon had said, he did not show it – but Gavalon knew well enough that this man, like every other assembled on the field, must have heard that there were a million other worlds like this one. The captain must have wondered whether, if that were true, and if the Changer of the Ways were interested in every one of them what right any petty local tribe could possibly have to think themselves his favoured children, or the chosen instrument of his vengeance.

But the Divine Schemer is a mighty god indeed, Gavalon told himself. If he suffers grubs and worms to become megascarabs, ogreflies and daymoths, why should he not suffer men to become his cherished champions, or daemons more powerful than exploding stars? And if he has his favourites among men, am I not one of them? Am I not, in fact, far more deserving of favour than a miserable wretch like Nimian? Surely I am destined for a better fate than he, even though he is the Vessel. For I, after all, am the Keeper and the Summoner, the Midwife of the Future. I am the Divine Schemer's Chosen One, his Child, his Champion.

He believed it, firstly because he had to and secondly – or so he had to tell himself – because it was true. The gods had to be trusted, because they had to be trustworthy, because they were gods. It was as simple as that.

THREE

THE JUDEYE FOREST was thorny but the ground was too dry and stony to allow the plants to grow densely together, so it was easy enough to pass between the trees uninjured. Most of the judeyes were mere bushes, and most of the leaves upon them were thin and wrinkled, seeming more thorn than flesh. It was not a good hiding-place if a fugitive might lie there undetected while small armies of ardent searchers passed them by, but it was not the kind of place that enemies would bother to search carefully unless they had a powerful reason.

Pater Saltana guided his party to a cave set into the side of one of the largest rocky outcrops in the forest. It must have been a natural cave at one time, but it had been further hollowed out by metal tools at some time in the distant past – the very distant past, long before the Imperium had fallen out of the sky. Its entrance was poorly concealed, but it was shady and cool and there was a water-barrel stowed in a hollow at the rear. Once the children had been safely herded inside, though, Dathan was enthusiastic to climb the rock-face to keep a lookout.

'You can't see the village from there,' Hycilla pointed out.

'No,' Dathan admitted, 'but I could see smoke rising into the air from the houses or the fields, and I could see men coming through the forest.'

'No one will come into the forest,' Saltana assured him, although the old man didn't seem very confident. 'They'd have to come on foot, and they won't leave their vehicles. They'll probably go straight through into the plain, hoping to catch Gavalon's forces by surprise, before they're fully gathered and battle-ready.'

'And if they don't?' Dathan wanted to know.

Saltana didn't answer. It was Hycilla who said: 'Kanak will send a messenger with further–'

That was when they first heard the sound of gunfire. It was a sound none of them had ever heard before, but Dathan knew immediately what it was. His first impulse was to wish that he had paused long enough at his house to find something that could serve as a weapon, but he realised immediately that if even a quarter of what he had heard rumoured about the guns of the Imperium were true, nothing the village had in the way of weaponry could provide a man with adequate self-defence. *Nothing* could oppose that kind of firepower but magic, and the village had little enough of that.

In fact, Dathan realised, almost all of what little magic the village did possess was lodged with him here, in the person of Saltana – perhaps also in Hycilla. That did not increase his confidence at all. Pater Saltana was surely the pettiest sorcerer imaginable, and even if Saltana's judgment of Hycilla's talent were correct, the talent in question had hardly begun to bloom.

Dathan had thought it absurd at first when Hycilla had told him that she might one day be a wise-dreamer. But in recent weeks he had noticed on occasion that a certain chill entered into places where she was, and that adolescents who had not been such fast friends with her as he had always been had begun to feel uneasy in her presence.

'I'm going up anyway,' Dathan said. 'I want to see whatever there is to be seen.'

He didn't wait for any further discussion, but set about scaling the rock-face. It only took ten minutes to clamber all the way to the top, but the effort left him short of breath and he had to lie down for a further minute or two before standing up beside the twisted trunk of a hundred-year-old tree, craning his neck even though he knew that the tallest chimneys in the village would still be invisible.

He was right about the smoke. Long columns were already rising from half a dozen different places, and more were appearing with every minute that passed. One column, to the west of the village, was a beacon fire set to warn the sentries on the look-out towers of Mancip and Elvenor of the attack. The remainder were all in the village, testifying to the ferocity of the assault that had been launched against it.

Saltana had, however, been wrong about the attackers sticking to their vehicles and ignoring the judeye forest. Two sinister shapes on foot were already visible, moving through the trees.

Had they not been so intent on looking to right and left, as if they expected every last tree to conceal savagely armed villagers lying in ambush for them, the soldiers might have caught sight of Dathan before he slipped behind the ancient trunk of the tree – but he did not think that they had. After a few heartbeats, he peeped around the trunk, determined to see what he could without being spotted himself.

The uniforms the two men wore seemed little more exotic to Dathan than the clothes worn by traders, and the men themselves – though they were obviously foreigners – were far more ordinary than he had anticipated. But they were carrying guns: heavy, wide-barrelled things that required two hands. Dathan had no idea whether the guns produced missiles or floods of fire, but he had no wish to find out. He had no idea, either, why the men had come into the forest, given that Kanak's men and the village women would have fled in any other direction but this one – but even if the enemy knew that, they might have considered it necessary to leave no ground uninvestigated.

The gunmen were already too close to allow Dathan to call out a warning without drawing attention to himself, and he knew that he could not climb down the exposed rock-face without being seen. For one reckless moment he considered the possibility of deliberately calling attention to himself in the hope that he might lead the soldiers away from the cave, as a mother-bird might lead a wolfox away from her nest, but he discarded the idea immediately. He had no idea what the range or power of the guns were, and if all that was needed to dispose of him was a single shot there would be no point at all in making himself a target.

The best thing to do, he decided, if he could possibly manage it, was to work his way around behind the two men. If they would only draw far enough apart, and if only he could creep up on one, and take him by surprise, and stab him with his eating-knife in such a way as to penetrate an artery...

He discarded that notion too. It was stupid, because it was impossible.

He looked around for a weapon, however makeshift, but there was nothing. Fallen boughs never lay long on the ground even in a place like this, given the village's ever-urgent need for firewood. There were a few loose stones of a convenient size for throwing, but they were mere pebbles, and it would have required more than a slingshot to make them into useful missiles. He picked up a couple anyway, simply because they were close at hand, lodged between the gnarled roots of the judeye tree.

Dathan had never felt so helpless. He had to hope that the gunmen would pass by the cave without suspecting that it was occupied. He prayed that Saltana and Hycilla had enough magic between them to keep the children quiet and contrive some kind of subtle concealment.

Perhaps it would have worked out that way, and perhaps not, but events took another turn. The gunmen had not seen any of the village's defenders running into the judeye forest, but the village's defenders had seen them, and had known what was at stake. The plan that Dathan had rejected as impossible clearly did not seem so to others, for the two enemy soldiers already had a pair of stealthy pursuers creeping swiftly up behind them, clearly visible to Dathan from his elevated position but quite invisible to their quarry. One was Relf the baker, the other a labourer named Pavot from the Tahiri farm.

Alas, though the men were as yet invisible to the invaders, they were not inaudible.

Dathan saw one of the soldiers start and turn, and knew that he was about to call out a warning. Instinctively, he hurled one of the stones he had picked up – not at the soldier, which would have been futile, but at the crown of a judeye away to the soldier's left. As the gunman voiced his warning the pebble rattled the thorny leaves, immediately drawing the man's attention away from the direction in which the threat actually lay.

Without pausing for thought, Dathan hurled the other stone at a tree to the right of the other soldier, and immediately dropped to his knees in search of more.

No sooner had he put his hand on another stone than he hurled it high and wide with all his might, not bothering to search for a target. He hoped that the confusion he sowed might persuade the gunmen that they were surrounded, and might perhaps create a margin of opportunity for their pursuers to attack.

The troops had not the slightest idea how many adversaries they might be facing, or how well they might be armed. In all likelihood, they had never seen even a judeye tree before, and had no idea what creatures might be lurking in a forest of them. They were taking no chances. They raised their guns – and what their guns unleashed was a kind of fire.

Living judeye trees were resistant to the heat of the sun, and to the kinds of fire-making apparatus the villagers had, but this kind of fire was something else. The crowns of the trees agitated by Dathan's stones, and two or three others besides, were instantaneously transformed into huge balls of flame. Their trunks exploded one after another, sending burning wood in every direction. The noise was frightful, all-consuming, like nothing Dathan had ever heard before. It only required those two shots to start a conflagration that promised to engulf the entire forest, and the two soldiers realised that almost immediately.

They did what must have seemed to them to be the sensible thing. They turned back.

The two villagers who had been attempting to creep up behind the gunmen would have had little or no opportunity to get close enough to use their blades, but there was no chance now of their being heard and the gunmen had set their own ambush by turning back towards them. No matter how powerful the guns might be, they were rather unwieldy, and the gunmen were momentarily off-guard.

Relf and Pavot pounced, their blades red with reflected firelight.

The Imperial soldiers reacted, but their first response had to be to use their guns as clubs. Had the villagers carried spears, or even real swords, one thrust might have been enough, but their blades were short, edged rather than pointed. Dathan thought that Relf, at least, had inflicted a serious cut, but neither man got the chance to inflict a second. The soldiers were trained; they had practised hand-to-hand fighting.

One soldier smashed the barrel of his weapon into Pavot's face. The labourer was a big man, well-used to heavy work, but he could not take a blow like that and remain standing. He fell on to his back, his arms sprawling. He kept his fist clenched about the hilt of his knife, but the weapon was virtually useless unless he could get up again. He could not: the Imperial soldier was far too skilled in his murderous trade to let an opportunity go, and he struck again with the barrel of his gun, driving it into Pavot's groin with all the force he could muster.

Relf, meanwhile, had been struck so sharply on the right arm that the bones had cracked. He dropped his weapon, but he could not have used it even if his nerveless fingers had maintained the grip. A second sweep of the heavy flame-gun took his legs away. He fell even more heavily, and even more awkwardly, than his bigger companion.

Now that both would-be ambushers had been laid flat, the Imperial soldiers calculated each further blow. Although they continued to use their bizarre weapons as instruments of crude, brute force, they did so with ruthless efficiency.

As Dathan watched the bodies jerk reflexively and the blood pooling on the dry soil, he knew that neither villager would ever get up again. It did not require much of his imagination to picture similar scenes repeated twelve or twenty times over. He could hear the sound of guns of a different kind, blasting and stuttering, and he could hear the sound of distant screaming, but in his mind's eye the massacre of his friends and neighbours was an endless series of repetitions of what he had just seen: strong men, well-trained and well-armed, beating the life out of helpless innocents – and then adding a few extra blows, for the sake of insult.

In the meantime, the children fled.

Saltana and Hycilla must have realised very quickly that they could not stay where they were in the middle of a forest fire, and they must have decided that their best chance of survival lay in running as quickly as possible in the direction opposite to the village – westwards. Whether they had actually decided to scatter, or whether it was mere panic, Dathan did not know, but scatter they had.

It would have been better, Dathan realised, if the Imperial soldiers had not been attacked. In that case, they would probably have continued their retreat without looking back. As things were, they were still looking around for other possible dangers when the children tried to make their escape.

The noise of the burning trees and the sounds of the conflict in the village was easily loud enough to cover the sound of running feet, and acrid smoke was already building a screen, but one of the troopers saw something, and immediately set off at a run in the direction the fugitives had taken. His companion hesitated, then followed.

The thick smoke rising up the rock-face forced Dathan back from the edge. His eyes were already smarting, and he knew that he had to find better air to breathe, so he too moved westwards, knowing as he came down the further slope of the outcrop that he would have to be very wary indeed when he reached the forest floor.

For the next ten minutes everything was confusion. The children were running as fast as they could, but Dathan did not dare to do likewise. He was too far behind them, and that put him far too close to the gunmen who had gone after them. He had to make more careful progress, taking whatever precautions he could, so he stayed close to the tree-trunks whenever he could, in spite of the thorns that were always reaching out to scratch his face and arms.

Unfortunately, the fire seemed to be travelling almost as fast as he was. He could hear its awful clamour behind him, and the pungent odour of smoke kept getting worse and worse.

He heard the soldiers before he saw them, and what he heard was the word: 'No!'

The sound was far too close for comfort, and he dropped to a crouch behind an unusually squat bush before manoeuvring himself into a position from which he could see the speaker and the companion to whom the speaker had spoken.

One of the soldiers, who was bleeding profusely from a cut in his shoulder at right-angles to the collar-bone, was standing over Pater Saltana, who was crouched on the ground with his arms protectively wrapped around Houlme. It seemed that the soldier had been about to dash out the priest's brains with the butt of his weapon, until he had been ordered to desist.

Dathan was glad to note that the other trooper also seemed to have been cut, if only superficially – his cheek had been slashed by a thrust that must have been less than a finger's-breadth away from taking out his eye.

'Take him alive!' said the man with the cut cheek, although he did not seem certain of his own instruction. 'Can't you see that he's some kind of priest? Look at his face, if his costume doesn't tell you. We might need the information he can give us.'

'What for?' demanded the other. 'If he's a sorcerer, all the more reason to kill the heretic scum!'

Dathan realised that the second man's voice was taut with anxiety, and that the reason the first had lacked conviction as to the reasonableness of his own argument was that he was afraid: afraid of Pater Saltana! Dathan had been afraid of Pater Saltana himself, but only in the way that any child might be afraid of his teacher. These were strong men – ruthless killers. Why should they look at an old man with such horror and trepidation?

Dathan thought again about the effect that Hycilla had begun to have on people who did not know her as well as he did. Was it possible, he wondered, that long familiarity had tamed his awe of Pater Saltana, making it seem less ominous than it really was?

'Don't be stupid,' the first soldier said, although there was still a manifest unease in his tone. 'We need local knowledge if we're to establish a supply-point here, and the rest of these stupid peasants probably don't know which way's up. We need everything he has in his head, and we need to tease it out very tenderly. We have to deliver him to the inquisitors.'

Dathan took the remark about 'stupid peasants' very personally. He had heard enough of town life to know that his people were poor, and he had heard passing merchants speak condescendingly of the ignorance of those who had never seen what lay beyond the horizon, but he was not stupid. The village had its craftsmen, who were legitimately proud of the quality of their work, and even its ploughmen and livestock-tenders knew more than the particular secrets of their work and worship.

'What about the child?' asked the man with the bleeding shoulder, although he must have known the answer.

'That we don't need.'

The soldier with the wounded shoulder had already reached out to yank Houlme out of Saltana's protective grasp. Saltana would not give him up, but when the second man joined in, the priest could not hold on.

The man with the slashed cheek took Houlme from his companion, held him by his ankles and swung the child's head against the bark of a tree, so forcefully that his neck snapped. Dathan heard the horrible crack quite clearly in spite of the background roar.

'Shit and corruption!' said the man with the wounded shoulder, clinging hard to Pater Saltana's limp body. 'It's not going to be easy getting out of here, even without this kind of burden.'

'Give him to me,' the other commanded. 'You lead the way. Just make sure you don't take us into any more ambushes – and if you have to shoot again, try not to devastate the entire landscape. That way, if we steer around the fire, we'll get back to the village easily enough.'

The man with the bleeding shoulder didn't wait before setting off, although he did say 'What about the others?' as he marched off.

'They're just brats. We can tidy them up later, if need be. In all probability, the fire will take care of most of them, and thirst and hunger will do for the rest. This is the one we need, for now. With luck, we'll have a few others, so there's a couple to spare when the questioning starts. And the women, of course.'

By the time this last sentence was completed the two soldiers had passed out of Dathan's sight.

If he had had a weapon, of any sort, Dathan might have followed them. As it was, he had enough sense to let them go. He went to stand over Houlme's broken body, feeling an impotent rage more terrible than any emotion that had ever possessed him.

He didn't notice Hycilla coming up behind him until she touched his shoulder. Then he whirled about, wishing that it might be an enemy – albeit an enemy that he was capable of fighting.

When he saw that she was not, he lowered his hands, but his fists were still clenched, the nails digging into his palms. He shuddered, but it was not because Hycilla's presence was disturbing – or so he told himself.

'We have to go,' Hycilla said. 'We have to go as far and as fast as we can – to Elvenor, if we can find the way. We have to tell someone who can get a message to Gavalon that the Imperium is establishing a supply-base here. It might be important.'

'We never had a chance,' Dathan whispered. 'None of us. Relf, Pavot, Pater Saltana – we're all as helpless as Houlme, just things to be destroyed, or tortured, or–'

Hycilla grabbed his arms and pulled him.

'If we don't go,' she said, 'we'll be meat. Cooked meat. Come on!'

Dathan knew that she was right. Even so, she had to lead him away, and he did not begin to run until she forced him.

FOUR

ORLOC MELCARTH STOOD on the balcony of the Governor's Apartment in the Imperium Tower, looking out over the city of Sostenuto, capital of the Civilization of Kalazendra. The news, relayed from Ierius Fulbra by a chain of vox stations spanning half a world, was good.

Fulbra's main forces had skirted the Amber Waste to the north and south, and his own company was now making rapid headway into Gulzacandra. The invaders had met no significant opposition, and Fulbra's armoured corps had been able to blast its way through the makeshift barriers that had been set up to impede its progress. Fulbra had left his slower-moving cavalry and loxodonts far behind, although they would have a great deal of valuable work to do in tidying up after him and making sure that the supply-routes across Yevelkana were properly maintained.

In the meantime, Fulbra had sent a smaller contingent of trucks racing straight across the Waste, with a view to establishing a supply-base at an insignificant village identified on the maps as Odienne. Melcarth knew that the decision to do so had been encouraged by Ragan Balberith, whose psykers had allegedly detected signs of trouble brewing in the wasteland west of the village, but that was a petty annoyance. If Balberith wanted Fulbra to mount an exploratory 'Operation Probe', he might as well have his way – it might keep his mind off more problematic matters.

The cultists' forces, which seemed to have been given no useful forewarning by magical means, were reported to be gathering together, although Fulbra had not managed to find out where, or what their plan of campaign was likely to be. Melcarth could not see that it mattered much. Fulbra would be on them soon enough, and even if they had contrived to muster ten thousand fighters they would be crushed. Many of them would be unintelligent and poorly-armed beastmen; even the human conscripts would be pathetically ill-equipped.

Everything was going to plan – and not just to Fulbra's plan, but to his.

Within a matter of weeks he, Orloc Melcarth, would be the ruler of the world: the emperor of the world, in all but name. Sostenuto would be the capital city of an Imperium that embraced the whole world, on which the sun never set, and he would be able to ride through it in triumph, celebrating his ascension to absolute power, with Fulbra at his side. He had an aircraft standing ready, first to carry him to the battlefield – once the crucial victory had been well and truly won – and then to bring him back with the general by his side, to establish him in the mind of every man in Kalazendra as a hero in his own right, and a great leader.

Once Gulzacandra was purged, Melcarth believed, the fugitive covens of Bulzavara, Zendamora and Yevelkana would be isolated and unsupported, easy targets for Ragan Balberith's agents and hirelings – or, more likely the agents and hirelings of the more reasonable man who would presently be replacing Ragan Balberith in the position of Chief Inquisitor.

Melcarth wondered, briefly, whether the title of Chief Inquisitor could be discarded along with its occupant. Perhaps the notion of a 'Chief Inquisitor' had too much of the True Imperium wrapped up in it. Perhaps it demanded – and, alas, commanded – rather too much respect. The cultists had to be hunted down, of course, and killed. They were too vile to live, and their magic posed a threat to the worldly Imperium – Melcarth's Imperium – but the memory and methods of the True Imperium were a little too carefully preserved by

Balberith's Inquisition. Perhaps it was high time for the entire institution to be replaced by something more suited to local circumstances. The way would then be clear for Orloc Melcarth to be emperor in name as well as in reality.

It was not the fact that he had not yet conquered Gulzacandra that had prevented Melcarth from claiming that title before, but rather that it would have caused such offence to the inner circle of Balberith's inquisitors, their agents and their allies. Given the way inquisitors worked, Melcarth could not be entirely certain how wide that circle was – although he was quite sure that its members would certainly regard his use of the title as a usurpation and a blasphemy, if he did not handle the matter with the utmost delicacy. Even Balberith was prepared to tolerate the fact that the aborigines had been encouraged to call the political institutions and armed forces at his disposal 'the Imperium', but that was because he still considered the worldly Imperium to be nothing more than a humble instrument and representative of a much grander Imperium: an Imperium that spanned the stars. That Imperium was, however – at least in Orloc Melcarth's opinion – nothing more than a distant memory, quite irrelevant to the world as he knew it.

Balberith always insisted on referring to the world as Sigmatus, but Melcarth preferred to think of it simply as the world – or, even more pleasantly, as his world. He was already the effective overlord of four-fifths of its land surface, and the conquest of Gulzacandra would deliver the greater part of the remainder. The rest – consisting of islands covered by impenetrable jungles, ice or volcanic ash – was not worth having, even though a few of the islands in the southern sea were inhabited. Aborigines were happy enough to scratch out a living anywhere.

In the distance, as he looked to the west, Melcarth could see the shell of one of the ships that had brought his ancestors to Sigmatus. The four that had been stranded when the stars began to shift again – or when the warpstorms of the Eye of Terror extended their outer fringes to embrace it again, as Balberith insisted on putting it – remained on display outside the four gates of the city, to remind everyone who passed through those gates of the proud heritage of their rulers. They were potent symbols of the awesome power that existed outside the world, in the great wilderness of the universe – but Orloc Melcarth was a determined realist, who knew that symbols were only symbols, and that real power had to be exercised within the world, with an immediacy that had to be obvious to anyone who ever thought to resist it. Once the Inquisition had been reformed, redesigned in a more subservient role, it would be time to begin dismantling the hulls of the ships, reclaiming the valuable metals bound up therein. It would be easy enough to turn the symbols into scrap, and once that was done the memory of the True Imperium would continue to fade, until it finally became no more than a myth.

'The Chief Inquisitor is here, excellency,' a voice murmured from the room behind him. 'He desires....'

'I know what he desires,' Melcarth said, casually interrupting the guardsman. 'Please ask him to join me.'

He liked entertaining Balberith on his balcony, because Balberith was slightly acrophobic. Heights made him nervous, and nervousness put pressure on him to cut his interference short. Unfortunately, devotion to imagined duty put pressure on him too, and that always encouraged him to extend his interference to the limit.

And that, no doubt, was why Ragan Balberith stepped out boldly onto the high balcony overlooking the capital city, despite the quiver of vertigo that must have run from head to toe as he did so. His bodyguards remained discreetly inside.

Under the gaze of Balberith's angry eyes, Melcarth had to remind himself that the title of Chief Inquisitor was merely an echo of something at best half-remembered, an imitation of a very distant original. Doubtless there had once been real inquisitors – men of authentic power and sanctity – but here in the real world there were only men who pretended to be inquisitors: men who merely played at being inquisitors, no matter how eager they might be to root out corruption, nor how efficient they might be in slaughtering the supposedly-cor-rupt.

'The news is excellent!' Melcarth said, before the other man had time to speak. 'Our plans are proceeding exactly as they should – all praise to the Emperor Magnificent.'

'All praise to the Emperor Magnificent,' Balberith echoed, dutifully – although his flashing eyes declared his awareness that Melcarth's use of the formula was tokenistic. 'I am told that General Fulbra has asked for the aircraft. He needs it for reconnaissance, to examine the enemy's disposition – but it is still in Kalazendra.'

Balberith had drawn himself up to his full height as he spoke, trying to make the most of the one-inch advantage he had over the governor. Melcarth observed that the inquisitor had even combed his hair in such a way as to make it stand up, trying to gain an extra quarter-inch that way – but the governor was not a man to be intimidated by an accident of stature. In any case, the inquisitor's ascetic habits ensured that he could not get the full benefit of his exercise regime, and Melcarth's muscles were much more solid.

'General Fulbra always has a tendency to overestimate his needs,' Melcarth said, smoothly. 'Soldiers rarely see very far beyond the next battle, and never see beyond a war's end.'

'But you've taken elaborate steps to ensure that the chain of refuelling stations is intact, and Fulbra's engineers are under orders to clear landing-strips wherever they make camp, in order that the aircraft can always get to them within twelve hours,' Balberith complained. 'Why do that, if the aircraft is not to be placed at the general's disposal?'

Melcarth wondered whether Balberith might have guessed the real reason for the careful preparations he had listed – which was, of course, to allow Orloc Melcarth to claim the fullest possible share of Fulbra's triumph. It did not seem to matter, either way: Melcarth was the only man who could order it to take off. The aircraft was the most potent example of Original Technology left to the Imperium of Kalazendra, and Melcarth had always been careful to reserve its use entirely to himself.

'The aircraft is too precious a resource to waste in mere reconnaissance,' Melcarth told the inquisitor. 'If it were a matter of life and death, of course... but it is not. Our tech-priests have had to work virtual miracles to maintain the craft's airworthiness, given the dearth of native resources, and we owe it to their loyalty and devotion not to squander the rewards of their endeavours.'

That was the way Melcarth had to talk to Balberith: it was the kind of language the inquisitor understood. Melcarth understood that Kalazendra's so-called tech-priests were mere tinkerers, whose forebears had remembered the prayers and rituals associated with the use of weapons far better than they had remembered the manufacturing skills necessary to reproduce and maintain them, but Balberith saw things differently.

'I don't think you fully realise, excellency, what kind of forces General Fulbra might be up against,' Balberith said. 'This is the cultists' last stand, and the coven-masters must have kept a few of their best tricks in reserve. Our forces are a long way from home, and it will be impossible to reinforce them if they get into serious difficulties. Worse than that – if they should get into difficulties it would undoubtedly affect the morale of our troops in the other conquered territories. The cultists may have been driven underground in the subject states, but they are not extinct even here. Corruption is far more widespread than you seem to believe, and the threat it poses far more insidious. If our communication-links were to be weakened…'

'But they aren't being weakened, Ragan,' Melcarth pointed out, stressing the name because he knew how much Balberith hated to be addressed in that manner rather than his title, especially by one who had the notional right to do it. 'Radio reception has never been better – every message comes through as clear as a bell, no matter how many relay stations are involved. Imagine what it would have been like ten years ago!'

'That's because the warpstorm appears to be abating,' Balberith said. 'But it's something over which we have not the slightest control. The enemy…'

'Have no more control than we have, for all that they have been tainted by the warp themselves. In any case, you've been exceedingly enthusiastic to see the stars stand still for as long as I've known you. Surely you're delighted that the warpstorm seems to be abating.'

'If it allows us to re-establish contact with the Imperium, it will be the most fortunate thing that has happened on Sigmatus for two hundred years, but…'

'Would that be local years,' Melcarth put in mischievously, 'or Imperial years?'

The year defined by Sigmatus's orbit around its sun and the day defined by its own rotation – the real year and the real day, as Melcarth thought of them – were both a little longer than the 'year' and the 'day' that had been built into the time-calculations of his ancestors, which Balberith still insisted on using in assertions about the supposed antiquity of what he thought of as the real Imperium.

'It doesn't matter,' Balberith said. 'If we can re-establish contact with the Imperium – as everyone should devoutly desire – then General Fulbra's exploits will become irrelevant. The Adeptus Terra will send more ships, and they will decide what needs to be done about the taint of the warp that affects Sigmatus. If they decide that the planet can be safely purged, and that its resources might then be useful to the Imperium, they will doubtless have the men and the tools to do the job. If the warpstorm recovers its vigour, on the other hand, it will be up to us to oppose the forces of Chaos with all our might. We must consider the possibility that the tide may turn against us, and prepare as best we can for that contingency.'

'Whether the stars will ever stand still again or not,' Melcarth told him, wearily, 'we must prepare for the contingency that we and our children and our children's children will have to rule this world for centuries, if not millennia. The weapons and equipment that our ancestors brought to this world are a very precious resource that must be conserved. We have contrived to manufacture trucks of our own, and guns of our own, but anyone who has ever used them knows how primitive they are by comparison with those our ancestors brought with them. Clearly, our tech-priests – good and worshipful men though they are – have only contrived to retain a few of the rituals and prayers that the manufacturers of the True Imperium know. Of course General Fulbra wants me to give him more and better guns, more and better ammunition, more and better vehicles and the use of our one and only aircraft. He's a general, and he hates to think that anything he might use should be kept in reserve for future contingencies – but you and I must acknowledge a higher duty, must we not?'

Balberith scowled at that, knowing that he was being mocked. Melcarth knew full well that the Chief Inquisitor took the prayers and rituals of the so-called tech-priests entirely seriously – as did the great majority of the tech-priests, whose status depended on the mystification of their work.

'I believe that you might be underestimating the enemy, excellency,' Balberith said, doggedly. 'My psykers–'

'You have not an atom of evidence for saying so,' Melcarth interjected, casually leaning back on the balcony, revelling in his own lack of anxiety. 'Your inquisitors have done a magnificent job of suppressing the agents of Chaos in Kalazendra and the subject civilizations. At every juncture, the magic of these so-called sorcerers has been defeated. We have suffered losses, of course, but they have always been acceptable losses. If there really is something brewing in the wastelands west of the Amber Waste – in addition, of course, to the gathering of a ragged army – then Operation Probe will tell Fulbra what it is, and Fulbra will deal with it.'

'It may not be so simple. My psykers–'

'Are as crazed as their counterparts on the other side, especially since you've taken to dosing them with the same drugs. You worry too much, Ragan. We have always generated resentment by the harshness with which we have opposed the cults – although I cannot pretend to understand why the aborigines feel so strongly about the children we put down when they seem quite oblivious of all those murdered by their own wizards or marred by their vile gods – but we always withstood their attempts to take vengeance, material and magical. History is on our side, as it certainly should be, given that ours is the side of right and justice, the side of the Imperium. We shall win this war, and win it gloriously.'

'If we had more history we might be better served,' Balberith retorted, resentfully. His eyes were fluttering from side to side now, as the mere consciousness of Melcarth's position began to excite his vertiginous imagination. 'The problem is that it is not merely the original artefacts that have been a wasting asset these last two hundred years. The knowledge and wisdom that our ancestors brought to this world was but a fraction of the wisdom and knowledge of the Imperium. They did not expect to be stranded here, and did not come prepared to be colonists. No doubt their efforts were heroic, and they must have done everything they could to tell their children everything they would need to know to fight the Eternal Enemy even on its own ground – but we do not know how much we do not know. We do not know what tricks this so-called Gavalon the Great might have up his sleeve.'

Melcarth sighed. It was all true, of course, but it was all irrelevant. No one could prepare for the unforeseeable: no general; no inquisitor; no governor; no emperor, even of the universe. 'We can only act on what we do know,' he said. 'Yes, it is possible that all the defeats our enemies have so far suffered were accepted in order to lull us into a false sense of security. Yes, it is possible that the last sorcerer we have to dispatch really is more powerful than all the rest. It is even possible that he has the power to move the stars or make their fire rain down upon this miserable world, turning every womb-held embryo into a ravening monster that will eat its mother alive. But all our experience tells us that we are the strong ones: the ones with the power to rule this world. We have the strength of will and purpose to exterminate all the residual stains of evil that are gathering together even now in their last wilderness redoubt. Fulbra does not need my aircraft yet.'

'*Your* aircraft?' Balberith was quick to pounce in the slip of the tongue, but the Chief Inquisitor's nerves were at full stretch now. There was cold sweat on his brow. He was edging back into the doorway, in spite of the fact that he could not confront the governor from that position while Melcarth insisted on standing sideways at his balcony, leaning out into empty space.

Melcarth decided that it was time to score a point, to continue the arduous process of securing his psychological ascendancy over his only possible rival for authority over the world. 'Yes,' he said. 'My aircraft. I am the governor, after all, sole heir to the authority of the First Governor, the star-born. You are the Chief Inquisitor, and the instruments of the Inquisition are yours. I make no claim upon them and would not dream of instructing you in the delicate arts of torture and the arcane mysteries of priestly magic. But I am the governor, and the apparatus of government is mine. The aircraft is mine.'

'Perhaps,' Balberith said, through gritted teeth, 'you think the whole world is yours, save for the monstrous manifestations of Chaos that I must dispose of for you.'

Perhaps! Melcarth echoed, in the privacy of his own thoughts. The man has known me all my life, and has worked alongside me for more than twenty years, and still he thinks that perhaps I think the whole world is mine. So great is his reverence for the Imperium of the stars – the Imperium from which we have not heard a whisper since my great-great-grandfather was born – that he can barely imagine the temerity of a mind that could leave it out of its calculations of ambition.

Aloud, he said: 'We are human, Ragan, and part of the Imperium of Mankind. Even the aborigines, who were here before the Imperium existed, are humans of a sort, however miserable that sort may be – and that means that they too are part of the Imperium of Mankind, even though they do not know it and are direly reluctant to be persuaded. It is our duty to save them from their ignorance, and to raise them to the same level of awareness of virtue, necessity and love of the Emperor that we possess. Whatever I must do to secure that aim, I will do, and I expect no less of you.'

Balberith had to know that Melcarth was insincere, but the governor knew that the Chief Inquisitor did not have the strength of will to quibble over such subtleties in a situation like this. Balberith continued backing away into the room, making strangled noises that were presumably supposed to indicate reluctant agreement with everything the governor had said.

If I have to live on this damned balcony till the campaign is over, Melcarth thought, I'll do it. I'm too close now to let Balberith get in my way – and once this famous sorcerer is as dead as all the rest, the Inquisition will have lost its most precious asset. With no bugbears looming over them, the rank and file will soon lose all respect for those who pretend to be our last and best protection against destruction by the forces of evil.

It was a comforting thought.

When Balberith and his bodyguards were safely out of the way, Orloc Melcarth condescended to return to his desk and sit down, ready to receive more obsequious visitors – or, if none came, to attend to the routine business of government.

There was always routine business: papers to read, budgets to approve, and orders to sign. It was even more dangerous to delegate too much than to delegate too little. A ruler had to be seen to rule, especially by his immediate subordinates. If any one of those subordinates ever got the idea that he could do the job as easily as his master, he would immediately cease to be a subordinate and would become a threat instead. A good ruler had to be always busy, always attentive, always interested, always on top.

And while there was only one original aircraft in the world, it had to be his.

Within thirty minutes of his sitting down, however – local minutes, not Imperial ones – Melcarth was interrupted by

Kerforo, one of his best spies, bearing an urgent message. It really was an urgent message, too, unlike many of those his spies brought him out of anxiety that they might be thought to be falling down on the job.

'One of Balberith's psykers claims to have made contact with an Imperial warfleet,' Kerforo reported. 'Balberith will have the news by the day's end.'

'What kind of contact?' Melcarth wanted to know.

'Only dreaming, so far,' the spy told him.

The 'so far' was probably an attempt to exaggerate the importance of the news, but Melcarth wasn't such a fool as to ignore its implication. Balberith's psykers were optimists of exactly the same stripe as the Chief Inquisitor, and their optimism was always prone to pollute their dreams. It wouldn't be the first time that a psyker had thought that he had sensed the nearness of Imperial forces when he had only been dreaming hopefully... but radio reception was coming in as clear as a bell, and the stars seemed to become quieter in the sky with every night that passed. If the warpstorm were to die down, and Balberith's psykers were actually to obtain some authentic telepathic intelligence of the Imperium of Mankind, it might only be a matter of time before they got a message out... and then everything really might change.

'Well,' said Melcarth, pensively, 'I suppose everyone is entitled to a pleasant dream now and again. Just keep your ear to the ground, for now – but if the psyker makes any significant progress, you'd better make sure that it comes to an abrupt stop.'

'That won't be easy,' Kerforo was quick to say. 'Balberith's organization is too tight. We don't have ready access to the cells – and anyone who broke cover would never get out alive.'

The subtext of what the spy was saying was that he was the only person who had a reasonable chance to dispose of the inconvenient psyker, but that he probably wouldn't get away with it – and that his capture would deprive Melcarth of his most useful pawn in Balberith's camp. Melcarth also had to bear in mind the fact that Kerforo was terrified of psykers, and hated being anywhere near them even when ordered to keep an eye on them. Everybody hated psykers – even Balberith's priestly allies, who were obliged to keep them company when they were exercising their power.

'Arrange an accident,' Melcarth said, coldly. 'You're an ingenious man.'

'There might be a possibility of food-poisoning,' the spy suggested, tentatively.

'Not reliable enough,' Melcarth told him. 'What's worse, it's said that partial poisoning sometimes stimulates psyker power. A broken neck would be better. Even psykers use the stairs. If he doesn't get ambitious, though, you can leave him alone. We might need Balberith's psykers if Fulbra really does run into trouble taking out this so-called Gavalon the Great – and if he doesn't, I dare say we'll be able find uses for them once the Inquisition has been reformed in the wake of the Final Victory.'

Kerforo smiled, but there was neither joy nor humour in the expression. 'I dare say we shall,' he said, unenthusiastically. As he got up to go, he added: 'All praise to the Emperor Magnificent.' He didn't go so far as to wink his eye, but Melcarth caught the irony.

'All praise to the Emperor Magnificent,' the governor echoed, dutifully, 'and death to all his enemies.'

The words sounded good in the mouth of a realist, he thought. And if all went well, they would sound even better in times to come.

FIVE

Hycilla led Dathan directly towards the setting sun, which grew redder in colour as it approached the flat horizon. It seemed to grow in size as it touched the rim of the plain, and its face was no longer so bright that it was impossible to look at it for more than a fraction of a second.

It was possible to see, now that the sun's face was neither still nor featureless, that the entire sphere was perpetually turbulent, seething like a cauldron. As the colour of the sky darkened from soft violet to deep purple it too began to reveal the movements that were ordinarily cloaked by brilliance. Even though the stars had hardly begun to shine, the sky began to shimmer like the surface of an oily pool.

The entire universe was restless, Dathan thought. That was the truth of the matter. It surely could not be alive, any more than the wind-stirred air or the desert sands were alive, but neither was it quiet. It could no more settle into silence and stillness than a baby racked by hunger and fear. Perhaps the stars themselves had their hungers, and the void between them its fears.

'We should stop to rest,' he said to Hycilla, when he saw that she was utterly exhausted – but she would not listen. The strangeness that intimidated people had taken hold of her, and even Dathan felt unease stirring the depths of his being.

'If we stop here we'll never get up again,' Hycilla said, brusquely. 'We need to keep going while the light lasts. We need to reach Elvenor, if we can, to find shelter – and if we can't, we must find water.'

That was far more easily said than done. The plain was not a desert like the Amber Waste: grasses grew here in profusion, and bushes of many different sorts, but the rainfall was sporadic and this was the dry season. There were herds of wild horses and pigs in the wastelands – although Pater Saltana had told them that there had been no such creatures in the world before the first humans came – as well as ghazals and loxodonts, but they were few and far between. The village men often mounted hunting expeditions in the autumn, and the game they sought was just about abundant enough to ensure that they rarely came home empty-handed, but as Dathan scanned the terrain laid out before him he could not see a single animal of any kind. There must be water-holes somewhere, and common sense suggested that they ought to reveal themselves by imparting a lusher complexion to the surrounding vegetation, but the plain's colours made a mockery of the other meaning of the word 'plain'. They were far too confusing to permit easy discrimination.

The further Dathan and Hycilla had come from the burning forest, the more confusing the plant-life had become. The fields planted by the villagers were green, and so were most of the plants that grew wild in their vicinity. Judeye trees – which had been in the world long before the first humans came, a thousand generations ago – were not so very different from the trees that grew in the neighbouring orchards. Dathan realised now, though, that the village might have been built where it was precisely because the location seemed uncommonly hospitable, and that the plain across which he had Hycilla were now trudging was devoid of permanent human habitation precisely because it was not. Here, there was as much red and purple foliage as green, and a good deal of ochreous yellow.

The fruits on the bushes – which seemed so tempting to Dathan, because he was hungry as well as desperately thirsty, even though they were far past ripeness and shrivelling on the bough – were white and red and black and glorious sky-purple. He had been taught to avoid them, not so much because almost all of them were bitter and a few frankly poisonous, but because hardly any of them had much nutritional value to human beings. Some cautionary folktales of his people told of children lost on the plain who filled their stomachs time and time again with tempting produce, and starved to death even with their bellies crammed. Ghazals and loxodonts – not to mention countless smaller creatures – grew fit and fat on such produce, but the horses and pigs that had escaped human control in the distant past had to be more discriminating.

Even so, Dathan thought, the fact that some animals could live out here proved that humans could too, if they could only develop similar powers of discrimination.

The most striking thing of all about the vegetation of the plain was not so much its colour as its variety. It was not uncommon to see bushes which supported leaves of a dozen different shapes, and flowers of a dozen different conformations.

The crops the villagers grew were stubborn in that regard; each one clung to a single basic pattern. With only a few exceptions, the plants that had developed here enjoyed a remarkable freedom of expression, within and between generations. They seemed far more susceptible to disease, deformation and death, but they compensated for that sensitivity with exuberance.

'We could pick fruits and crush them, then throw away the pulp and drink the moisture,' Dathan suggested, as the last thin slice of the sun's disk slipped out of sight and left them to twilight.

The western horizon was flat, save for a ragged semicircular shadow just to the south of the point at which the sun had gone down. The shape was suggestive of an artificial structure, but there seemed to be vegetation of some sort growing on top of it, so it was probably just an oddly-shaped hill.

'We need water far purer than that,' Hycilla told him, after a few moments' thought. 'Even if there were no poisons dissolved in it, there'd be other substances, which our bodies would have to excrete. It would be like drinking seawater.'

Dathan wondered how she could possibly know this. She wasn't talking like a village child any more; she was talking like

someone to whom secrets had been revealed by some mysterious inner process. Like Dathan, Hycilla had never seen the sea,
and probably never would, so how did she know what drinking seawater would be like, and why was she using a word like
excrete? Everyone liked to hear stories of piracy and adventures
in far-flung lands, of course, and of desperate castaways
marooned on desert isles, but Hycilla seemed to be speaking
with an authority derived from a very different source.

Dathan was beginning to understand why people sometimes took a step back when Hycilla was like this – and he had
never known her be like this for so long. Would she ever return
to her true self, he wondered, or had she been changed forever
by the arrival of the Imperium?

'We'll never find pure water,' Dathan said, bleakly. He
wished that he had not breathed in so much smoke when the
judeye forest caught fire. Surely he would not feel as thirsty as
he did if his throat had not been scorched.

'Yes we will,' Hycilla told him, as she marched relentlessly
towards the place where the sun had disappeared.

'What's the point, anyway?' Dathan demanded. 'Everyone
we ever knew is dead, and our home is gone. Where are we
going? Where is there to go?'

'There's an army out here somewhere,' she told him. 'An
army gathered to fight the invaders.'

'Pity they weren't in the village,' Dathan said, hoarsely. 'They
could have fought them today.'

'I doubt that this was the only place where the soldiers
crossed the wastelands. Most travellers avoid the Amber Waste.
Even if they have camules, they usually go the long way round
to the north or the even longer way to the south. These men
had trucks that could move much faster than a camule train,
but we were unlucky even so.'

'Unlucky! We're supposed to be the ones with magic on our
side. We have sorcerers and wise-dreamers, and they don't.
Why weren't we warned?'

It wasn't intended to be a personal attack, but Hycilla could
hardly help but take it personally. She was the village's most
favoured child, said by Pater Saltana to have been touched by
the true god.

'I see so much in my dreams,' she said, flatly, 'but none of it
clearly. Even the greatest sorcerer in the world can be lost in

confusion, or betrayed by illusion.' Dathan knew that she was quoting Pater Saltana.

'So much for the gift of further sight,' Dathan muttered, 'or the honesty of the true god.'

'You're wrong to mock,' Hycilla told him, 'and foolish to blaspheme.' Her voice was oddly intense. She wasn't quoting Pater Saltana any longer, but Dathan had the impression that her words weren't her own – at least, not entirely.

'The reason the wisest dreams are so confused,' Hycilla went on, 'is that the future is not yet made. It exists, at present, as a near-infinite set of possibilities, whose likelihood changes with every second that ticks away. The mere fact of looking into that sea of possibilities affects the likelihood, so everything we glimpse changes as we try to focus on it, because we've glimpsed it, and because we're trying to focus on it. If we saw it any other way, the god which grants us sight would be lying.'

Dathan decided that he had liked Hycilla better when she was just a girl, untouched by any outside force. It was only to be expected that wise-dreamers would become wiser, but this was definitely scary.

'You might think that my talent is too uncertain to be useful,' she continued, as if she were still trying, wonderingly, to make sense of what she were saying, 'but imagine the alternative. Imagine looking into the future and seeing it all mapped out, fixed and definite, perfectly ordered and unalterable. What benefit could we gain from such insight as that? It would only tell us that we were utterly helpless to change anything, utterly impotent to make anything of ourselves other than what's already made.'

Aren't we? Dathan thought – but Hycilla was lost in her own private wilderness, and wouldn't have heard him if he had spoken the words aloud.

'It would tell us that we're machines,' Hycilla said, with an odd edge to her voice which suggested that she was beginning to frighten herself, 'or puppets, acting out a ritual we can neither change nor understand. What kind of mind could such a seer have? What kind of thoughts and feelings could she have? Her experience would be pure horror, a sensation of absolute and inescapable entrapment. That's what the enemy want to make of the future, Dathan, and of the whole of existence.

They want to bring order to the world. Well, I'm glad that when I dream wisely, I see confusion. If I couldn't see confusion, I wouldn't be free and I wouldn't be human, and the god whose gift I bear would be the most monstrous tyrant imaginable.'

She didn't sound at all glad. She sounded as if she felt that she ought to be, but couldn't quite find the courage. In her own way, Dathan thought, she must be as frightened as he was – but the fact that her way was so different from his was frightening in itself.

So much, Dathan thought, for being free. So much for being human.

As dusk fell, though, they found their guide. While the sun shone they had seen birds of several kinds fluttering about the branches of the bushes or darting from one to another, but now the dark was gathering the birds were gathering too, into unexpectedly huge flocks which took to the air en masse, wheeling this way and that as they piped their various calls, and then set off for their roosts.

'There!' said Hycilla, her finger following the direction taken by one of the flocks, some way to the north of their westward course. 'That's where we'll find water. It's out of our way, but I don't think we can reach Elvenor tonight – we'd do better to make the detour.'

'Let's hope it's not far,' Dathan said – but he swiftly realised that if the water had been too far distant they would not have been able to see the birds descend. He and Hycilla actually contrived to increase their pace, in spite of their fatigue, as urgency spurred them on.

As the night became absolute the two fugitives arrived at the rim of a saucer-shaped depression. In the middle of the depression was a pool surrounded by rushes and chimerical flowering plants. They were far stranger than any that Dathan had ever seen before.

There was a saying in the village which bade children beware of the gardens of god. Its meaning had never been clear to Dathan, but as soon as he saw this bizarre array of flowers he thought he understood what kind of garden the god of Gulzacandra might maintain. Alas, he could not exercise due caution. The need to drink overrode all other considerations. He forced his way through a clump of rushes and threw him-

self down on the edge of the open water, scooping up hand-
fuls and filling his avid mouth.

All around him, the birds were chattering – but even as he
drank their conversation ceased.

When he had had enough, he made no attempt to get up,
but simply rolled on to his back and looked upwards at the
sky.

The stars were out in force now, as restless as ever. They were
shifting this way and that, apparently at random, changing
colour very slightly as the quality of their light altered.

Dathan wondered whether they were as restless now as they
had been when he was a little child. Everyone said that they
were becoming quieter – that throughout his lifetime they had
been growing steadily less irritable – but Dathan could not
tell. He could not remember a time when the movement of
the stars had been noticeably more vigorous. Was it possible,
he wondered, that it was only anxiety that made his elders
think that the stars might be settling down?

The last time the stars had stood still, it was said, the
Imperium had fallen out of the sky: a dire punishment meted
out to the world. Were they to stand still again, it was said,
then the Imperium would come again. Today, of course, the
Imperium had come – but when Pater Saltana was at his scari-
est he would sometimes speak of an Imperium beyond the
world's Imperium: a True Imperium, vaster than anyone
could imagine. The world's Imperium could be fought, Pater
Saltana had always assured them – although Dathan was no
longer able to believe it – but the True Imperium was irresistible. If the god of Gulzacandra were ever displeased with
the prayers and sacrifices offered by his people, Pater Saltana
had prophesied, while his eyes had grown sulphurous and
terrible, then the god would merely rest his hand, the stars
would stand still in the heavens and death would rain down
from the sky.

According to Pater Saltana, in his quieter and gentler
moments, the stars did not really move at all, any more than
the sun moved around the world. The sun only appeared to
move across the sky because the world was turning, and the
stars only appeared to be restless because the world was in the
grip of a curious kind of storm: a storm whose winds stirred
the fundamental fabric of space, making waves in the void.

Even so, death could descend from the sky like a storm of hail, if the people of Gulzacandra were ungenerous in their sacrifices and unenthusiastic in their prayers.

All three moons had risen now, and all of them were full. Dathan had seen all three of them full at the same time on two previous occasions, but they had been far more widely distributed about the sky. He did not think that he had ever seen them so close together, even as crescents. By the time they reached their zenith, he judged, they would be even closer, arranged in a tight triangle whose sides were of equal length.

'*Dathan!*' Hycilla screamed, so loudly that he sat bolt upright.

It was as well that he did. He heard the sound of jaws snapping shut, so close that a little gust of foul breath stirred the hairs in the back of his neck.

Dathan didn't waste time looking around. He dived away from the poolside, sprawling among the rushes.

By the time he did turn round there was nothing to be seen on the pool's surface but a vast circle of spreading ripples.

Hycilla's silhouette loomed above him, blotting out a few of the stars. He couldn't see the hand that she was extending to him, but he knew it was there. He took it, and Hycilla helped him up. There was something in her touch that made him quiver, but he was grateful nevertheless.

'What was it?' he asked.

'Nothing I have a name for,' she told him. 'It had a long neck and a head like a snake's, but it seemed to have a big body submerged below the surface. I don't think it will come out of the water, and it'll probably move sluggishly if it does, but we'd better leave a wide margin just in case.'

Dathan was glad to observe that Hycilla sounded more like herself now. 'There's a place forty or fifty paces that way where we can lie down,' she added. 'The ground's not bare, but the grass isn't too tall or spiky, and we can make mattresses of a sort by cutting rushes. You have a knife, I suppose?'

'Only a little one,' Dathan told her, remembering how dreadfully inadequate it had seemed when he had needed a weapon. It proved, however, to be quite adequate to the task of cutting rushes, once he had broken the rigid stems.

'We should eat something,' Dathan told Hycilla, when they had made a makeshift bed on which to lie. 'Even if it isn't real food, it'll stop us feeling hungry.'

'No,' she said. 'The risk's too great. We'll find something tomorrow, when we're on the move again.' She knew the village saying as well as he did, and she must have jumped to the same conclusion about the nature of this place as he had. She was supposed to be a favourite of the true god, but even she didn't dare to eat the fruit of his garden.

Dathan was sure that his hunger would keep him awake, and not at all sure that he wanted to sleep, given that the pool was bound to attract predators from the plain as well as those that already lurked beneath its placid surface. He had underestimated the extent of his exhaustion though; almost as soon as he laid his head down, he fell into a shallow sleep as restless as the stars and full of inconvenient dreams.

Dathan had never shown the slightest sign of magical ability. Like every other village child, he had dutifully reported his dreams to Pater Saltana almost as soon as he learned to speak, and he still remembered how disappointed he had been to have them rejected as items of little interest. Hycilla's reported dreams had not sounded any different to his untutored ear, and he had been jealous when Pater Saltana began taking a greater interest in them.

Now, Dathan dreamed of ships in space: ships shaped like detached fingers, or fabulous eyeballs, or chicken-bones, but made of polished metal. He dreamed of whole flocks of ships, wheeling this way and that in unison, shooting forth fire that burned whole worlds and sent spears of lightning into the hearts of the gods themselves – but he knew all the while that this could not be wise-dreaming. It was only a froth of imagination born of horror, fed by fear, and made grotesque by the feverish heat of his blood.

Hycilla was even more restless than he, and Dathan was very conscious of the fact that she never fell still beside him. She was always turning from one side to the other, drawing her knees up to her belly at one moment and stretching her legs as straight as she could at the next. She was muttering too, although he could not make out what she was saying to herself – and the intermittent murmur wove itself into Dathan's own dreams as the voice of some hidden companion who was desperate to be understood but could not communicate its warnings. The voice became ever more frustrated as the failure continued. Dathan knew that it was not really Hycilla's voice.

It was the voice that had merged with hers when she made her long speech about wise-dreaming: the voice of something strange and scary.

Dathan wasn't at all sure that he wanted to listen to that voice, whether Hycilla were awake or asleep, but he couldn't stop himself.

Eventually, Dathan began to think that he could make sense of at least a few of the words whispered into his ear, but even when he came to that conclusion he couldn't decide whether it was the voice itself that was becoming clearer or whether his own dream was imposing a kind of clarity upon it.

Alas, much of what he discerned seemed to consist of the names of people and things, some of which were familiar and some of which were not.

Gavalon was the name most frequently repeated; that one he knew.

Another, almost as frequent, seemed to be Sathorael; that one he had never heard before. Kanak he knew, Fulbra he did not, nor Ecclesiarchy. Nor ork, nor Astronomican.

The one name he did not hear, no matter how hard he tried, was Dathan.

In the end, although the murmurous voice never died away, Dathan's attention was distracted by something far more disturbing: a great red-rimmed eye that seemed to fill his field of dream-vision, as if it were the eye of the sky itself. The iris of the eye was a thin rim of pink around a huge black hole, which poured forth a kind of light like one that Dathan had never seen with his waking eyes: light which withered everything it touched; the light of instantaneous decay.

That light seemed to be everywhere, the glare of the eye unavoidable.

'No matter how much confusion you see when you dream,' his dream-self told Hycilla – although she was not present in his dream as a listener – 'you cannot ever be free, and no matter what aspects of the future remain unmade and uncertain, the ultimate fate of everything is fleeting decay and absolute annihilation. Nothing endures and nothing can, and no matter what power the Imperium of Mankind may obtain and use, it is doomed to fall apart and vanish within a single moment in the great forever of Universal Time.'

He knew, though, that it was only a foolish dream. Dathan had never been touched, so far as he knew, by the god of his people. He had neither wisdom nor magic of his own, and he could not reasonably expect that Hycilla's whispering voice might transform the essence of his soul, no matter how much he loved her.

SIX

THE PLACE APPOINTED for the summoning was the crest of a curious semi-circular hill, which seemed very obviously out of place in the plain that formed the heartland of Gulzacandra. Gavalon assumed that it was, in fact, a huge circular object that had tumbled out of the sky in the distant past and embedded itself halfway into the continental bedrock.

Most meteors, Gavalon knew, exploded on impact with the ground if they had not already been evaporated by the friction of their passage through the atmosphere, but this one had merely had its outer and softer layers stripped away, leaving a dense metallic core so fiercely magnetic that it made compasses misleading for two hundred miles in every direction – a fact which, he hoped, was still unknown to the invading forces.

In spite of its awkward shape and texture, the protruding part of the star-shot had been covered in due course by native vegetation. Nothing could take root in the hill itself, but great creepers rooted deep in the surrounding soil had extended their branches over it, and the dead wood around the living heart had become a soil-substitute in which many other species could take root. As the leaves of the folding creepers died and rotted into the nooks and crannies of the wooden crown their litter provided further nourishment to parasitic and saprophytic plants – which provided food in their turn to a rich variety of lizards, snakes and giant centipedes, all of which were venomous to unprotected humans.

The crown of the hill was one of the true god's most private gardens, and had it not been for the fact that Gavalon had extended his own magical immunity to his retinue of beast-men – and, of course, to the Vessel – they would never have been able to reach the place where the ritual was to be conducted. Had the numerous preparatory sacrifices not been required well in advance, it would have been a very awkward task bringing the victims to the altar in a fit condition to be murdered, but the all-wise and ever-patient Changer of the Ways was always prepared to hold spilled blood to the credit of his agents, so that they might store up power for important rites. It was even rumoured that he paid interest on such accounts, and that ten gallons of blood leeched by clever torture a month in advance of its magical deployment would have the power of eleven by the time the design of the spell was completed.

This spell was not only the most intricate that Gavalon had ever attempted, but the most intricate that any sorcerer had attempted since humans first arrived on the world that the Imperium's star-maps had called Sigmatus. Gavalon had been working on the spell – gradually divining its shape and purpose as well as making the necessary preparations for the final ritual – for seven long years. He strongly suspected that from the viewpoint of the god he served the seven years in question had been merely the final phase of a much longer process.

To a god, of course, seven years was a mere eyeblink, and even two hundred years was little more than a moment. Gavalon suspected that the roots which the ritual had within the mysterious otherworld of the warp went back at least as far as the brief interval of spatial calm that had allowed the Imperial ships to land, and perhaps much further. He could not help wondering whether everything that had happened since those ships arrived might, in some fashion inconceivable to merely human beings, have been part of one of the legendary schemes of the Changer of the Ways. He could not help wondering, too, whether the sorcerer appointed to bring that scheme to its climax might be destined for better things than to remain merely human.

After all, Gavalon thought, if a miserable wretch like the Vessel could be transformed into a powerful daemon – albeit at the cost of the utter annihilation of his own personality – why should a steadfastly loyal sorcerer of no mean ability not be elevated at least to petty daemonhood?

Oh to be a Lord of Change!

What an ecstatic existence that must be!

The night was well advanced by the time the party reached the summit, but the stars were bright and the three moons were all full. The moons were all close to their zenith now, arranged in an equilateral triangle – a narrow conjunction which would not occur again for three hundred and twenty-seven years. This light was more than adequate to illuminate the ritual, in spite of the residual unsteadiness of the unusually quiet warpstorm.

The Vessel had to be stripped naked and laid out within the cup of a vast golden flower, whose pollen-bearing anthers obligingly made room for him, and then began to caress him gently.

Nimian, alas, had to be conscious throughout – and being the imbecile that he was, he could not help giggling a little as the anthers tickled him. Mercifully, he was far too terrified to try to say anything.

The beastmen took their places with the calm obedience expected of somnambulists. Gavalon had not had to waste any of his own energy in hypnotising them; the scent of the night-blooming flowers had delivered them smoothly into a trance while they climbed the side of the natural dome. Gavalon was free, therefore, to concentrate all his attention on the words of the incantation and the accompanying gestures.

In truth, this component of the spell was not as difficult as others he had worked to much lesser effect – or so it seemed when he struck his opening pose and began to chant.

Gavalon held a dagger with a wavy blade in his right hand and a lighted torch in his left, both of which would have to be introduced to his flesh at the appointed moments. He was no stranger to constructive self-mutilation, and it would not be the first time that he had put out an eye or cut off a designated appendage. Provided that one had faith, and the favour of

one's divine master, such excisions rarely hurt as much as one
might expect, and the damage was always repaired, after a
fashion. Indeed, his twice-regrown left eye saw far more, and
far more keenly, than the one he had been born with, even if
it was by far the uglier of the now ill-matched pair.

At least it was the right eye that he had to burn out this time,
so there was a slim chance that he would end up with two that
were not so conspicuously unalike. As for the other appendage
he had to remove – well, that had never been part of a pair and
it was so rarely on public view that it hardly mattered how
bizarrely distorted it was or how strangely complicated its
inbuilt sprinkler had become. It still remained perfectly serviceable as an instrument of ravishment, and might even be
considered to be all the more effective for its thorniness.

When the appropriate points of the ritual arrived, therefore,
Gavalon the Great did not hesitate or tremble. Nor did he
begrudge the god he was proud to serve the last and least of
the many sacrifices he had offered in pursuit of this particular
end.

The pain of his newly-incandescent eye was a little worse
than usual, but that discomfort had to be offset against the
remarkable changes of colour that the torchlight underwent
while consuming it, which his left eye found quite beautiful.

The other cut hardly hurt at all as the razor-keen serpentine
blade sliced through old scar-tissue, and the blood which
fountained from the liberated veins was so thick and rich that
it reflected the starlight wonderfully.

It would have been pleasant to be able to mutilate the flesh
of the Vessel too, but that was not Gavalon's prerogative. As
the syllables of the rite spilled out into the quiet night, the
petals of the golden flower folded about the boy, drawing him
into a kind of womb – a womb from which he was destined to
be very soon reborn, the gestation of the spell having already
come to the brink of its full term.

Even before the incantation was complete, Gavalon felt his
right eye grow again within his head, and felt sight return to it.
As he looked up into the glorious sky, he knew that this was
an eye that would see far more, and far more keenly, than its
twice-renewed counterpart.

He felt his other wound turn to scar-tissue too, and felt the
scab swell with awesome pride as it was rough-hewn into a

tumour, and then into something for which even the secret language of sorcery had no ready-made name.

Oh to be a Lord of Change! he thought. Oh to be a master of metamorphosis, defiant of common decay! What bliss it is to serve the true god, and to be free!

He knew in his heart, of course, that he was not free at all – that he was, in the final analysis, no less a slave to fate and fortune than the Vessel or the stupidest of beastmen – but he was convinced that those who willingly accepted slavery, and chose their masters very carefully, were as fortunate as any merely human being ever could be. And he was convinced, too, that his was the only course that could ever lead a man to a destiny that was more than merely human.

When the penultimate phase of the incantation ended Gavalon paused, letting a minute's reverent silence elapse – and he looked eagerly at the tightly-closed flower, agog to see what manner of being would be reborn therefrom. Then he spoke the final word, and brought the spell to its conclusion.

The final word and ultimate purpose of the ritual was: *Sathorael*.

Gavalon felt the rock beneath his feet vibrate very slightly.

Even through the thick detritus of many generations of creepers and all the secondary growth that the creepers had facilitated, Gavalon could see that the huge sphere had begun to glow. While the vibration increased, until it resembled a heartbeat, the glow brightened from vermilion to crimson to vivid scarlet, and finally to a lividly luminous shocking pink.

Gavalon realised that the half-buried star-shot was some kind of egg, and that the folded flower was more akin to a birth-canal than a womb. That which was being seeded in the Vessel's body was far too great a thing to be long contained in any structure of flesh, no matter what kind of metamorphosis it could achieve.

The petals of the flower began to unfold, peeling back with stately slowness to display their cargo.

Gavalon had to suppress a pang of disappointment to which he knew he was not entitled. Nimian had been laid down within the flower and Nimian was still there, so languidly extended that he might have been sent to sleep by boredom. His flesh seemed fresher, to be sure, but it was just as pale as it had been before, an egg-shell white unburnished by the sun.

When the Vessel began to sit up, his movements seemed more supple, but his limbs were as scrawny as ever. It was not until he opened his eyes and met Gavalon's inquisitive stare that Nimian gave the slightest indication of being something more than human.

Nimian had never dared to meet Gavalon's intimidating eyes before, but he looked into them frankly now. His own eyes had become pools of shadow, quite devoid of iris or white.

'Gavalon?' he said, curiously wrapping his tongue around the syllables, as if uncertain of their exact significance – or if determined to savour the gift of speech.

'Your humble servant,' said Gavalon, insincerely. Given that the daemon-to-be was still wearing Nimian's body, the words sounded slightly absurd as well as indecent, but propriety had to be maintained. Even if he were still addressing Nimian, the Final Sacrifice, and not Sathorael, the Instrument of Vengeance, he had to be polite. It was slightly galling to think that this stupid boy had suffered so little by comparison with his fellow sacrifices, or even by comparison with Gavalon himself, but the sorcerer knew that his faint resentment was probably undue and certainly ought not to be voiced.

'Feel strange,' the boy said. 'Not myself.'

That worried Gavalon. It was obviously Nimian who was speaking, his soul by no means fully obliterated. Was that because the soul in question was fated to be devoured slowly, so that it might savoured like any other experience of the flesh? Or was it possible… could it possibly be… that something had gone wrong? Had the ritual been imperfect? Was Nimian's metamorphosis going awry?

No, Gavalon decided. This was the way it was supposed to happen: slowly, languorously, indulgently. It had to be. The alternative was unthinkable.

'Better,' the Vessel said, after a moment's pause. 'Feel better. But not myself.'

'Understandable, lord,' said Gavalon. 'Such a transformation must be difficult, even for a daemon-to-be.'

Nimian giggled at that. 'Lord!' he repeated, wonderingly. 'You called me lord! Gavalon the Great called me lord!'

It was unthinkable, Gavalon reminded himself, firmly, that anything could possibly have gone wrong. This must be seen as a test of his patience. However much of the boy remained within the Vessel, the eyes revealed the truth. The eyes were the windows of the soul, and there was nothing in them now but a void impenetrable even to Gavalon's augmented sight: the void of the warp itself.

'Your army awaits, lord,' Gavalon said, patiently. 'The enemy has already crossed the wastelands, faster than we anticipated, and the final battle will not be long delayed. It is time to show these bastard children of the Imperium whose world this is, and always will be.'

'Army?' repeated the boy, still making the most of every syllable. 'Do I need an army?'

Did the daemon-to-be really need an army? Gavalon wondered. Perhaps not. On the other hand, given that he had gone to such pains to provide the daemon with an army, it would surely be slightly churlish of the daemon and the Changer of the Ways to spurn its services. Was there not to be a war of vengeance? Were the Imperial soldiers to be allowed to put Gulzacandra to the sword without the Gulzacandrans having the opportunity to retaliate? The dead of Gulzacandra were sacrifices of a sort, of course, whose deaths would therefore be pleasing to the god for whom they died – but surely the god would not let too many of his worshippers perish, especially while they included such worthy champions as Gavalon the Great. Was not the daemon-to-be here to turn the tide of battle? Should the daemon not be eager to review his troops?

Gavalon was acutely conscious of the fact that he did not know the answers to any of these questions. He had spent three long years divining the sequence of the spell and the pattern of its rituals, but he had never been shown the climax of the god's plan. The simple and deeply embarrassing fact was that he did not know exactly what the daemon-to-be had come to do, or how, or to what extent it would alleviate the peril in which the faithful of Gulzacandra presently stood. He had made the best guesses he could, but they were only guesses.

'An army is a very useful thing, lord,' Gavalon pointed out, anxiously. 'There is nothing quite so adept at spilling enemy blood as an army. And there must be bloodshed, must there not? The Imperium must be made to bleed, and suffer, profusely.'

'Don't know,' said the boy – which was, Gavalon reflected, quite the most disturbing thing he could have said.

Gavalon could not imagine that Sathorael would ever have said such a thing as 'Don't know'. He reminded himself, however, that what was before him was not yet Sathorael, even though Sathorael was plainly incarnate in those lovely eyes of darkness. Nimian obviously still held a measure of dominion over his own flesh, and his own mind. And why not? If this metamorphosis had been more than two hundred years in the making, why should it not proceed to its terminus in a leisurely fashion. How many other opportunities would the daemon have to taste the petty pleasures and paradoxes of a human being?

Perhaps, Gavalon thought, a human body and soul – even a human body and soul as miserable as Nimian's – was a meal not to be hurried: a meal worth savouring to the full.

But the army was waiting, and the enemy was coming, far too rapidly for comfort – and the final battle could not be long delayed, if there were indeed to be a final battle.

'There must be bloodshed, lord,' Gavalon said, deciding that if the daemon-to-be needed help, then it was his duty to be helpful. 'There must be abundant bloodshed, not only by way of sacrifice but for the sake of delight. The outworlders have been busy breeding for ten generations, and it is time for the harvest. On the other hand, the descendants of the first new-comers in Kalazendra, Bulzavara, Zendamora and Yevelkana have been breeding for a thousand generations, and their next harvest season is surely more than due. Yes, lord, there must certainly be bloodshed, and it must be very generously distributed. It is time for the casual slaughter of the guns and the iron discipline of the new overlords to be countered, and balanced. An army is a very useful device for work such as that, lord. I have put a hundred thrall-wizards, two hundred coven-masters and all manner of beastmen at your disposal. They have the means to provide you with a great deal of pleasure, as well as the kind of food that you will doubtless need and desire.'

'Food,' the naked boylike thing repeated, in a tone which made Gavalon regret his choice of the word 'doubtless'. The sorcerer realised, belatedly, that he did not actually know what kind of nourishment Sathorael would need to complete his metamorphosis, or what taste-sensations he might desire.

The daemon-to-be obviously had ideas of his own on that score. 'Good idea,' he said. 'Want food.' He seemed a little larger now, and a little sturdier, as if even the mere idea of food had set him a little further along the road to daemon-hood.

As soon as he had voiced his desire for food, the daemon-to-be began to look around. Then he moved, pouncing upon a snake that had been sleeping beneath the golden flower. He lifted the snake high into the air, his illimitably dark eyes fixed upon it with a kind of greed that only a void could manifest.

The snake hissed, and opened its mouth to expose poison-dripping fangs, but the daemon-to-be lowered its dangling head into his mouth and closed his teeth upon it, then fed the two-foot tail inch by inch into the same ravenous maw.

'Better,' he said, when the snake had completely disappeared into his throat. 'Much better.' The metamorphosis of Nimian's flesh had clearly begun. He was still pale, but the beginnings of a pattern had begun to emerge on his skin, like the ghost of the snake he had just consumed.

The boy darted away to the left, then to the right. Within five minutes he had consumed two more snakes, a warty crested lizard and a centipede the size of a beastman's belt. The meal seemed to give the newborn creature considerable satisfaction.

'Water,' said the daemon-to-be, thirstily. 'Need water.'

'We shall have to go down to the plain to find water, lord,' Gavalon said. 'I fear that I neglected to bring a flask, even for my own use.'

He had not noticed until he said it how thirsty he had become. Burning an eye out always made him thirsty, now he came to think about it, but he had not yet done it often enough to have come to a full appreciation of the correlation. How thirsty, the,n was the daemon-thing?

The boy who was no longer a boy had found a globular fruit half-buried in the flesh of a growth. It looked like a cross between a giant cactus and a toadstool. He wrenched it free without apparent effort and cracked it like an eggshell, drinking the fluid contained within its core. He offered the last few drops to Gavalon, but finished them off when Gavalon shook his head.

'Still thirsty,' the daemon-child announced. 'Go down now.'

Gavalon was quick to agree, and he signalled to the beast-men, who had not yet recovered from their trance state – but as he turned to lead the way the boy straightened, pricking up a pair of ears that suddenly seemed twice as large as they had before, lavishly tufted with orange hair. The face was still Nimian's face, apart from the eyes and ears, and the limbs were still Nimian's scrawny limbs, except that both the arms and the legs now seemed at least a hand's-breadth longer, but the patterned whole was unmistakably not Nimian – and the voice, when it spoke again, had a very different timbre.

'Soldiers are coming, Gavalon,' the newborn said. 'I can hear and see them, only a few miles off. The trucks are driving through the night, using their headlights to find a way across the plain. They will be here before morning – a little too late... but the margin of that lateness might be inconveniently little... or perhaps inconveniently great...' The voice trailed off, as if the mind behind it could not bring all the possibilities into focus.

'Yes, lord,' Gavalon said, feeling a distinct undercurrent of anxiety mingling with the tidal surge of his relief. 'Your army awaits you, lord.'

'Gavalon,' said the embryo of the daemon Sathorael, slowly and rather dreamily, 'you have not the slightest idea what awaits me, and nor have I. Let us hope that we shall both have an interesting time finding out.'

And without waiting for an answering comment, the Vessel suddenly set off down the precipitous slope, running at a reckless pace that no mere man or beastman could hope to match.

Suppose he falls! Gavalon thought – but the idea that the Vessel might be broken before the daemon it had been born to contain had time to emerge was too horrible to contemplate. The dawning awareness that the Vessel was already out of sight, and that Gavalon had not the faintest idea where he was going, or why, was quite bad enough to be going on with. Gavalon was not vain enough to think that the daemon-to-be really needed him, but he was not in the slightest doubt that he needed the daemon-to-be. Without the daemon to help him, even an army led by the greatest sorcerer in Gulzacandra could not hope to make a stand against the kind of weaponry Ierius Fulbra had.

'Well, don't just stand there,' Gavalon howled at the stupefied beastmen. *'Follow him!'*

SEVEN

DATHAN WOKE UP with a start, astonished and alarmed to discover that he had been asleep. Hycilla was sleeping beside him, deeply but not restfully. She lay still, but she was muttering feverishly, as if engrossed in some tense argument. He could see her face quite clearly, illuminated as it was by the lamps of the three full moons. They had passed their zenith now and their tight formation had begun to break as the nearer ones gradually pulled ahead of the most distant.

How long would it be, Dathan wondered, before they came so close to a perfect alignment again? But he had no time for such abstract questions; the more urgent issue was what had woken him up. Dawn was still some way off, and the environs of the pool seemed perfectly still. The only sound he could hear was a muted hum, like a swarm of bees around a hive.

Bees? In the dead of night?

Dathan sat up, trying to figure out which direction the noise was coming from. He settled on east. Then he stood up – and once he was upright peering over the bushes, he saw the lights. There were three bright ones, arranged like the midnight moons in a tight triangle with a horizontal base and a bright apex – but there were others behind, half-hidden.

The muted hum was the sound of distant engines; already it was growing towards a roar.

Dathan knelt down and began shaking Hycilla urgently.

'Wake up!' he begged her. 'They're coming after us! A convoy of trucks, using headlamps and a searchlight to guide them across the plain.'

It wasn't easy to rouse her; wise-dreamers slept more deeply than ordinary folk, even when they were dreaming as foolishly as anyone else, and Hycilla had matured as a wise-dreamer during the last few hours. Once Dathan had dragged her to her feet, however, and pointed to the approaching lights, Hycilla soon realised the extent of their danger.

'That's silly,' she said. 'Why chase us?'

Dathan had already realised that his first assumption was probably wrong. 'They must be heading for the water-hole,' he said. 'They must have a map. An invasion force would need good maps – and they must have been preparing to invade Gulzacandra for a long time.'

Hycilla didn't answer immediately – her lips were forming the shapes of numbers as she tried to count the trucks, but it wasn't easy while the others were lined up behind the lead vehicle.

'There aren't that many,' Dathan told her. 'Five or six, maybe seven. An advance party – probably scouts. There's a hill up ahead – maybe they want to occupy it for use as an observation-post. It's the only high point for many a mile, and they won't know that there's nothing to be seen from the top of it but more wild country.'

'We don't know that,' Hycilla pointed out. 'For all we know, Gavalon's army might be camped within a mile of it.'

'If it were,' Dathan retorted, 'our people would probably have occupied it already. The point is, what do we do? The best hiding-places are close to the pool, but if we don't get far enough away and they decide to stop for water, they'll be far too close for comfort.'

'We ought to try to find out what they're up to,' Hycilla said, although she didn't sound very positive. 'It might be important.'

'It won't do any good to find out if we can't pass the information on,' Dathan said – but he knew that they had already argued too long. The way the trucks ate up the ground was quite amazing to someone used to watching caravans of camules plod across the Amber Waste. He grabbed the sleeve of Hycilla's shirt and pulled her in a direction directly opposite to the pool – which happened to be a little east of north.

The further they went the less cover there was, but Dathan knew that they had to make the best compromise they could, without any further hesitation. The searchlight was already within range, and although their blue and brown clothing was reasonably dark, the light only had to pick out their pale faces to alert the approaching Imperial soldiers to their presence.

'Here!' Dathan said, as he found a clump of bushes that seemed reasonably dense but not at all thorny. Hycilla ducked down readily enough, but stiffened suddenly.

'They'll see the cut reeds,' she hissed, anxiously. 'They'll know we're here.'

It was far too late to do anything about their makeshift beds, and Dathan wasn't sure that they could have done very much even if they had thought of it sooner. The only alternative they had now was to run as fast as they could into the night and keep on running – but they might not be able to outrun the reach of the searchlight no matter how quickly they moved.

The trucks fanned out as they approached the pool. More searchlights came on, raking back and forth across the fertile patch of ground. Half a dozen animals broke cover and ran from the light, and there was a brief crackle of gunshots. Dathan heard one creature come crashing to earth, and shuddered slightly at the realisation that he had not had the slightest idea that anything so massive was lurking nearby.

'I hope the meat poisons them,' Hycilla muttered – but wild pigs were good eating, even though they often fed themselves on plants that were not, and ghazal meat was harmless even though it was somewhat lacking in nutritional value.

They heard orders barked back and forth as the men disembarked from the trucks – orders which suggested that the enemy soldiers did not intend to pause for long once they had laid in stocks of water. Some, however, were told to take torches and search the bushes for 'anything useful' – presumably meaning anything edible.

The trucks had so many lights that Dathan could see the Imperial soldiers quite clearly. Like the two men he had seen in the judeye forest they wore tightly-fitting grey uniforms. The weavers in his village were skilled, but they could not turn out clothing so neatly-tailored. Dathan had always thought his clothes perfectly adequate, but he had never been able to compare their fabric with such cloth as this.

The boots and belts the soldiers wore were even more impressive. There was no tanner in the village, so all the leather-goods its people possessed had to be bought, but Dathan was lucky enough to have a pair of boots that no more than a dozen boys before him had discarded, having recklessly grown out of them. By comparison with the high boots these men wore, though, Dathan's were horribly shoddy. In addition to their well-stocked belts, the soldiers' uniforms had pockets and buttons. They were decorated with all manner of insignia, whose meanings Dathan could not begin to guess.

Dathan had not had time to study the men in the forest before hurrying to distract them with stones, and he had kept his head so fixedly down while they were murdering Houlme that he had hardly caught a further glimpse of them. Now that he could see them clearly, though, he realised how very unlike him the Imperial soldiers were. Everything they wore or carried was better-designed and better-made.

Gulzacandra was a civilized land, Dathan had always been told. It had preserved a useful measure of the learning brought to the world by the very first humans – but he doubted that there was anything in Gulzacandra's cities to match the clothes the Imperial soldiers wore, let alone the guns that they carried.

'Lie low and lie still,' Dathan warned Hycilla. 'Don't look up if the light shines our way.' It was obvious enough, as much a reminder to himself as an instruction to her. She didn't answer, and didn't bother to tell him to be as silent as he was still.

Dathan heard splashing sounds as soldiers gathered by the pool-side, doubtless jockeying for position as they lowered containers into the water. They seemed greatly relieved to have found the pool, and Dathan wondered why their supplies were so low when less than fifteen hours had passed since they had captured the village well. Could Kanak possibly have spoiled the well? If so, then the village was dead as well as defeated; without a reliable well it could never be rebuilt.

The night was rent by a sudden scream, and Dathan remembered his lucky escape. There was a quick blast of gunfire, combining the rattle of a dozen shots with the sinister, sizzling hiss of a kind of weapon to which he could not put a name. There was a new fusillade of orders and curses. Even the curses the Imperial soldiers used seemed more impressive than those Dathan had heard in the mouths of labourers and tradesmen, referring to an Emperor and a Throne. Was there an Emperor in Kalazendra, Dathan wondered, or were the soldiers preserving lore of their own, which their ancestors had brought with them when they fell from the sky?

Most of the shouted orders were reminders of the need to conserve ammunition. When the panic had died down, though, there was a residual moaning which suggested that the lurker in the pool had not only drawn blood but inflicted a serious casualty on the enemy.

Gulzacandra strikes back! Dathan thought, exultantly.

His exultation did not last long. Two soldiers were coming in his direction, shining their torches about them – all the more urgently, now they knew that danger lurked in the shadows. These were not the feeble torches that villagers occasionally improvised from oil-soaked rags. Their beams were white and penetrating. They were machines which had seemingly domesticated the light of the sun.

Unfortunately, there were animals hiding in the undergrowth, whose instincts commanded them to lie low until they were exposed – and then to run in panic.

No animal that was not panic-stricken would ever have run into a thicket where humans were hiding, but these torches were too obvious a breach of normal circumstance. A sow and a litter of half a dozen piglets broke from their own hiding-place and ran straight for the densest cover around – which was, alas, exactly what Dathan had picked out as an ideal hiding place.

The sow ran right into him, pursued by gunfire. He had no alternative but to roll sideways as the animal realised her mistake and turned to fight as only a desperate mother would. Had two gunshots not taken her down immediately she would probably have done him some damage, but as it was she only contrived to give him away to the men with torches, who were as quick to pounce on the two villagers as they had been to shoot the pig.

'Lie still, peasant!' Dathan was ordered, as a booted foot came down heavily on his back, pinning him down. He heard a second and identical order, and knew immediately, even though his face was pressed down into the soil, that Hycilla had suffered the same fate.

Moments later, he was hauled to his feet as his captor shouted back the news that 'two hostiles' had been captured.

The Imperial soldiers dragged Dathan and Hycilla to the back of one of the trucks, and shoved them up against the tailboard. Six or seven torches were shining in their faces, and they were blinded by the dazzle.

'They're unarmed,' one voice pointed out.

'There may be more!'

'There's some rushes over there, sir, cut to make a mattress of sorts. Only big enough for two.'

'Doesn't mean there weren't four or six – might have been taking turns to sleep.'

'Just make sure you cover the area, sector by sector. You! Where do you come from?'

There didn't seem to be any point in lying. 'The village,' Dathan said.

'Which village?'

'The village.'

Whoever had asked the question didn't like that answer. The shadow of a rifle-butt flickered in the blaze of light and clipped Dathan on the chin – but the man who had struck out at him had already been interrupted and hauled back.

'He's just an aborigine kid. His village is the whole bloody world. He's probably never seen a map, let alone heard the names on it. Which way were you coming from, kid? Away from the sun or towards it?' They obviously thought his ignorance extended to not knowing east and west by their proper names, which just went to prove that they were the stupid ones – city-bred merchants always assumed that farmers and rural tradesmen were idiots, and soldiers must be even more confident of their intellectual superiority.

'We're from the village you attacked yesterday,' Dathan told them, his voice fractured by anger and despair. 'We were in the judeye forest when you set it on fire. There was only one way to run.'

'And only one place to aim for, at least on day one,' his questioner concluded, seemingly satisfied that his powers of deduction were little short of awesome. 'Did you meet the critter in the pond? Or did you know it was there?'

'I didn't know,' Dathan said grimly. 'If Hycilla hadn't screamed, it would have got me.'

More than one of them laughed at that.

'You ever been this far from home before?'

'No,' Dathan said.

'You're Hycilla?' the questioner said, turning his attention to his second captive. 'You ever been this way before, Hycilla?'

'Not this far,' Hycilla said. Dathan didn't know whether she was lying, but he suspected that she might be. He hadn't had to, but she had spent time alone with Pater Saltana lately, and not in the village.

'There's supposed to be a hemispherical formation west of here – that's like half a ball, as if the ball were buried half-way deep in the soil. You see anything like that before the sun set?'

Hycilla didn't answer, and Dathan sensed movement within the blaze, as if the rifle-butt were being readied for another blow.

'I saw it,' he said, quickly, knowing that it couldn't possibly make any difference. 'It's a long way off.'

'If you could see it,' the questioner said, still exceedingly self-satisfied, 'it's close enough. We aren't savages walking barefoot – we have trucks… horseless carts. Vroom vroom.'

Dathan didn't bother to point out that he and Hycilla were wearing boots. He had already realised that the soldier's opinion as to what might constitute a serviceable pair of boots was likely to be different from his own.

'Should we kill them now?' another voice wanted to know. 'There's something weird about the girl – might be a mutant.'

'No,' said the questioner, who was presumably an officer. 'We've got water now – and we can assume it's safe to drink, as these two must have tried it out hours ago – but we still need food. They know better than we do what's edible.'

'We've got a converter.'

'Sure we do – and the prayers to go with it. But even the tech-priests admit converters aren't much good if they're only converting local crap that's as much use to us as wood-shavings. This place is full of mutants, plants and animals alike. I've been out in the wilderness before, and I know the value of local knowledge.'

'What local knowledge? They said themselves they haven't been out here before. They grow their own, just like aborigines everywhere. Even if they did know anything, they'd lie. I can see the point of keeping the girl a while, unless she really is a mutant, but we ought to kill the boy regardless.'

'Didn't you kill enough kids yesterday? Have a bit of patience, why don't you? He's a farm-boy, not a sorcerer. So how do you fancy jobs as head interpreter and number one poison-taster, kids? Bearing in mind that you just heard the alternative.'

'It won't help you,' Hycilla said, her voice unnaturally calm. 'Your leaders shouldn't have sent you out here like this. You'll never get back alive, with or without our help. You'll all be dead by sunset.'

That changed the mood of the men who were ranged about them in a semi-circle. Such good humour as they had exhibited was only a defence against their anxiety. They knew well enough that theirs was the riskiest position of any so far taken up by the invading army. 'May the Emperor protect us,' muttered one man, reflexively. 'Praise Him,' echoed another.

'Who's going to kill us?' the officer who had been asking the questions wanted to know – but his voice had changed slightly now that he had heard Hycilla speak. He could not possibly know that the voice she had used was not entirely her own, but there was something in it that had disturbed him. He was apprehensive.

'You won't even see them,' Hycilla continued. Her voice was thick, as if she had not fully emerged from the wise-dream whose confusion had overflowed into the mutterings Dathan had heard.

'Are you talking about your precious coven-masters?' the officer demanded. 'Or the horde of beastmen they're supposed to be gathering? Is that what they tell you, to keep you in their thrall – that when the evil day comes, they'll use their power to destroy your enemies? Well, I've got news for you. We've got inquisitors and tech-priests, and prayers that work, and our power outweighs all the petty tricks your hedge-wizards can turn. We're the Imperium.'

'That you are not,' Hycilla replied, gravely, in a voice so unnaturally deep that Dathan could find none of the old Hycilla in it at all.

'What do you know about it?' the officer wanted to know – but his unease seemed to have increased.

'I said she was a mutant,' another voice put in. 'I say kill them both, now.' This time it was the barrel of a rifle that came out of the wall of light to prod Dathan in the chest and thrust him painfully back against the tailboard of the truck.

'He's right – we ought to kill them now,' said a third voice.

'Wait!' said the officer. 'If she really does know something, I want to learn what she knows about this thing that's going to kill us all before next nightfall. If you want to live, girl, you'd better tell me something I need to hear. Give me a reason to hold on to you a little while longer.'

As promises went, Dathan thought, it was distinctly lacking in generosity – but Hycilla was still in the same trance-like calm.

'Nothing I can tell you will be the least use to you,' the voice that was not hers said, indifferently, 'but if you think differently, your exterminator is already within two hundred paces, approaching very quickly from the west.'

'What?' The officer plainly didn't believe it – but even if he had, Hycilla was right. The information was no use to him. Neither the officer nor any of his men had time to begin another sentence before the screaming and the shooting started.

The noise was coming from the west side of the camp – and Dathan suddenly felt certain that whenever the name of the Emperor was voiced now, it was voiced in desperation and superstitious terror, not in careless and casual disregard of its true meaning.

Dathan knew that he hadn't a second to spare – and he knew that he couldn't trust Hycilla to act rationally while she was in this state. He ducked down, dragging her down with him, and then he folded his arms tightly around her as he rolled between the back wheels of the truck, under the chassis.

The lights had moved away in alarm; where there had been a wall of light directed at him there was now only confusion as the turning soldiers dazzled one another. The group had already begun to scatter, its members getting their weapons ready to fire.

It would only have required one of the soldiers to kneel down and unleash a quick burst of any kind of fire beneath the truck – but no one gave that order and no one took the burden of responsibility upon himself. Like the sow that had betrayed the two villagers, the soldiers were creatures of instinct and trained reflex – and Hycilla's melodramatic announcements had pressed all the right buttons. As soon as the screaming broke out, the soldiers ran to face the prophesied enemy that had come to kill them.

'What is it that's coming?' Dathan whispered, urgently, in Hycilla's ear. 'What in the world is it?'

'I don't know,' Hycilla said, in her own voice, while trembling with stress and more than a little fear, 'but I felt it coming, and it's powerful. The trouble is – I don't know if it knows the difference between them and us. We're hardly big enough to be noticed, and if it doesn't notice us…'

The tenor of the multiplying screams and the wild desperation of the gunfire persuaded Dathan that Hycilla might well be right. He did not need an atom of talent to tell him that whatever had come had not come to save them, no matter how convenient its timing had been.

It had come for its own reasons, the first and foremost of which was to kill.

EIGHT

'INCREASE THE DOSAGE.'

The priest, whose name was Carro Alpalhao, looked up anxiously at Ragan Balberith. He maintained his position, kneeling beside the bed of the stricken man, although the cell was so small that he had to crane his neck awkwardly to meet the Chief Inquisitor's gaze.

'It's dangerous,' he said, fearfully. The objection was highly ambiguous, although the statement was undoubtedly true. The drug that Alpalhao was using in the hope of stimulating the psyker's ability was a local product, identical to the one that the cultists used to stimulate their own 'wise-dreamers'. Even their priests – who had used the stuff for centuries, if not for millennia – occasionally overdosed their charges, with fatal results.

The drug was doubly dangerous. It was toxic, and its toxicity was a mutant product of the warp. The second danger opened up the possibility that any information a psyker of pure immigrant stock derived by means of its use might be tainted at the most elementary level. It wasn't just the possibility that the drug would have the wrong effect that had frightened the priest, though. Balberith knew that Alpalhao was also fright-

89

ened that it might have the right effect. Nobody liked being around a juiced-up psyker, not even a priest.

The priests who had been aboard the ships that had brought the Imperium to Sigmatus must have been made of sterner stuff, Balberith supposed. They must have been far more steadfast in their faith, far more certain in their trust in the beloved Emperor and the power of his blood. Castaways isolated from civilization for generations, cross-breeding all the while with aborigines who were faithless at best, could hardly help losing knowledge, but the gradual loss of faith was surely the more dangerous erosion. He and his predecessors had done everything in their power to ensure that the aborigines with whom Imperial blood was mingled were only faithless, not actually tainted by the creeping corruption of Chaos, but how could he be certain of his own success, let alone that of his forebears? If contact with the True Imperium were not restored soon, so that authentic inquisitors and priests could be put in place of those who presently bore the name, Sigmatus might be doomed even if Ierius Fulbra's campaign in Gulzacandra were successful.

That was a thought that Balberith could not tolerate. Sigmatus must be reunited with the True Imperium, and properly purged. Only the priests and inquisitors of the True Imperium could be trusted to judge the exact extent to which corruption had permeated Kalazendra, Sostenuto, and Orloc Melcarth's so-called palace.

Balberith knew that Orloc Melcarth must have heard by now that the psyker had reported the approach of the Imperial Fleet. He had spies everywhere.

Although Balberith had no proof, he was certain in his own mind that Melcarth had ordered the assassination of other psykers, not so much because he feared what they might learn as because he feared what they might communicate. Orloc Melcarth believed that his army was winning the war of conquest – and so it was, if one took a limited view of what 'conquest' meant – but he must know perfectly well that the men who were still proud to call themselves the Imperium could not win the war against the forces of mutation that had contrived the slow corruption of this world, unless they had help.

Melcarth might pretend that Gulzacandra was the last refuge on Sigmatus of sorcerers and coven-masters, but it was only pretence. The governor was no fool, and he knew perfectly well that the sorcerers and coven-masters of the puppet states had merely been driven underground, and that Sostenuto was by no means free from the taint of Chaos, despite being the capital of Kalazendra and the first base of the immigrant community.

Orloc Melcarth, to whom the word 'Imperium' meant power of a perfectly straightforward kind, saw no problem in describing himself as the Planetary Governor and his administrative apparatus as the Imperium. Ragan Balberith, by contrast, knew that the word Imperium meant faith, purity and discipline, and he was very keenly aware of the vanity of describing himself as a Chief Inquisitor, even though he was heir to a long chain of appointments that must have begun with an authentic inquisitor.

Balberith often wondered what that authentic inquisitor would make of the present situation on Sigmatus. When formulating his own strategies, he often asked himself: 'What would the First Inquisitor of Sigmatus want to achieve, and how would he go about it?' Sometimes he thought that he knew the answer. Mostly, alas, he knew only too well that he did not.

Two hundred years – even if they had been 'real' years instead of slow local years – was too long a separation. Far too much had been lost as vital knowledge had been handed down from generation to generation. The descendants of the colony ships' crews had tried with all their might to learn everything their fathers had to teach them, and to offer up their prayers with all due conviction. Every generation had tried with all its might to pass on the whole truth – but even the truth needed reinforcement by context. Even the strongest faith was bound to weaken when the power of the Emperor was not manifest in everyday circumstance.

The raw power of the Imperium had weakened as the guns imported by the ships developed mechanical faults, or ran out of ammunition, but that slow decay had been visible and easily understandable. The decay of faith, purity and discipline was far less easy to map out, and far more mercurial. No one knew – not even the Chief Inquisitor himself – exactly how much, or in what precise ways, the spiritual aspects of the Imperium had decayed during the Sigmatus exile. The tech-priests still said their prayers, but as the technologies the prayers helped to maintain were subject to a slow decay, so was the faith that sustained the prayers. That was why the dosage of the drug that was being fed to the psyker had to be increased, no matter what dangers the increase might involve.

If there really were an Imperial Fleet nearby, contact had to be restored – or everything would eventually be lost.

Balberith knew that the war of conquest was necessary, given the nourishment that Gulzacandra's coven-masters lent to their fugitive kin in the other four continents, but he knew that it would not be enough. No matter how well it would serve Melcarth's selfish vanity, it could not save the Imperium of Sigmatus – and if Melcarth's vanity were as great as it sometimes seemed, Fulbra's triumph might even serve to accelerate that petty Imperium's decline.

In the longer term, even if Fulbra were victorious, Sigmatus would surely be lost to Chaos. The only thing that could possibly prevent that was to restore contact with the Imperium – and Ragan Balberith was painfully well aware of the fact that the window of opportunity that had recently been opened by the recent abatement of the warpstorm might not be open very long.

There was, of course, another danger, which the Chief Inquisitor felt as keenly as any man: the danger that if he managed to alert the real Imperium to the state of affairs on Sigmatus the response might be an order of Exterminatus. Balberith was, however, one of very few men left in the local Imperium who could accept that fate with philosophical resignation if it were deemed necessary.

Perhaps, Balberith thought, that was the danger on the priest's mind as he continued to hesitate, with the phial containing the drug in his hand – but it seemed unlikely. The priest was the kind of man who was more easily frightened by obvious possibilities. Unlike the psyker, the priest was a half-breed. There was nothing in their names to indicate the difference – the psyker's name was Deir Ajao – but it was real nevertheless.

In fact, Balberith thought, that might well be the real root of the problem. The ships that had landed on Sigmatus two hundred years before had been sent on an investigative mission. They had been well-staffed with soldiers and functionaries of the Adeptus Terra, but their crews had been ninety per cent male. The soldiers had left an abundance of descendants, but nine hundred and ninety-nine out of every thousand now living had at least one aboriginal mother in their bloodline. The Adeptus Terra had been more careful, but there was a limit to what caution could achieve when the original breeding-stock had been so limited. The second pure-bred generation had been fifty-per cent female, and so had every generation since, but the limitation of the original stock had been too severe. The 'immigrant community', according to its usual definition, was less than a tenth pure-bred; the rest were half-breeds – and the vast majority of the marginal mass of fighting-men and privileged servants had no more than an eighth or a sixteenth of authentic Imperial blood. The priest had only a quarter.

'Do it,' Balberith commanded, sternly.

Alpalhao could not keep hesitating forever, and he knew it. The priest finally condescended to extend his skinny arm so that the claw-like hand put the phial to the psyker's lips. The psyker's eyes were closed, although he did not appear to be asleep, but when the rim of the little bottle made contact with his flesh he lifted his head slightly, avid to drink.

The psyker was already in the unsettling trance-state fostered and refined by the drug. His senses were now unresponsive to that tiny fraction of the mundane world that was confined in the monkish cell, but they were becoming highly attentive to the other worlds that existed in parallel to the dimension of normal space-time.

In some of those other dimensions, Balberith had been assured by his teachers, sight was so remarkably augmented that a man might see clear across the void to look out upon the worlds of other stars. More importantly, the manner in which a man could speak his thoughts silently within the privacy of his own head was so remarkably augmented that he could speak those thoughts directly into the mind of another, and hear thoughts that were spoken into his from thousands, millions or billions of miles away.

That was what was required. This pure-bred psyker had to make contact with others of his own kind, preferably – although the necessity was not absolute – aboard a ship of the Imperial Fleet that was close enough to Sigmatus to reach it in a matter of hours.

The psyker drank, and the room grew cold. The phial in Alpalhao's hand cracked, and the priest laid it down lest it should shatter. The priest's hand was shivering furiously, as if it were being shaken by some external force. Balberith felt a frisson seep through his own body, causing his blood to seethe in his veins and unusual emotions to stir in his heart. He fought for self-control.

The psyker knew what was required of him, although Balberith had never been at all sure that knowing what was required was more likely to enhance the chances of success than to diminish them.

As the drug took effect the psyker's face began to contort. Sweat began to ooze from the pores of his forehead and cheeks, and his eyeballs fluttered wildly behind his closed lids. Carro Alpalhao raised a tremulous arm to his own face, so that the sleeve could mop his nose – but it was blood, not snot, that stained the cloth.

'I told you so,' muttered the terrified priest, without the least hint of self-satisfaction. 'All you've done is expose him to the hellworlds.'

Balberith had long suspected that the warpstorm enclosing Sigmatus was a strangely delicate thing. The evil painter of destiny worshipped by the aborigine coven-masters seemed to him to be using the lightest of all his brushes upon it, to create intricate and elusive effects whose subtlety probably could not be appreciated by any mere mortal. Although the world was on the fringes of the so-called Eye of Terror it had never been subjected to the garish effects which legend attributed to the worlds that actually lay within the Eye. It was, however, close enough for wise-dreamers to glimpse those unfortunate worlds far more frequently and far more revealingly than the myriad worlds of the Imperium of Mankind.

'Hellworld' was a notion which certainly had not been forgotten by the inquisitors of Sigmatus; nor had its significance been lost.

Immigrant psykers had sometimes been driven mad by such sights. Worlds where the atmosphere was permanently aflame and worlds whose oceans of blood were alive were of little relevance to humankind, for the life they supported was entirely alien, and worlds sculpted in the form of screaming humanoid heads were mere cosmic scarecrows, but there were other hellworlds where creatures possessed of minds and souls could exist, and did exist, in perpetual torment.

Balberith had never been entirely sure how that could happen. Surely a creature shaped by natural selection for life in a world that seemed hellish to a human being would be adapted mentally as well as physically to its environment, so that local conditions would seem perfectly normal, distressing only when they strayed towards hazardous extremes? Even if such a creature's pain responses were permanently excited, how long could pain endure before it became a familiar aspect of experience, impotent by virtue of its everpresence?

Alas, the Eye of Terror was part of the Empire of Chaos, and common sense was useless in its appraisal. There were doubtless matters which only the Emperor of Mankind himself was privileged to comprehend.

Balberith nudged Carro Alpalhao with his knee to indicate that the priest should make room for him – which the quivering priest did, despite the narrowness of the space to which he was confined. Balberith knelt beside him, and took the psyker's hand in his own. The hand was limp and feverish, but by no means unresponsive. The psyker's trance had not made him any less excitable – quite the reverse. The very air around him was beginning to crackle, as if his body were possessed of a fiery invisible aura. When Balberith exerted pressure with his fingers the pressure was immediately echoed.

'Listen to me, Deir,' Balberith said, stifling the horror that flowed from the other's hand into his own being. 'The hellworlds are a psychodrama – an entrancing corruption, posted at the interface of the dimensions to distract the pure in mind and heart. You do not need to look at them, and you do not need to focus on them if you do chance to look. You have to look beyond them. No matter what the Chaos-worshippers call their rogue psykers, you are the only dreamer on Sigmatus who can be reckoned truly wise, and you must use your wisdom. If any part of the Fleet is nearby, you must find the ships – and when you have found them, you must make contact with their guiding minds. We need to know whether they are aware of our plight – and if they are not, we must make them aware of it.'

Balberith wasn't certain that his words could penetrate the barriers that had been erected between the psyker's dreaming consciousness and the regular dimension, but he knew that it could do no harm to say them aloud. He felt that the speech worked to his benefit, even if it had no effect at all on the man adrift among the dimensions, haunted by hellworlds.

Perhaps the words did have an effect, because the eyes moving behind the closed lids were no longer roaming so fervently, and the sweat evaporating from the face was no longer being replaced quite so profusely. Indeed, the entranced man seemed to be trying to shut his eyes even more firmly, screwing them up as if in concentration. He was unmistakably awake and active, for his whole body now seemed to be alight with strange consciousness. The walls of the cell were weeping, and so was Carro Alpalhao – but the priest's tears were pink.

'He's trying,' Balberith whispered to his stricken companion. 'Pray for his success.'

'I am,' the priest assured him, speaking through gritted teeth.

The psyker's lips began to stir, as if he were trying to speak – but no words were audible and Balberith could not read the sketchily ill-formed movements of the lips.

'Louder, Deir,' he muttered. 'Louder, or more precise.' The horror that flowed out of the dreamer had changed its quality now: it was more subtle, less brutal. Logically, it should have been less intense, but it did not seem so.

Balberith had to exert even more mental force to quell the panic that was trying to take hold of him. He felt that the vessels feeding his heart were trying to tie themselves in intricate knots.

The dreaming psykers of Sigmatus were often incapable of forming sounds, and their users had to be highly-skilled lip-readers. Unfortunately, the psykers were often incapable of clarity when they were miming, and even the most expert readers sometimes produced garbled accounts of what they were trying to say. Balberith did not know whether this was a universe-wide problem or some freak of local circumstance.

Gradually, though, the flutter of Ajao's lips became calmer and more definite.

'Sigmatus,' Balberith read, aided by the murmurous sounds spilling from the psyker's lacerated lips. 'Castaways... Assimilated... War continuing... Possibility of redemption... Danger... Landing may be feasible... Temporary blink... Danger... Remain on hold... Danger... Balance of probabilities... Danger... He's through, Carro. He's through. Tell them,

Deir. Make them hear you. Tell them that we need help – that the world needs them desperately, but that everything would be well if only we had their firepower and their spiritual leadership. Tell them that we need reinforcements: Space Marines, inquisitors. Tell them that the echoes of the Imperium that still endure here deserve support and salvation. Make them hear! Make them see! A victory might yet be won here, if they can only act swiftly and well.'

Balberith had no way of knowing whether Ajao could hear him, or whether the psyker was capable of following the instruction, but he needed hope as much as he needed faith. He was, after all, surrounded by enemies, including many of those who were supposed to be his closest collaborators. He needed reinforcements to help his own inquisitors and priests against Orloc Melcarth, as well as reinforcements to help Ierius Fulbra against the sorcerers of Gulzacandra. Most of all, he needed the hope that such reinforcements might come, and that they might come in time.

Deir Ajao's lips were moving again, but they were not trying to pronounce words. They were indicating pain and sore distress. There were tears of blood leaking from the corners of the psyker's screwed-up eyes and his tremors were turning into a full-scale fit.

'He's over the edge,' Alpalhao said, while urgently mopping his own face with an extremely unsteady hand. 'He's falling. We have to try to bring him out.'

'Not while he's so close,' Balberith said, through gritted teeth. The walls of the cell were shivering feverishly, displaying a riot of colour that no human hand armed with a paint-brush could ever have contrived – but there were, alas, no readable graffiti.

Balberith knew, in any case, that trying was all that he and the priest could do. There was no antidote to the aboriginal drug, and a psyker's trance-state was not the kind of altered consciousness that could be banished by mere shaking. Ajao was trapped, a prisoner of his own strange nature. If he fell within his waking dream, he was the one who had to stop the fall. His innate wisdom was the only means by which he could acquire the kind of wings that would let him fly, or the kind of lightness that would let him float.

But the hand that Balberith had gripped was now gripping Balberith's fiercely, taut with desperation.

'Come on, Deir,' Balberith said. 'Take control. You have to take control.'

Unfortunately, it seemed to be the case that no dreamer, however wise, was skilful enough to pilot his own dream. Perhaps, Balberith thought, another thousand years of Imperial dominion over the galaxy would produce a purer and more careful breed of psyker than anything wild and corrupted Chaos could ever produce – but that time had not yet come.

The tears of blood continued to flow, and it was obvious that the eyes flickering from side to side behind the screwed-up lids were looking into some sort of hell – perhaps a kind of hell far worse than any mere world aflame or sea of boiling blood.

The psyker's complexion had always been uncommonly pale, even for a purebred immigrant, but it was paper-white now. The tracks of his tears looked like a line inscribed in red ink, writing the history of civilization on Sigmatus in a long-lost language older than the world itself.

Balberith's priorities had shifted now. As he returned the vice-like grip of the sleeping man's right hand he began to whisper a new and far simpler set of instructions into the psyker's ear.

'Don't die,' he commanded. 'Hold on. Don't die. Live to dream another day. Don't die. Try to sleep. Don't die. Close your inner eyes and your inner ears to all the temptations of the enemy. Come home. And above all else, don't die!'

He could only hope that it would be enough.

Tomorrow would be another day – and tomorrow might not be too late to win salvation, for himself if not for the world of his birth. Desperate times required desperate measures, and Ragan Balberith was keenly aware of his own desperation.

NINE

IT WAS VERY dark at first beneath the truck. Half a dozen searchlights had been quickly switched on, so that their beams could
sweep back and forth across the dense vegetation surrounding
the pool, but that only made the shadow in which Dathan and
Hycilla lay seem all the deeper. Dathan couldn't see Hycilla's
face, but he was certain that she was at least half-entranced. She
wasn't still, but her movements were spasmodic and unco-
ordinated; she made no attempt to move into a position from
which she could see a little more of what was happening.

Perhaps she had a clearer view with her eyes shut, he
thought. Perhaps, whether consciously or not, it was she who
had unleashed the forces that were blasting and harassing the
hapless soldiers, who clearly did not know which way to turn
to find an enemy at which they could fire back.

Dathan had no inner sight to rely on, so he scrambled forwards in a prone position, lifting his head until it bumped on
the truck's front axle-housing, then raising it again as soon as
he had worked his way past the obstacle.

There was not a great deal he could see without actually coming out of hiding – and he had no intention of exposing
himself to gunfire – but he could see something of what the

99

soldiers on the ground were doing. They were crouching down, keeping almost as low as he was, while the gunners on the trucks fired over their heads. He could see the white traces of missiles zooming into the bushes, but these weren't like judeye trees and they didn't explode. Fires were started in half a dozen places, but they seemed reluctant to start and even more reluctant to continue. They smouldered crimson or blue, emitting thick clouds of acrid smoke, but they didn't flare up and there didn't seem to be any danger of the entire area being caught up in an unstoppable conflagration like the one that had devastated the judeye forest.

Dathan couldn't see any visible sign of returning fire: no muzzle-flashes, no soaring arrows, no beams of natural light. What he could see, though, was that the soldiers on the ground were taking casualties.

He saw one man rolling on the ground with his eyes bugging out of his head, foaming at the mouth as if his brain were boiling in his skull. The man was obviously trying to bring himself to a halt, because he was scrabbling at the ground with his hands with such urgency that he was tearing his own fingernails away from the quick, and yet it seemed to Dathan that it was his own muscles that were causing him to roll over.

In striking contrast, another man was bolt upright, standing to attention with astonishing rigidity – save only for his arms, which were moving very slowly to reverse the direction of the weapon he held in his two hands, bringing the barrel of the lasrifle slowly but inexorably towards his head.

Not until the barrel was aligned did the man open his mouth and slide the muzzle between his chapped lips and yellowed teeth. Dathan could see his eyes quite clearly, although no light was shining directly upon them, and he could read the terror in them as the soldier's finger, though bent at an excruciating angle, began to tighten on the trigger of his gun.

Dathan saw another man catch fire, as if a taper had been applied to some mysterious fuse within his abdomen. Little jets of flame were bursting out of the soldier's skin and burning holes in his uniform. He, unlike the others, was free to scream, and he took full advantage of the opportunity.

Dying quietly was not, it seemed, a dignity that many men could maintain.

This is magic, Dathan thought. This is the way it is supposed to be. This is the fate that ought to befall invaders who came as these men came, to slaughter the innocents of Gulzacandra. He knew that he ought to be delighted, or even exultant – but it seemed that he too must be caught by a kind of spell, because all he felt was sick. Dathan was incapable of hating anyone or anything more than he hated these men, but the sight of their dying horrified him. If Hycilla really is responsible for this, he thought, thinking himself a traitor for thinking it, then I wish that she would stop.

On reflection, however, Dathan rejected the idea that Hycilla might be responsible. No matter how rapidly her progress as a wise-dreamer had been accelerated by the events of the previous day, she could not possibly have turned into a sorcerer. In any case, none of the tales that Dathan had heard of the most powerful sorcerers who had ever lived had included scenes like this. Whatever was at work here was surely more than human.

An escalation of more distant screaming assured Dathan that the men on the trucks had no protection from this kind of assault. The fire pouring from the big guns mounted on the machines became increasingly random as the soldiers' situation became more desperate.

Someone was shouting orders, trying to organise the firing-pattern to cover the whole of the surrounding area, but the response was distinctly uneven.

Dathan crept a couple of inches further forward, drawn by curiosity, but Hycilla suddenly grabbed him round the waist and pulled him back.

'This way!' she hissed. 'No time! We stay, we die!'

Dathan realised that by 'this way' she meant that they were to move to the left. She was already on that side, so she scrambled out from under the truck first, plucking at his shirt in order to make him follow her. Dathan didn't know whether she was entranced or not, but he had no ideas of his own and the assurance that they would both die if they stayed where they were rang all too true. Whatever was killing the soldiers didn't seem to need a clear sight of them; death, like the smoke of the reluctant fires, was in the air.

There seemed to be no alternative but to run, trusting to luck to preserve them against the attackers and defenders alike – except that running was not what Hycilla had in mind. Instead of haring off into the night as fast as her legs could carry her she turned on her heel and groped for the handle of the door that would let her into the front part of the truck – the part that was presumably equivalent to the driver's bench of a cart.

Dathan didn't suppose that there was anyone in the driver's covert, but it didn't seem to him to be a safe place on that account. If the raised sides of the truck's rear couldn't protect the artillerymen manning the big gun, the transparent shield in front of the driver's seat was hardly likely to be able to ward off the malign force that was wreaking havoc in the soldiers' midst.

As soon as Hycilla had the door open, though, she leapt up into the covert and reached back to offer Dathan the support of her arm. He took her hand and clambered up behind her.

By the time he got in, Hycilla had already scrambled across to set herself in the further seat of a matching pair, behind the big wheel that was the cab's most prominent internal feature.

'But you can't work a thing like this!' Dathan said, foolishly. He had always known that such things as trucks existed, and had heard descriptions of them from people who had actually seen them, but no such description could have prepared him for the reality of being inside one. This confined space seemed to him to be an utterly mysterious and profoundly alien environment – but when Hycilla turned towards him to tell him to be quiet she didn't need words. Her eyes were large and luminous, brightly lit by moist reflections even though the pupils were widely dilated. Her lips were formed into a ferocious snarl, making her once-lovely face into a hideous caricature.

There was a lever sticking up from the floor of the truck between her seat and the one into which Dathan had settled, and Hycilla was already wrenching it back and forth as the truck's engine roared into life. As soon as the wheels began to turn she spun the wheel that presumably served much the same function as a guiding-rein, forcing the vehicle into a tight arc that carried it away to the left.

There were two soldiers lying prone in front of the truck's new course. They leapt to their feet, but only one was stupid enough to try to signal to the driver, imploring rather than commanding her to halt. The other man was content to throw himself out of the vehicle's path – which saved him from being run down.

Even if the driver had been one of his own men, Dathan thought, the dead soldier had been a fool to think that he would stop in a situation like this. Even as he formed that thought he realised that theirs was not the only vehicle that had come to life. Whether a retreat had been ordered or not, men who had seen the manner in which their companions were dying had evidently decided that any other place in the wilderness was a better place to be than the environs of the pool.

That's good, Dathan thought. They won't know it's us. They won't chase us.

He worried, though, about what might be going on immediately behind them. How many armed men were in the back of the truck? What weapons did they have? And what would they do when they found out who it was that had abstracted them from the battlefield?

Hycilla was in no condition to consider such niceties. She was spinning the wheel again, sending the truck into another, entirely different arc. Dathan had already lost track of where the pool was, and wondered whether she might have had to turn so suddenly in order to avoid driving straight into it. She was making no attempt to stick to better ground, and there was nothing visible through the windscreen but the crowns of bushes and exotic flowers – a veritable tide of vegetation that seemed to hurl itself forward and dive down beneath the vehicle with reckless alacrity.

It was an optical illusion, of course; it was the vehicle that was moving, mowing down the vegetable flesh as it went, lurching madly from side to side as it bounced over the bases of clustered stems.

Dathan heard the sounds of people – or perhaps inanimate objects of some unidentifiable kind – being thrown about in the back of the truck, impacting with each of the raised sides. There was no indication that the gun mounted in the back was still being fired.

There were no more soldiers to be seen now, but the evidence of their presence was all around, in billows of smoke and lines of hectic light scrawled upon the surface of the starry sky.

'Open the door!' Hycilla screamed at him. 'Move over!'

Dathan didn't understand. He would have asked why, but as soon as he looked towards her with the question in his eyes she looked towards him – and what there was in her eyes was definitely not conducive to asking questions. It was an order that permitted no dissent.

Helplessly, Dathan felt his hand shoot out from his side to grapple with the door-catch. He had never encountered one like it, so it required a few seconds of inexpert fumbling, but in the end he managed to spring the catch and hurl the door open – and then, without any pause for thought or reinforcement of the command he moved over into the narrow gap between the two seats.

For a moment, Dathan could not believe that there was anyone in the world agile enough to leap on board the careering truck, or anyone brave enough to try. His scepticism could not endure, however, when a human figure did exactly that, leaping out of the onrushing vegetation to land sure-footedly on the floor of the truck, arms extended to catch the side and top of the door frame, so that a single fluid movement might deliver the slender body into the space that Dathan had cleared.

The newcomer closed the door himself. He said nothing at all, but Hycilla obviously knew well enough what to do without verbal instruction. She was spinning the wheel yet again, hurling the truck into an arc so tight that it came up on two wheels. Dathan was scared that it might tip over, but the fear was insufficient to override his astonishment as he stared at their new passenger.

It was a boy, seemingly no older than himself. The boy was stark naked, and his skin was faintly but strangely patterned. His physique did not seem particularly remarkable, although the appearance had to be deceptive, given the amazing gymnastic trick he had just performed, so it was his face that attracted and held Dathan's attention.

It was getting much darker inside the truck now that they were heading away from all the lights, but it seemed to Dathan that the particular darkness within the newcomer's eyes was no mere shadow. His ears were also unusual: they were pointed and tufted, like the ears of a wolfox or a scrublynx.

Even in the village, which was said to be uncommonly lucky in such matters, freak births sometimes occurred. Dathan had been allowed to look at dead animals with seemingly human features, but he had only heard hushed whispers regarding human babies with animal features which had had to be taken away. This was the first time that he had been near a human with animal stigmata.

'Who are you?' Dathan managed to stutter, when he got his breath back.

'You and you,' was the boy's cryptic reply – and as he spoke he reached out with both arms towards his saviours. The long fingers of his right hand touched Hycilla's forehead, while the knuckles of his left rested briefly on Dathan's cheek. Dathan felt a strange thrill pass through him. It wasn't painful, but it wasn't pleasant either; he felt as if some kind of thread had wound itself around his heart.

'What's your name?' Dathan asked, in case the boy hadn't understood the first question.

'Don't know. Too tired,' was the only reply he received.

Even in the near-darkness, Dathan sensed that the astonishing eyes were already half-closed. The boy slumped in his seat, his strange head – tufted ears and all – coming to rest upon Dathan's shoulder. Dathan did not dare to shrug him off, or even to run the risk of inconveniencing him by turning his head to look towards Hycilla, but he could and did keep stammering away.

'Who is he? Hycilla? What is this? What's happening?'

'Don't know,' said Hycilla's voice, like an eerie echo. 'Too tired.'

But she, at least, wasn't falling asleep. She kept right on driving, hurling the truck through the night.

They were heading out into the wilderness now, and the ground was more even. The tide of vegetation no longer seemed to be hurling itself suicidally beneath their wheels. The light of the headlamps allowed them to see something of where they were going, although the truck was surely going far too fast to be able to stop in time if some obstruction suddenly loomed up out of the night within the headlamps' span.

'Uh oh!' said Hycilla's voice, suddenly. It really did sound like Hycilla's voice, although Dathan couldn't be entirely certain that she was the one in charge of her arms and legs.

Dathan couldn't turn around, but from where he sat in the middle of the truck's seat he could look into the mirror that was positioned above his head to allow the driver to look back through the portal in the back of the cab. He couldn't see anything but lights, but that was enough to tell him that the truck was being followed – or perhaps pursued.

The lights were too bright to be mere headlamps, Dathan concluded. He reasoned, therefore, that the spotlight on the back of the following truck had to be working, and it was trained on their own truck. Which meant that the gun mounted on the back of the other truck was probably working too, and probably trained on the target that the searchlight had picked out. Which probably meant that if anyone on the other truck had seen the naked boy leap aboard, or had any other reason to be confident that it wasn't being driven by an Imperial soldier, the three of them probably only had as long to live as it would take any Imperial soldiers left on the back of their own truck to jump clear... which they had probably already done...

Dathan stared into the mirror raptly, even though there was nothing to be seen but dazzling light. The hairs on the back of his neck were standing up.

Then the dazzling light became even more dazzling. The mirror seemed to flare up, as if it were itself a bubble of incandescent gas.

I'm dead, Dathan thought, although he knew that it was absurd to think it.

He wasn't dead. The gun mounted on the pursuing truck hadn't fired – or if it had, it had misfired. The gun mounted on the pursuing truck had exploded, and the truck itself had been blasted to smithereens by the force of the explosion.

The shockwave tilted their own truck, but didn't tip it over.

'Uh oh!' said Hycilla's voice. Dathan had never realised before what a wealth of hidden meanings a phrase such as that might be able to contain. The nonsensical syllables sounded completely different the second time around, anxiety and irritation having given way to triumph and amusement. But Dathan realised, as the truck zoomed on into the darkness, that the triumph had been cloaked in weariness, and the amusement in exhaustion. He saw that Hycilla was slumping over the wheel now, not even looking where the truck was going – not, at least, with her eyes.

'Hycilla!' Dathan said, uneasily, wondering whether he could bring her back to a normal state of being – and whether he should if he could.

After all, he thought, if she recovered her old self now she might suddenly discover that she hadn't the slightest idea how to drive an Imperial vehicle, and now would not be the best time for her to make that discovery. Dathan decided, on due reflection, to keep quiet. If Hycilla had been driving in a magical trance since they first got into the cab it was probably best not to disturb her.

When a few more minutes had passed, though, the pressure of that chimerical ear upon Dathan's shoulder, and the tickle of its elongated hairs against his neck became unbearable. Very gently and very carefully, he eased the other boy's body over to the right, so that the strange head eventually shifted. It lolled against the back of the seat, supported to the side by the frame of the door. The position looked uncomfortable, but not unbearable.

That allowed Dathan to turn towards Hycilla, and to watch her as she balanced her head on her knuckles, while her hands kept the truck on a steady course. The course in question took them into darkness and the unknown, but seemed nevertheless to have been carefully plotted and selected.

The darkness did not last much longer, though. Within another twenty minutes the sky behind them acquired a silvery glow, and then the rosy pink of sunlight reflecting off low cloud.

They were not heading directly away from the as-yet-unrisen sun, but their course was only slightly displaced to the south.

The war has begun, Dathan thought. I was present at the first battle, and the second. I've survived both, without taking any wound worse than a common-or-garden bruise. But this is only the beginning. The soldiers who attacked the village were numbered in their hundreds, the ones in the trucks in their dozens. When the big battle begins, there'll be thousands on each side, and the firepower…

He realised that his world had already ended. The village had been smashed. If the fields had been burned and the well poisoned, it could never be rebuilt. If his mother was lucky enough to be alive, she would be a homeless refugee lost in the wasteland. What had happened to the village would now happen to the smaller towns, and eventually to Gulzacandra's cities. Whoever won, nothing would ever be the same. The world would be new, and life would be different.

Dathan understood that the adulthood at which his boyhood had always been aimed had been cancelled at a stroke, and he would never be the man he had always intended to be. He was a fighter now, whether he wanted to be or not. He was an enemy of the Imperium, a defender of his homeland. He might live or he might die but the one thing he could never do was go back to being himself. He was different now, and he had to discover a whole new way of being.

Dathan watched Hycilla's hands and feet, wondering if he could figure out how to drive while he was awake. It looked easy enough, but so many things had looked easy while he watched others do them that had turned out not to be easy at all, when he came to try them for himself. He knew that he couldn't afford to entertain childish illusions now that he was a grown man. He looked around again, to watch the dawn through the rear window of the cab.

The pink clouds extended themselves across the sky like the wings of a giant vulture – and then the rim of the sun peeped over the flat and seemingly featureless plain, as if the sky had been split by a sword-thrust to let out the blood of the stars. The stars that shone in the night-sky were already fading out, swallowed up by the violet blaze of day. That blaze was not yet bright enough to seem uniform, though. The clouds that blistered its face with grey seemed as solid as oatmeal gruel against a background stirred by the restlessness of space itself.

Dathan had only the vaguest notion of what those ripples were. He could see nothing but inexplicable uncertainty – and he could feel ripples of a similar sort within his own inner being, stirring his very soul.

'Well,' he murmured, just loudly enough to have been heard if any nearby ear had been awake and attentive, 'I suppose they'll settle, or they won't. Either way, I'll have to do the best I can to move in harmony with them. I certainly can't banish them from my soul.'

TEN

GAVALON'S REGROWN EYE was hurting horribly, but it was not a blinding pain. Quite the reverse, in fact. The other eye already had better night-vision than ordinary human eyes – though not as good as that possessed by a few of his beastmen – but this one, perhaps by virtue of being grown by night, seemed to relish the particular textures of starlight and moonlight.

Even so, he had not been able to keep the Vessel's fleeting form in view once he was down on the plain. Nimian could never have run so fast, and Sathorael had hardly begun the process of metamorphic emergence, but their peculiar hybrid already seemed to have acquired a number of extraordinary powers. Gavalon had a few of those himself, but moving at great speed across problematic territory was not one of them. Even beastmen had their petty tricks, but none of the heavily-built members of his personal retinue could run like mowas.

Gavalon had no choice, therefore, but to follow the Vessel at his own pace, hoping that the limitations of a body that was still ninety-five per cent Nimian would cause the daemon-to-be to pause for rest before very long.

The sorcerer had glimpsed the flashes of light on the horizon while descending the slope of the rounded hill but he had been unable to form a firm conclusion as to what they were. Once he was at ground level the lights were obscured by vegetation, and he did not see them again until the firefight began, at which time they became far more prolific. He guessed immediately what had happened.

'Imperium soldiers!' he hissed to his followers. 'They must have vehicles to have come so far so fast. Not battle-tanks imported by the first invaders, just light trucks, assembled in Kalazendran factories – but they're still dangerous.'

The nearest beastman nodded its shaggy head, but Gavalon knew that its understanding of the danger was limited. The creature had never seen a motor vehicle.

How sophisticated, Gavalon wondered, was Nimian-Sathorael's understanding of the enemy he had raced off to fight? It would be a terrible tragedy if the nascent daemon were to lose its Vessel before it had a chance to develop more than a tiny fraction of its power. According to the wisest of his wise-dreamers, Sathorael was to bring about the destruction of Gulzacandra's invaders, and of Kalazendra's cities, and more… more, apparently, than the Divine Schemer cared to reveal even to the most loyal and devoted of his worldly servants.

Gavalon had to suppose that if the Divine Schemer's divine scheme somehow went awry, Gulzacandra would suffer, and so would he. It would not matter whether or not there was anything he could do to save the daemon-to-be from premature destruction while it was, in effect, a confused infant; he and all his followers would still be held responsible.

'Weapons ready,' he said to the beastmen, as they continued to hurry forward. 'Approach by stealth. Seize guns as and when you can and turn them on the Kalazendrans – but whatever else you do, see that no harm comes to the Vessel.'

That was, he knew, far easier said than done – but they would all have to do their utmost to turn words into action.

He had expected a few more seconds to prepare, and to select a pathway into the heart of the battle, but the battle came to him instead when two soldiers ran from the bushes, in full flight from an enemy they could neither see nor number.

The enemy soldiers did not see Gavalon and the beastmen either, at first, which gave the running beastmen time to mount a pincer movement to either side of them. By the time they finally did catch sight of Gavalon and the yak-head that had remained by his side they were too slow in raising their guns to take aim.

One of them got off a shot at the sorcerer, but it was fired from the hip. Gavalon needed neither luck nor magic to avoid the bullet, which whizzed harmlessly over his head. The man was then dragged down by the claws of a beastman, whose talons tore the flesh from the right side of his face. The soldier tried to bring the muzzle of his gun around so that he could fire into the beastman's belly, but the creature's descending mass was too great. The life was crushed out of him.

The second soldier might have done better had he actually contrived to fire, because he had brought his gun up to his shoulder first, but the yak-head who had remained with Gavalon had already hurled its spear with superhuman force. The serrated obsidian head of the weapon cut through the human's ribs like a carving knife. The soldier fell backwards, his body carried ten or twelve feet by the momentum of the impact.

Gavalon let the beastmen who had felled the two men harvest the guns and ammunition they had carried. The weapons were neither Imperium originals nor high-quality Kalazendran imitations, but they would be a welcome addition to the firepower of his own army. Fulbra's battle-tanks were mostly crude by comparison with their original models, their engines fuelled by alcohols distilled from wood and their caterpillar tracks compounded out of an unsavoury mixture of Yevelkanan rubber and native plant-fibre, but armour was armour and their advance would be inexorable if Gavalon's thrall-wizards could not fortify their own exotic resources with the kind of brute force that only heavy metal could deliver.

Gavalon signalled to the beastmen to spread out in both directions, while he and his immediate companion moved carefully forward, making full use of the abundant cover.

The next gunman to run into Gavalon was not quite so panic-stricken, and he was alert to the possibility that there would be enemies lurking in the outermost circle of the bushes surrounding the pool. The Kalazendran had some kind of light-gun, which made him at least doubly dangerous, but he had already used it at least once, and his vision was still slightly confused. The shot he fired would have been well-enough

aimed had it had an ordinary target, but Gavalon was a sorcerer, blessed with a deceptive presence. The hot beam was
close enough to singe his shoulder, but such little pains were
momentary spice to Gavalon and only served to sharpen the
sense of triumph he felt as he hurled himself forward to grapple with the man.

The Kalazendran was tall and muscular, and might have put
up some sort of resistance even to a bull-shouldered beastman, but he had no chance at all against a sorcerer blessed
with as many mutations as Gavalon the Great. Gavalon
ripped the soldier's right arm clean out of its socket before
using his fingernails to slash the man's throat – a cutting blow
so effective that it shredded all the flesh in front of the backbone. Gavalon paused just long enough to pry the
convulsively-locked fingers of the dead arm away from the
handgrip of the exotic weapon before bringing his prize
around and charging forward.

The bushes surrounding him were already sputtering fitfully
and belching smoke, but Gavalon's new eye did not seem
prone to weeping. It stung as badly as ever but it gave him the
sight he needed to pick out enemies running this way and that.
He shot one, and watched in fascination as the soldier's uniform and flesh melted together as they burned. A second
returned fire, but he too was confused by Gavalon's deceptive
presence, and a beastman's blade made him pay for his confusion. Gavalon shot a third himself, but he still had not caught
a glimpse of the Vessel.

The engines of at least three trucks were roaring now, and
their searchlights were probing in every direction. Gavalon
heard a frightful bellowing scream that had to be one of his
beastmen. He moved reflexively towards it, on the assumption
that it must have come from the place where the fight was
most fiercely-contested and the enemy most securely-
entrenched, but still he could not see the skinny naked form
of the nascent daemon.

The trucks were on the move now, seemingly headed in several different directions. One was coming directly towards
him, and Gavalon poised his weapon, ready to fire. He was
confident that no single human could pose a mortal threat to
him, but a two-ton truck with a heavy gun mounted on its
back was a different matter. He could have moved sideways to

take cover in a cluster of head-high flowering plants and let the vehicle pass by, but that would have allowed the truck and its personnel to get away, and at least two vehicles were already in the process of doing that. So he stood firm and took aim.

The truck's searchlight picked out the sorcerer almost immediately. Had the vehicle not been heading straight for him already its driver would presumably have altered course in order to run him down. Fortunately, Gavalon's new eye was far less sensitive to the harsh glare of the searchlight than the delicate tints of starlight and moonlight, and he could easily make out the helmeted heads of the man swivelling the searchlight and his companion stationed at the big gun.

Gavalon shot the gunman first, and then the searchlight operator. He watched their heads explode with grim satisfaction – and then turned his attention to the one with what was now the most dangerous weapon of all at his disposal: the truck-driver.

As the vehicle hurtled towards him, the intervening distance vanishing yard by yard, Gavalon fired a third time.

Unfortunately, the plastic of which the windscreen was made turned out to be somewhat resistant to the kind of fire the light-weapon produced. It did not shatter and it did not melt – not quickly enough, at any rate. Gavalon knew that the splash of the discharge must have dazzled the driver, but the truck was so close to its target that the driver's loss of sight was irrelevant. Gavalon had only a split second to dive clear.

Had he been wearing his battle-armour he might not have been able to do it, but the costume required by the ritual was much lighter.

He threw himself sideways, and just managed to get his boots out of the line followed by the off-side front wheel, thus saving his feet from pulverization.

The truck careered on for forty or fifty yards, and for a moment Gavalon thought that it would disappear into the night and be lost – but then the brakes were applied and the vehicle was thrown into a tight U-turn. The sorcerer realised that the driver had no idea that the men on the back of the truck had been killed; the man obviously thought that he was still at the wheel of a powerful battle-wagon, a veritable cannon on wheels.

Gavalon got up, but made no attempt to hide himself. Instead, he backed up slowly, looking around himself all the while for further signs of trouble. No one came at him, and there were no more screams.

As soon as the truck was fully turned around, the driver hit the accelerator hard. The engine screeched and the truck lurched as its solid tyres bumped their way through a dense thicket, but it hurtled forward nevertheless.

Gavalon knew that a second shot might well succeed where the first had failed, the fabric of the windscreen having already been weakened – but he also knew that it might not, and that ammunition was precious. He kept the stolen gun in his left hand, but his right reached down to pluck a dart from his belt. He had not come fully-armed to the ritual, but he never went anywhere without adequate defences, and the dart was charged with a magical energy that would multiply its momentum a hundredfold, if it were thrown with the proper skill.

He threw it, with the proper skill.

The dart smashed through the truck's windshield as if it were made of spidersilk and vanished into the startled driver's open mouth. He jerked back in his seat as the point of the dart sliced between the base of the skull and the first cervical vertebrae before embedding itself deeply in the steel wall of the back of the cab – but the truck kept coming. The dead driver's hands were still holding the wheel in place, and the truck was still headed straight for the spot where Gavalon stood.

Gavalon cursed the necessity of diving sideways for a second time, but he had no time to do anything but dive, so that was what he did. This time, the tyre missed his booted foot by a clear six inches.

The truck careered on into a huge stand of rushes, whose brittle stalks crackled as they gave way to its mass – but they could not slow it down sufficiently to stop it driving on into the pool, where it arrived with an almighty splash.

The water thrown up by the impact was hurled in every direction, and Gavalon reflexively raised his arm to shield his eyes from the fraction of the cascade that landed on him.

One last scream sounded then, but it was neither a human scream nor the agonised howl of a bovine beastman. It was the scream of some monstrous pool-dweller, deeply resentful of the rude invasion of its normally-quiet home.

After that, relative quiet resumed. The sound of the other engines was already reduced by distance to a hum. If any of the Kalazendran soldiers were still alive, they were not firing their guns.

'Search the area,' Gavalon shouted, as the yak-head who had not strayed far from his side helped him to his feet. 'Find any fugitives and kill them – but above all else, find the Vessel.'

He did not doubt that the beastmen did their best to obey the order, and he certainly played his own part in what became a mopping-up operation, but by the time dawn came he knew the awful truth.

Nimian's naked form was nowhere to be found, dead or alive. He had come and gone. Unless the larval Sathorael had discovered an altogether unexpected ability to fly – and to fly unpractised and untrained – he must have been on one of the trucks that had escaped the skirmish by driving off into the night.

Gavalon was certain that at least three trucks had gone, but he could not be sure that only three had gone – and there was no way to be sure which direction the one carrying Nimian had taken. How could he possibly return to his gathering army with the news that he had lost the ally who was supposed to provide their most powerful antidote to Imperial firepower? What were a few captured guns by comparison with a lost daemon? How would the daemon-to-be fare without the guiding voice and wisdom of Gavalon the Great?

The yak-head uttered a grunt of solicitous concern.

'I'm all right,' Gavalon assured the creature. 'In fact, so far as I know, everything is all right.' He tried to reassure himself with a few further thoughts in the same vein. What need had a daemon of human guidance, when it had the grace and favour of the great god? The plan was not his, strictly speaking, but the Divine Schemer's – and who was he to judge that it had gone awry? Perhaps it was proceeding perfectly. Perhaps there was no perhaps about it. How could the gods be subject to the whims of chance?

He was not convinced. The daemon-to-be might not need him, but he certainly needed the daemon-to-be. The daemon-to-be might not need to receive his guidance, but he certainly needed to give it.

The yak-head grunted again, and three other beastmen joined in the chorus.

The beastmen seemed happy enough with the pile of guns they had gathered from the corpses of the Kalazendrans – as well they might, given that there were more than enough for them to take one each, and that their own casualties amounted to no more than two walking wounded.

If I knew how to control one of these abandoned vehicles, Gavalon thought, looking at the three trucks that remained and were seemingly still usable, I might return to my army in such style that they would applaud my triumph.

What he eventually said out loud was: 'We need more than the guns and ammunition. We need all the supplies they were carrying. What we cannot carry ourselves we'll gather into a cache, and send a detachment of pack-horses out to collect it. When you have done that you can sleep for an hour, perhaps two if you're quick. We cannot spare any more time than that. The enemy is moving fast, hoping to get at us before we're ready. We have to move fast too.'

The beastmen's nods and grunts of agreement were over-enthusiastic, as was invariably the case when he told them things they were too stupid to understand fully.

Once the beastmen had returned to work, though, Gavalon could not help reverting to his original train of thought. If the gods were not subject to the whims of chance, he thought, then the world would surely be a much more predictable place than it was. A good deal of its disturbance might be due to the conflicts of the gods, but the unpredictability of circumstance was no mere matter of opposed and contending wills. As a sorcerer, with a sorcerer's powers of foresight, he knew better than any mere dullard how wayward the ways of chance really were, and how vulnerable even daemons might be to freaks of circumstance.

As a man who aspired to become a daemon himself, if he could only serve his god bravely and cleverly enough, Gavalon was desperately well aware of how little he knew about the ways and powers of daemons, but one thing he did know was that they could only enjoy worldly existence for a brief time before returning to whatever dimension it was that they were entitled to call home.

As Sathorael grew into his heritage he – or should that be 'it'? – might acquire the power to blast continents, or to put out the sun, but he, or it, would not have that power long, and its use would hasten the moment of the daemon's departure.

Without Gavalon the Great to guide him – or it – how could the daemon possibly know and understand how best to deploy that awesome power in the interests of Gulzacandra?

Without Gavalon the Great's guidance, was there not a possibility that the daemon might deploy that power in such a way as to contrive the ruination of Gulzacandra as well as the petty Imperium that had been established in Kalazendra since the fall from the sky?

Gavalon put up a hand to cover his aching eye, protecting its tenderness from the hot light of the risen sun.

The sight of the palm of his hand seemed strangely comforting, that being one of the few areas of his outer flesh that had not changed appreciably since his apprentice days. The fingers were longer and thicker, their nails much more claw-like, but the palm was still engraved with the same pattern of criss-crossed lines: the pattern in which his destiny was written, if only he could master the art of reading it.

Alas, for all its marvellous powers of sight, his new eye did not come with any enhanced ability to read.

Even Gavalon the Great, the most powerful sorcerer to walk the surface of Sigmatus for a thousand generations, could not read the finer details of the promises inscribed by his parent god in the frail fabric of his own flesh.

Know thyself was, alas, far from being the easiest of the sorcerous commandments to keep, even in respect of those aspects of the self that were not subject to continued evolution or arbitrary alteration.

'But we will win,' Gavalon muttered, too softly for the yak-head to hear. 'We must.'

ELEVEN

DATHAN WOKE UP with a start as the truck lurched to a stop. The engine sputtered and died. He realised, somewhat to his surprise, that the sun was now high above the horizon, only a little to the left of the truck's heading. Several hours must have passed, although it did not seem to him that he had slept for more than a few minutes.

Hycilla raised her head too, and turned to peer at him. Her eyes had lost their scary quality, and he knew that she was no longer entranced. She seemed far more surprised than he was by their circumstances. Whatever memory she had of having driven the truck had obviously faded into that oblivion to which dream-memories were usually consigned, and she seemed quite nonplussed by the presence of the boy with the tufted ears, who was just beginning to wake up in his turn.

'Where are we?' she asked.

'I haven't the slightest idea,' Dathan told her. 'A long way west of the pool, and some way to the south. I have no idea which way Elvenor might lie. We're in the middle of nowhere.'

Hycilla turned to look out of her side window then, but she couldn't see far. The truck was in a forest of sorts, although its 'trees' looked like huge red-and-black corn cobs sheathed in pale yellow leaves with silver spikes. The undergrowth on both sides was fairly dense, but the truck had been following a road of sorts – or perhaps an animal trail, if there were animals hereabouts as big as loxodonts.

Hycilla turned back. 'Who's he?' she said, meaning the boy who was rubbing the sleep from his eyes. Those eyes had been even scarier than Hycilla's when he had first leapt aboard, but they looked merely human now. Even the ears did not seem as remarkable as they had before, and the dirt-stained body seemed even skinnier. Dathan wondered whether the pattern he had seen on the naked body when the boy leapt aboard had been merely a trick of the confused light.

'I suppose he must have been hiding in the scrub around the pool, just as we were. When the soldiers were attacked and everything started burning he must have panicked. Maybe he was close enough to see us being captured and knew that we were friendly.' It wasn't until he'd said all this that Dathan realised that there might be an easy way to get a more accurate answer. 'Who are you?' he said to the boy.

'You and you,' said the boy, seemingly quite mystified by his own existence and capacity for speech.

'Where do you come from?' Dathan asked, still hopeful of finding a question that might elicit a comprehensible answer.

'Hungry,' said the boy, as if making a vital discovery.

'Yes,' said Dathan. 'So am I. But what's your name?'

'Nimian,' the boy replied, as he wrestled with the door-catch. As soon as he had the door open he dropped to the ground and scuttled into the undergrowth. He was lost to sight almost immediately.

'I think his name's Nimian,' Dathan said to Hycilla, although he knew that she must have heard the terse word as clearly as he had.

Hycilla opened her own door and stepped down gingerly. Then she went towards the back of the truck. Dathan got down on the other side and moved around to join her at the rear.

There was a dead soldier on the back of the truck, laid out in a supine position between the gun-mount and the side-wall. It wasn't immediately obvious how he had died. There were no gaping holes in his uniform and there seemed to have been no conspicuous spillage of blood, except for two trickles that extended from his closed eyes like tear-tracks. He did stink, though, and not merely of shit. It was as if putre-faction had already set in deep within his flesh. When Dathan had clambered up on to the back of the truck he pushed back one of the dead man's eyelids, but when he saw the ruin beneath he shuddered and snatched his hand away.

'Magic,' he said, tersely. Then he remembered that Nimian must be a wise-dreamer, at least, and perhaps a sorcerer. He wondered, for the first time, whether the boy could have had anything to do with the attack on the Imperial soldiers, If so, he had saved Dathan's and Hycilla's lives before they had saved his – if they had saved his.

'Never mind him,' Hycilla said. 'What's in the boxes and canisters?'

Dathan looked over the cargo that had been stowed in front of the gun-mount. 'Lots of water,' he said. 'Some food, and what looks like ammunition. No guns, though, except for this monster. If the truck stopped because it ran out of fuel, we certainly can't take that with us… and I wouldn't know fuel for what it was even if I saw some. Where has the boy gone? Didn't he say he was hungry?'

Nimian reappeared then, as if on cue. He was carrying a two foot-long lizard in one hand and something that Dathan couldn't put a name to in the other. While the boy lifted his right hand high above his head so as to dangle the head of the living lizard into his mouth, and then swallow it whole, inch by wriggling inch, Dathan had time enough to study the second creature more carefully.

It looked like a grotesquely over-inflated woodlouse with horns and a spiky tail. Dathan couldn't imagine that it was edible, whether it was poisonous or not – but when the lizard was safely packed into his gullet Nimian proceeded to stuff the creature into his mouth, exoskeleton and all. This time, he condescended to do a certain amount of biting and chewing – both of which were noisy processes – but the final effect was the same. The monstrous arthropod was completely consumed.

'Ah,' said Nimian, with what seemed to Dathan to be a parody of satisfaction.

'There's some real food here,' Dathan said, numbly. He had found biscuits, compressed fruit and corned beef.

Nimian's refusal to take his pick of the treats on offer seemed disdainful. Instead, he grabbed the dead man by the boots and hauled him off the back of the lorry. He quickly stripped the man of his uniform and boots.

For one horrid moment, Dathan thought that the boy was going to start feeding the soldier's limbs into his unnaturally capacious maw – but it was the clothes he wanted, for now. By the time he had put them on they weren't quite as ill-fitting as Dathan had expected; Nimian seemed to have grown taller and wider since he had first jumped into the truck.

Hycilla had opened one of the water-canisters and had taken a drink before passing it to Dathan. When Dathan had quenched his own thirst he passed it on to Nimian, half-expecting the offer to be refused – but Nimian drank from it with astonishing avidity, consuming at least half a gallon in no more than half a minute.

When he put the canister down, the improbable boy said 'Still hungry' and promptly disappeared into the undergrowth again.

'What is he?' Dathan asked Hycilla.

Hycilla did not question Dathan's use of 'what' instead of 'who'. She was as apprehensive as he was. She would probably have been terrified – as Dathan would have been – had they not endured so much horror already that she had lost the capacity for further excitement.

'I don't know,' she said.

'A mutant?' Dathan prompted. 'I've heard people say…' He trailed off. Where the secret matters of the covens were concerned, he had only heard people say things that he wasn't supposed to hear. He was a man now, but he had been a boy all his life, shielded and excluded from all adult affairs.

Hycilla, who had hardly begun her preparation for education as a wise-dreamer, seemed to know only a little more. 'I don't think he's an ordinary freak,' she said. 'Something else. Something more. Did I really drive the truck for half the night and nearly half a day? I can't imagine how.'

'You were at the wheel,' Dathan said, choosing his words very carefully. 'Maybe he knows who was really driving. I wish I'd got to those good boots before he did – but I suppose I'd have had to hand them over. Whatever kind of something else he is, he isn't the kind of something else that people like us can say no to. How much danger are we in, do you think?'

'Not as much as we were in when the soldiers had us, I suppose,' Hycilla said, uncertainly. 'They'd have shot you within another couple of minutes – and they'd have shot me too, after another couple of hours, or however long it took.'

'But he is dangerous.'

'I think he is,' Hycilla said, pensively. 'Whatever he is, he's definitely dangerous. But he's on our side, isn't he? His enemies are our enemies, which must make him our friend – and us his. We ought to get some food for ourselves while we can.'

Dathan knew that Hycilla was right, probably about everything. He wished that he were able to think clearly, but the overload that had obliterated his capacity for fear and horror seemed to have slowed him down in every respect. He ate mechanically, unable to taste the food and seemingly unable to do anything but move his hands mechanically back and forth from his mouth. Whatever danger Nimian posed was simply set aside; Dathan was unable to contemplate it, let alone to reason it out any further than he already had.

Dathan and Hycilla had finished their meal by the time Nimian appeared again, and this time he didn't bring his meal with him. Either he had figured out that his eating-habits were so disconcerting to others that they were best indulged in private or he had been too hungry to delay his satisfaction.

The stolen uniform appeared to be even better-fitting now that it had when he had disappeared. If the boy really had grown into it, Dathan thought dully, he had done so with astonishing alacrity. Nimian's eyes and ears seemed more distinctly unhuman now, and there was hair on the back of his hands that had not been there before. His teeth were noticeably sharper, and there seemed to be ridges growing on his skull, their tips already showing through his silky hair.

'Can you understand me, Nimian?' Hycilla said. She had obviously recovered more fully than Dathan.

The boy didn't answer, but he swivelled his incredibly black eyes to fix his gaze upon her.

'I'm Hycilla and this is Dathan,' she told him. 'We ran away from our village when it was attacked. We ran away again from the pool – but we have no idea where to run to. We're lost, and alone. We need help.'

The boy listened to all of this, and then seemed to set about thinking it over – but it appeared that the effort was a trifle painful, because he raised his hands to his forehead, closing his eyes momentarily.

'You and you,' he said. 'Us now. All together. Grow together. Burn together.'

Hycilla pondered these remarks for a moment or two, then shrugged her shoulders, admitting defeat. She turned back to Dathan. 'This is a road of sorts,' she said, kneeling down to inspect the surface. 'I can feel the ruts of cart-wheels. It's not well-used, but it is a road – which means that it must lead somewhere, probably to Elvenor or Mancip. Maybe all we have to do is follow it, until we come to a town – or, at least, a village or a farmhouse.'

Dathan looked at the giant parodies of corn-cobs that were growing beside the roadside, and wondered briefly whether they could possibly be a crop of some kind. He decided that it was highly unlikely. They were native, of little nutritional value if not actually poisonous. The tales told to the village children sometimes referred to 'nightshade forests' as places of even more extreme danger than the 'gardens of god', but he had never managed to obtain a clear notion of what a night-shade forest might look like. Maybe, he thought, this was one.

Or maybe not.

'Walk,' said Nimian, suddenly, having apparently completed his cogitations. 'Battle to fight. Stars stand still. Then… whoosh.' His voice trailed off, uncertainly.

'Whoosh,' Dathan echoed, looking to Hycilla for guidance.

'There's a battle to fight, and then the stars will stand still,' Hycilla said, trying hard to import the proper sense into Nimian's clipped utterances. 'That's bad, I think, if I've got it right.'

'Bad,' Dathan repeated, thinking that it sounded all too plausible.

'There was something in a dream I had,' Hycilla went on, 'something Pater Saltana said… if the stars stand still, more enemies might pour out of the sky. They'd annihilate us, and there'd be nothing Gavalon and the other coven-masters could do to save us.'

Nimian seemed to have become confused again as he tried to follow this speech, but his expression cleared as he caught one word that was evidently far more meaningful to him than the rest.

'Gavalon,' he repeated, nodding his head urgently. 'Lost Gavalon. Too hungry, too angry, too fast. Lost Gavalon. Bring him. Touch him. Do his part.'

'If he knows Gavalon,' Dathan concluded, uncertainly, 'he must be from Gavalon's army.'

'I don't know,' said Hycilla, even more uncertainly. 'If that's so, maybe we ought to help him get back to it. But we don't know where Gavalon is.'

Dathan felt slightly better now that he had food in his stomach – but feeling slightly better only paved the way for feeling much worse, as he found the ability to be afraid again. He hopped back on to the rear of the truck, intent on rooting around to see what he might be able to carry away. 'We have to go,' he said. 'One way or another, we have to go. Why did the Imperium have to come to Gulzacandra, to destroy everything we had and everything we were? What did we ever do to them?'

'I don't know,' was the only reply Hycilla could offer.

Nimian was still listening, apparently trying to digest what was being said. He seemed to be making progress intellectually as well as physically. 'Imperium,' he said, seizing for a second time upon a word that had ready-made significance for him. 'Men at war with themselves, at war with everyone else. No peace. Never can be. Always war. Always game.'

'It's not a game, Nimian,' Dathan assured the boy – whose neatly-fitted Imperial uniform now seemed almost as disconcerting as the traces of unhumanity that had appeared in his face. 'It's real. People are being killed.'

Nimian smiled then. It was the first time Dathan had seen him smile, and he got the odd impression that it might have been the first time the boy had ever smiled.

'Everything dies,' the boy said, as if he were imparting a precious hidden truth. 'Only matters how.'

'That's not true,' Hycilla put in, as she too set about making up a pack to carry. 'Everybody dies, but it matters when as well as how – and what matters even more is what the dead can leave behind. Knowledge, tradition, discipline. Everybody dies, but villages outlive individuals, and civilization can continue forever.'

Hycilla was parroting Pater Saltana's teachings, but her voice was beginning to take on that peculiar extra timbre; Dathan deduced that she too was beginning to feel better – but that she was no longer the kind of person who could feel better in the perfectly ordinary way that he could.

Dathan had felt comfortable in Hycilla's company for so long that it seemed utterly preposterous that she should now appear alien – but that was the truth of the matter.

'Only darkness is forever,' was Nimian's reply to what Hycilla had said. 'Men die, villages die, civilizations die, empires die, universes die. Ashes to ashes, dust to dust. Ashes of stars, dust of stars. All darkness in the end – but while we burn, we must burn. Will see. Will all see. You and you and…'

Nimian's eyes seemed to flare up from within while he delivered this speech, but the light died away in the void as confusion reasserted its hold on his head and his heart. 'Hungry,' he muttered, after a pause. 'Need food.' But this time he did not dive into the undergrowth in search of hideous prey.

'I think this is all I can carry,' Hycilla said to Dathan, showing him the pack she had made up. There was enough food and water to see them through several days – twice as many when the resources of Dathan's own self-selected burden were added in. Had there been a manageable gun, Dathan would certainly have taken it, and plenty of ammunition, but the dead man hadn't been wearing a sidearm.

'It's enough,' Dathan said. 'Let's go.'

Nimian hadn't prepared a pack of his own, and showed no inclination to help Hycilla or Dathan with theirs, but nobody offered any objection to his travelling light. The three of them set off along the road, and the truck was soon lost to sight behind them.

The forest wasn't extensive – not, at least, in the direction they were heading. They had only gone a few hundred paces when the cob-like plants gave way to a more varied vegetation: grassland much like the one which they had trekked across the previous day, interrupted by clumps of spiry silver-leaved trees.

It was beautiful, in a way, but Dathan was not in a mood to appreciate its beauty. The imaginary thread around his heart seemed to be tightening its grip upon him. He could not find words to describe how he felt. Like a prisoner within his own body? Not quite. As if his flesh were no longer entirely his? Almost. Odd, at any rate. Very, very odd.

A family of mowas sprinted away across the grassy plain as the three travelling companions emerged into plain view. They looked like eight-foot chickens but their gait was remarkably steady and very speedy. Further away, Dathan saw a herd of ghazals. They were too far from the track to feel threatened by human presence, and they continued grazing.

There was no immediate sign of cultivation or of any human dwelling, but Hycilla pointed to a thin spiral of smoke on the horizon. 'Maybe a house-fire,' she said.

'If so, we should see the chimney soon enough,' Dathan said.

'There can't be enemies ahead of us,' Hycilla said, uncertainly. 'The trucks were the spearhead – and now that's been broken off, they won't be so keen to get ahead of themselves again.'

'If it's the remains of a beacon-fire,' Dathan said, hopefully, 'maybe we can get the keepers to rebuild it, and send a signal to Gavalon's army.'

'Gavalon probably has better means of finding us than we have of finding him,' Hycilla told him. 'He has wise-dreamers and thrall-wizards, and divination spells. Reaching us might be difficult – but the army must have fast horses, and maybe other runners even faster.'

Dathan didn't want to question her as to the nature of those other runners.

'Hungry,' said Nimian, yet again. 'Need food.' This time he did make a detour, although he came back quickly enough, with what appeared to be the tail of a fast snake still dangling from his lips.

'So hungry,' Nimian reported to his companions, in a semi-apologetic manner. He seemed to have grown another two inches taller. It was no longer possible for Dathan to think of him as a boy. He had started out shorter and slimmer than Hycilla but he was considerably bigger than both of them now.

'That's all right,' Dathan said. 'Just keep right on eating.' To Hycilla, he whispered: 'All that stuff we were taught about native produce filling you up but not doing you any good doesn't seem to apply to him. He's thriving on those horrors.'

While Dathan was speaking, Nimian drifted off again, presumably in search of yet more food.

'So I see,' Hycilla agreed. 'But the native predators don't bother with scales and bones and armour-plate. Whatever he is...' She stopped abruptly, as if she had suddenly realised what he might be.

'Go on,' Dathan prompted.

Hycilla didn't take up the thread of the sentence, and Dathan had no way of guessing what she might have been thinking. He had to provide his own continuation.

Whatever he is, Dathan thought, perhaps we ought to be grateful that he's on our side. The thought was less comforting than he had hoped. After a moment's pause, he asked Hycilla another question. 'How big is he going to get, do you think, if he keeps on eating?'

'Very big indeed,' Hycilla replied, fearfully. 'And he might change in other ways too. If he's just a kind of grub, imagine what the fly might look like when it finally hatches out.'

It seemed to Dathan to be a peculiar comparison to make, but Hycilla was a wise-dreamer, a lot better at sensing possibilities and jumping to conclusions than common folk like him. Even the commonest folk could sometimes see strange possibilities, though, and even the commonest folk could sometimes jump to ominous conclusions.

'He's something really horrible, isn't he?' Dathan said, anxiously. 'Something out of the kind of tale that children aren't supposed to hear.'

Dathan had already begun to wonder whether the tales he had contrived to hear while he was everybody's helper and nobody's apprentice might only be a tiny fraction of the tales that adults kept to themselves. What horrors might there be in the world that had been successfully hidden from him?

That made him think of his mother, and everything she had tried so hard to hide from him in order to protect his innocence – and for the first time, the fact that his mother was probably dead stood starkly clear in the forefront of his consciousness. Now he was able to be afraid again, and terror struck at his heart like an icy spear.

'Not yet,' Hycilla replied to his question, stressing the yet ever so slightly. She seemed utterly oblivious to his reborn terror. 'But if he means what he says about having to burn while he can, we might have to be very careful indeed not to be caught in the flames.'

TWELVE

THE ASSASSIN CAME out of nowhere. Ragan Balberith was descending the staircase towards the foyer of the headquarters of the Adeptus Terra of Sigmatus – in what was supposed to be a completely safe environment – when the aborigine suddenly appeared at the foot of the stairs and started shooting.

Perhaps he would have succeeded had he not started shooting quite so soon, before taking proper aim, but it seemed likely that he had not had adequate opportunity to practise using the weapon. It was not so very uncommon in Kalazendra for aborigines to possess and use stolen guns, but they lacked training opportunities.

Even so, the assassin got off four shots before one of Balberith's bodyguards put him down, and one of those shots lodged in the thigh of the second bodyguard, who had been quick to do his duty by serving as a human shield to the Chief Inquisitor.

Balberith's first thought, as he watched the gunman collapse, was that it was as well that what passed for the Adeptus Terra on Sigmatus had contrived to maintain a proper measure of loyalty and discipline. Had his bodyguards been less than fully committed to his protection, one of them would surely have been bribed by now to do Orloc Melcarth's dirty work. As things were, Melcarth had to rely on aboriginal petty criminals to serve as triggermen, and kitchen staff or cleaners to get them into a shooting position.

There would have to be an investigation, however time-consuming it might be. The rat within the walls had to be identified and annihilated – after proper interrogation, of course. Melcarth was too careful to leave a trail that might lead back to him, but an example had to be set. There was, of course, a possibility that the assassin hadn't been sent by Melcarth, and that he really was a local anarchist with a grudge against everything Imperial, but Balberith had always found it politic to assume the worst until he was presented with proof to the contrary.

While servants hurried to help the wounded man and summon a doctor, the bodyguard who had shot the would-be assassin knelt beside the dying man, demanding to know who had sent him. Having checked that the bullet-wound in his protector's thigh was unlikely to be fatal, Balberith followed the other man down the stairs. He knew that it would be futile to question the gunman. Even if the failed assassin had breath enough to answer – which was unlikely, given the size of the hole in his chest – he would waste it in a brief exhalation of spite. In all probability, the man wouldn't have the slightest idea that he was Melcarth cat's-paw even if that was the truth of the matter. He probably thought that he was a good servant of the Revolution, working for the destruction of the Imperium, and he might be right.

Even Balberith had only the vaguest idea how many of the supposed Revolutionaries were really spies, because he could only make an educated guess as to what proportion of the infiltrators were Melcarth's rather than his. He did know, though, that the whole movement could be tidied up in a matter of days if it were ever in the interests of the Imperial community to do so. One of the few points of strategy on which he and the governor were wholly agreed, however, was that a carefully-managed and subtly-manipulated opposition was a far more useful political tool than a much smaller organization that really did operate in secret.

'He's dead,' the bodyguard reported. 'Never said a word.'

'Anything on him?' Balberith asked, as the bodyguard began to search the dead man's pockets. He was certain that the answer would be negative, and so it was.

'Word of Ajao's breakthrough must have leaked out,' the bodyguard opined. 'They know that if we can establish contact with the Fleet, everything will change.' He carefully didn't specify who 'they' might be. 'Shall I double the guard in the psykers' quarters?'

'If you can be absolutely certain of the new men,' Balberith said. 'And I mean absolutely certain. Even the strongest minds are apt to become agitated down there – it's a duty that requires exceedingly strong nerves.'

'No problem. I'll get the best possible replacement for poor Makri, too. Do you want to wait until he gets here?'

'No. I've got to see Melcarth now.' Balberith stood up as he spoke and moved towards the door, where his car was waiting.

'Is that wise?'

'It's necessary. Anyway, the so-called palace is just about the safest place in Kalazendra – he couldn't afford to have anything happen to me there. He thinks he has enough support to make himself ruler of the world, but he knows how fragile some of that support is. He can't afford to let the rumour get around that he cares far more for his own personal glory than the safety of the Imperial community.'

'It's getting around anyway,' the bodyguard said, as he held the car door open for the Chief Inquisitor, looking round all the while for further dangers – of which there were none.

'That's a pity,' Balberith said, as the bodyguard took his own seat and closed the door so that the driver could get under way, 'because I'm not sure that we can afford a split in the ranks at this point in time, any more than he can. If we can't re-establish contact with the Imperium we need to win this war in Gulzacandra – and if we can, we need to be able to persuade the real tech-priests and inquisitors that we're worth saving. What we need is to rein Melcarth in and make him see sense.'

'No reprisals, then?' the bodyguard said.

'We don't even know for sure that it's him,' Balberith said, tiredly. 'It's not as if we're short of enemies, is it? The aborigines hate us more than they hate the governor's guardsmen and the army, because we're the ones trying to exterminate their foul religion. They don't understand the kind of war we're fighting.'

It was only a short ride to the governor's palace. It would
have been easily walkable, but custom dictated that the Masters
of the Imperium didn't walk. They were the True Men, citizens
of the galaxy still, despite the fact that they had been out of
touch for seven generations. Walking was for aborigines.

As the elevator rose to the floor where Melcarth's offices
were, Balberith hoped that he wouldn't have to go out on that
damned balcony again. He didn't like Melcarth playing with
him, or even knowing that he was vulnerable to being played
with. One day, he thought, Melcarth would lean out just a little too far and lose his footing – but not, of course, while the
Chief Inquisitor was standing next to him, or even in the
building. Now was not the right time – but times changed,
sometimes rapidly, and if Deir Ajao was right they might be
about to change very dramatically for the better. Within a
week, if only the warpstorm would condescend to become
dormant for long enough, Sigmatus might have a real
Planetary Governor – and the importance of its Chief
Inquisitor's loyalty and determination would receive due
recognition at long last.

Orloc Melcarth was not on his balcony. He was at his desk,
entertaining other guests: three of the army's senior officers,
and a vox-caster operator who must have delivered fresh news
from the front. The expressions on their faces told Balberith
that the news was not good.

'What went wrong?' he asked.

'Operation Probe,' replied Major-General Vorch, succinctly.

That brought a frown to Balberith's face. Operation Probe
had not been his idea, but its presumed necessity had been
based on intelligence provided by his psykers. The vision in
question had been unfortunately vague, but it had seemed adequate to establish the tactical importance of a certain hill west
of Odienne. The decision to take Odienne and hold it as a supply depot had been taken independently, but once that was in
Fulbra's plan, the desirability of occupying the allegedly-signif-
icant position without delay had seemed clear.

'The cultists must have occupied the rock already,' Colonel
Balila put in. 'Fulbra's men must have ridden straight into an
ambush.' There was more than a hint of accusation in his tone.
Military men, who had no understanding of the problems of
dealing with psykers, could never quite come to terms with the

limitations of the intelligence Balberith and his fellows were able to gather. Having been warned that the rock might be important, Fulbra's men should have been alert to the possibility of an ambush.

'What were they ambushed with?' Balberith asked, combatively. 'Field artillery? Assault rifles?'

'We don't know,' Vorch admitted. 'There don't seem to have been any survivors to report back. Something nasty. Something horrible.' He meant *magic*, but he couldn't even bring himself to pronounce the word.

'If there was no one to report back,' Balberith said, faking a contempt that he was not quite able to feel, 'we have no reason to assume that it was anything out of the ordinary, do we?'

'It must have been,' Vorch retorted, sombrely. 'They were good men – travelling light, but well enough armed against any foreseeable contingency.'

'Even if it were something horrible,' Balberith said, 'its use will cost the enemy dear. This might be a setback, but we have to press on regardless. It's the fact that we're fighting to destroy something horrible that makes it absolutely necessary to fight this war – and win it. We have to send the aircraft now, so that Fulbra can make use of it.'

'The Chief Inquisitor is right about this being a setback,' Orloc Melcarth put in, swiftly, 'but it's not serious. We've lost a handful of trucks and thirty men – but we can take it on trust that they didn't die easily. They must have inflicted some damage on the enemy. It leaves the position at Odienne weaker than we could have wished, but it would have been weak anyway, given that the locals managed to poison the well. The incursions to the north and south have proceeded much more smoothly – our casualties are insignificant, while the enemy has already lost thousands.'

Thousands of ill-armed peasants, Balberith thought. The first real battle has yet to be fought. 'But General Fulbra is still asking for air support, isn't he?' he said, doggedly. 'The refuelling points are all in place. We should dispatch it without delay.'

Melcarth casually ignored the statement, as if it had been a mere suggestion of no importance. 'What news do you have, Chief Inquisitor?' he asked instead, looking Balberith straight in the eye. If he knew that there had been an attempt on Balberith's life he gave no sign of it.

'Ships of the Imperial Fleet are definitely nearby,' Balberith said, boldly. 'They are certainly aware of the situation on Sigmatus. If the abatement of the warpstorm continues...'

'Are you telling us that you've actually got a message through to the Fleet?' Melcarth wanted to know. 'Have you begun a dialogue?'

'Not exactly,' Balberith had to admit. 'What we seem to have contrived is to eavesdrop on a few relevant exchanges within the Fleet's internal communications. We're trying to establish a telepathic link, but the warpstorm...'

'Is still a barrier, and might become impenetrable again at any minute,' Melcarth finished for him. 'We can't afford to wait, Chief Inquisitor. We have to press on with our own plans. We've been isolated for two hundred years, and we can't pin all our hopes on the possibility that the isolation might soon end.'

You certainly can't, Balberith said to himself, silently, but I'm not sure that I have any alternative. Aloud, he said: 'We can't ignore the possibility either. If the warpstorm does remain quiet, the Fleet's commanders will have to decide whether it's worth their while trying to help us. It would be a risk, because they wouldn't know how soon warpstorm activity will increase again, or how violent it might become. If they think we're beyond help, or undeserving of it, they might decide that the safest course of action is Exterminatus.'

'I can't believe that,' said the major-general, bluntly. Balberith realised that it was perfectly true. Vorch was literally unable to believe that the Imperium – the real Imperium, of which this one was but a feeble and distorted echo – was in the business of obliterating whole ecospheres, making no discrimination at all between Chaos worshippers and those who opposed them.

To men like Vorch, the Imperium of Mankind was a distant memory, preserved in a set of stories handed down from his great-great-great-great grandparents, more speculation than history. Vorch thought of himself and men like him – in which category Vorch presumably included Ierius Fulbra and Orloc Melcarth – as the Imperium, and took it for granted that his own notions of authority and strategy were universal. The inner core of the organization that was still proud to own such names as the Inquisition and the Adeptus Terra was the only place on Sigmatus where accurate knowledge and true faith still survived. Alas, the twisted mind of Orloc Melcarth, who would prefer that contact with the real Imperium was never resumed, was not so very remarkable in a community which had strayed so far from the path of righteousness.

'Our task,' Melcarth said, smoothly, 'is to oppose the forces of the enemy with all our might. To do that, we must win this war, swiftly and completely. I don't suppose, by any chance, that you have any more information to offer about this mysterious rock in the wilderness? Our men are dying out there.'

The last thing Balberith wanted was to make Melcarth's support any less fragile than it was. 'I'll do what I can to obtain further intelligence,' he promised, 'but the tech-priests and inquisitors accompanying General Fulbra may be better placed to do that, especially if they can capture a few of what the aborigines call wise-dreamers. If you were to send the aircraft...'

'If Operation Probe hadn't gone so badly awry,' Vorch said, in a vexed tone – doing Melcarth a service whether he knew it or not – 'we might have been better placed to capture a wise-dreamer or two without exposing our men to undue risks.'

'Nobody expected this campaign to be a walk-over,' Balberith pointed out. 'However inflated the reputation of this Gavalon the Great might be, he's as powerful as he is vile. We, who are pious and virtuous men, can have little or no idea of what horrors he might be able to unleash – but we are the Emperor's men, no matter that we have been cast away on this pustulent planet, and we have right on our side. We were always going to take losses in this campaign, and we always knew that those losses might be heavy – that's why we waited until our forces were strong enough to be irresistible. My people will do their utmost to help with the primary assault – but their real work will begin afterwards, when we have to root out every remnant of Chaos-worship throughout the continent. That will be a long and uphill struggle, unless we can obtain reinforcements from the Imperium.

'If we can get those reinforcements soon enough, we might be able to cut General Fulbra's anticipated losses drastically. That's what we all want, isn't it? More than anything else, we want to save the lives of our soldiers, and make the work of our priests that much easier – which is why I have to continue trying to make contact with the Fleet, and why every small success in bringing that end closer is worthy of celebration, and why we really ought to send the aircraft to Gulzacandra without further delay.'

Balila was already nodding agreement to the main points of this speech, and Vorch's expression had softened considerably. Even Orloc Melcarth had to make a show of approval, no matter how determined he was not to take up the final suggestion. Balberith had begun to understand that Melcarth wanted the aircraft for himself – and that made him determined to make sure, one way or another, that he didn't get it.

'You're right, of course, Ragan,' the governor said. 'But let's not put all our eggs in one basket, shall we? General Fulbra will do everything he can to figure out why Operation Probe went wrong, and what the implications are for the next phase of the battle. We do need to know what the enemy has in store for us, and your people represent our best hope of finding out. It's not as if Gulzacandra is like Kalazendra, with a spy on every street of every town – and if the reports from Odienne are anything to go by, even our best interrogators will find it hard going extracting useful information from the local peasants, whose stupidity is only exceeded by their stubbornness. We're relying on the Adeptus Terra, Ragan. We need you now more than ever before.'

Melcarth's insincerity was palpable. It was easy enough for Balberith to imagine the governor adding, for his own ears alone: *and once we're through with this campaign, we'll never need you again.* He knew, though, that the Imperium would need him again. If Chaos were to be annihilated rather than subjected to a merely temporary defeat, the rulers of Sigmatus would need to maintain the strength of its remnant of the Adeptus Terra, and its strength of purpose too. And what the local relic of the real Adeptus Terra needed more than anything else was a healthy injection of new strength and new purpose from the real Adeptus Terra, the backbone of the Imperium of Mankind.

It would be foolish, Balberith thought, even to try to redirect Deir Ajao's attention from authentically important matters to such trivial questions as who or what had ambushed Operation Probe, and why a lump of rock in the desert seemed to be of some tactical significance to Gavalon the so-called Great. 'If you need me so much,' Balberith said, grimly, 'it's a pity your police force couldn't stop a native with a gun getting into my headquarters this morning. One of my bodyguards took a bullet that was meant for me.'

Major-General Vorch and his junior officers seemed genuinely shocked, but it was hard to believe that Melcarth's pantomime of horror had any genuine sympathy in it. Balberith couldn't believe that it had, even if Melcarth hadn't actually been behind the assassination attempt.

'The cultists still have agents in Kalazendra,' Melcarth observed. 'Until their organization loses its head, we'll never be able to obliterate them entirely – but once Gulzacandra is ours and this Gavalon is safely dead, along with all his disgusting followers, the underground will wither away. Once victory is ours, we'll all be able to sleep safely in our beds. Would you like me to lend you some men to reinforce your bodyguard, Ragan? I'd be only too happy to help.'

'I can take care of it,' Balberith said, drily. 'I can take care of everything – depend on it.'

'I will,' Melcarth assured him, insincerely. 'We all will.'

I'll bring the Fleet here or die trying, Balberith told himself firmly. You can ignore the possibility if you want, my dear governor, but you won't be able to ignore the ships when they come down – and then we'll see who can take care of themselves and who can't. All praise to the Emperor Magnificent – and death to all his enemies, whoever and wherever they may be!

THIRTEEN

IT TURNED OUT that the smoke Dathan and Hycilla had seen was not the residual smoke of a dead beacon-fire. It was coming from the chimney of a small house set in the middle of a square patchwork of fields, which had remained invisible far longer than seemed likely because it was situated in a narrow valley.

There had been grain growing in two of the fields, lentils in two more and potatoes in the remainder, but the grain had all been harvested and all but a few of the potatoes had been unearthed. Even the sturdily-fenced chicken-run behind the house had been emptied. Dathan assumed that the birds had been taken by the quartermasters serving Gavalon's army. If so, that army could not be far away.

The farmer's family had gone, presumably to seek refuge in Elvenor – if, in fact, Elvenor was the nearest town. If rival armies were to clash upon the plain, the farmer had presumably reasoned, it was best not to remain in an isolated building that either side might find it convenient to occupy and hold against bombardment.

From Dathan's point of view, on the other hand, the possibility of temporary shelter seemed very welcome. Because he

141

had hardly slept during the previous night the morning's trek
had soon exhausted his reserves of strength. Hycilla seemed to
need rest even more than he did, and he was afraid that she
might slip back into a trance state at any moment. Nimian,
who had slowed their progress considerably while he took any
and every opportunity to feed his unnatural appetite, seemed
stronger and more alert than either of them, but he too was
beginning to show distinct signs of confusion in his eyes.

Nimian might be alert, Dathan thought, but it was not
merely – and perhaps not primarily – his immediate surroundings that he was alert to. Other things, whose nature
was beyond Dathan's comprehension, seemed to be clamour-
ing for his attention.

When they had searched the little house and its outhouses
thoroughly, not so much to make sure that no one was hiding
there as to determine whether they could renew their supplies,
Dathan and Hycilla settled down on the hearth before the last
glimmering embers of the previous night's fire. They ate a reasonably hearty meal.

Nimian ate too, although the Imperial soldiers' rations did
not seem nearly as much to his taste as the various disgusting
items of native fauna he had been chasing and devouring
since dawn.

'How do we go about finding Gavalon?' Dathan wanted to
know.

Hycilla didn't answer immediately; the meal had made her
more somnolent than before. 'I don't know,' she said, weakly.

'The only thing I can think of,' Dathan said, not at all satisfied with this feeble response, 'is trying to find and follow the
tracks left by the wagons that took the grain and potatoes
away. They must have been heavily laden, so it shouldn't be
too difficult to pick up their trail. Or we could just go on following the road until we reach the next village.'

'Fine,' Hycilla said, unhelpfully.

Dathan turned to Nimian in exasperation. 'What do you
think?' he asked, not expecting much in the way of a reply.

Nimian stared at him in a most disconcerting fashion, but
he did at least appear to be considering the question with all
due seriousness and with a measure of intelligence.

Dathan noticed that both halves of Nimian's stolen
Imperial uniform were now straining at the seams; he

doubted that they would last more than an hour before they were torn apart from within. No one could possibly have called Nimian 'skinny' now; he had muscles that a blacksmith would have envied.

'I stay here,' Nimian said, eventually. 'With her. You go. Bring Gavalon. Bring wizards. Sacrifices will come. I will bring ships.'

The word 'sacrifices' seemed ominous. It was, however, the final word that seemed the most surprising to Dathan.

'Ships?' Dathan said. 'We're hundreds of miles from the sea. How can you possibly bring ships?'

'You bring Gavalon and wizards,' Nimian said, impatiently. 'I bring ships.'

'You mean starships, don't you?' Hycilla put in, having apparently experienced a sudden flash of enlightenment. 'Like the ones that brought the Imperium here, two hundred years ago.'

'You bring wizards,' Nimian repeated, still looking at Dathan with his illimitably dark eyes. 'Sacrifices will come. I will bring food. Lots of food. Then ships. Whoosh.'

'I don't want to leave Hycilla,' Dathan said, wondering how stubborn he dared to be, given that he was talking to someone who was gradually turning into a giant, or something far stranger and far worse.

'Safe here,' Nimian replied. 'Safer than anywhere. Need her here. She can see. She knows. She is me. So are you. Go.'

'Hycilla's supposed to be a wise-dreamer,' Dathan persisted, stubbornly, 'but she's very young. She's just an apprentice. She doesn't know anything.' He was uneasily aware of the fact that he had no idea what Hycilla might know, or even how she might have come by the information.

'Needs help,' said the boy who was no longer a boy, nodding in agreement. 'And rest. Stay with me. You go.'

Dathan wasn't convinced. Didn't he need rest just as much as Hycilla did, maybe more? And how could anybody be better off staying with whatever Nimian was becoming? This was, after all, a being who didn't think that it mattered when a person might die, but only how – a being who reckoned that when the time came to burn, one had to burn.

Pater Saltana had once told Dathan that all life was like fire, and that food really was a kind of fuel, whose energy was released and reclaimed by slow combustion. The trick of being human, Pater Saltana had said, was to burn as slowly and as steadily as one could – but the trick of being more than human, as wizards and wise-dreamers were, was to burn brightly as well.

Dathan knew nothing about wizards except what he had heard in fantastic tales, but he had a nasty suspicion that when Nimian spoke with such relish of burning he was thinking of the kind of fire that could compete, if only momentarily, with the sun.

Dathan didn't want Hycilla to burn like that. He didn't even want her to be standing near to anything – or anyone – that did. He wanted Hycilla to be safe, and slow, and steady, and not to risk anything for the sake of brightness. He had loved her for a long time and he didn't want to stop just because she was becoming strange, and wasn't always entirely herself. He was convinced that he could love her, if only the world could be restored to proper order.

If only...

'Go on, Dathan,' Hycilla said, opening her eyes a little wider. 'Do what Nimian says. It's for the best.'

Was it really Hycilla talking, Dathan wondered, or was she under the control of someone else – something else? It was a frightening thought, but he had grown so used to fear by now it was difficult to conceive of any thought sufficiently powerful to add an extra measure to the terror he already felt.

'I wouldn't know which way to go,' Dathan objected, in a low tone. 'I need you to come with me.'

'Give you guide,' said Nimian. He reached up to his head and pulled out one of the hairs from the top of his head. Then he wrapped it twice around the little finger of his left hand, and used his teeth to knot it tight. Dathan noticed that the fingernail had grown longer, thicker and darker, so that it was now more like a claw.

When the knot was secure, Nimian-the-monster – as Dathan was beginning to think of him – took the base of his own left little finger between the thumb and forefinger of his right hand, and casually snapped it off.

No blood flowed from the wound.

Nimian got hold of the free end of the hair and held it up, so that the severed finger dangled freely. It swivelled left and then right, oscillating for a second or two before settling down.

'That way,' said the monster, blandly. 'Follow the finger. Find Gavalon. Bring wizards. Soon. Sacrifices will come.'

'What kind of sacrifices?' Dathan asked, although something inside him was trying to tell him that he really didn't want to know. He couldn't bring himself to reach out his hand to take the proffered charm.

'When is time to burn,' Nimian replied, 'we burn.'

'Take the finger, Dathan,' Hycilla said, dully. 'Show it to Gavalon – he'll understand what it means. He'll know what to do.'

'I'm not sure…' Dathan began.

'You don't have to be sure,' Hycilla told him, brutally. 'You just have to do it. For me. For the village. For the world.'

'I don't want to leave you.'

'It was only an accident that brought us together in the first place,' she said. 'I have to stay here, to play my part. For you. For the village. For the world. For the god of Gulzacandra.'

'You're not safe with him,' Dathan persisted. 'Whatever he is, whatever he becomes, he's not safe to be around.'

'There is no safety,' Hycilla told him. 'There's only war – only the game.'

'It's not a game,' Dathan insisted. 'It's life and death. Especially death.'

'Go,' she said. 'Do what you have to do. For us. I am he and he is you. For all of us. For *me*.' This time, Dathan noticed, she had left out the village and the world – and the god of Gulzacandra, who was sometimes called the Changer of the Ways, the Divine Schemer. It was a good ploy; Dathan wasn't sure what he was willing to do for the village, the world and the god he had worshipped since birth, but he did know what he was willing to do for Hycilla.

Anything.

Gingerly Dathan took the charm that Nimian was still holding out to him, and wrapped the free end of the hair around his right forefinger, so that the darkened nail of the dangling finger could point whichever way it wanted to. Then he picked up an open canister of water and took a deep swig before screwing the cap back on and returning it to his pack.

'How far do I have to go?' he asked.

'I don't know,' Hycilla said. 'Rest when you have to – ten minutes every hour, as best you can calculate – but don't stop to sleep. Keep going. There isn't much time.'

Dathan was convinced by now that although Hycilla's mouth was forming the words, there was another intelligence behind them – perhaps, however paradoxical it might seem, the same intelligence that couldn't yet persuade Nimian's vocal apparatus to form a proper sentence.

Dathan looked hard at Nimian, but all Nimian said was: 'Very hungry. Must bring food.'

Dathan didn't want to think about what that might involve, but when he condescended to be pushed outside he soon got a clue.

A family of mowas – probably the same ones that he had seen running away when he emerged from the red-and-black forest – was sprinting towards the farmhouse. They were only flightless birds, but the adults were taller than any man and they were very stout around the waist. Dathan suppressed a vision of Nimian breaking their necks and chopping them up before wolfing them down one by one – feathers, talons and all.

The stolen uniform would have no chance at all of containing the subsequent expansion, but Dathan didn't suppose that clothes were going to be a significant priority once the hungry boy's legs and torso began to follow the example of his ears and find their eventual form. He remembered the pattern he had glimpsed on Nimian's naked body when he had first seen him, and realised that it might have been a pattern in more than one sense of the word. It might have been a plan, like those that carpenters and weavers scratched in the sand while trying to organise their thoughts.

It wasn't just the mowas that were coming towards the house, either, although the rest were reptiles and megascarabs. Apparently Nimian wasn't hungry enough to tackle a loxodont yet, but there didn't seem to Dathan to be much comfort in the cautious 'yet'.

Some of the reptiles passed right by him, but none of the snakes hissed at him or reared up to threaten a strike. The finger seemed to be doing more than point his way; perhaps it had protective power too.

Dathan did exactly as he had been told. There was a certain comfort to be found in the sense of purpose that obedience gave him. No matter how scared he was of what might lie at his journey's end, having orders to follow was better than having no idea at all what to do.

When he had been going for about an hour – he had no way of knowing the exact time – he stopped for a few minutes' rest. Once he had taken a drink, however, and rested his feet by sitting down on a giant mushroom for a while, he set off again.

He made steady progress, even though his legs were aching. While he was on the move he didn't feel unduly sleepy, so he kept moving. His conscious mind became dull and the flow of his thoughts became viscous – but his feelings were out of step, and there was a peculiar excitement in his belly. He lost track of time as he strode across the alien landscape, but there was something deep inside him that seemed to rejoice in his movement.

The sun was well into its afternoon decline when Dathan ran into the beastmen.

He was passing through a native wood at the time: one that was not quite as spectacularly odd as the corn-cob forest in which he had found himself when the truck ran out of fuel, but which was nevertheless peculiar. Some of the trees were domberries, which were as similar to imported vegetation as native vegetation ever got, but most had shiny scales that made their boles and branches look more like metal than wood, and their fruits were like medallions.

He had smelled the beastmen before he actually saw them, but he hadn't been able to recognise the odour, and only realised how foul it was when he found out where it was coming from.

Dathan was dumbstruck with terror, but terror seemed to have lost its meaning and he felt oddly clear-headed, oddly mechanical. The severed finger was still dangling from its thread beneath his own forefinger, but there was a paradoxical sense in which he seemed to be dangling from it, meekly following its direction, unable to do more with himself than point and proceed.

Under other circumstances, he would have been quite convinced that the monstrous beastmen were about to pounce on him, rend him limb from lim and make a meal of him, but with the finger to guide him he felt as if he, not they, were the real monster and that they, not he, stood in the greater danger of being rent asunder and consumed.

There were six beastmen in all – three with heads suggestive of lopsided cattle, one with a hawk's head, one that was more like a pig's than anything else Dathan could put a name to, and one with the face of some nightmarish caricature of an ape. They were all shaggy, except for the piggy one, and they mostly had legs like bears, except for the two mowa-legged ones. They were armed with an assortment of axes and spears, although there wasn't one of them that couldn't have torn him limb from limb with their bare hands – or claws, in the cases of those that didn't actually have hands as such. They had been sitting or lying down, but when they caught sight of him they all came to their feet and moved to bar his way.

On any other day of his life such a meeting would have caused Dathan to faint with horror, or to run away as fast as he could, hoping to hang on to the contents of his colon. Today, however, he simply stopped, and lifted his right hand a little higher in order to display the talisman that was dangling from his forefinger.

'I'm looking for Gavalon the Great,' he said. 'I have a message for him.'

The beastmen looked at him, their various eyes squinting slightly as they weighed him up. He moved his hand a little, trying to draw their attention to his uncanny compass. Their attention was duly drawn.

They grunted to one another, unhurriedly, but they didn't come any closer.

'Gavalon,' Dathan repeated, figuring that they were probably stupider than the average human. 'Do you know Gavalon? Can you take me to him? Don't worry if you can't – I'm already pointed in the right direction. All you have to do is let me pass. You will let me pass, won't you?'

The beastmen didn't reply, and they didn't move.

Dathan realised, reluctantly, that he would have to march right up to them and pass through their ragged line. The stink seemed suddenly overpowering, and the idea of coming within arm's reach of the creatures was extremely unappealing, but he knew that he had to do it and he knew that he could do it.

Nervously, he set one foot in front of the other – and then, figuring that he was committed, walked forward boldly. He extended his right arm so that the monstrous finger preceded him by as wide a margin as he could contrive. He made up his mind that he would pass between a bull-head with an axe and the spear-wielding ape-thing.

They didn't move until the last possible moment, but they did move sufficiently to let him pass without touching either of them. Their nearness was repulsive, but the fact of his being able to bear it was strangely exhilarating. As soon as he was through, while still within easy reach of a spear-thrust, he felt his heart leap.

I'm a brave man, he thought, rejoicing in the surprise of it. I really am a man, and brave. It was not the first time he had thought of himself as something other than a boy – far from it – but it was the first time he had had occasion to call himself brave. He had not been brave in the judeye forest, or at the pool, or at the farmhouse, but he had passed through the rank of beastmen with iron in his soul.

I am in this war, he thought, whether I like it or not. I am a fighter now, and I must do whatever I can to secure our victory. For the village. For the world. For glory.

On the far side of the wood, he saw the fringes of the encamped army: its myriad tents and wagons, and its multifarious coloured banners, flapping lazily in the breeze. There were other sentries to pass, but none so frightful as those he had first encountered, and he found men with voices soon enough, who not only understood the name of Gavalon the Great but were willing and able to reply to his enquiries.

'Who sent you?' asked one tall man – the first person on his own side Dathan had seen with a gun: a sleek rifle with a polished barrel.

'Nimian,' Dathan told him. 'That's what he said his name was, at any rate – before he began to change into something else.'

The man's eyes narrowed at that, but he was just a fighting man, not a wise-dreamer. He obviously knew little or nothing about what Nimian had been, let alone what he was becoming.

'We – that is to say, a girl named Hycilla and I – were ambushed next to a pool last night, a long way to the east,'

Dathan explained. 'We'd run away from the village when the Imperial soldiers came, hoping to reach Elvenor, but they came after us in trucks. I think Nimian killed them all, but I'm not sure. We got away in a truck.'

The rifleman was capable of understanding that. His eyes widened again. 'Trucks? Imperial soldiers?' he said. 'Come with me – you'll need to tell the commanders where and how many, and what guns they had. They're supposed to be some way off to the north, as yet. They're not supposed to be less than a day away in the east.'

'They aren't now,' Dathan assured him. 'If there were any left alive, they can't have numbered more than a dozen.'

If the rifleman believed him it didn't lessen his sense of urgency. He hustled Dathan through the camp, towards the tent that bore the most striking banner of them all: a huge eye that emitted an irresistible blast of killing force. Dathan realised that he had seen it before, in his dreams. Did that mean that he was a wise-dreamer now? He couldn't believe it, and told himself that he must have seen something like it before, when he was too young to remember.

Inside the tent, Dathan saw Gavalon the Great for the first time. He had no difficulty whatsoever in picking the sorcerer out from the crowd that surrounded him; he had never seen anyone so spectacularly ugly, or anyone with such monstrous eyes.

Dathan watched the rifleman stammer out his story, and saw Gavalon wave a huge hand negligently, as if to indicate that the news was no news at all. Then the sorcerer turned, to direct those awesomely intimidating eyes at Dathan. As Gavalon came towards him, Dathan the valiant drew himself up to his full height and displayed the finger that had brought him here.

As soon as Gavalon saw what Dathan was holding aloft before his face the sorcerer's broad mouth broke out into an expansive smile, exposing two great rows of jagged yellow teeth.

'Where is he?' Gavalon wanted to know. 'We must find him – there's no time at all to lose. Fulbra is coming at us full tilt, and we do not have arms enough to hold him off. Is he well and strong? Where is he?'

'He wants you to come to him,' Dathan said, a little breathlessly. 'Bring wizards, he said, and–'

'And what?' Gavalon the Great was avid to know.

'He said something about sacrifices,' Dathan concluded, reluctantly. 'He said that sacrifices are coming... and that he will bring ships.'

FOURTEEN

IERIUS FULBRA PULLED a blanket over his head and shoulders and crouched down in the ditch as the explosive charges went off. He winced slightly as great gobs of mud rained down on the blanket, almost tearing it from his hands. A general had to protect his uniform, or what kind of example would he be setting to his men? He had not merely to appear to be the bravest of the brave, but also the neatest of the neat. He was fighting for order, after all, against the insidious and horrific ravages of Chaos – and if that thought imported a little dread into his own trained mind, how much more dread would it import into the minds of his less enlightened followers?

Fulbra knew that his followers would be glad to be on the move, glad to be in action, glad to be doing the holy work of the beloved Emperor – how could it be otherwise when the anticipation of that gladness had been so thoroughly drummed into them? But they would be apprehensive too. If the thought of Ragan Balberith's psykers was enough to bring them out in a cold sweat, what would the prospect of facing a continent full of alien psykers do to them, if the notion were allowed to take root? They would say their prayers and perform their rituals and fire their guns with all the mechanical regularity their drill-sergeants had been able to contrive, but every time they had a moment's pause for thought there was a possibility that doubt, the most insidious of all the enemy's weapons, might come to occupy it. At least the killing had so far been easy, and profuse. There was nothing like a good massacre to maintain morale. Blasting barricades apart wasn't quite as satisfying, though. It was often tedious work, without the hint of a thrill.

The barricade was the sixth they had encountered today but only the second that had required explosive charges to be set within it. Shells fired by bolters had been adequate to take care of the others. It was a waste of good ammunition, of course, but necessary. Although the trucks carrying Fulbra's vanguard – even the ones carrying the precious caterpillar-tracked battle-tanks – were theoretically capable of handling rough terrain, they moved a great deal faster if they stuck to what passed for roads in these barbarian parts.

Fulbra gave the filthy blanket to an orderly and moved swiftly back to his armoured car, signalling Colonels Hamera and Diambor to follow him. Like most of the other vehicles in his retinue the car was locally-built. Fourteen of the tanks and sixteen of the troop-carriers were originals, Leman Russ and Chimeras and Salamanders, but no fast-moving vehicles had survived the two hundred years since the landing except for the aircraft that Melcarth would not let him have. Even the motor-cycles his scouts used had come out of Kalazendran factories, although their relative simplicity meant that they were much more similar to original designs than the heavier vehicles.

The Salamander command vehicle that Fulbra used while the brigade was on the move was lightly armoured, but it was more manoeuvrable than its lumpen kin – much more so than the fortress-on-wheels to which he would retreat when the serious fighting started. Given that the enemy had vastly inferior fire-power, he had decided that mobility was his first priority for the moment, which was why his heavy tanks had been loaded on to trucks instead of lumbering into Gulzacandra at their own stately pace.

It was obvious to Fulbra that Colonel Hamera would have preferred to sit safely inside an original tank even when there was no obvious need, but Hamera valued his position as the general's chief aide-de-camp too much to raise any objection –

all the more so with Diambor ready to step into his shoes at a moment's notice. Fulbra was all in favour of jealousy and competition among his senior staff – it sharpened up everyone's performance and added a necessary seasoning of recklessness to their battle-tactics. Envy, if properly channelled, could be just as useful in its own fashion as piety. A good officer had to be taught to love the Emperor, hate heresy, and keep very careful account of the progress of his rivals.

Unfortunately, the enemy also seemed to know that mobility was the invading forces' first priority, and the swine were doing everything they could to slow the invaders down. They were setting fire to their fields as they retreated, burning wooden bridges, tumbling boulders into narrow canyons and scattering caltrops in the hope of puncturing the tyres of the Imperial vehicles. There was a barricade in every village, no matter how makeshift, and if the village were large enough there would be snipers posted on the roofs of the houses beyond the barricade. Only one sniper in three had a rifle, but those who used bows were skilled archers and their arrows could do nearly as much damage as a bullet if they hit unarmoured flesh. So far, casualties on his own side had been trivial, but time was on the side of the defenders, for now. Once the victory was won, the victors would have all the time in the world to hunt down the tainted and slaughter the lot, but until then...

'News?' Fulbra barked at the vox operator as soon as he had taken his seat again.

'Nothing from the scouting-party sent out from Odienne, sir,' the operator replied, as the car got under way, taking its customary slot in the column. 'The village itself is secure, but the commander hasn't heard a word from the men sent to find the dome-shaped rock.'

'It must be an equipment breakdown,' Hamera put in. 'How could an ambush have taken them out so quickly that they didn't even get a chance to call for help?'

'That's what I'd like to know,' Fulbra growled. 'Don't make the mistake of thinking that these people are helpless, or tactically incapable. They're not honest fighting-men, like us – they're nasty, corrupt and underhanded. Tell the commander at Odienne to find out what happened, and to make sure that when his men have found out, they get the news to us immediately. Anything else, corporal?'

The vox operator hesitated momentarily, but then said: 'There's been an attempt on the life of the Chief Inquisitor. Unsuccessful, thanks be to the Emperor.'

'Expectable,' Diambor said. 'The locals might be separated from the sites of the First Conquest by thousands of miles, but the cults have their own lines of communication. There was bound to be an increase in terrorist activity in Sostenuto when things began to get hot hereabouts. Our men have the measure of them, though – all praise to the Emperor Magnificent!'

'I suppose so,' said Fulbra, dubiously. He had his own theory as to who might be responsible for the attempted assassination of Ragan Balberith, but he knew that it wouldn't be politic to mention it here and now. He cursed suddenly as an arrow bounced off the plastic window to his left, leaving an ugly scar in the transparent pane.

It was a wasted shot – the car had only a few square inches of surface vulnerable to the kinds of missiles that snipers had at their disposal – but it was not without a certain symbolic value.

The sharpshooters in the turrets of the leading Chimera troop-carriers were blasting away in every direction, but Fulbra couldn't see whether their shots were having any effect because there was too much smoke. The houses hereabouts were mostly built of wood and even those that were made of stone or brick often had thatched roofs, so the fires set in the fields usually spread to the dwellings and gutted them if the wind pushed them in that direction.

'Imbeciles,' Hamera commented. 'They're destroying their property and their future livelihoods for the sake of slowing us down by a couple of hours a day. If they'd just let us through and lend us a little support they might be able to keep what they have – under new management, of course, once we've secured the territory. Why should they care who rules in Rintrah, or whichever of their shabby towns becomes the new capital? Do their current masters treat them any more kindly than we would? No. Much worse, probably, given that they're evil-worshippers. Peasants! Shit for brains, the lot of them.'

Fulbra knew better than Hamera what would happen when the conquest was complete. Once the inquisitors got busy the owners of the fields hereabouts would be under the new management of whatever vile afterlife their foul god cared to provide for them. Some few of them might conceivably be untainted, but how could anyone be certain which? Best to kill the lot and let the gods sort them out.

A final punctuation mark was appended to Hamera's speech by the spang of a bullet ricocheting from the steel-plate surround. Hamera muttered a supplementary curse, then shifted slightly in his seat as he added a quick prayer.

'They've been taught to hate us with a passion that defies all reason,' Diambor said, laconically. 'They can't begin to understand that the Imperium of Mankind is the only thing that stands between the forces of corruption and dominion over the entire universe. It's hard even for our own people, given the duration of our isolation.'

'We are still part of the Imperium of Mankind, praise be to the Emperor,' Fulbra growled, remembering why he kept Hamera in place as his second-in-command, even though Diambor was the more intelligent man. 'Seven generations of separation and the necessity of manufacturing our own ordnance don't make any difference to our purpose. We're the Emperor's trusted servants, and we must never forget it. One day – perhaps in our own lifetimes – contact with the Fleet will be restored. If and when that glorious day comes, we have to be able to hold our heads high and say: We did what was expected of us. We held to our duty, no matter what obstacles were put in our way.'

'It's not exactly news, sir, but...' the vox-caster operator put in, tentatively.

'But what?' Fulbra wanted to know.

'There's a rumour that ships of the Fleet are nearby, waiting for the warpstorm to ease sufficiently to permit a landing.'

'What do you mean, a rumour?' Fulbra demanded. 'Either we have vox contact or we don't. If this is true, it's the most vital news that we've had in centuries. This could change everything.'

'A psyker is said to have made contact of a sort, sir,' the vox operator said, failing to suppress a slight shudder. 'The word is that any ships that are out there must be too far off to get vox messages back and forth without an unacceptable time lag, even if the storm wasn't garbling the signals, although Melcarth's tech-priests are trying as hard as Balberith's people.'

Fulbra's reply to that was diplomatically wordless. He wouldn't allow tech-priests in his own armoured car, no matter how useful their prayers were to the maintenance of equipment and morale, because the two things he hated most of all were backchat and confused priorities. No one could accuse tech-priests of lacking discipline, but it wasn't military discipline, and no matter what anybody might say about unity of method and purpose, there was still an obvious difference between men who said their prayers as they passed and used their ammunition and men who merely said prayers. Fulbra didn't like psykers any more than the next man, but he knew that Balberith's psykers were far more likely to establish telepathic contact with Imperial ships than Melcarth's tech-priests were to get a vox message through, even if Melcarth's men were really trying.

Let it be true! he said to himself. For the love of the Emperor, let it be true! Then he reminded himself, dutifully, that it was only a rumour, and that he had battles to fight and massacres to manage. He also reminded himself that any intelligence gained by Ragan Balberith's psykers ought to be reckoned dubious, given that their powers had to be boosted by the same drugs that the aborigine dreamers used – drugs that were undoubtedly tainted.

Despite the poverty of their equipment and their relative dearth of true purestrain immigrant blood, Ierius Fulbra had every confidence in the fact that the fighting-men of his army were just as brave, just as determined and just as well-trained as the agents of the First Conquest – but that confidence did not extend to the so-called inquisitors of the so-called Adeptus Terra. He respected Ragan Balberith as a man, but he was not at all sure that Balberith would be as easily recognisable as a cog in the great machine of the Imperium of Mankind as he himself would, or even Orloc Melcarth.

According to the secret history carefully handed down to Fulbra by his forefathers, the psykers of the galaxy-spanning Imperium of Mankind were the glue that held the Imperium together. They maintained the Astronomican, transmitted messages over interstellar distances and navigated starships. What they did not do, unless his more immediate forefathers had contrived to lose the relevant information, was to function as what the aborigines of Sigmatus called 'wise-dreamers'.

The handful of psykers who had accompanied the original exploratory mission had been attached to it in order to relay

information about Sigmatus back to the Fleet, so that a reasoned decision could be made as to how the world ought to be
developed. Once that purpose had been nullified by circumstance, even more so when the original psykers had been
replaced as one generation gave way to another, new roles had
had to be found or designed for them. The Chief Inquisitor's
psykers were just as intimidating as their forebears had presumably been, and their business was equally shrouded in
mystery; Fulbra knew that they had become an important element of the war against the aborigine cultists, but he was not
convinced that their role was entirely orthodox. Balberith was
as steadfast a servant of the Imperium as anyone now alive on
Sigmatus, but Fulbra sometimes wondered whether he might
have made a terrible mistake in trying to turn the methods of
the Gulzacandran cults against them.

Perhaps, he thought, this supposed news is a vile trick,
worked by our enemies in order to deflect our hopes and our
intention from our present mission. Who knows what hideous
subtleties these horrid sorcerers may be capable of?

The armoured car had finally cleared the fields surrounding
the village, and Fulbra was grateful to be able to draw fresh air
into his lungs again. Now that they had passed through the
swirling smoke, visibility was good, although the range of his
vision was limited by the density of the local vegetation.

Ierius Fulbra had been born in the hills of northern
Kalazendra, and he had grown up with jagged horizons of distant peaks. The trouble with flat plains, he thought, was that
they had no standpoints from which a man could see for many
a mile. Even when there were no clumps of nasty vegetation in
the way, it was difficult to see for more than a few hundred
yards, and in this kind of warp-exposed landscape, clumps of
nasty vegetation were very common indeed. There were plenty
of trees that were recognisable as trees, although their foliage
was sometimes peculiarly coloured and their fruits exotic, but
there were far too many bulbous growths like giant fungi or
twisted cacti.

Long before the Imperial forces had arrived, the not-so-great
aborigine civilizations of Kalazendra, Zendamora and
Bulzavara had overplanted all but a few enclaves of native vegetation with earthly produce. By contrast, the two kinds of life
had always rubbed shoulders in Yevelkana, and alien life still

ran riot in Gulzacandra, whose indolent and corrupt inhabitants had always been content to down tools at the boundaries of their own fields. The terrain over which the invaders were now speeding seemed more profoundly alien than anything Fulbra had ever seen before.

'Bikes reporting in, sir,' the vox operator said. 'The road's clear for the next five miles, but then there's a bridge down. Slow-moving river at least twelve feet deep, twenty-five yards across. The engineers ought to be able to work unimpeded, though – there's no cover for snipers on the other side and a couple of bolter-blasts should take care of the flanking vegetation.'

'What's beyond the river-crossing?' Fulbra wanted to know.

'More of the same for at least a mile. Then a cluster of roofs – another village. Can't see beyond that.'

'How am I expected to make plans if I'm blind?' Fulbra complained. 'I need that aircraft – and why in the Emperor's name am I clearing makeshift airstrips every time I pause if those fools in Sostenuto don't intend to send it? How am I to find out where the cultists' army is, or how numerous it is, or what its disposition is, if I don't have the aircraft?'

'They're mostly farmers with pitchforks and beastmen with axes,' Hamera said. 'It won't matter all that much how many there are and how they're distributed.'

'It will if we can't catch up with them and inflict massive casualties while they're massed together,' Diambor pointed out. 'If they realise once they've got a good look at us that the only sensible option is to wage a guerilla war, it might take us years to gain control of the region. It won't be easy to move colonists from the other continents to support our troops, given that the locals have destroyed so many of their homes and farms.'

'But they are massing for a pitched battle, however misguided that may be,' Hamera pointed out. 'We know that much, and we can probably figure out where. Surely they'll want to intercept us before we can bring up the cavalry and the loxodont corps. They must intend to prevent us from linking up with the southern contingent.'

'It's not easy to figure out what they intend, or why,' Diambor mused. 'Why fight a battle you can't win, when you could wear down the opposition by attrition? If they have nothing up their sleeves, what can they be thinking? And if they have, why haven't Balberith's psykers found out what it is? There's something not right about this supposed gathering of the enemy forces, and I wish I could figure out what it is.'

'The answer might be simpler than it seems,' Fulbra told the two colonels. 'In Kalazendra, small groups of guerillas really could live off the country for months or years, because most of what passes for wilderness there is earthly produce – but look around you! Without their fields, there's no way these people can find enough food to keep them going. They know that if our supply-lines are broken we'll be in trouble – but in order to put us in that kind of trouble, they have to put themselves in it too. They can't fight a long drawn-out guerilla war because there aren't enough places where they can safely hole up. They have to isolate us if they can – but once they've isolated us, they have to deal with us as quickly as possible. If they have a chance to do that, no matter how slim, they'll probably take it. Attacking tanks and armoured cars with hand-held weapons might seem futile to any sensible strategist, but if they can only get enough fighters to close quarters, they might do a lot of damage with spears and clubs, let alone the kind of vile tricks that only heretics and mutants would use. That's why I need to know their exact deployment.'

'In all fairness to Governor Melcarth,' Diambor put in, 'air surveillance wouldn't necessarily give us the information we need, given the abundance of cover hereabouts. If the trucks that set out from Odienne hadn't got lost, they would probably have been more useful to us.'

'But they did get lost,' Fulbra pointed out. 'And if that many trucks carrying that much firepower can vanish on the instant, without even contriving to tell us what hit them, we might find a similarly unpleasant shock awaiting us.' But sorcery can be exhausted, just like any other kind of firepower, he thought, during the pause that followed. And if the Fleet really were on the brink of restoring contact, all the sorcery in the world would be impotent. If we could summon a ship to our aid, imagine what that could do to the enemy!

The command vehicle was slowing now as it approached the broken bridge, but the flame-throwers mounted on the leading troop-carrier had already burnt back the neighbouring vegetation, and the far bank was so empty that the motorcycle scouts hadn't even bothered to take cover. The engineers were already extending the main girders that would form the steel frame of a temporary bridge.

'Tell the quartermaster's people to test the water before renewing our supplies,' Fulbra instructed the vox operator, although he knew that such precautions were routine. 'And send the bikemen out again as soon as we can get them across.'

'Yes sir,' the vox operator replied. 'All praise to the Emperor Magnificent!'

Fulbra contemplated getting out of the vehicle to stretch his legs, but he didn't need to and it was probably better to let his men see that this was a thoroughly routine operation. They would have their own anxieties, and rankers were notorious for their ability to interpret every tiny circumstance as a cause for apprehension. Oh for a platoon of Space Marines, or even Imperial Guardsmen! What an example they would set to his feeble imitations!

What his men needed, of course, was more action: another easy massacre, conducted with brutal efficiency and no losses. Unfortunately, the local yokels no longer seemed to have the least inclination to make themselves available for slaughter – not, at least, by the enemy they had been taught to loathe.

What, Fulbra wondered, could possibly have happened to the advance party sent ahead from Odienne? How could trucks carrying that kind of firepower have run into trouble in the Gulzacandran wilderness, even if they were few in number? And why, against all reason and calculation, did he have the insistent creepy-crawly feeling in his stomach that he usually got before fate sprang a particularly nasty surprise?

FIFTEEN

'CAN YOU RIDE?'

Dathan blinked at the unexpected question. 'I've ridden a horse, sir,' he said, wondering whether he ought to admit that he had only ridden a very slow horse at a very moderate pace, and not very often. He also wondered whether it was adequate to address a man as powerful as Gavalon as 'sir' – but he had never been told the proper way to address a sorcerer, let alone the supreme head of all the covens in Gulzacandra. Mercifully, Nimian's finger still seemed to be exerting its benign influence over him, maintaining his equilibrium far better than he could have maintained it himself.

'Good,' said Gavalon. 'I need to get to the Vessel as soon as possible. Our attempts to delay Fulbra and string out his forces have failed miserably. His engineers are too good – rivers, ditches and burning fields can't make significant obstacles, and our fighting-men can't get to close quarters with his unless they can find a better way to stop his trucks. It would be a dire irony if the outcome of this conflict were to be settled by the number of spare tyres he's carrying and the speed with which they can be changed. You'll have to show me where this wretched farm-house is. My beastmen can follow at their own pace, but I need to get Sathorael to understand what is required of him, as soon as he's able to listen.'

'I'll do my best, sir,' Dathan promised.

He began to regret this promise as soon as he saw the mounts that Gavalon's servants had prepared. There were four in all; although Gavalon was prepared to hurry ahead of his retinue of beastmen he was compensating for their temporary loss by taking two of his thrall-wizards, Abdalkuri and Maldayak. The steeds were definitely horses, but they were coloured far more garishly than any horses Dathan had ever seen, orange and kingfisher-blue being the predominant colours, and their heads were elaborately horned. Their tails were not made of ordinary horsehair, being more like rats' tails, and their unshod hooves were massive. The saddles and bridles with which they were fitted were conventional enough, but they had no bits in their mouths. They seemed as bizarre to Dathan as the thrall-wizards, whose faces were scarred and painted and whose leathery armour was brightly striped in red, yellow and green.

'Don't worry, Dathan,' Gavalon said, when he took note of the boy's anxiety. 'They're more amenable than they seem, and more intelligent than any animal you've ever encountered. Once constrained to obey you, this kind of steed will serve you very well.'

Dathan hesitated again when the time came to mount. He was a whole foot shorter than the least of his companions and the stirrup seemed impossibly high – but one of Gavalon's beastmen came forward to make a step with his huge hands, and Dathan managed to scramble into the saddle.

I have monsters to wait on me now! he thought. Yesterday I was no one, but today I am the emissary of a very powerful person indeed!

Gavalon paused to shout a few more instructions to his commanders. Then they were off, moving swiftly from a walk to a trot to a canter.

Within minutes, the four coloured horses were galloping faster than Dathan had ever imagined possible. As he bounced in the thigh-stretching saddle he wondered what would have happened if he had told Gavalon that he couldn't ride. In all probability, he guessed, Gavalon would simply have taken the direction-finding finger from him and left him behind – and that was definitely not what he wanted. He was anxious to get back to Hycilla as soon as possible. If he had to learn to ride the hard way, so be it.

Mercifully, his mount was well-accustomed to carrying riders and it was exceptionally sure-footed. Dathan only had to twitch the bridle to suggest a change of direction and the instruction was obeyed. This delicacy allowed him to free the hand to which Nimian's severed finger was attached, so that it could instruct him as to the pathways that needed to be taken.

Gavalon rode alongside him to begin with, to make sure that he was capable of identifying and taking the correct path, but after ten minutes or so the sorcerer dropped back, content to follow where he led.

Once his mount had settled to a steady pace the ride became smoother, and Dathan found that if he kept his eyes fixed on the horizon ahead of him rather than glancing sideways at the bushes and cacti that were whizzing hectically past he did not feel quite so sick. It was, in any case, so long since he had eaten a substantial meal that he could not believe that his stomach contained anything to throw up.

When Dathan had been on foot, even with his mind unusually dulled, the distance between the isolated farmhouse and Gavalon's camp had seemed very long, but the horned horses covered the ground at such a remarkable pace that the miles seemed to melt away. Dathan had only just begun to get used to his unlikely situation astride the bizarre animal when he saw the chimney of the farmhouse – smokeless now – loom into sight.

For a moment or two, Dathan thought he might somehow have got the wrong farmhouse. The environment looked wrong – but the roof of the house was familiar, and Dathan realised that the discrepancy was in the surrounding vegetation. New plants were springing up in the shadow of the walls: native plants, not cultivated ones. Some were thorny bushes and a few were fungal masses, but the majority seemed to be creepers intent on climbing the walls of the house and all the other walls and fences marking out the territories and possessions of the farmer's tiny domain.

Dathan knew that some forms of local vegetation could grow very quickly indeed, but Pater Saltana had told him that was because they could draw energy directly from the sky. It was something to do with the force that made the stars appear to change colour and move. Given that the movements of the stars were slower now than they had ever been before in Dathan's lifetime – or, he suspected, in Pater Saltana's – this did not seem a likely season for the encouragement of plant-growth, but all the normal rules of expectation had been set aside within the last twenty-four hours.

It was more likely, though, once Dathan thought about it, that the growth had something to do with Nimian's arrival at the house.

When Dathan dismounted and tethered his steed to one of the gateposts of what had once been the kitchen garden he realised that the ride had not been quite as short or as smooth as he had thought. His legs seemed to have been bent out of shape, and walking had become painful.

This did not stop him running into the cottage to find Hycilla.

Hycilla was easy enough to find. She was, however, quite alone.

This circumstance did not please Gavalon the Great at all. 'Gone?' he repeated, impatiently, when Hycilla began to offer a tentative explanation. 'Gone where?'

'Perhaps he wasn't expecting you quite so soon,' Hycilla said, anxiously. 'He said that he was hungry, although how that could be possible after what he did to those birds... He's a lot bigger now. If he'd stayed here much longer he probably wouldn't have been able to get out of the door. He had to get rid of the Imperial uniform he was wearing – the rags are over there – but his skin doesn't look like human skin any more. He's more like some kind of enormous reptile than a man, although he talks much more fluently.'

Dathan noticed while Hycilla was stammering out her excuses that she too looked taller than before, even though she certainly hadn't been dining on mowas and megascarabs. Nimian's unnatural growth seemed to have a certain communicable generosity about it, which extended to people as well as to native plants.

'This is bad,' Gavalon said, fretfully. 'He should never have run away from me in the first place, even if he had sensed enemies closeby. He shouldn't have got aboard the truck, and he shouldn't have sent the boy to fetch me instead of coming himself. How will he know what I need of him if I can't tell him? Fulbra is coming too quickly, in good order. If we have to fall back we'll expose too many towns and too many roads. If the Imperial forces can occupy a strong position, and gather in supplies, we'll never winkle them out. How did the Vessel seem mentally? Has his true consciousness begun to manifest itself within the wreckage of Nimian's soul?'

'I don't know what you mean,' Hycilla said, faintly – but Dathan knew that she was only being cautious. She had already said that Nimian had begun talking more fluently.

'What had he to say for himself?' Gavalon demanded, impatiently

'Not much,' Hycilla said, worriedly. 'He told me to wait. He didn't actually say that he'd return, but I thought that's what he meant. After all, he'd told Dathan to bring you here, so that... He said that he needed to touch you.'

Gavalon considered this for a moment or two. 'I need to get to him as soon as possible,' he murmured. 'He can have anything he wants once he's back at the camp, but...' He turned abruptly to look at the device that was still attached to Dathan's finger, having noticed that the severed finger was no longer horizontal. As Gavalon's interrogative gaze lingered upon it, the knot in the hair by which the finger was suspended suddenly came undone, and the direction-finder fell to the floor.

It did not lie there as it should have done; instead, it began to wriggle like a worm, moving awkwardly towards Gavalon. The sorcerer reached down, laying one of his hands flat on the ground, palm upwards. The severed finger was growing longer as it moved, and it was long enough now to wind itself around Gavalon's finger like a compound ring.

Gavalon stared at it, and continued to stare after rising to his feet. His stance suggested incomprehension, but the expression in his amazing inhuman eyes was quite unreadable.

Well, Dathan thought, I suppose that he has now been touched. Perhaps the monster is close enough to work his will without putting in an actual appearance. As soon as he had thought it, though, he wondered how he had formed such a strange conjecture. It had been his thought – he was sure of that – but it seemed to have seized upon a feeling that was not his, or not entirely his. He remembered Nimian's less comprehensible mumblings, and wondered for the first time whether

there had been far more meaning that seemed likely in the
reply of 'you and you' that Nimian had twice made to the question, 'Who are you?'

Dathan shivered, and decided that he really ought to think
about something else. He looked up.

'Am I mistaken,' Dathan asked Hycilla, in a low voice, 'or is
the ceiling a little higher than it was before?'

Hycilla looked up too, apparently not having noticed any
change in her surroundings until Dathan spoke. 'I believe it is,'
she said, pausing before she added: 'but I don't seem to be any
further beneath it than I was before.'

'Everything's getting bigger,' Dathan said, hesitantly. 'Even
the stone in the walls. Everything he's touched – except me.'

'No wonder he's hungry,' Gavalon said. 'But he mustn't waste
his power, accidentally or deliberately. I don't know how much
energy he'll have at his beck and call when he reaches maturity,
but it won't be infinite and he won't be long in his prime. We
have to smash the Imperial forces, so decisively that they'll
never recover. If we don't, this world will never be safe for worshippers of the true god.'

'What about the ships?' Hycilla asked.

Gavalon's remarkable gaze had been relatively subdued until
now, but Dathan saw its fire flare up slightly then, especially in
what looked to be the younger and fresher eye.

'Spaceships?' Gavalon queried.

Hycilla nodded. 'I've seen them in my dreams,' she said, 'but
never so clearly as last night. Nimian mentioned them – he
says they're coming closer.'

'Are these Imperial ships?' The question came from one of
the thrall-wizards – Maldayak, Dathan thought.

'Not necessarily,' Gavalon replied. 'The true god has his
spacefleets too, as do other gods to whom the Imperium is
opposed. There are other races which can navigate between the
stars: eldar, tyranids, tau... The names mean little enough, but
they have been revealed to me, so that I may know something
of the war in which I am a part. What did the Vessel say about
the ships?'

'Firstly that he would bring them,' Hycilla reported.
'Secondly that they were coming closer. He seemed pleased.'

'Bring them?' Gavalon repeated, pensively. 'And he seemed
pleased!'

'The warpstorm is retreating,' said the thrall-wizard who was probably Abdalkuri. 'If ships serving the Changer of the Ways could come to our aid…'

'We might obliterate the Imperium once and for all,' his multicoloured companion finished for him.

'The Imperium is too vast to be obliterated,' Gavalon corrected him, scornfully. 'The little fragment of it that has been lost here for two hundred years was always a small and sickly thing – but yes, that could be obliterated, once and for all. If the warpstorm has retreated far enough, forces might be gathering in space to dispute possession of five or fifty worlds: worlds full of men, and sorcery, and who knows how many descendants of stranded Imperial investigators? This phase of the great game may be taking place on a larger stage than I had imagined… but that only makes it all the more important that Sathorael should follow my lead, and act under my direction.'

'Most certainly,' said Abdalkuri.

'Absolutely,' said Maldayak.

It seemed to Dathan that both voices rang slightly hollow. The thrall-wizards were, he assumed, completely bound to Gavalon's ends and means. They were his obedient servants, and nothing more. But whatever it was that the so-called Vessel now held was a great deal more: far more than they were, and far more than even Gavalon the Great was. Dathan realised that the two thrall-wizards might not be entirely displeased were some freak of fate to reduce Gavalon to their own ignominious status, even if their own were further diminished in the process.

But we are all mere servants of the true god, Dathan reminded himself, or was reminded by something not quite himself. He is the Divine Schemer, and he decides where each and every one of us should fit into his scheme. We are all potential sacrifices, it seems. Again he wished that Pater Saltana had had time to tell him more about the secrets of the cult and the rituals of his people.

'I suppose we must wait a while,' Gavalon concluded, reluctantly. 'Have you, perchance, any food fit for human beings to eat?'

'We have what we took from the Imperial trucks,' Hycilla admitted. Her reluctance, Dathan knew, was due to the fact that she knew very well how difficult it might be to come by further food supplies in the next few days.

'Good,' said Gavalon. 'We'll eat, and hope that the Vessel's hunger will be as easily satisfied as ours.'

Dathan and Hycilla had no alternative but to place their packs at Gavalon's disposal, and to watch the sorcerer and his thrall-wizards make short work of the greater part of their hoard.

After settling his own hunger pangs Dathan walked stiffly out into the walled enclave in front of the house, intending to water the horses and stretch his legs in a more familiar fashion than that in which they had recently been stretched.

Hycilla followed him out and stood by while he tended to the horses. She looked around, studying the native vegetation that was springing up all around the house. It was a remarkable sight. The most avid creepers were already half-way up the walls of the house, and spiky growths to either side of the low garden wall had already made it into a far more impressive barrier than it had been before. The roof, which seemed steeper now than it once had, was covered in mossy parasites.

'What will become of us, do you think?' Dathan asked, when he was able to join her.

'I don't know,' she said. 'My head tells me that the closer we are to Nimian, the safer we're likely to be when the fighting actually starts, but my legs would rather be nowhere near the fighting – or Nimian.'

'They have need of you because you're a dreamer,' Dathan pointed out. 'But what use am I now, even as an errand-boy? I don't even have the magic finger any more.'

'It makes no difference,' she told him. 'Gavalon has us now, and he'll use us both as he can. If he gives us up, then Nimian – Sathorael – will use us instead. Gavalon seems to think that the creature's here to do his bidding, but I don't think it's here to do anyone's bidding. I think it has a purpose of its own – and that you and I have been caught up in that purpose, by accident or by design.'

'If even Gavalon the Great is here to be used at Nimian's whim,' Dathan muttered, amazed at his ability to discuss such matters at all, let alone so calmly, 'you and I could be in real trouble.'

'We already are,' she reminded him. 'But we wouldn't be here at all if Nimian hadn't turned up in time to stop the Imperial soldiers doing what they wanted to us. We have to think of every minute that passes as pure good fortune, no matter what the future might bring. If we die tonight, we're still a day ahead of the game, aren't we?'

'Which is what you meant when you told Nimian that "when" mattered as much as "how",' Dathan murmured. 'And you're right, of course. But it's not going to be easy, is it?'

'I don't know,' Hycilla said, with a tiny shrug of her shoulders, in a voice that was no longer her own. 'Maybe it will be easier than we imagine, if we can only learn to look at it the right way. When you come right down to it, if you have to burn you might as well try to burn brightly.' She was noticeably taller now than she had been when she followed him out of the farmhouse, and her eyes were aglow again.

Hycilla was still beautiful, but Dathan wasn't sure that her beauty would last. Having seen what the exercise of magic had done to Maldayak and Abdalkuri, let alone to Gavalon the Great, he suspected that she might not age as elegantly as women who did not dream wisely.

'I'm afraid,' Dathan confessed. 'If I thought that gaudy horse would consent to carry me, I'd be tempted to ride away into the sunset as fast as I could go – but it's Gavalon's, and while I have it, I suppose I'm Gavalon's too.'

The sun was indeed setting again, although the day seemed to Dathan to have flown by, and its disc would soon be gone. Hycilla looked around, presumably hoping to catch a glimpse of the giant that Nimian must now have become, but there was nothing to be seen moving upon the world's surface.

Dathan looked up into the sky, at the first of the moons to rise and the few fugitive stars that had begun to twinkle in the east. He tried to estimate the strength of the force that stirred the stars – the force the Gavalon had called the 'warpstorm' – but his merely human eyes weren't up to the task.

'Whatever kinds of ships might descend from the sky, it wouldn't be good news for us, would it?' he said. 'Whatever allegiance they own, they'll only come to rain down destruction.'

'Perhaps,' she said. 'But the Imperium only has firepower. We have something better.'

'Is it better?' Dathan asked, wondering why he was the only one who didn't seem to be growing in response to the crisis. 'Or is it worse?'

'Of course it's better,' Hycilla assured him. 'We're the victims here. We deserve help, and we should be grateful for any
we get, no matter how scary it may seem.'

'I suppose we have to go on hoping that it'll all turn out
right in the end,' Dathan agreed, 'no matter how ugly it gets.
I suppose Nimian's still getting uglier as well as bigger?'

'You should have seen him dismembering those birds,'
Hycilla told him, with a slight shudder that seemed to have
more delight in it than fear. 'He's eaten five or ten times his
own weight since we met him. I've not seen much of what
Imperial firepower can do, but I'm beginning to be able to
imagine what he might do, when he's fully grown.'

Hycilla's eyes were glowing even more brightly now that the
sun was down, and Dathan felt that she was already slipping
away from him into the exotic consciousness that he would
never be able to comprehend, let alone to share. There was an
oracular quality to her pronouncements now; she had been
growing inwardly as well as outwardly since the moment that
Nimian had crashed into their lives.

'Will we come through it in one piece?' Dathan asked, hoping that he might be speaking to something better placed to
give an accurate answer than a mere village girl.

'It doesn't matter,' she told him. 'All this is profit, beyond
our due. We must make the most of every precious second,
and begrudge nothing.'

It was, Dathan supposed, easy enough for her to say, given
that she was no longer the person he had known all his life.

For his own part, he still nursed a hunger for life that was
very far from satisfied.

SIXTEEN

'I SIMPLY COULDN'T get to him, excellency,' Kerforo reported, uneasily. 'Since the assassination attempt, Balberith's guards have been even more vigilant than usual, and the fact that every inquisitor in Sostenuto is convinced that contact with the Imperium Fleet is imminent has caused a veritable explosion of piety.'

The spy was sweating a little and squirming uneasily – as well he might, given that Orloc Melcarth had decided to conduct the interview in the vaults of Sostenuto's main prison.

Their immediate surroundings were not unduly threatening, and might even have been described as festive, but the room was a guardroom most of the time and it was only a few dozen paces away from accommodations that were infinitely more unpleasant, and from which few tenants ever moved on.

There was always a party in the prison on the eve of mass executions, when Melcarth distributed petty favours to the members of his inner circle and servants who had served him well, but Melcarth rarely trifled with the condemned, no matter how pretty they might be. He preferred to use such occasions as opportunities to do business. He was, in any case, firmly of the opinion that attractive aborigine women owed whatever glamour they had to the taint of Chaos, and that they remained direly dangerous to good and honest men, even – perhaps especially – when they were due to be hanged or burned in the morning.

'An explosion of piety?' Melcarth echoed, wryly. 'Somehow, I can't quite imagine an explosion of piety.'

'Then you don't know the kind of power that Chief Inquisitor Balberith wields over his own people, excellency,' Kerforo said. 'You and I might be prepared to believe that the waking dreams of a drug-sodden psyker are meaningless, and not at all anxious to see contact with the greater Imperium restored, but the instruments of the Inquisition think differently. They really are desperate to be welcomed back in to the Imperial fold, restored to the bosom of the beloved Emperor. The possibility has made each and every one of them consult his conscience, and to resolve to make up for the slightest lapse or relaxation of faith with a new flood of devotion. They're entirely sincere, sire, and it's the kind of sincerity that doesn't compromise. It's not conducive to... diplomacy.'

Kerforo did not, of course, consider himself to be a mere spy, let alone a hired assassin. He liked to think of himself as a diplomat.

'That's inconvenient,' Melcarth admitted, chewing his lower lip reflectively. 'And I suppose we have to face the possibility that the psyker really is on the brink of making contact with an Imperial starship. It's a contingency we have to prepare for, just in case. If there were to be another landing... Well, if Balberith appears to be a good and efficient chief inquisitor, then I must appear to be a good and efficient planetary governor. It shouldn't be too much of a problem, given that I've just launched a holy war against the heretics of Gulzacandra. A successful holy war, which General Fulbra is winning – all praise to the Emperor Magnificent!'

Kerforo was still sweating, and squirming even more. There was obviously something else on his mind, as well as his obvious incompetence in the matter of arranging assassinations.

'What is it?' Melcarth demanded.

'Well, sire,' the spy stuttered, 'it's just that my people... your humblest hirelings... do have their fingers on the pulse of popular rumour... and even though they do everything humanly possible to monopolise the starting of rumours, they can't help the fact that other rumours do get about, and...'

'Oh, spit it out!' Melcarth growled, impatiently.

'Well, excellency, there's a rumour going round that... how shall I put it?... That you've not been as enthusiastic in your support of General Fulbra as you might have been. The little people, in their ignorance and foolishness, seem to think that Balberith has been more ardent in that cause than you. There's a whisper on the streets about your refusal to provide the general with the aircraft he's requested, in spite of the fact that it's ready to take off at a moment's notice – a whisper which my men have naturally tried to quell, without success. Which wouldn't be so bad, except that news is somehow getting about that one of the general's operations has gone awry and that a whole platoon's been lost... and the two stories have become connected in the public mind, in the awkward manner that such things often do, in a way that simply can't be helped... or hindered.'

Melcarth considered this intelligence carefully. It would all have been irrelevant, of course, if Kerforo had done his job properly. If the psyker had been disposed of, or if Balberith had been wounded by the assassin, there would be no space on the street for any other topics of conversation. The common people weren't supposed to know anything about the aircraft's state of readiness, and they certainly weren't supposed to know about the failure of Operation Probe, but if someone who did know such things had a motive for letting the news out, there was no way to keep it in. It appeared that someone did. Ragan Balberith, it seemed, was already making preparations for the second landing of Imperial forces on Sigmatus, and one set of preparations he was making involved undermining the governor's reputation and position.

'Perhaps I took him out on that balcony once too often,' Melcarth muttered. 'I shouldn't ever have let him see how much I hated and despised him, but I simply couldn't resist the temptation. But it's not a disaster. There's an obvious countermove, if we're quick enough. I always intended to take the aircraft over myself as soon as the time was ripe. All that's happened is that the time has become ripe a little sooner than I expected. You'd better get over to the airbase as quickly as you can, and tell Techmaster Sauldron that I want the aircraft ready to take off at first light.'

'You're sending the aircraft to Gulzacandra, sire?' Kerforo said, letting his astonishment show. 'You're putting it at Fulbra's disposal?'

'No,' Melcarth said, patiently. 'I'm taking the aircraft to Gulzacandra and keeping it under my disposal. I'm going to be a war hero. With luck, the battle will be fought before we get there, but even without... the aircraft is an original. It's the finest original left to us, and it has been scrupulously maintained. We'll be quite safe.'

'We?' Kerforo echoed, nervously.

'Oh, not you,' Melcarth said, appalled by the other man's apparent cowardice. 'I'll take Vorch and the cream of the palace guard.'

Kerforo was still looking at him in open astonishment. The silence was broken by a long drawn-out howl of agony, only slightly muffled by the thick stone walls of the prison. Someone was obviously having fun. Melcarth smiled, but his smile was mirthless. Unlike Ragan Balberith, Kerforo had not the slightest fear of heights, but there was obviously something about the idea of flying – even in a prime example of original Imperial technology – that terrified him. Melcarth had flown in the aircraft four times, admittedly for less than an hour each time, but he had only been afraid the first time, and then only slightly. He loved the idea of flying. What kind of ruler would he be if he did not?

'My grandfather used to tell me tales about skimmers,' Kerforo said, trying to speak lightly, 'but they were stories he'd had from his own grandfather, about the Emperor's finest. Your aircraft isn't a fighting-machine – it's just a transporter. Are you sure it's capable of a twelve-hour flight, excellency? Are you sure it's safe to even take it into a battle zone?'

'I'll leave all the actual shooting to Fulbra's men, of course,' Melcarth told him, wearily. 'The point is that I'm going to his aid, personally. I'm so firmly behind him that I'm taking personal responsibility for finding out what happened to Operation Probe. I'm the kind of governor that generals can depend on, after all. I'm the kind of governor that deserves the loyalty of all his subjects.'

'What if you can't find out what happened to the missing trucks, sire?' the spy asked, in frank perplexity.

'Who cares what happened to the missing trucks?' Melcarth said. 'The point is that everyone in Sostenuto will see me set out to join General Fulbra. We'll circle the city twice to make sure that they do. The mere sight of the aircraft will be enough to send most of them into paroxysms of awe. The news that I'm aboard it will make any vile whispers spread by Balberith's agents instantly redundant. Once I'm out of sight and out of mind – and as soon as General Fulbra has actually joined battle with the Gulzacandran forces – mere details will cease to be of any importance. I'll fly back with news of our first great victory, which I'll deliver personally from my balcony... and the triumph will serve me just as well if the miracle happens and the Imperial Fleet does make contact as it will if we're left to our own devices, responsible for the making of our own history. It's perfect. Why are you still sitting there? Why aren't you on your way?'

Kerforo leapt from his chair, his face suddenly clearing as he realised that he was under orders – and, at least for the moment, safe from his master's wrath. He left the room in a hurry.

It was a pity that the spy would have to miss the climax of the party, Melcarth thought, but he hadn't really seemed to be in a party mood. Nor should he be in a party mood, while matters of such importance hung in the balance.

When Kerforo had left the prison, Melcarth instructed one of the senior guards to find his driver, put an immediate stop to whatever fun he was presently enjoying, and tell him to bring the car to the rear entrance of the prison. If the guard was surprised, he gave no indication of the fact.

As he made ready to depart the governor found that he was getting more and more excited.

I've been scheming too long and delegating too much, he thought. I've forgotten how exhilarating it is to be a man of action. I always used to be a man of action, before I became tangled up in too much politics. I should have built this expedition into the plan from the start. It's exactly what I need.

As he hurried through the corridors of the prison he heard a new chorus of screaming raised from a dozen agonised throats. It was music to his ears. He felt a warm glow of satisfaction at the thought of the entertainment that his most loyal supporters would obtain while the long night lasted, and of the further

increase in loyalty that the reward would undoubtedly produce. He was glad, though, that he had more urgent business
to attend to. The despoiling of the condemned, no matter how
imaginatively it might be carried out, was too easy to rank as an
authentically piquant pleasure, especially for a man of action.

He instructed his driver to return to the imperial palace, in
order that he might pack a bag, select a retinue of bodyguards
and organise a motor-cycle escort for the motorcade, but he did
not linger long over the task. His car was careering through the
darkness again within the hour, with a second vehicle in the
rear and six motor-cyclists in attendance. He sat in the back,
with his chief bodyguard, Thorold, beside him.

The journey through the city streets was not as smooth as it
might have been. The Imperial forces stranded in Kalazendra
had improved Sostenuto's roads dramatically during the first
years of their tenure, but regular maintenance had been left to
the aborigines when the Imperium's engineers moved on to the
business of conquest. The central streets were in good repair,
but those in outlying districts had been deteriorating for as
long as Melcarth could remember.

It was the same with the buildings, Melcarth thought, as he
watched the shop-fronts and the factories go by. Nothing new
had been erected in this neighbourhood for more than a century, because everyone knew that new buildings were far
inferior – in design as well as quality – to those that the reluctant colonists had made. Although factories had been
established to turn out copies of the vehicles the Imperial
forces had brought with them the copies had always been poor,
and the copies of the copies even poorer.

Balberith's people believed – or pretended to believe – that
the steady deterioration was mostly due to the fact that the tech-
priests of two hundred years ago must have been word-perfect
in all the prayers and rituals which today's tech-priests had
never quite contrived to master, but Melcarth was sceptical. He
was more inclined to blame the quality of their raw materials
than the limitation of their practical skills. Not that it mattered
much either way; whatever the reason, the simple fact was that
the descendants of the original castaways had been unable to
prevent the long, slow decline of their material wealth.

Nowadays, the margin that separated the lifestyle of the
majority of so-called Imperials from that of the richer

aborigine city-dwellers was very thin indeed. The Imperium still kept its monopoly on vehicular transport, but there were so few vehicles on the roads of Sostenuto that it was fast becoming a distinction without a difference for everyone but the governor's personal staff and the army.

Melcarth stared out of his window at the streets through which he passed, trying as hard as he could to take pride in his capital city, but it wasn't as easy as he would have wished. Now that the car had passed out of the heart of the city, where the Imperial castaways had built according to their innate sense of grandeur, his route was flanked by houses that the aborigines had built for themselves, using stone, cement and wood in seemingly haphazard combinations. The streets were lit, if they were lit at all, by smoky oil-lamps, and the people moving through them – in a city like Sostenuto the streets were always full of people, even at night – were mostly ugly, drunk, miserable and ill-dressed.

By day the aborigines made more of an effort to ape the imported manners of the Imperium, pretending as hard as they could to be virtuous, well-disciplined and fully devoted to the great causes of order and civilization, but by night they relaxed into their age-old habits of slothfulness. They should have been far more grateful for the effort that the Imperium had invested in saving so many of them from the vile clutches of the coven-masters that had been their erstwhile rulers, but Melcarth suspected that many of them were secretly nostalgic for the long-gone days before the advent of the Imperium, having completely forgotten how brutal, dangerous and degenerate the life of their ancestors had been.

There were, so far as Melcarth knew, no cults or covens still active in Sostenuto, but one item of conviction on which he and Balberith were in complete agreement was the knowledge that the corruptions of Chaos were as subtle as they were insidious. The people who turned their heads, with as much hostility as curiosity in their predatory eyes, to watch his car pass by were the victims of a very bad inheritance. No matter how hard they tried, they could never be entirely convincing as models of rectitude and piety. No matter how often the population was purged by the Inquisition, it never seemed to become entirely pure, and probably never would.

When Gulzacandra had been purged, the most prolific well-spring of the world's malaise would run dry, but Melcarth knew that no matter how strictly the purge was carried out, it would not and could not put an end to the eternal war. There would always be a need for organizations like the Inquisition and men like Ragan Balberith to run them – under the proper supervision of more sensible men, of course. Everyday life had to be maintained too, and the business of government was far too broad and complicated to be left to obsessive zealots.

Melcarth started suddenly as a stone hurled from a shadowed side-street hit the window out of which he was peering. The bodyguard sitting beside him also reacted, but soon settled back into his seat as a member of the motor-cycle escort roared off into the side-street to make certain that there was no real threat.

The motor-cyclist reappeared a moment later. Melcarth watched through the rear windscreen as the man signalled to his companions that all was well.

No significant injury had been done to the car, but the enormity of the insult filled Melcarth with a sudden rage. The missile had probably been thrown by an unruly child, with no more motive than pure mischief, but it seemed nevertheless to be symptomatic of a disrespect more terrible than any ingratitude. Had these wretched aborigines no idea how much they owed to the Imperium? Had they no understanding of the enormous enrichment the Imperial castaways had brought to their shabby culture, in addition to the enlightenment that turned the tide against the awful corruptions of Chaos? How could they not recognise such an obvious superiority of manners and mores? Were they really stupid enough to hanker after the reign of coven-masters who not only offered daily tributes of their blood to the vilest of gods but welcomed their own slow transformation into mad and monstrous mutants?

'Perhaps Balberith is half-right,' the governor murmured, in a highly exceptional moment of generosity, as he continued to stare out of the rear window. 'The only thing worth fighting for is the Imperial ideal, and that would be a great deal easier to uphold if we were not cut off from our starfaring brothers. If only the man could understand that the very best embodiment of that ideal in our own world is me, we might be friends instead of adversaries!'

'Excellency?' said the normally taciturn Thorold, just in case the remark had been addressed to him.

'Is that a third car, Thorold?' Melcarth asked, having suddenly caught sight of the glimmer of headlamps behind the motor-cyclist who had temporarily detached himself from the protective formation. 'I thought Vorch contrived to cram the other guardsmen into his.'

The bodyguard turned to peer into the gloom. 'Yes, excellency,' he said. 'I believe it is. Shall I have it stopped?'

'Not yet – let's find out who it is first. Tell your colleague in the front to use his vox-caster to find out whose it is.'

This order was relayed through the glass screen that separated the rear section of the governor's car from the front seats. After a few moments, the answer came back.

'It's the Chief Inquisitor's car, excellency,' Thorold reported.

'What?' Melcarth was dumbfounded. 'Where is he going?'

Another minute went by, seeming much slower than its predecessor, before the second answer came back – this time directly from the driver's companion. 'He says that he's coming to help you, excellency,' the guardsman reported. 'As soon as he heard news of your heroic endeavour, he thought it necessary to pledge his full support, and to share the danger.'

Melcarth became uncomfortably aware that his jaw was hanging open. He shut his mouth with an abrupt click, gritting his teeth while he considered the situation.

He wondered briefly whether Kerforo might have been turned, but quickly decided that it must have been the vigilance of Balberith's own secret agents that had alerted the Chief Inquisitor to Melcarth's hastily-improvised plan. Balberith must have reacted instantly, just as impetuously as Melcarth himself. Having understood the game that Melcarth was playing, and the decisiveness of this latest move, Balberith had responded reflexively – and very recklessly.

He's played right into my hands! Melcarth thought. *What a stroke of genius it was to hasten my departure!*

Melcarth could see nothing but advantage in allowing Balberith to 'share the danger' of the aerial expedition – provided, of course, that his own retinue outnumbered Balberith's by at least two to one. If it were to transpire, after his timely return to Kalazendra, that the expedition had suffered casualties while in Gulzacandra, would that not serve to demonstrate his bravery in going, and the true extent of his triumph in returning safely? And what a magnificent funeral he could stage for the heroic Chief Inquisitor, whose life had been so tragically lost...

'How much extra space will there be aboard the aircraft, once our own men are accommodated?' Melcarth demanded of Thorold.

'As much or as little as you desire, excellency,' was the swift reply, as the bodyguard immediately realised what his master was thinking. 'We can depend on Techmaster Sauldron to set as narrow a limit as you might care to suggest.'

'Good – send him instructions to make sure that our people outnumber Balberith's by three to one. Tell him to be as apologetic as he needs to be, but to make sure that there are abundant good reasons why there simply aren't enough spare places to accommodate more than a couple of his pet thugs. Make sure it's all sorted out before we arrive.'

'Yes, excellency,' Thorold replied – and immediately leant forward to take the vox-caster's speaking horn from his colleague.

Having grasped this unexpected opportunity, Melcarth settled back into his seat to make further plans. He was amazed that Balberith was even prepared to contemplate joining him on the flight, given the Chief Inquisitor's aversion to heights, but now that the possibility had been raised, his main fear was that Balberith would suffer a last-minute attack of cowardice and pull out. That, he thought, would be a real anti-climax. It would be wise to delay any hostile action until the aircraft had actually landed in Gulzacandra. It would be entertaining too, if Balberith did turn out to be as deeply discomfited by flying as by standing on a high balcony – but once they were on alien soil... on hostile soil... it should be easy enough to extract the thorn from his side permanently, and make up a story that would work to his advantage...

'It seems, excellency, that there won't be a problem,' Thorold reported. 'Apparently, the Chief Inquisitor left his apartments in a hurry. He's already told Techmaster Sauldron that he has only three men with him – and only one of them is armed. We have eight men fully-armed, plus the pilot and the aircraft's vox operator, both of whom are completely trustworthy. But why is he doing it, excellency? Surely he must know that it's suicide.'

'Must he?' Melcarth wondered, aloud. 'Perhaps not. Perhaps he really does not understand how matters lie. Or perhaps he is merely desperate. In either case, everything is going our way. How the Emperor must love us, Thorold – all praise to his glorious name!'

'All praise to the Emperor,' Thorold echoed.

Even when Melcarth reached the airbase and discovered what he had not thought to wonder or to ask before, he was still exultant, still convinced that he had the favour of the gods. After all, he thought, the only thing that would matter once the aircraft was aloft, was the number of guns aboard and the loyalty of their carriers.

What difference could it possibly make to his unfolding scheme that Ragan Balberith had elected to bring along a priest and a psyker as well as a bodyguard?

Was it not, after all, the greatest gift that circumstance could offer a future ruler of the world, that the psyker who had come so close to making contact with the Imperial Fleet should be delivered into Orloc Melcarth's hands along with his troublesome master, the Chief Inquisitor Ragan Balberith?

SEVENTEEN

WHEN HYCILLA WENT back into the farmhouse Dathan stayed outside. He told himself that he was 'keeping watch' but he didn't really believe it. He knew that when Nimian – or Sathorael – returned, there would be no need to offer Gavalon an early warning of his approach.

He was, therefore, taken utterly by surprise when he heard the noise of the approaching trucks.

It had never occurred to Dathan that the soldiers who had taken the village might set out to discover what had become of their companions, or that once having found the wreckage by the water-hole they might also find the tracks made by the truck Hycilla had driven away, and follow them until they found the truck that had run out of fuel – at which point, the Imperial soldiers would naturally continue along the road, anxious to know what had become of the vehicle's driver. Once he realised that the trucks were actually coming, though, Dathan understood immediately that all this had been obvious, and that he had been a fool not to expect it.

Dathan understood, too, the awful significance of the fact that Gavalon the Great was in the farmhouse, with only two thrall-wizards and two unarmed villagers for company. It

would be utterly disastrous, he knew, if the defenders of
Gulzacandra were to lose their leader before the expected battle had even begun.

For this reason, he ran back into the house shouting: 'Mount
up! Mount up! We have to get away! More trucks are coming!'

The response was immediate, but it was not quite what
Dathan had expected. Instead of running for the steeds that
had carried them from the encampment, the sorcerer's first
move was to whirl around to face Hycilla.

'Where is the daemon?' he demanded. 'How near is he?'

Dathan's first assumption was that Hycilla had no way of
knowing what the answer was – but when he saw the way that
she met Gavalon's intimidating gaze, he remembered that she
had known far more than she should even before Nimian had
made his spectacular appearance in their lives. Ever since the
boy had touched her, she had been growing – and the physical
change was merely symptomatic. When Nimian had touched
her, he had claimed her; she was his now.

He touched me, too, Dathan remembered – but was swift to
add: *but I am no wise-dreamer, and she is*. There was already
something in her, waiting to be claimed.

Gavalon's eyes were dark and bulbous; looking into them
was like looking into a stormy night – but Hycilla's eyes were
larger now, and much darker. Anyone who met her stare would
be frightened – anyone, except a man like Gavalon.

The sorcerer and Hycilla met one another's eyes very steadily.
Gavalon reached out as if to seize Hycilla's arms in his remarkable fists – but Hycilla was too quick for him. She reached out
and placed her own recently-elongated hands on his forearms,
and she stared into his face with the full glare of her suddenly-
supernatural eyes. Gavalon was taken aback – but he was
obviously satisfied with what he saw within or behind Hycilla's
eyes, for he nodded his shaggy head. Then he stepped back,
releasing himself from her unresisting grip.

'Maldayak, with me!' the sorcerer shouted. 'Abdalkuri –
mount up! Take the boy with you. The beastmen cannot be far
away. Ride to meet them and bring them forward as fast as you
can.'

Dathan was momentarily confused by these instructions, but
as Abdalkuri grabbed his arm and pulled him back towards the
door he realised that Gavalon intended to make a stand, and

that he must intend to keep Hycilla with him as well as Maldayak. He opened his mouth to protest, but the words died in his throat as he realised how futile a protest would be. He did not want to leave Hycilla in a place of danger, but he was in no position to demand of her, let alone of Gavalon the Great, that she should come with him.

By the time Abdalkuri had dragged Dathan out to the yard where the horses were tethered, the leading truck had already come to the crest of the ridge, from which the farmhouse was clearly visible. Dathan knew that he must be visible too – and that their vivid orange and blue colouring would make the horned horses stand out boldly even against the exotically tinted vegetation of the plain.

'Don't be afraid,' the wizard hissed, as he thrust Dathan towards one of the horses. 'They have guns, but we have glamour.'

Dathan had no idea what this reassurance was supposed to mean, but his attention was fixed on the task immediately before him – which was to get up into the saddle. The stirrup seemed even higher than it had before, and the possibility of using it as a step even more remote. The horse knew him this time, though, and although it could not bend a knee to make the step easier it stood stock still, looking back at him with what seemed to be a trustful eye.

Mustering all his courage, Dathan reached up to take hold of the saddle-horn, and lifted his left foot as high as he could. Somewhat to his surprise, he managed to get his boot into the stirrup. He pushed off with his other foot, while using the strength of his arms to haul himself up.

Amazingly, it worked. He found himself in the saddle.

Although he no longer had Nimian's severed finger to help him, the horse seemed perfectly content to recognise Dathan as its master, or at least as its ward. He had to admit that there was no real exercise of mastery in the fact that the horse turned and trotted out of the yard, breaking into a canter as soon as it was clear of the gate. If anyone were actually the master, he quickly realised, it was the horse – but at least the horse seemed enthusiastic to have him on its back.

Abdalkuri's mount was already ahead of them, but as soon as its direction was obvious the trucks coming over the hill began to draw apart, two of them leaving the road on an interception course.

Dathan judged that the trucks were too far away to be able to cut Abdalkuri off, but he saw that there were men swarming around the guns mounted on the backs of the vehicles. He had no doubt that he and his companion were already within range.

The firing began immediately, although it was the smaller arms that opened up first; the bigger guns remained silent while the men attempting to aim them fought to get them properly aligned.

Although he heard the whine of one bullet that passed close by, Dathan saw that the trucks which had peeled off were bouncing too violently on the uneven ground to provide a good platform for marksmen. With a little luck, he thought, and given that the ground could only get worse the further the trucks went from the road, his sure-footed mount might be able to carry him out of range before he was hit.

Unfortunately, his sure-footed mount did not seem to see the matter in that light at all. While Abdalkuri's horse galloped full-tilt for the horizon, aiming for the point at which Gavalon's retinue of beastmen was due to appear as they plodded after him, Dathan's mount wheeled about and charged away at a right-angle, exposing the whole of its wide flank to the gunners on the two trucks.

The trucks were close enough by now for Dathan to sense the gunners' delight at finding such a target, and he knew full well that they did not need to hit him to seal his fate. If they brought down the horned horse while it was galloping the subsequent fall would certainly disable him, even if it did not kill him.

Now the big guns opened up, both together, at what their operators thought was an easy target.

They were wrong.

Dathan felt the blast-wave as the shells sailed past him, but when they finally came to earth and exploded they were more than a hundred yards behind him. The rifles continued to blaze away, but he could not even hear the whine of their bullets now that he had been deafened by the cannon. He suddenly understood the meaning of the enigmatic reassurance that Abdalkuri had given him, and the significance of the fact that the horses' colouration – not to mention the thrall-wizards' costumes – would make them stand out so sharply against any easily-imaginable background.

Glamour must be a kind of illusion. The horses and their customary riders were supposed to attract fire – but their apparent position was somehow deceptive. Missiles aimed at them would always go astray.

Or, if not always, then mostly.

No sooner had Dathan figured out the manner of this trickery, though, than the horse changed its tactics again. It wheeled around, and this time it charged towards one of the trucks, on an interception course of its own.

Because they were approaching one another at an angle there seemed to be no danger that the horse would actually run right into the front of the truck, but as the range diminished rapidly the gunners on the back of both trucks became even more excited. The big guns swivelled urgently, while the riflemen continued to fire.

Dathan did not know what to do, except duck. He pressed his face into the horse's mane, dropping his arms in order to grip the animal around the neck. The reins were still clutched tightly in his right hand, but they were exercising no restraint whatsoever on the horse. He shut his eyes reflexively, having not the slightest idea what would happen – and when the horse's unnaturally massive hooves suddenly ceased to beat upon the ground he thought for an instant that he had been hit by a bullet and robbed of all sensation, for he was still quite deaf.

Then he realised that he was still alive, and whole, and that his mount was sailing through the air in an unimaginably prodigious leap. It jumped right over the careering truck, as disdainfully as if it were clearing a waist-high wooden fence.

The landing jarred him badly, but Dathan did not fall, and the sheer exultation of being alive more than compensated for the shock. The joy in question was quickly compounded as the front wheels of the truck he had leapt over fell into a drainage ditch and brought the vehicle to an abrupt halt.

At least, the sudden descent into the ditch would have brought the truck to an abrupt halt had the ditch not been quite so wide and deep, and had the mass of the big gun not been mounted so far back. The combination of the speed at which the truck had been travelling, the precipitousness of the descent and the imbalance of the load ensured that inertia plucked the back wheels from the top of a low ridge and sent the entire vehicle into a cartwheel.

The sheer weight of the vehicle slowed the ascent of the back end, but could not slow it quite enough. Almost as soon as the radiator at the front of the truck hit the dirt the back end attained the vertical, and the vehicle began to topple forwards.

The men on the back tried to jump clear. The jumping was easy enough, but landing was a very different matter. They came down somersaulting, their limbs flailing madly, and four out of the five fell very badly indeed.

The fifth fell quite well, and might have been uninjured had the tailboard of the falling truck not caught the top of his skull, killing him instantly.

The other truck that had left the road was in trouble too, although not nearly as much. Its driver, forewarned, had managed to steer sideways as the vehicle approached the drainage ditch. He had managed to keep one of the front wheels clear – but one was not enough. Given a second more warning, he might have been able to keep the other clear too – but as it was, the left front wheel tipped over the edge. The left rear wheel followed it. The truck did not tip and topple like its predecessor, but it skidded and shuddered to a slanting halt, incapable of further movement in any direction.

All the guns on the second truck kept blazing away at Dathan's brightly-coloured mount, but the horse continued to present a deceptive target. Two more explosive shells blasted enormous craters in the farmer's ravaged fields, but Dathan remained miraculously untouched.

For a moment or two, Dathan was carried back towards the roadway, where more enemies were gathered – but that gave him the opportunity to see that there was another fight in progress, far less equal than the one in which he had been engaged.

In order to attack the farmhouse the other trucks had drawn up in a line, and Imperial soldiers had swarmed out of them, heading for the building where Gavalon, Hycilla and Maldayak were waiting. It had been a rash move – but how could the soldiers have known that the plants which grew in such strange profusion around the house had been growing with such astonishing and unnatural fervour for hours?

Those plants were giants now, and they were active too. For a moment, Dathan thought that they might hold back the attackers and murder the lot of them, but they were only plants. They slowed the attackers down, but it did not seem to Dathan, at first glance, that they could hold them for long.

Some of the soldiers had flame-throwers like the ones that had burned the judeye forest, and were quick to use them. The plants seemed to devour flame, and to love the taste of it, but the blasts persisted and soon turned the tables, devouring them in their turn. Others among the soldiers had blades as well as guns – blades that were sharp enough to strike a man's head from his shoulders in a close fight – and they were even more effective, in their fashion, than the flame-throwers.

When the plants were hurt by being cut it seemed to Dathan to make them all the more avid to entwine their stems and branches around the limbs and the bellies of the soldiers, in order that they might squeeze and crush and strangle them. Once they lost their connections to their roots, though, they lost most of their strength.

But we're winning! Dathan thought, desperately, as his mount changed direction yet again. *We're holding them!*

Alas, it was not as simple as that. There were still artillerists manning the big guns on the trucks that had drawn up along the road, and they opened fire on the farmhouse.

The clamour of the cannonade blended almost immediately with the crashing of falling masonry and the splintering of wooden beams, but it was all so muted in Dathan's deafened ears that it sounded very distant and rather strange.

Nor were those gunners the only ones still capable of firing. The truck whose left side was perched on the edge of the ditch was listing at an angle, but that tilt was not so steep as to prevent the big gun from being brought to bear, and the riflemen still had their weapons. They were still firing at Dathan's glorious mount, although the noise of their weapons seemed so faint as to be slightly absurd.

Alas, that absurdity was no armour against the damage they could do.

Their aim was still confused, but Dathan realised just a fraction of a second in advance of disaster that if well-aimed shots were certain to miss a target, then badly-aimed ones still had a chance of finding their mark. There was a peculiar instant, in which he thought he heard another sound, utterly different from the explosive gunfire and much more horrible, but he had no opportunity to wonder what it might be if it were more than mere illusion.

His horse was hit, and he had no attention to spare thereafter for anything but himself.

Had the horse been hit in the shoulder or the head it would have gone down immediately, and Dathan would have been sent somersaulting through the air in exactly the same fashion as the men hurled from the truck that had turned over. Although the wound the animal took was no less mortal, the point of impact was close to the stock of its ratlike tail. Instead of cartwheeling, the beast lost its back legs and slithered, while its front legs continued to strive gallantly, but vainly, for purchase.

The deceleration seemed horribly abrupt to Dathan, and the descent to the ground was bruising, but even as he fought to avoid being thrown he realised that fortune was still on his side. He had a chance to jump clear and roll, and if he could only control the tumble well enough to avoid breaking a limb he could still fight on – fight being the operative word, now that he was fully exposed and quite without glamour.

He dived, and he rolled.

The ground was better than it might have been, firm without being unduly hard. His muscles were jarred and his nerves were jangled, but Dathan eventually came to rest lying on his side, with all his limbs intact. He was not even winded, and he had the presence of mind to look up before trying to get up, in order to see exactly where he was and where his enemies were.

Perhaps the clever horse had contrived it and perhaps it was mere chance, but Dathan found, to his delight, that he was little more than ten yards away from the truck that had overturned, and that the body of the truck was shielding him from the fire that would otherwise have been streaming from the other one.

There was a man with a gun not a dozen feet away: a living man, whose eyes were fixed on Dathan and whose arms were trying to bring a rifle round so that its muzzle would be pointing at his face. But the man had broken a leg and an arm as he fell awkwardly, and he could not do what he was trying so very hard to accomplish.

Dathan launched himself forward and wrestled the gun free from the stricken man's one good hand – and then he smashed the butt of the weapon down on the soldier's head.

That's for Houlme! he thought.

Dathan's brain, unprompted, completed a calculation which told him that there must be a hundred and thirty villagers still to avenge, but there was a pain in his heart that was not in the least concerned with calculations. His mother was among those who might have been murdered, and he knew that these were the soldiers who had taken everything from him that he loved, and everything that he knew. Even Hycilla was lost to him now, having become Nimian's creature, and the agony in his heart told him that he was utterly alone.

It was the agony in his heart, not the calculation in his brain, which reversed his grip on the rifle and sent him sprawling into the ditch, peering around the upturned truck in search of targets.

The other truck was less than thirty yards away, and it was full of targets.

Dathan never paused to remember that he had never fired a gun in his life before, and that did not even know how. Nor did he pause when he felt the first recoil tear into his shoulder muscles, more painful than the jolting he had received when his horse collapsed.

He felt the discharge of the gun, but he could not hear it at all.

He fired, and he kept on firing – and when the gun ran out of ammunition, he scrambled back to the upturned truck, determined to find another gun if he could not find the wherewithal to reload the one he had.

He found another rifle, and took advantage of the cover afforded by the vehicle to resume firing.

The soldiers from the more distant truck had begun a charge as soon as they were certain that he was out of ammunition, but they were charging at the wrong position. Dathan shot two of them down before they realised their mistake.

Then the beastmen arrived.

Gavalon's laggard retinue came charging across the fields like stampeding cattle, howling more loudly than Dathan would ever have thought possible – loudly enough, in fact, to cut into his deafness where even the crack of the rifle had failed. Even muted, as they were to Dathan, the beastmen's howls were terrible, neither human nor animal but both at once – everything at once, mingling in a scream so sharp it seemed to have the power to lacerate and carve.

Dathan howled too.

Although his yell of anger and triumph was a feeble thing by comparison with the howling of the beastmen, quite inaudible to him, it must have added its force to the tumult.

Dathan felt that he was one with the beastmen, a sharer in their power and their determination.

He came out into the open then, to join in a pitched battle, choosing his targets now with the utmost care, lest he should hit one of his allies instead of an enemy.

He was sure that he had killed at least one more enemy before he was struck down himself – and when he fell, feeling a curtain of hot wet blood gush like a waterfall over his forehead and into his eyes, he felt nothing at all but astonishment: no pain, no sorrow, no regret.

Why, he thought, as his senses spun away from him, *I thought I was invincible. I really did!*

EIGHTEEN

WHEN HYCILLA SAW the trucks split into two groups – two of them chasing Dathan and the thrall-wizard, while four continued to approach the house – her first thought was a flash of hope that Dathan's steed might be able to carry him out of range of the guns. She had no doubt that Gavalon could defend himself, and anyone who remained with him, although the sorcerer did not appear at first glance to be carrying any weapon adequate to deal with the impending threat.

Even Gavalon seemed slightly distressed, for a moment or two – but then she realised that he was intensely annoyed.

'I had hoped to save the horn for the real battle,' he said to Maldayak, 'but a blast sufficient to deal with these reckless fools should not deplete its power too much. Protect your ears – no matter how well I direct the weapon, there's certain to be leakage at this range. You must do likewise, child, no matter how well Sathorael has strengthened you. Your ears are growing nicely, but they'll still need to be stuffed with something virtuous. Give her a strip from your jerkin, Maldayak.'

Gavalon seemed quite unhurried while he made this speech, but Maldayak showed a greater sense of urgency as he tore strips of bright yellow cloth from his decorated jacket, passing two to Hycilla with a slightly ill grace before he began stuffing his own ears with protective wadding.

Hycilla copied him, while Gavalon detached the horn that hung from the right side of his belt, opposite his heavy sword.

Hycilla had heard that the horns of loxodonts were sometimes used as signalling devices when it was inconvenient to make beacon-fires, but the only wind instruments she had ever heard were delicate and fluty, made from the little horns of ghazals. Gavalon's horn did not seem so very large, and it certainly was not as curly as the horn of an old ram, but it was intricately carved and elaborately enamelled in a hectic mixture of reds, yellows and blues.

As the trucks screeched to a halt and the soldiers swarmed from them bullets began to pour through the windows of the farmhouse, forcing Hycilla and Maldayak to duck down. Almost immediately, though, the firing became confused.

Peeping over the window-sill, Hycilla saw that the native weeds that had invaded the farmyard in such numbers were not as easy to trample down as the booted soldiers had imagined. Only a few had grown fast enough to reach head height, but many were waist high and many more had extended creepers six or eight feet along the ground. As soon as the soldiers were within the confining wall of what had once been the farmer's herb-garden they found themselves under attack.

When the purple and pink stems and creepers began to grapple with the legs of the charging soldiers, the soldiers were quick to fight back. Four who had flame-throwers ready – presumably to flood the rooms of the house with fire and force its inhabitants out into the open – immediately used their weapons to counter-attack, but they had to be extremely careful not to injure themselves or their companions. The enemy was already at close quarters, and the engagement was far too intimate to allow the reckless use of flaming liquid.

For a moment or two, the plants actually seemed to be thriving on the flames, as if the burning liquid were some kind of spicy nutriment – and when the vegetation did begin to burn, it was the plants which were not actively involved in the conflict that suffered most.

The soldiers carrying rifles had to stop firing in order to free their right hands to reach for their knives. Once clear of their scabbards and deployed with reasonable skill, the blades cut through the branches and creepers readily enough – but the severed ends continued to harass their victims, squirming and squeezing as best they could.

Without anchorage, alas, there was little enough the severed branches could do, although those with thorns dug deep enough to penetrate the skin beneath the soldiers' uniforms, and a few of those that were perfectly smooth leaked corrosive sap. Three or four of the attackers began to howl with pain – but none of them fell, and their howling soon had as much rage as anguish in it.

Because the attackers seemed to be having such extreme difficulty getting to the wall of the house, Hycilla was bold enough to lift her head a little higher, but she regretted her rashness as the big guns on the trucks opened up.

The gunners had aimed high in order to avoid hitting their own men, so she was in no danger of taking a direct hit, but the shells punched gaping holes in the masonry and tore into the beams holding up the roof. The house had not been badly built, but its structure had not been designed to withstand a collective shock of this magnitude. The ceiling immediately began to crumble and debris began to rain down on Hycilla's shoulders.

She ducked, putting her hands to her head in order to protect her skull. It was as well that she did, for the move made it easy for her to clamp her forearms over her wadded ears when Gavalon returned fire.

All the sorcerer did was to blow his horn – but the horn was loaded with a power far greater, in its own subtle fashion, than the enemy guns.

Hycilla could not have described the note sounded by the horn in musical terms. She could not tell whether it was high-pitched or low, more like a trumpet or more like a reed pipe. Had she been required to say what it was like she could only have compared it to pain, but even then she would not have been certain what kind of pain it was. Perhaps it was simply that she had not had enough experience of different kinds of pain, but it seemed to her that this was a kind far purer than anything generated by a blazing fire, a piercing dart, a thundering headache or a bone-slicing blade.

The Imperial soldiers had probably had far more opportunities to become discriminating connoisseurs of pain than

Hycilla had, but she could not believe that they would have done any better.

Even though the building was still crumbling, Hycilla lifted her head again as soon as she was sure that the artillerists aboard the trucks had ceased firing. She saw immediately that the holding action conducted by the plants had been a great success in spite of the plants' inadequacy as warriors. Not a single soldier had reached the wall of the house, and it seemed obvious now that none would. All but two of those who had come into the yard had fallen, at least to their knees.

Most of the attackers had dropped their weapons – knives as well as rifles – in order to clasp both hands to their ears, but the precaution had been woefully inadequate. Several were in the grip of convulsive fits that seemed likely to shake them apart. Others were foaming at the mouth, the foam turning red as it was flooded with blood from tongues bitten through.

The gunners on the trucks had not been quite as badly affected, and the drivers of the trucks even less so – the latter had the protection of their windowed cabs to thank for that – but the two remaining men on the most distant of the four trucks seemed to be the only ones still capable of conscious action. While the gunner struggled to recover his poise and his position the driver threw the truck into reverse gear and began to draw away.

Hycilla became aware that Gavalon had taken hold of her – and the thrall-wizard too – and that he was thrusting them towards the window.

'Out! Out!' he yelled.

Hycilla realised that the horn had almost paralysed her, and Maldayak too – and that their weakness put them in great danger, given that the house was still collapsing in upon itself.

She knew that she had to help Gavalon, and made a supreme effort to take charge of her own limbs. Had her arms and legs been as scrawny and weak as they had been two days before she would have had some difficulty climbing through the window, but her limbs were far longer now, and possessed of a strength that she had not yet tested. She took hold of the sill and leapt through the narrow gap with a single bound, more gracefully than she would ever have thought possible.

Gavalon's intention had been that Maldayak would follow her. The sorcerer was already yelling a further instruction to his thrall-wizard, telling him to mount his horse and chase the truck – but the instruction was worthless, because Maldayak's limbs were by no means as lithe as Hycilla's. The wizard tried to climb, but he could not co-ordinate his actions. Somehow, he became wedged in the window.

The remainder of the roof finally fell in.

Then the wall collapsed outwards, carrying Maldayak with it.

Gavalon was still inside.

Hycilla had to leap backwards in order to avoid being trapped by the falling wall, but her backward leap carried her a dozen feet. She landed beside one of the disabled soldiers, who was still thrashing about in an attempt to dislodge a dozen feeble but inconvenient vegetable serpents from various parts of his body. Hycilla picked up his discarded knife – a keen blade more than two feet long – and slashed his throat.

He continued thrashing, but harmlessly. The plants drank up his lifeblood greedily.

Hycilla hardly spared him a glance, staring instead at the place where Gavalon the Great had disappeared under a mass of falling masonry.

A mere man would probably have been killed, or at least knocked unconscious, but Gavalon was no mere man. He rose up from the rubble, sending bricks and mortar cascading in every direction, more angry than hurt – but he had not lost his power of calculation, and he had not forgotten that he was in the middle of a battle.

His first impulse, it seemed to Hycilla, was to pull Maldayak out of the wreckage, so that the wizard could obey his order, but it took him only a couple of seconds to realise that Maldayak had been caught at a far worse disadvantage than he had.

The thrall-wizard was not dead, but he had broken at least one leg and at least one arm. He was useless.

Gavalon's eyes immediately fixed on Hycilla, questioningly.

'I'll follow them!' she said, when she realised that he was waiting. 'I'll kill them.' She was amazed by her own words. How could she possibly make such a promise?

Gavalon nodded, immediately acquiescent, and seemingly devoid of any doubt as to her ability to chase a truck and kill its passengers.

'The one who was fully exposed will not be very dangerous,' he said, 'but the other might… be careful, I beg of you. Go! Go!'

Hycilla turned. Without bothering to question the sense of the action or the magnitude of the task she had accepted, she began to run – and as soon as she settled into her stride, she realised that Gavalon must know her new capabilities better than she did. She glanced back once, not so much to see what Gavalon was doing as to see what had become of Dathan.

Her heart leapt into her mouth when she saw that Dathan's horse was down, but then she saw that he was on his feet, and armed. Like her, he was carrying the fight to the enemy. He had not grown at all since Nimian had touched him, and did not appear to be changing in any way whatsoever, but he had risen to the occasion nevertheless.

He is a hero! she thought. *Even a boy like him may become a hero, when disaster strikes!*

She saw Gavalon, too, but only very briefly. The sorcerer was running towards the youth, presumably to help him. Then she heard a strange noise, which somehow contrived to penetrate not only the coloured wadding in her ears but the aftershock of Gavalon's horn.

It was an eerie and frightful noise, and she had the impression that under other circumstances, it might have seemed loud and blood-curdling, but she had to bring her head back round then in order to maintain her balance as she sped along the road, faster than she had ever seen any human being run.

But I am no longer human, she reminded herself. I have been touched by the creature that Nimian is becoming. I have been touched by a Lord of Change more powerful than any other, and there was something in me that responded to its touch. I am more than human now. I am burning far more rapidly, and far more brightly, than I could ever have done as a mere wise-dreamer.

She realised as she settled into an even, carefully measured stride that the truck was not drawing away from her. Even though the driver had taken the first opportunity to turn it around, so that it was moving forwards instead of backwards, it was not moving any faster than she was.

Hycilla knew, having sat in a driver's seat – even though she had been in a very strange state of mind at the time – that the driver would be able to see her image in the mirror set in the centre of the cab, above his head. He would know, therefore, if he cared to look, that he was being pursued.

Perhaps that would not frighten him, given that she still looked like a young girl, in spite or her increased stature – but perhaps it would, given that no mere girl could be doing what she was doing without magical aid.

The man on the back of the truck could see her too, and she could see him quite clearly. He had fallen down when the horn's blast hit him, but if he had experienced a convulsive fit, it was over now. There was no sign of blood or foam at his mouth, and he looked as if he might be able to stand up again if only he could find the strength. Hycilla did not doubt that he was trying to find that strength with all his might, but for the moment it was a losing battle. He could not draw himself into a sitting or kneeling position, in spite of having the plinth and mount of his gun to hold on to.

His eyes were firmly fixed on the vehicle's pursuer, and there was terror in them.

Hycilla took a certain satisfaction from that terror, but she knew that it would have been more to her advantage if the man had been laughing. Terror might help him gather his strength. Terror might help him bring his weapon to bear – and no matter how much unhuman strength Nimian's touch had given her, a well-aimed shot from a cannon like that would blow her to smithereens.

Gavalon had told her that the man would be helpless for some time, but Gavalon had not factored the terror into his calculation either.

Hycilla tried to accelerate, but it wasn't easy. She knew that she mustn't exhaust herself too soon, and that she had to pace herself in anticipation of a long chase. She also knew that she had to begin to close the distance separating her from the truck.

She accelerated, but so did the truck. The driver could see her – and he was afraid.

Now, though, the truck could go no faster. But Hycilla still had reserves of strength untapped.

Steadily, yard by yard, she began to eat into the distance separating her from the stricken gunner. While he stared at her, she stared at him, not terrified at all, nor even slightly apprehensive.

Her confidence made the gunner try even harder to rise to his feet. Finally, he managed to sit up. The effort cost him dearly in pain, but it seemed to be a price he was willing to pay. He braced himself for an even greater effort, gritting his teeth in anticipation of paying an even higher price. Had he been a coward, he would have failed, but he was a brave man.

If he had a god, Hycilla thought, he must have offered up a particularly powerful prayer. Against all the odds, he began to haul himself to his feet.

Once he was erect, Hycilla knew, the rest would be so much easier. He had only to adjust his position, and aim the gun. The gun was swivel-mounted, easily manoeuvrable. It would not be easy to aim from the back of a vehicle moving at full tilt over such an ill-made road, but he would not have to be very precise.

She was only twenty yards away now, and still closing. By the time he could get the gun aligned, she would surely be less than ten yards away – unless she abandoned the chase and moved off the road into the corn-cob forest which they had just re-entered, in order to follow more discreetly.

It was her choice.

She accelerated again, throwing every last vestige of her strength into a final sprint. The intervening distance lessened dramatically, forcing the gunner to a further effort of his own.

His legs were not as willing as hers. He stumbled.

That lost him at least ten seconds, and ten seconds was more than Hycilla needed. By the time he had recovered his former pose she was leaping up on to the back of the truck, hauling herself over the tailboard with an improbably fluid motion.

There was a rifle in the corner, but it was out of reach. Hycilla slammed into the gunner even as he turned, and the impact must have filled his body with paralysing pain all over again. His body hit the back wall of the cab like a sack of grain, and bounced.

The soldier collapsed, turning as he fell to face her again with his terror-stricken eyes.

Hycilla knelt over him and pressed the point of her blade to his throat.

'One question,' she whispered. 'Why did you destroy my village, and kill everyone in it?'

She used her left hand to tear the rags out of her ears in order that she might hear his reply.

He looked at her as if she were mad – as if anyone who asked such a question as that must be mad. There was horror and loathing in his eyes too, but they were outweighed by astonishment.

'I... I was following orders,' he said, as if it were absolutely obvious and something of which a man might be proud.

Hycilla had been intending to slash his throat as she had slashed the throat of the man whose knife his once was, but when she heard that reply she changed her mind, and deftly used the point of the weapon to blind him in both eyes.

Then she picked him up as if she were a labourer with powerful muscles hauling a sack of grain on to a sturdy shoulder, and hurled him over the side of the still-speeding truck, hoping that he might live long enough to bring himself to his feet again and stagger off into the hostile forest – whose predators would doubtless dispose of him at their leisure.

NINETEEN

DATHAN DREAMED THAT he was taking part in a great battle, whose fire and fury stretched from horizon to horizon of a vast plain. It was the dead of night, and the only illumination apart from the faint and hazy light of the three moons and the multitudinous stars was provided by the muzzle-flashes of countless guns. He had a gun himself, which he was firing repeatedly and mechanically, always finding shadowy targets at which to aim but never knowing whether any of his shots struck home.

He was surrounded by beastmen and other monsters: creatures that had once been human but were human no longer, having suffered terrible mutations and mutilations. Such armour as they had was brightly-coloured, but the colours seemed oddly drab in the dim light. Only a few had guns, while the rest wielded massive blades of various bizarre shapes. They too fought shadows, but the shadows they fought had guns of their own, and blades too. No matter how many shadows faded or fell, there seemed to be an infinite number rising anew from the muddy ground.

The mud was not compounded out of soil and rainwater, but out of soil and blood.

He awoke with a start to find that someone was shaking him by the shoulder. He could not open his eyes at first because they were sealed shut, but he rubbed them and forced them open. The knuckles with which he had rubbed them were dark red, and he realised that it had been dried blood that had caked his eyelashes and locked his eyelids shut.

When he lifted his head he discovered that the alarming eyes of Gavalon the Great were staring at him. It was Gavalon who had shaken him awake.

Dathan put his hand up to his head then, to feel the wound that had felled him. His matted hair was in the way, but his fingertips traced the length of a ridge of horny scar-tissue that arched across his head an inch or two behind the hairline. It wasn't painful.

'Did you heal me?' he asked the sorcerer. 'Did you bring me back from the dead?'

'Healing isn't one of my talents,' Gavalon growled, 'and no one comes back from the dead as hale and cheerful as you seem to be. But yes, I sealed the wound. It's a great deal less pretty than it would have been had it healed of its own accord, but I couldn't wait – you might have slept till tomorrow, and I need you now.'

'What for?' Dathan wanted to know. He was already hauling himself to his feet and looking around. The battle was over, but the beastmen were still moving rapidly back and forth over the ground, scavenging for weapons.

'The trucks,' Gavalon said. 'We need them, so we need to know how to make them work.'

'How would I know that?' Dathan asked, in frank astonishment. 'I'm just a villager – not even a craftsman's apprentice.' He noticed that there was a rifle at his feet, and remembered using it. He touched the fingers of his left hand to his right shoulder, where the weapon's persistent recoil had left a bruise. That still hurt more than a little, but the twinge released a surge of pride as he remembered what he had done. He might not have been appointed an apprentice, and might never have become a true craftsman even if his life had clung to its rut of normality, but he was a man now. He was a warrior.

'You watched the girl,' Gavalon said. 'You saw what she did.'

'I don't remember!' Dathan protested. Then his voice dropped as he added, more honestly: 'I wasn't paying attention.'

'That doesn't matter,' Gavalon said. 'The girl was guided, and you were beside her. The Vessel touched both of you, and drew you into the process of his maturation. With you beside me, I can easily recall an echo of the guidance the girl received – and I've power enough to share what I learn with those in thrall to me. One truck got away and one broke an axle, but the army needs the other four. You're the key.'

Dathan was confused by this speech, but when its import became clear he saw its most worrying implication.

'Where's Hycilla?' he demanded. 'Why can't she show you what to do?'

'Not here,' Gavalon admitted, with a slight sigh. 'She followed the men who drove away, because she was the only one who could. Perhaps I could have demanded that she stay, if I had had sufficient presence of mind in the heat of the battle, but she is not in thrall to me any more than you are. She was responding to a higher call, and I would only have confused her by trying to prevent it, and so I urged her to go. But all will be well, I trust – because I have you.'

Dathan was astonished by this speech, as much by the confession that a man and a sorcerer as powerful as Gavalon could lack presence of mind in the heat of battle as by the implication that he had somehow become an important element of Gavalon's scheme. To cover his confusion he knelt down to pick up the rifle – his rifle, by right of conquest. As soon as he had his hands on it, though, the impatient sorcerer pulled him upright again, and thrust him towards one of the trucks. It was the one whose wheels had slipped sideways into the ditch, but it was no longer stuck. Gavalon's beastmen must have used levers to prise it out and set it to rights. Dathan remembered shooting the man who had fired the big gun at him.

'Where's Nimian?' Dathan asked.

'He didn't come back,' Gavalon replied, as he increased his pace, pulling Dathan along with him. 'I dare not wait any longer. He'll find us easily enough when he wants to – if he wants to. I ought to get these weapons to the army. Fulbra will be on us soon enough, and I must place myself in a position to shape the encounter as best I can. Every gun will be desperately needed, no matter what part Sathorael intends to play. The Changer of the Ways will doubtless let me know what my part is to be when the time comes.'

The sorcerer thrust Dathan into the cab of the truck, and climbed up behind him as soon as Dathan had scrambled over to the passenger seat. Gavalon put his misshapen fingers to his ragged lips and whistled an ear-splitting signal to his retinue of beastmen. Through the side-window of the cab Dathan could see that they responded as one, running to the trucks with the last of their booty.

'Why didn't you use magic the moment you saw the trucks?' Dathan asked. 'Why did you let them get so close and do so much damage?'

Gavalon looked at him sharply. Had the sorcerer's face been more human, Dathan thought, he would have been wearing exactly the same expression that his mother and Pater Saltana had put on when he had asked one question too many – but unlike them, Gavalon didn't seem to begrudge him his curiosity.

'Had you had an atom of talent, boy,' the sorcerer said, 'we might have made a wizard out of you.'

It was obviously meant to be a compliment, but Dathan couldn't quite see the logic of it. Was asking questions a qualification for wizardry? Surely not. He opened his mouth to speak again, but Gavalon placed a clawlike hand upon his shoulder, and the massive talons dug into his bruise just hard enough to shock him into silence.

'Try to remember, Dathan,' Gavalon said brusquely. 'Try to relive the moment when you first got into one of these things. Remember what Hycilla did. Remember the expression on her face.'

If it had been anyone else but the sorcerer beside him, Dathan would have had difficulty collecting himself – but it was the sorcerer, and the words seemed to flow into his head, exercising an awesome power of command.

As soon as Hycilla had the door open she had leapt up into the empty space, and had then reached back to offer Dathan the support of her arm. He had taken her hand and clambered up behind her. By the time he was in she had scrambled across to set herself in the further seat of a matching pair, behind the big wheel that was the cab's most prominent feature...

The confined space had been an utterly mysterious and profoundly alien environment, but when Hycilla had turned towards him to tell him to be quiet she hadn't needed words. Her eyes had been uncannily large and strangely luminous, brightly lit by moist reflections even though the pupils had been widely dilated. Her lips had formed themselves into a ferocious snarl, making her lovely face into a hideous caricature...

There had been a lever sticking up from the floor of the truck between her seat and Dathan's, and she had already begun wrenching it back and forth. The truck's engine had roared into life. As soon as the truck's wheels had begun to turn she had spun the steering-wheel, forcing the vehicle into a tight arc that carried it away to the left...

'Not so distant,' Gavalon murmured. 'Relive it, as if it were now.'

Hycilla spun the wheel again, sending the truck into another, entirely different arc. She was making no attempt to stick to better ground, and there was nothing visible through the windscreen but the crowns of bushes and exotic flowers – a veritable tide of vegetation that seemed to hurl itself forward and dive down beneath the vehicle with reckless alacrity...

There were no more soldiers to be seen now, but the evidence of their presence was all around, in billows of smoke and lines of hectic light scrawled upon the surface of the starry sky...

'Open the door!' Hycilla screamed. 'Move over!'

His hand shot out from his side to grapple with the door-catch. He had never encountered one like it, so it required a few seconds of inexpert fumbling, but in the end he managed to spring the catch and hurl the door open – and then, without any pause for thought or reinforcement of the command, he moved over into the narrow gap between the two seats...

A human figure leapt out of the onrushing vegetation to land sure-footedly on the floor of the truck, arms extended to catch the side and top of the door frame, so that a single fluid movement might deliver the slender body into the space that Dathan had cleared...

Hycilla spun the wheel yet again, hurling the truck into an arc so tight that it came up on two wheels. Dathan was scared that it might tip over, but the fear was insufficient to override his astonishment...

He became lost, then, as two different times seemed to over-
lap and merge, so that his old self briefly confronted his new
self. Dathan was astonished to discover that his old self was
contemplating his new self with as much horror as astonishment, but he told himself – his new self, of course – that his
old self was only a boy, and was not capable of understanding
the man that he had become, even though the process of metamorphosis had taken little more than a day.

Gavalon's hand lifted from his shoulder, and Dathan came
back to the present with a peculiar rush, as if he were being
thrown clear of a vortex in which hours and minutes had mingled with centuries and millennia.

Dathan looked sideways at the monstrous sorcerer, and
recognised the trance-state into which Hycilla had slipped
when she had been required to perform a task that she had no
idea how to do.

This, Dathan supposed, was magic – and yet the Imperium
had no need of magic to propel and steer its vehicles. The soldiers had been trained to drive, and simply did so. But if the
people on his side needed magic to do what the enemy found
simple, what chance did they have in the impending battle?

'We have Sathorael,' Gavalon said, as if he had heard the
unvoiced question. 'We shall not have him for long, and his
behaviour has been annoyingly mercurial, but he is the key to
everything.'

The sorcerer's voice sounded strangely mechanical, and
Dathan wondered whether Gavalon was actually awake, even
though his strange eyes were fixed on the ground ahead of
them – the ground over which they were travelling at a surprisingly rapid pace.

Dathan was surprised that he had not noticed the truck's
engine roaring into life, let alone the commencement of the
journey, but his curiosity was further intrigued by the fact that
Gavalon had answered a question that Dathan had not even
voiced.

But what is Sathorael, exactly? he wondered, taking care to
form the question clearly in his mind even though he did not
say a word.

'I wish I knew more precisely what Sathorael is,' Gavalon
said, in that same mechanical manner. 'I had expected a Lord
of Change, but I now suspect that it may be more than that,

although it may be that the lore of the covens is defective in its understanding of what a Lord of Change is. I had hoped that it would provide me with a daemon familiar, such as favourite champions of Chaos are said to be granted to aid their own apprentice daemonhood, but even the Vessel Nimian did not conduct himself as a familiar should once the ritual was complete. I had hoped to be allowed to know far more of my Divine Master's mind once I had brought his plan into its final phase, but it seems that I was more ignorant than I knew, and still am.'

But he – it – will help us to win the battle, Dathan thought. *That much has to be certain, has it not? He – it – will make the Imperium pay dear for invading our lands, and save Gulzacandra, will he not?*

'I hoped that Sathorael would make our victory certain,' Gavalon said, his voice becoming slightly more distant and oddly plaintive. 'I thought I knew what strategy my Divine Master was following, but I am no longer so sure. Much had been revealed to me in my dreams, but still I had the temerity to think that what happened on this world, to my people, was of paramount importance. Perhaps I should have realised that this is but the tiniest corner of a vast arena, and that whatever happens here is of scant importance, if it does not bear somehow upon the whole. If Imperial ships are coming… Sathorael may have a higher purpose than the salvation of Gulzacandra.'

Dathan struggled to make sense of this, not very successfully. *But we are heroes,* he reminded himself, *and we have magic. The Imperium has guns, and trucks, but I have faced them twice and – admittedly with magical aid – have beaten them twice. We are heroes, fighting for our homeland, and Gavalon the Great is a powerful sorcerer. How can the enemy possibly win?*

'The secret of whether the enemy can possibly win may be the darkest secret of all,' Gavalon said, his sonorous voice becoming even more distant and ruminative. 'Darker than the secret hidden by the Golden Throne itself. Everything we know and believe, of course, tells us that the Imperium cannot possibly win in the end. In the fullness of time, the only possible victory is that of Chaos. In the fullness of time, the only possible fate for humankind is extinction. And yet the Imperium fights on – and who knows what petty victories they might win in the meantime, or what the true value of those petty victories might be?

'We who are proud to be dwellers in Gulzacandra and followers of the Changer of the Ways might say, and might even believe, that we are the heroes of the eternal struggle – but we know in our hearts that it is not true, and that the Imperium has the monopoly on heroism. We fight out of choice, driven by pride and lust and fury, and everything we do hastens our own end and the end of our species. They fight for duty, driven only by faith. They know that they cannot win, but they fight on, determined to survive for another hour, another year, another century… even though they know that they cannot survive forever. It is they, not us, who maintain the game and make it worth the playing. It is they, not us, who are the game.

'The ultimate triumph of Chaos, which lies so far in the future as to be of little concern to short-lived creatures such as you and I, is absolutely certain. The ruination and destruction of all mankind is but a tiny part of that culmination. The Imperial forces have nothing to fight for but a trivial postponement, and yet they fight. They have made their emperor a god, and are surely right to do so, for if anyone less than a god could ever deserve to become one, what other kind of man could it be than an emperor? The Imperial forces are the heroes, because they have nothing to win but a momentary eyeblink in the hour of eternity, for the sake of which they have sacrificed every freedom, every thought, every hope and every pleasure. They will never know how grateful my Divine Master and those like him must be for all their sacrifices, or what the true value of their petty victories must be.

'That, I am convinced, is the darkest secret of all.'

Dathan would have liked to feel privileged to have been admitted – even by accident – to this 'darkest secret of all'. Alas, he could not begin to fathom what Gavalon meant. Even the elementary secrets of the cults, known to Pater Saltana and Kanak, and perhaps by now to Hycilla, had been denied to him. And yet, he now had the word of Gavalon the Great that the lack of an atom of talent was all that had prevented him from being apprenticed to a wizard, thus entering into the special favour of the god of Gulzacandra, whose name was too ominous ever to be spoken aloud.

What an achievement that would have been, for his mother's son!

'And what an achievement it has been,' said the entranced Gavalon the Great, more mildly than Dathan would ever have thought possible. 'I have regretted nothing, no matter what my career may have cost me. I would not trade places with anyone, no matter what my fate is yet to be. I have lived; I have chosen; I have led. Can any commander of the Imperium – even the True Imperium – say more? Can any daemon? There are those, I know, who believe that the gods which are served by men like me are compounded out of human evil, but I cannot believe it. There was Chaos long before humankind was dreamed of, and there will be Chaos long after humankind is vanished from the universal stage. Humans who think themselves vital to the cause and course of Chaos are the vainest of the vain; we live but a moment and die forever, unable to encompass infinity and eternity even in the ambition of the imagination. I have dreamed; I have seen; I have understood. If I die tomorrow or the next day, as I likely shall, I have nothing to begrudge.'

It was at this point that Dathan realised, belatedly, that Gavalon was not talking to him at all, but only to himself, and that the questions he was asking were serving as prompts to Gavalon's exploration of his own interests and intrigues. Dathan saw that he was a mere eavesdropper on a private conversation that he could not hope to understand, even if it were all true. Perhaps it was not. No matter how great a sorcerer Gavalon was, he was only human, more than capable of believing that he knew and understood far more than he actually did.

And yet, Dathan had to suppose, there was valuable knowledge to be gained here, if he could only phrase a question simply and carefully enough.

What, he wondered, would become of him?

'All men die,' Gavalon murmured, still lost in the cold depths of his reverie. 'Some live to be old, others die as babes. In a world like this, in a time like this, no one can be sure that he will survive the morrow, and everyone should conduct himself accordingly. There is no future but war. There is no hope but postponement of disaster. There is nothing a man can do to help himself except to fight, unendingly, with every weapon he can command.'

And having said that, with the myriad banners of his army already fluttering mutely upon the horizon, Gavalon suddenly shook himself, and coughed. Then he turned to look at Dathan, and said: 'Better wake up now, boy. We're almost there. It's good that you've slept – you needed the rest. Get yourself washed now, and fed. Then pray. Fulbra will surely be on us soon enough, and I must do what I can to bring Sathorael to the field, in order that he might unleash the wrath of the Changer of the Ways.'

'Can I keep the rifle?' Dathan asked, meekly.

'It's yours, boy,' Gavalon said, in a gruff voice very different from the one he had used – unwittingly, it seemed – before. 'Yours by right. You'll be issued with ammunition. Use it well.'

TWENTY

As soon as Hycilla had sent the blinded soldier tumbling over the side of the truck, the vehicle's driver slammed the brakes on.

If he had done it a minute earlier he might have rendered some useful assistance to his friend, but he could not have known how badly the gunner had been hurt by the blast of Gavalon's horn. Although he had been able to see Hycilla close in on the gunner by means of his mirror, the driver must also have seen his comrade struggle to his feet. Either he had thought that the other man was capable of putting up a fight, or he had been afraid that a sudden stop would cause his friend more distress than it would cause Hycilla. Now that the blind man was gone, though, and Hycilla was off guard, the driver must have thought that the time had come for him to take a hand.

Hycilla had not been standing awkwardly when the truck suddenly decelerated, but she was thrown completely off balance nevertheless. Had she been only a few inches closer to the rear end of the gun she might have succeeded in grabbing it, and using its mass to steady herself, but her groping hand missed it by a whisker and her momentum sent her cannoning into the back wall of the cab.

Had the cab been higher or had she been only as tall as she had been mere hours before she would only have bruised herself, but as matters stood the bulk of her mass was too high to be readily arrested. Her legs were swept from under her and she tumbled forward, rolling over the roof of the cab and falling down on the other side.

Her back hit the hood of the vehicle hard, spoiling her second desperate grab for purchase, and she fell again, right in front of the truck.

Had the driver waited where he was and accelerated as soon as he saw her fall from the hood he might have run her over, breaking at least one of her limbs, but he had not waited. Instead, he had chosen to hurl himself through the door, with a long blade in his hand, ready to run his enemy through.

And had Hycilla been only human, she would have had little strength left with which to resist the driver's angry charge, but she was far more than human now – as he should have understood when he had seen her pursue him on foot and catch him in spite of all his efforts to pull away.

Even so, it was a close run thing – it was only at the last possible moment that she raised her own blade to block the soldier's thrust.

The soldier cursed, seemingly surprised that Hycilla had contrived to hold on to her own weapon while she described her involuntary somersault, or that she had done so without inflicting the smallest cut upon herself. She met his pale blue eyes, lit by terror and desperation, and saw him flinch from her own gaze, as if her eyes had the power to wither him. She was aching in every limb, and her spine was a river of fire, but the burning sensation was exhilarating rather than debilitating. Although she was down on the ground while her adversary was standing, the soldier could not make the most of his advantage.

He thrust again, and then again, but Hycilla parried both thrusts with enough force to make him unsteady on his own feet.

Rather than risk falling on top of her, the soldier moved sideways to regain his balance, giving her a moment in which to alter her own position. She was still on one knee when he attacked again, but as she blocked his fourth thrust she borrowed a little of the force of his attack to prise herself upright

– and now she had the advantage, for she was several inches taller than he was, and had a considerably longer reach.

The Imperial soldier should have been confident. He was, after all, a trained man, and Hycilla was young as well as female – but the man's eyes told the real story. He could hardly bear to look at her, so frightful had she become. Nor was it her lack of prettiness that appalled him; he knew and understood that she had been touched and transformed by sorcery. He was a brave man, though. Mouthing what was probably a prayer, he attacked again, with all the courage of a man who was fighting for more than his life.

Hycilla had never trained with any kind of weapon, but she had played the same games as Dathan and her other peers, and it was to her advantage now that it had always been the boys who decided which games to play. She had played at sword-fighting, with branches and broom-handles, and now that she had strength to supplement her quickness of hand and eye her reflexes were good enough to check the increasingly desperate thrusts of the Imperial soldier.

For three or four minutes Hycilla was content to check him – and then she took up the tempo of the fight, and went after her opponent.

His training had equipped him with skill enough to fend off half a dozen thrusts, but it had not granted him skill enough to save his life. Although she was still aflame with pain, Hycilla had the stride, the reach and the diabolic strength to finish him.

First she slashed his arm, rendering him unable to make further use of his weapon, and then she stabbed upwards through his belly, pushing the blade through his intestines and liver to puncture his diaphragm.

He died more swiftly than she might have hoped, and was certainly unconscious before the creature that had once been Nimian walked carelessly out of the alien forest, picked his body up in two massive hands, and bit his head off.

The pattern that Hycilla had first seen on Nimian's skin as a mere sketch was now clearly manifest in coloured scales and a cape of feathers. The creature had wings now; they were furled for the moment, but she estimated their span as thirty feet at least. They too were brightly coloured. The monster's hands and feet were vast taloned claws, but its face still held an echo of humanity – and was still just about recognisable as

Nimian's – even though the nose and mouth had been twisted and wrenched to form the shape of a beak.

Had she seen such a sight two days earlier Hycilla would have been utterly aghast, perhaps paralysed by terror, but having seen so many of the stages of this strange metamorphosis Hycilla felt almost that she was looking into the face of a friend – a friend she knew better than anyone else ever could or would, and who could probably have said the same about her. This peculiar being had touched her, and that touch had been no casual salute or caress. She had been drawn into its evolution. She was in thrall to it – but she did not feel like a slave or a victim. She felt proud, as if she had more mastery of her fate now than could ever have been granted to her former, lesser self.

'You might have helped me,' she pointed out, as the monster continued to make a meal of the bloody corpse.

'There was no need,' it said. The voice seemed to materialise out of nowhere; the creature's beak-to-be was obviously incapable of forming the same sibilants and plosives as human lips, but the words were clearly audible and their pronunciation was perfect. Nimian had not been nearly as articulate. Hycilla had only to wonder where the daemon's new command of language had come from to know the answer, as if by an inspired guess. This was no longer Nimian but a Lord of Change: a very powerful Lord of Change. It could hear the thoughts of human beings... no, not hear, exactly, but share. No secret was safe from its presence, language least of all.

It shared the language of those it had touched and those it had not, not entirely but in fragments. It shared aspects of each person's intellect, and each one's imagination, hope, anxiety, ambition. It possessed her completely, but even Dathan had something in reserve, and the minds more distantly glimpsed and grasped had even more; nevertheless, the sum of all the disparate parts over which it had dominion was not merely a whole mind but a whole far greater than any mind. It was a crazy patchwork, a vast confusion, but it was a million minds and a single mind at one and the same time: a mind befitting a daemon.

Hycilla realised, as she looked into those bleak raptor's eyes, that the daemon was glad to be possessed of such a fine fragmented mind, and utterly fascinated by the extent and complexity of its thefts and borrowings. The daemon knew, as it had to, that it would not live long – but that only increased the piquancy of its experiences, and the particular feeling of power it obtained from knowledge.

There was a sense, she realised, in which the daemon was a brute: a thing of raw power whose destructive potential was still undeveloped. But there was a sense, too, in which it was an infant: a being possessed of youth, and all the zestful curiosity of innocence. She knew this because there was a further sense in which she was now a part of the daemon: not merely an extra limb but an extra intelligence.

Hycilla leaned back against the radiator of the truck, exhausted by the sum of her physical and mental efforts. The grille was very hot, but the heat did not seem uncomfortable. Her body soaked it up, and the fire inside her burned a little more brightly. She felt very tired, but she was determined not to sink to the ground while the monster was looking down at her. She did not want to run the slightest risk of being mistaken for another toothsome morsel, more use as nourishment than as a living being.

'What shall I call you now?' she asked, in the hope of giving further evidence of the fact that she was not for eating. 'Master, or friend?'

'Sathorael,' the monster replied.

'Sathorael,' she repeated, mechanically. 'Who gave you the name? Gavalon?'

The monster seemed to consider that question very carefully, as if it were a matter that it needed to get straight in its own mind. Hycilla wondered if she really ought to be thinking of the creature as 'it', or whether it would be more appropriate to revert to 'he', but she decided that it probably did not matter much.

'A Lord of Change requires a true name,' the giant told her, eventually. 'I am a great Lord of Change: a very, very great Lord of Change. The name is mine, ingrained in every fibre of my being.'

'Well, Sathorael, Lord of Change,' Hycilla said, faintly amused by her own temerity, 'you certainly seem to have changed me.'

'True,' said the monster, echoing her amusement. 'I change everything. That is my nature, and my purpose. I change. I change myself. I change the world. I change the game. I am

change. Change concentrated; change crystallized; change clarified. Thank you for asking.'

'Why?' she asked, taken slightly aback.

'Why what?'

'Why thank me for asking?'

'Change clarified. How am I to know myself, if no one asks
the questions? I can know everything that you know, everything that anyone knows, but there is so much, and all so
confused. I should like to know myself more clearly. I shall not
exist for long, and there is so much to do. May I offer you a
ride?'

'A ride?' Hycilla echoed, still tying to catch up with the unexpected course that the conversation had taken. 'In the truck,
you mean?'

'No. I am too heavy, and it is best that we take a straighter
course than the truck could follow in the forest. On my shoulder. You could lean back upon my furled wing and rest a while.
There may not be another chance.'

'Where are we going?' Hycilla asked, making no move to step
into the huge claw that the monster had extended, invitingly.

'We are going to burn,' the giant said. 'More gloriously than
you could ever have imagined – more gloriously than anyone
of your kind could ever have imagined.'

'Do I have a choice?' she wanted to know.

'Yes. We all have a choice; that is our greatest strength and
our greatest folly. We perish by choice, gloriously or inglori-
ously. You may fight, or you may run. You may fight the little
fight, or the greater fight. You may come with me, or not. It is
a choice not many have, and fewer still would want, but you
must make it now. Time is pressing, and I must make the most
of myself when I am fully grown. For that, I must prepare.'

Sathorael was already three times as tall as Hycilla, who was
no longer small. She shuddered as she received a sudden but
fleeting impression of the extent of the growing that it had yet
to do.

'Are you going to Gavalon?' she asked. 'Are you going to help
him against the Imperial invaders?'

'I shall do what I must,' the monster said – and when it said
it, Hycilla divined that even Sathorael did not know exactly
what its purpose was, and would not until its identity was fully
revealed.

Hycilla stepped forward into the embrace of the waiting claw and allowed Sathorael to pick her up and place her on its shoulder. When it stood erect again, she was well above the canopy formed by the spurs and tassels extending from the crowns of the corn cob-like plants. From this vantage the forest looked very different, rather like a field of clover painted and enamelled in red, black and purple, interrupted by exotic weeds like twisted clumps of nails and curly icicles. She could see for miles – or so it seemed – and she could see the waste-land beyond the forest's edge as a blurred and bobbled patchwork quilt, in which fugitive greens and yellows mingled with the harsher colours. There was not a trace of human habi-tation, or of the plants and animals that the first humans had brought with them thousands of years ago.

'Everything has changed,' she said. 'In two days, my whole world has been torn apart and turned upside-down. I am not what I was. What am I now, Sathorael? What have I become?'

The daemon thought about this for a moment as it began to thrust its way through the native foliage, using its massive hands to part a way for its lumpen thighs and awkwardly-furled wings. Eventually, Sathorael said: 'Familiar. You are familiar.'

'You seem strangely familiar yourself,' she said. 'But that's not what you mean, is it?'

'Yes it is,' he said. 'That, and only a little more. Be glad of it; you are more than you were or could ever have become.'

'Because you would have eaten me by now, if I weren't famil-iar?'

'That too – but be glad for what will come. It will only be a moment, but it will be more than a lifetime of merely human existence.'

Hycilla got the distinct impression that the monster was try-ing to rouse a gladness in itself that it had not yet learned to feel. Even daemons, it seemed, could be anxious. She won-dered whether she ought to help in the morale-building exercise, or challenge its fundamental assumption. Eventually, she said: 'Forgive me for saying so, but I'm not sure you're the best judge of the value of merely human existence.'

'Who is?' Sathorael countered.

Hycilla had insufficient confidence to make any claim on her own behalf. 'We are going to win this battle, aren't we?' she said, instead. 'With you on his side, Gavalon has the advantage, has he not? We call the enemy the Imperium, but they're really just castaways, aren't they? They've used up almost all the weapons their forefathers had. They're no match for the kind of power you can unleash.'

That required an even longer interval of thought. It was almost as if the monster were relaying the more difficult questions to some further source.

'Never underestimate an enemy,' the great beast said eventually. 'These soldiers are brave. They think of themselves, modestly, as little more than a travesty of their true Imperial forebears, but they are better men than they can credit. Because they lost so much, they had to learn to improvise. The warriors of the true Imperium are fine fighting men, but they are never called upon to understand their weapons. The invaders of Gulzacandra have had to learn so much that they have had no alternative but to substitute cleverness for faith. That has weakened them, in one way, but it has strengthened them in another. They do not know the extent to which they have laid themselves open to corruption, but they should not be despised. They are worthy sacrifices.'

'Worthy sacrifices?' Hycilla echoed. 'In other words, you intend to kill and eat the lot of them.'

'There will not be time for that,' the monster replied, a trifle regretfully. 'Gavalon's army must do its share of killing, and of dying. Everyone must do his part. And hers.'

'The true Imperium is coming, isn't it?' Hycilla said, slowly. 'That's what you – or Nimian – meant when you said that you would bring ships. What happens in Gulzacandra doesn't matter to you at all. You aren't here to save us, are you?'

'That which you used to call "us",' the creature told her, peeping sideways at her from a vast eye that seemed to have become even more predatory since she had met it squarely on the road, 'is but a petty legion of the dead and a greater legion of the dead-to-be. Now, there is only me, and that which is familiar to me.'

Hycilla swallowed hard as she realised what the full implications of this statement were – but she was not as distressed by it as she might have expected. There was only one sad thought that pricked the vestiges of her conscience.

'Is Dathan dead already?' she wanted to know.

This time, the giant's response was immediate. 'Can you expect me to concern myself with such trivia as that?' it demanded. 'Time is; time was; and time will soon be gone.'

Hycilla saw then that they had been moving so rapidly that there was something new to be seen on the horizon, far beyond the soft blanket of purples, pinks and golds that lay beyond the forest's edge. It was no less gaudy than the forest or the plain, but it was far more fragile.

It was, in fact, the wind-fluttered banners of Gavalon's army, waiting impatiently for the descent of the foe.

Hycilla reached out her right hand to touch the daemon's enormous ear, as tenderly as anxiety would permit.

'Have you no fear?' she asked. 'Are you not horrified by the thought of extinction, after such a brief existence?'

She expected an automatic, if slightly insincere, denial. She did not know how welcome she would have found such a denial, until she heard the actual answer.

'I am immune to fear and horror, for the moment,' Sathorael said, 'just as you are. But when the time comes – and now that you have chosen to unite your wise-dreams more fully with mine, it will come to us both as one – we shall know the true meaning of fear, and of horror, and of death. Until then, we can only guess. Is it not fascinating to know that we shall know – and so very soon?'

TWENTY-ONE

Dathan was astonished, when he awoke, to find that the tent was being dismantled around him.

'What's happening?' he asked – but the men who were busy with the ropes and canvas ignored him. He had to pick up his gun and go outside into the bright morning light in search of an answer. There he found that the entire army was making ready to march. He could not see Gavalon, but Abdalkuri was nearby, placing a pack on his colourful steed. Abdalkuri treated Dathan with some respect now that he had been admitted into Gavalon's inner circle.

'What's happening?' he asked, again.

'A change of plan,' the thrall-wizard told him. 'Fulbra's stopped his advance. We don't know why. He may simply be resting his men, but he might be waiting for something.'

'Reinforcements?' Dathan guessed.

'He'd have to wait months for that, unless the reinforcements can fly,' Abdalkuri said, drily. 'He's probably waiting for his scouts to report on our positions.'

'Is that why we're changing them?'

'One reason. Given that we already know their positions, Gavalon might have seen an opportunity to attack.'

Dathan remembered what Gavalon had said to him in the truck. Perhaps the sorcerer had received further enlightenment from the god he served as to what his part in the unfolding drama was to be. Perhaps, on the other hand, he was merely confused. Perhaps he wasn't sure that he had time to wait, even though Fulbra apparently had. Perhaps Fulbra had stopped because he had got wind of the daemon's existence, and had a scheme of his own to counter its influence.

At any rate, Dathan thought, Gavalon's own plans had gone awry the moment he had lost sight of Nimian. The sorcerer was desperate now, and likely to remain so.

'Are you going to saddle up?' Abdalkuri asked. 'You won't be riding in the truck this time.'

Dathan was surprised by the question. He hadn't expected to be allowed to ride into the battle in a truck, but he hadn't expected to be allowed to ride at all.

'The horse I rode before was killed by a stray shot back at the farmhouse,' he reminded the wizard.

'Maldayak won't be needing his,' the other pointed out. 'He'll need to be carried into battle on a litter, if he can take any part. It's over there. Don't worry – it can sense the daemon's touch as well as I can. It'll serve you as well as the other.'

The daemon's touch! Dathan thought. Is that what I am, now? Something touched by a daemon, set aside from all my fellow men, save for initiates of a cult whose secrets I was never permitted to hear?

He knew, though, that it was an envious position to be in, given the circumstances. The closer he was to Gavalon and Gavalon's thrall-wizards, the closer to the heart of the enterprise he would be. He would be no safer for being close, and probably quite the opposite, but such closeness was a thing to be desired in and for itself, given that he was fatherless – perhaps motherless too – and all but friendless besides.

If he had to go into battle, he reasoned, was it not far better to go mounted on a clever and deceptive steed rather than on foot, especially when he had thoughtlessly missed a second opportunity to scavenge a better pair of boots from among the prizes taken at the farmhouse?

The coloured horse stood meekly, with its horned head bowed, while Dathan placed the saddle-cloth on its back and buckled the saddle in place. The stirrup was just as high as it had been on previous occasions, but Abdalkuri made a step for Dathan with his hand before stepping up on to his own mount.

'Shall I follow you?' Dathan asked,

'That would be wise,' the thrall-wizard replied, calmly. 'I may yet be grateful for the nearness of your gun.'

Dathan had not noticed before that the thrall-wizard seemed to have no weapon of any kind, but while he settled himself in his saddle one of the beastmen brought Abdalkuri a long lance with a wad of cloth – presumably a furled banner – behind its spearhead.

'And you,' the thrall-wizard added, 'might have cause to be grateful for my nearness.'

'Is that your magic?' Dathan asked curiously.

'Gavalon's magic,' Abdalkuri said, 'which I am privileged to wield on his behalf. He has the withering eye, of course, as well as the horn of agony and other tricks. Mine is a mere standard, but a potent one.'

Dathan remembered the banner he had seen billowing in the breeze above Gavalon's tent when the beastmen had brought him to the camp. It had seemed an ominous device even then, although he had not realised that it was magical. If the name that Abdalkuri had given it signified its power, it might be interesting to see its magic released – always provided that its force could be directed away from Gavalon's allies, entirely towards the enemy.

'What does your banner do?' Dathan wanted to know.

'It is a hellfire standard,' Abdalkuri told him. 'Its power is great – much greater than those flame-throwers the Imperial soldiers had – but soon exhausted. Invaluable in a skirmish, less so in a protracted battle.'

'But you believe that the battle we have to fight now – tomorrow if not today – will be a protracted one,' Dathan said, to make sure that he had taken the wizard's meaning.

'Very,' said Abdalkuri, sombrely. 'I have a few tricks of my own – I'll not die easily when the standard decays into a mere spear. You'll be in far greater danger than I, unless the daemon that has touched you deigns to protect you.'

'Is that likely?' Dathan wanted to know.

'How would I know?' was the only answer he got, as Abdalkuri shook the reins and urged his mount into motion.

Dathan had only to touch the neck of his own animal; it seemed to know its business at least as well as he did. It fell into step behind the other horse, and the column was soon joined by other riders, arranged two or three abreast.

As Dathan rode through the busy ranks he was able to get a far better idea of the size and nature of Gulzacandra's army. Because he had seen so many beastmen and stigmatized wizards in Gavalon's entourage he had formed the impression that the majority of its soldiers must be only half- or three-quarters-human, but now he saw that his first impression had been misleading. By far the majority of his fellows were as ordinary as he – more so, if the effects of Nimian's touch were as obvious to everyone else as they were to Abdalkuri and the decorated horse.

None of the men had uniforms like those the Imperial soldiers wore, unless the vivid livery of Gavalon's thrall-wizards could be counted as such. These fighters still wore the costumes of civilian life: labourers who toiled in the fields; husbandmen who kept herds of livestock; the varied raiment of carpenters and smiths, weavers and thatchers, chapmen and cobblers. Only perhaps one in ten was privileged, as Dathan was, to carry a gun, and some of those guns had obviously made their way to Gulzacandra long before the current invasion – perhaps fifty or a hundred years before. Those who had neither guns nor magic mostly carried swords and half-pikes – good weapons, so far as Dathan could tell, applying the standards set by his village, but unlikely to be a match for the Imperium's firepower unless the men wielding them could actually get among the enemy, to fight virtually hand-to-hand.

He could not see the trucks that he had helped to capture, but that was not surprising. Dathan knew that even if they had managed to salvage the trucks left behind after the massacre at the water-hole, the army's total stock of vehicles was unlikely to be more than a dozen. However many there were, they had already been moved out.

Most of the men on foot who glanced in the direction of the riders as they passed by did not let their glances linger long upon the furled standards and their multicoloured bearers, but a few gazes which did settle on the anomalous figure of Dathan almost hardened into curious stares. Dathan could not see another person as young as himself, although there might have been a few hidden by the nearer crowds. Anyone younger was presumably deemed a child, unready for the role of protector of the land – but their turn to fight would surely come, in a year or two.

Everyone seemed to think of the coming battle as *the* battle, the crucial one that would determine the fate of Gulzacandra once and for all. Perhaps it would be – but whatever its outcome, Dathan thought, day would follow night again and again and again, as it always had. Whoever won the battle, or survived it, would have to fight another day, and another, and another. While there were people in the world the war would go on, every settlement a remote prelude to a new rebellion or a new conquest. The Imperium would never eradicate the followers of the true god while the stars swam in the sky, and the followers of the true god could win no final victory either while the possibility remained that more ships would come bearing more Imperial colonists.

In the long run…

Dathan knew that he would not be around in the long run. Nor would any man here, whether he survived the impending battle or not. Any difference he or they might make was a temporary affair – but what man, in what world, could ever say anything different? What difference could the mightiest sorcerer or the greatest commander make, even to a single continent of a single world?

Dathan shivered as these thoughts took hold of him – but he knew that they were his thoughts, born of his fears and calculations. He had been touched by a daemon, but he was still the master of his own mind. If he had never encountered thoughts like these before, it was not because he had been incapable of formulating them, but because there had been no necessity to do so.

The necessity was upon him now. He was going into battle, and would probably be killed. He would have no other chance to interrogate the meaning of his fate – and that, too, was the work of a man. He was a warrior now, and a brave one, but a true warrior had to be more than a mere killer. He had to know what his bravery, and his likely sacrifice, might signify.

He did not doubt that Ierius Fulbra's men were about the same business, but he could not know how differently they saw their own situation, or what resources they had for making sense of it.

In the end – as Gavalon the Great had told him, without quite meaning to – Chaos would win. The only true heroes were those who fought to postpone the moment of its victory, whichever god they served. There was nothing for any man to fight for but a narrow margin – a little more life than he might otherwise have, whether it be measured in years or hours or minutes – but a real man, truly human as well as truly brave, also had to consider the question of how best to use that margin.

'Well,' said Dathan, although there was no one but his uncaring steed to hear, 'if that's the case, we are all heroes, no matter which side we are on, so long as we fight instead of lying down. If the daemon comes to save me, all well and good. If not... I have a gun. I am more fortunate than I could ever have dreamed of being when I was a masterless boy. I have a gun.'

The cavalry column had passed beyond the limits of the camp now, and was making its way across the plain. The red bushes and purple cacti to either side of their path, though not very numerous, grew tall enough to loom over them, casting long skeletal shadows wherever they eclipsed the still-rising sun – but the shadows did not seem unduly dark or cold.

They had been riding north for two hours without breaking into a trot when Dathan saw a dozen other riders approaching from the north-east. He recognised Gavalon at their head. Like Abdalkuri, Gavalon was carrying a lance, but his was larger than anyone else's and the withered eye banner furled about its head was a bulkier mass than any 'mere standard'. Dathan realised that the sorcerer must be immensely strong, although the strength in question was surely not the product of hard labour and a healthy diet.

He wondered, briefly, how old the sorcerer was. He knew that the mutations of Gavalon's form must have obscured the usual signs of ageing, but it was impossible to think of a man of his sort as very young or very ancient. He wondered, too, if Gavalon had fathered any children – and what had become of them, if so. That was an oddly discomfiting question, whose answer he suddenly did not want to know.

'Hold and dismount,' Gavalon ordered Abdalkuri. 'We must wait here for support, where the cover is dense enough to keep us hidden from prying eyes. They're busy clearing the land around their present camp to make sure that there's no easy approach, which suggests that they don't intend to move on today. They've chosen their ground well enough, but they have kept so carefully to the road that they'll be awkwardly strung out for hours yet, and it will likely suit us even better than it suits them. They have formed a wide arc to make sure we cannot outflank them, but that leaves them more vulnerable to a frontal assault. If we can move enough men forward quickly enough, we might surprise them.'

Abdalkuri bowed his head in acknowledgement, but his voice was apprehensive as he said: 'It will take all afternoon to move the men and organise a formation, magister. The men will be tired.'

'And the Imperial soldiers will get wind of our presence soon enough,' Gavalon agreed, 'but they're in mortal dread of our magic, if not our firepower, and a night attack might work more to our advantage than they'd expect. They're still being harried from the rear, and they can't know for sure how few the snipers are. The faster we can move, the better our chances are. We must wait and see how quickly and how skilfully our forces can be assembled, but if we don't start the fight ourselves this evening, the enemy will have the opportunity to pick their own time.'

Abdalkuri bowed again.

Dathan dismounted when he saw the other riders do so, and looked for a place to tether his horse. The surrounding plants were unfamiliar to him, but the thrall-wizard helped him yet again.

'How do you feel, Dathan?' Gavalon asked, when he too had dismounted.

Dathan knew that the sorcerer was not interested in the state of his health. He was being kept so close because he had been touched by the daemon, and Gavalon hoped that he might somehow be able to provide news of the daemon's position and condition.

'I don't feel anything,' Dathan reported, reluctantly. 'If Nimian's nearby, I can't tell.'

'It's not Nimian any more,' Gavalon told him. 'At least, I hope not. We might have to attack regardless – you do understand that?'

Dathan was taken aback for a moment, but then realised that Gavalon must be hoping that even if Dathan could not bring

news, he might still be able to transmit it. The long explanation
Gavalon had given Abdalkuri had been more for his benefit
than the thrall-wizard's.

'I understand,' Dathan said. 'If Nimian – or whatever he now
is – knows what I know, he knows that he's needed urgently.'

Gavalon nodded his terrible head, and turned away.

If Nimian knows what I know, Dathan thought, then he
knows far more about me than I'd care for any man or woman
to know. I suppose I must hope that he only cares about the
battle and the war, and not about my deepest hopes and fears.

With that, he sat down in the shadow of a huge spiny plant,
like a rolled-up hedgehog that had taken root. He tried to
purge his mind of all seemingly-dangerous thoughts.
Unfortunately, the more he dwelt on the problem of what
thoughts might be dangerous, the more crowded his mind
became with thoughts of potentially dangerous kinds.

'I pray that Hycilla be kept safe,' he said to himself, as soon
as he settled upon it as a thought that as not merely safe but
sincere. 'Whatever happens to me, I pray that Hycilla may be
spared. Grant me that, if nothing else, oh mysterious god of
Gulzacandra, whose name I have never been permitted to
know.'

TWENTY-TWO

ORLOC MELCARTH WAS mildly displeased to discover that Ragan Balberith seemed more comfortable aboard the aircraft than he had ever been while standing on the balcony of the governor's apartment in Sostenuto. Even so, the Chief Inquisitor didn't appear to be in the least inclined to look out of the window. Nor did the psyker he had brought with him – but psykers always seemed to be on the verge of hysteria, so it was possible that the fact that he was aloft in an aircraft wasn't making much difference. The priest, Carro Alpalhao, gave the impression that he would have been comfortable if he hadn't had the psyker beside him.

The three members of Balberith's party were huddled together in the rear part of the main cabin, keeping as much distance as they could between themselves and Melcarth's entourage – an arrangement which suited both groups.

Melcarth's aides and bodyguards also seemed to have been experiencing some problems, although they were sleeping in shifts and were fresher than any of those who had been awake throughout the journey. Melcarth assumed that the guards-men's nerves had more to do with the presence of Deir Ajao than the distance separating them from the ground – or, for the moment, from the ocean.

The aircraft had not flown in a minimal arc from Kalazendra to Yevelkana; it had been necessary to take a slightly crooked path in order to refuel at the base on Zendamora's westernmost cape. Fortunately, there was no need to stray as far north as Bulzavara; once they had crossed the northern coast of Yevelkana they would be able to cross the central desert at its narrowest rather than skirting it as Fulbra had been forced to do. They would arrive in the Gulzacandran wastelands with enough fuel left to carry them to the airstrip that Fulbra's engineers should have cleared by now, perhaps passing directly over the place where Operation Probe had run into trouble.

Major-General Vorch emitted an audible sigh of relief when Techmaster Sauldron reported that they were crossing the coast of Yevelkana. Melcarth could not see that it made much difference – indeed, if the aircraft were to let them down, they would presumably fall more gently on water than on land, and the Amber Waste had the reputation of being an exceedingly inhospitable place. The spectra of other people's fears never ceased to astonish him.

Almost as soon as Vorch had been reassured, though, the general's eyes began roving yet again, in an agitated fashion.

'Is it safe to have that man aboard?' he muttered.

That man was, of course, Deir Ajao. Melcarth understood that kind of apprehension much better than a fear of heights or flying. Psykers were authentically scary – and while a psyker in a subterranean cell was discomfiting enough, a psyker in an aircraft was something else entirely, and the fact that Alpalhao was obviously in some distress was bound to amplify the anxieties of Melcarth's companions.

Melcarth was not entirely immune to such anxieties, but he was prepared to live with them in exchange for the opportunities that Balberith's insistence on joining the expedition had opened up. He had no intention of starting trouble while the aircraft was in flight, but he was convinced that once it had set its wheels down on alien soil, ridding himself of Balberith would be easier than he had ever dared to hope.

The aircraft's pilot, Jal Moberg, had objected to the idea of carrying a psyker, and the vox operator who shared his cockpit had also seemed distinctly discomfited, but both men had spent their lives in preparation for a flight like this, and they had been easily persuaded that the risk was minimal. Both crewmen had flown a dozen times before, often with Melcarth aboard, but all those flights had been brief training exercises. This was the real thing. This was what the plane had been designed and built for, by those mysterious and godlike tech-priests who had manned the starships of the great Imperium of Mankind. This was what Moberg, in particular, had been looking forward to ever since he was favoured with the rank of pilot.

'How soon will we be there?' Melcarth asked Techmaster Sauldron.

The techmaster consulted his timepiece, and made a show of elaborate calculation. 'About four hours, excellency, if all goes well,' he finally replied. 'If our charts are accurate, we'll be over the Amber Waste for three hours, then we'll reduce our airspeed and descend to a lower altitude as we move across the Gulzacandran border. We'll have to refuel before undertaking any actual reconnaissance, but Fulbra's men should have everything ready for us – they've had plenty of time.' He didn't sound entirely certain.

'Is there any reason why things shouldn't go well?' Melcarth asked him.

'Well, no sire – except that Gulzacandra is a nation of sorcerers.'

'All of whom, if our intelligence can be trusted, have joined Gavalon the so-called Great in the wasteland, conserving all their resources for the impending battle against Fulbra's forces. Even if there were a few malign magicians left in the deserts, how could they possibly bring down the plane? It's an original, not something your so-called craftsmen knocked up in one of your so-called factories.'

The techmaster winced at that.

So far as Melcarth knew, there was no such rank as 'techmaster' in the True Imperium's Adeptus Mechanicus, but the True Imperium's Adeptus Mechanicus employed whole worlds as factories, and were in full possession of all the knowledge and ritual required to produce an infinite supply of what he and his people were now required to call 'originals'. Unfortunately, the Adeptus Mechanicus had been so drastically under-represented among the castaways, and so direly under-resourced, that subsequent generations had been forced to create an entire class of improvisers, with their own invented titles, whose produce was notoriously shoddy. In Melcarth's view, a techmaster ought to be exceedingly grateful for any opportunity to travel safely, comfortably and rapidly in an authentic original rather than being condemned to crawl along the surface at a snail's pace in a variety of machines manufactured by his own inept kind.

'Yes, excellency, of course,' Sauldron said, weakly. 'But sorcery is sorcery, and who knows what its masters are capable of?'

'We know that they're not capable of standing up to Imperial firepower and Imperial resolution,' Melcarth told him. 'Isn't that so, Vorch?'

'Yes, excellency,' Vorch was quick to say. 'All praise to the Emperor Magnificent – but even so, sire, this has been a very long flight, and by the time we arrive at Fulbra's position we'll have precious little fuel left – and there's the problem of landing. We have to bear in mind, excellency, that although this is an original it's a very old original. It's been two hundred years since our forefathers arrived here. And how much real experience can the pilot have had, given that the craft's hardly been up in the air for more than an hour at a time for generations, And then…'

'That's quite enough, Vorch,' Melcarth broke in, disgustedly. 'Moberg, did you hear all that?'

'Yes, excellency,' the pilot replied.

'Is this craft capable of flying long distances? Are you capable of landing it safely?'

'Yes, excellency,' Moberg replied, dutifully. 'Always provided, sire, that General Fulbra's engineers have prepared the landing-strip properly, and that…'

'Oh, be quiet!' Melcarth commanded, sternly. 'Is there no one here who has faith in Imperial workmanship?'

'Indeed there is,' put in a new voice, slightly spiced with irony. 'I am delighted to hear the question on your lordship's lips.' It was, of course, Balberith, who had crept forward in the stealthy manner typical of an inquisitor. For once – and, he hoped, for the last time – Melcarth was almost glad to see him nearby.

'Chief Inquisitor,' Melcarth said, resisting the temptation to employ a nakedly sarcastic tone. 'How kind of you to join us.

Are your people as impatient as mine to reach the battlefield where the fate of the world will be decided?'

'We certainly are, excellency,' Balberith replied – and he sounded entirely sincere, to Melcarth's ear. 'We are as eager as you are to see the matter settled, and to play our part. Deir Ajao is ready, and I feel confident that proximity to so many evil magicians is exactly what he needs to spur him on to the final breakthrough. I am convinced that before the day is out, contact with the Imperial Fleet will be firmly established. They will know of our need, and they will send help.'

'You won't let him do anything while we're still up in the air, will you, Chief Inquisitor?' said Vorch, who seemed almost ready to panic if he did not receive a reassuring answer.

'Of course not,' Balberith replied. 'Like the heretic enemy wizards, he is hoarding his strength – but once we are on the ground, and the battle is joined, the moment will be propitious. Fear not, major-general. We will not fail you. It has been a very long day, but now that evening is upon us we may anticipate an equally long night.'

Strictly speaking, that was not true. The reason the day had seemed so unnaturally protracted was that the aircraft had been heading west, away from the rising sun. Given that they had been airborne for more than eight hours, and had less than three to go, the impending night could not be extended to the same extent as the day had been.

'The moment will indeed be propitious,' Melcarth murmured. 'But I wonder whether your psyker might not be better employed in lending assistance to General Fulbra, helping to counter the vile effects of enemy magic. He has the psykers and inquisitors you assigned to him, of course, but I wonder whether it was really wise – or dutiful – to reserve your most powerful instrument for your own purposes?'

'My own purposes!' Balberith repeated, feigning shock. 'What higher or more dutiful purpose could there possibly be than to restore contact with the Imperial Fleet?'

'None at all, if it were possible,' Melcarth said. 'But can we really afford such reckless hopes when there is such an obvious enemy close at hand? Is not our first duty to crush this Gavalon fellow and the cults at whose head he stands, then to purge Gulzacandra of the taint of hideous evil? Would the divine Emperor forgive us if we were less than wholly successful in cleaning our own house because we yearned so much to be reunited with our distant cousins?'

'Could we ever forgive ourselves,' Balberith countered, 'if we were to sacrifice a once-in-a-lifetime chance to make contact with the greater Imperium? Besides...'

Balberith was interrupted by the vox operator. 'Messages incoming, sire,' he said to Melcarth. 'We've just come within range of General Fulbra's field-transmitter. He's within a few hours' march of what appears to be the enemy's main contingent but he's waiting for the aircraft before pressing forward any further. He's made camp for the night. Aerial reconnaissance after dawn tomorrow will give him a much better picture of the enemy's disposition than his motorcycle scouts – but it appears at present that he has an overwhelming superiority of arms and armour.'

'Excellent,' said Melcarth.

'What news is there of Operation Probe?' Balberith put in. 'Has he found out why it went wrong?'

The vox operator returned to his apparatus for a few minutes, while Melcarth waited impatiently.

'The investigators sent out from Odienne encountered substantial enemy forces,' the vox operator reported, eventually. 'They sent back word quickly enough that the first expedition had been attacked at a water-hole in the wasteland, apparently by means of foul sorcery, but that some trucks appeared to have got away. They were following the trail of the escapers when they too were attacked, and the only message they were able to transmit before contact was lost was garbled – something about men in brightly-coloured costumes riding coloured horses with horns. If we want to keep that supply-route, Odienne will have to be reinforced soon.'

There was a moment's silence after this speech ended, broken by Vorch. 'It now seems to me,' the major-general said, 'that General Fulbra made a serious tactical error in sending such a small force directly across the Amber Waste, and then splitting it twice more.'

Were Fulbra to be found in any way negligent, Vorch would be next in line to take his place as supreme commander, so Melcarth could not consider this an unbiased judgment.

'The real issue at stake,' Balberith was quick to point out, 'is that my psyker was obviously correct in his identification of the wasteland west of Odienne as a significant location. Whatever is going on there, it's something the cultists are desperate to hide. They're not reckless enough to deploy powerful magic against scouting parties unless there's something they don't want the scouting parties to find.'

'That would be a sound deduction if the scum we're facing were strategists like us,' Melcarth said, pensively, 'but they're slaves of ruin, as mad as they are evil. We can't be sure that their motives and tactics make sense.'

'Even if they are strategists,' Vorch put in, 'this might be a ploy – something to distract our attention from the main threat.'

'Or from the main opportunity,' Balberith added. 'If Gavalon knows that the Imperial Fleet is nearby, he might risk everything – even sacrifice everything – to prevent us from restoring contact with the greater Imperium. He must know that his vile kind might have a chance of survival, even if the battle against Fulbra is lost, provided that the forces of the greater Imperium cannot intervene.'

'We are the Imperium here,' Melcarth said, sternly. 'We must do everything humanly possible to win this war with our own resources, and then to scour this continent clean. This is our world, and we are the ones who must rule and defend it.'

Balberith obviously did not want to continue the argument. 'I must try to get some sleep,' he said. 'You were wise to let your bodyguards rest, excellency – we have been awake too long. I may not get another chance.'

It was a reasonable observation, but Melcarth was immediately suspicious. *Does he intend to try something?* he wondered. *He would be mad, given that he is so heavily outnumbered, but he is here for a reason, and not to commit suicide.*

'Perhaps we should take the opportunity to close our eyes now that night is falling,' was all he said aloud. 'We shall be more use to the general if we arrive refreshed.'

Vorch seemed grateful for the permission, and so did Sauldron – but Melcarth only pretended to relax. He let himself sag in his seat so that his head was resting sideways – a position from which he could open his eye very slightly and see not only Balberith but both of Balberith's companions.

Ajao and Alpalhao both seemed to have taken Balberith's advice – but the fact that Balberith had come forward to offer it seemed deeply suspicious to Melcarth.

He's going to let the psyker try something, Melcarth thought. Irrespective of the risk, the tech-priest's slipped the madman a dose of that vile drug while Balberith was distracting our attention. But why? Does he think that it might be easier to contact the Fleet from a high altitude?

Through lids that were not quite closed Melcarth studied Deir Ajao very carefully. He could not believe that the psyker was asleep, but if he were he was certainly dreaming, and none too comfortably... almost as uncomfortably as the guardsman sitting next to Melcarth, who was similarly stirring in his sleep and muttering incoherently under his breath.

There's something not right here, Melcarth thought. Something...

He lost the thread of the idea. In spite of himself, he drifted away from consciousness – and when he snapped back again, he knew that he had made a mistake. He knew that he had lost a substantial fraction of time – perhaps as much as three hours. Everything seemed to be much as it had been before, save that Vorch and Sauldron were in fact asleep, but he knew that time had elapsed, snatched away from him by some trick of...

Magic.

For a moment, the enormity of what he was thinking overwhelmed Melcarth's imagination. He had always been convinced that it was a bad idea to amplify the powers of the Imperium's mixed-breed psykers with the native drugs that the aborigine 'wise-dreamers' used, because he had always felt sure that they were not neutral instruments: that they were, in fact, polluted by the corrosive evil of the covens. Now he was utterly convinced. Whatever Balberith was trying to do, and whatever the psyker was trying to do, the result could only be a catastrophe... and the time that he had lost had brought him to the very brink of that catastrophe.

He stood up suddenly, although the effort made him dizzy. He began to shake the man beside him with one hand, and reached out with the other to bestir Major-General Vorch, but his eyes were still fixed on Balberith and the psyker. The psyker was still feigning sleep, and still seemingly victim to a nightmare, but Balberith's eyes were wide open.

'What have you done, Ragan?' Melcarth demanded. 'What have you done?'

Balberith didn't answer. The Chief Inquisitor merely smiled – but the smile said more than a thousand words. It said that Balberith had never intended to be a passenger on this expedition, submitting meekly to whatever fate Melcarth could prepare for him at their intended destination. It said that Balberith's desperation had been more extreme than Melcarth had imagined, perhaps more extreme than Melcarth could have imagined.

No sooner had that ominous smile spread to its full extent than the aircraft seemed to become horribly unsteady, lurching alarmingly to the left and downwards. Melcarth felt his stomach muscles clench defensively, and knew that if his own reflexes were alarmed those of his companions were likely to be terror-stricken – but most of his companions seemed to be fast asleep and dreaming.

'Moberg?' Melcarth said, anxiously.

'It's only turbulence, excellency,' the pilot said. 'We're leaving the Amber Waste and moving into more temperate country. It's just a downdraft. Nothing to be alar–'

His final word remained unspoken as the aircraft lurched again, more violently than before.

Vorch awoke and came to his feet immediately, his own voice fracturing as he squealed: 'What's happening?'

'Sit down!' Melcarth commanded – but Vorch was in no mood to take orders.

'I knew this damn monstrosity wasn't safe!' he howled. 'It's two hundred years old! We're going to crash!'

Techmaster Sauldron was awake too by now. He, at least, had the presence of mind to launch into a prayer rather than giving way to panic, but Melcarth knew that he had been driven to it by terror rather than any conviction that the prayer might be answered.

Melcarth thrust himself into the cockpit, into the narrow space behind the pilot's seat. The aircraft was still shuddering drunkenly, and its nose was dipping even lower.

'What is it, man?' he demanded of Moberg.

'I... don't know, sire,' was the only reply he got.

Melcarth realised, a little belatedly, that it didn't really matter whether the craft had fallen victim to some crazy plan of Balberith's, or to some enemy sorcerer's spell, or whether there had simply been a mechanical malfunction. The question at stake was whether Moberg could do anything about it.

All of a sudden, Melcarth saw the sense of the anxieties of which he had previously been so contemptuous. The aircraft was an original, forged by the real Adeptus Mechanicus, but it was also two hundred years old. Faith in Imperial manufacture was one thing, he realised, but faith in worldly maintenance was quite another. Sauldron's predecessors had doubtless been uncommonly careful to keep the machinery in good order as well as preserving the letter and form of all the necessary rituals, but two hundred years was a long time to keep the components of the craft free from corrosion and metal fatigue. Jal Moberg was a well-schooled pilot, but how good could a pilot really be when his experience of actual flying had been limited to a few fugitive hours, never straying more than a hundred miles from Sostenuto?

I have been too trusting, Melcarth thought, marvelling at the fact that even he could make such a mistake. I have been too reckless, too impulsive – and now I am in danger of losing everything, having come so very close to ruling an entire world. 'You have to land us safely,' he said, tautly, to Jal Moberg. 'Whatever it is, you have to set us safely down.'

'What the hell do you think I'm trying to do?' Moberg complained, with frank disrespect. 'I'm up here too, aren't I?'

The craft was still shaking, but its dive had not steepened. Melcarth stared out of the cockpit's narrow windows, trying to see what lay ahead of them. The night was well-advanced now, but the terrain seemed very confused from this height. There were very few lights in sight – nothing that might signal the presence of a substantial town, although there were one or two that might be the illuminated windows of isolated farmhouses. Melcarth knew, though, that the lands between the farms would be wild, thickly overgrown with all manner of native vegetation.

The native vegetation of Gulzacandra, Melcarth knew, was warped vegetation, subtly tainted for thousands or millions of years by the faint corruption that was in the sun-, moon- and starlight, and in the very air. He had never seen considerable expanses of it – the soil of Kalazendra had been almost entirely usurped by human crop-growers long before the Imperial cast-aways had arrived there – but he knew well enough what the vast shadow below the aircraft concealed.

'You have to find somewhere flat,' he told Moberg. 'Somewhere we can land.'

'I know that,' Moberg replied, through gritted teeth. 'But I can't see.'

'I've informed General Fulbra of our situation, excellency,' the vox operator said. His voice was more controlled, although the effort required to maintain its evenness was obvious.

From the cabin behind, Melcarth could hear shrieking. At first the thought it might be Vorch, having completely lost control, but he realised soon enough that it was Deir Ajao.

'*The great beast!*' Ajao was screaming. '*The daemon! The daemon! It's ripping the sky apart!*'

The starlit sky above them, to Melcarth's eye, seemed uncommonly quiet and certainly unripped – but the air through which the craft was passing seemed to be becoming increasingly disturbed. The plane was bouncing up and down, vibrating horribly. Moberg seemed to be fighting the controls – and losing.

Sauldron was shouting now, as if he were trying to drown Ajao out. He was saying something about parachutes, but Melcarth had no idea what a parachute was. Techmasters were custodians of all kinds of arcane notions whose meanings had unfortunately been lost.

'You can do this, Jal,' Melcarth said, throwing protocol to the winds. 'You can set us down safely. None of us is going to die.' Except that snake Balberith, and that crazy psyker, he added, silently. He was desperate enough now to begin a private prayer of his own, but he left Ragan Balberith out of it, even though he knew full well that Balberith might seem a more righteous man to the Divine Emperor's all-knowing gaze.

The dive had not grown steeper but still the aircraft was losing height. It was just possible now to see the ominous shadow-shapes of the tallest alien plants, whose awful profusion seemed infinite in the near-darkness.

'May the Emperor be with you, Jal,' Melcarth whispered, more sincerely than he would have thought possible an hour before. 'May he guide you safely to ground. You can do it, Jal. You're a pilot. You can do it!'

But while the dark well of the Chaos-tainted wasteland reached up, as if to swallow them, Orloc Melcarth was secretly convinced that the well-schooled but poorly practised pilot couldn't do it at all.

Damn you, Balberith, he thought. *You've destroyed us all!*

TWENTY-THREE

DATHAN HAD ONE more brief conversation with Gavalon before the sorcerer gave the order to attack. He had almost ceased to be afraid of Gavalon, even while the sorcerer was standing near to him, but the sorcerer's presence seemed, on this occasion, more intimidating than it had ever been before.

Although his banner remained furled, for the moment, his eyes gave the impression that they too could wither at a glance and the mutations of his flesh had made noticeable progress. He was more hideous than Dathan could ever have imagined, his skin a patchwork of leprous patches, tufts of fur and sprays of serpentine scales.

'Can you sense Sathorael's presence in the world?' Gavalon wanted to know. 'Do you have any idea where the daemon might be? I must obey the commands that I have been given, but they will lead us all to destruction if Sathorael does not add his power to ours.'

Dathan had been thinking of little else for several hours. He had tried to will himself into the kind of trance state that Hycilla had been in when Nimian had first made mental contact with her, but he had never had her talent and could not do it. There was a vague sensation that he had never experienced

245

before somewhere at the back of his brain, but every attempt
he had made to bring it into clearer mental focus had had the
opposite effect.

'I can't tell,' Dathan said. 'I wish I could, but I can't.'

Gavalon scowled, making his hideous face even more
appalling. Dathan quailed before the sorcerer's annoyance, but
Gavalon's eyes were not yet fixed on him. They seemed to be
searching for some further target, lost in infinity.

'Then we must find another way to work the oracle,' the sorcerer said. 'This may hurt, a little, but it will not last long and
you will be stronger thereafter. Come closer.'

The last thing Dathan wanted to do was step closer to the
sorcerer while he was in such an uncertain state, but he had no
alternative. He obeyed the order, trying not to tremble too
much.

Gavalon placed his ungainly hands on Dathan's shoulders.
He had done it before, but not both of them at once, and not
while Dathan was standing directly in front of him. This
time, Dathan knew, the sorcerer intended to look into him –
into his mind and into his soul – and he felt sure, as he studied those huge, unnatural and ill-matched eyes, that the
sorcerer's scrutiny would not leave his mind and soul
unchanged.

This might do worse than hurt me, he thought. Nevertheless,
it was by choice that he met Gavalon's horrid and inquisitive
stare with his own meek eyes, and by choice that he let the
champion of Chaos into his mind and soul.

In fifteen years, it had never occurred to Dathan to wonder
how like or unlike other minds his own might be. He had not
always been content to be himself, but he had always accepted
that he was what he was, and that the question of exactly what
he was – and how that compared with what other men were –
did not require to be raised, let alone contemplated at length.
Now, he suddenly felt utterly different.

Dathan understood, abruptly, that he was a very frail and
fragile thing, of a sort that might be banished from the core of
his own being, or twisted into something utterly different, on a
momentary whim of a more powerful creature. He understood
that Gavalon the Great could have destroyed something like
him with a bitter glance – not entirely without cost to himself
but at no great loss – and that the only reason Gavalon

tolerated his further existence in the world was that he might be useful, not for a lifetime, but perhaps for a day or two.

After that, he would be nothing, or less than nothing. He would be turned into a quantity that was not merely negligible or negative but strangely twisted: irrational at least, if not imaginary. And he was useful now not because of anything he could actually do of his own volition, but because of something written in his flesh in an arcane language that he could not read: something that merely used him, as if he were smoothed-over sand in which a casual sketch might be made, erasable by time, or the wind, or an equally unthinking process.

It did hurt, in more ways than one – but Gavalon had not lied to him. Although the after-effects of the sorcerer's stare left him gasping and retching when the demanding gaze finally shifted, Dathan knew that there was a perverse sense in which he was stronger. He had been close to death in any case – he already knew that – and he was by no means capable, as yet, of utter indifference to his fate, but he had now taken a step closer to an indifference that embraced damnation as well as death.

He had begun to see what the daemon meant when its Vessel had told him that it only mattered how a life might burn, and not for how long.

When Dathan looked up again, Gavalon's eyes were far less dreadful. The sorcerer seemed to be puzzled.

'What is it?' Dathan dared to ask. 'What did you learn?'

'I do not understand where Sathorael went, or why,' the sorcerer confessed. 'I do not know why the daemon would not come to me sooner, or why it wants me to attack the Imperium before it comes – but one thing is certain. Sathorael will come. My victory will be the victory of Change; my fulfilment, the fulfilment of the Great Metamorphosis.'

It was not a helpful answer, but Dathan was glad to have received it.

'Mount up,' Gavalon said to him, quietly. 'The time has come.' Then he repeated the order, a little more loudly, for the benefit of others. Without ever being raised to a shout, the whisper passed through the entire troop – not merely the horsemen, but the various contingents of infantry that had been drawn up to either side of them.

The sun's disc was already obscured by the western horizon. Dathan knew that the twilight would fade quickly. Two moons had already risen, and he judged by the rare steadiness of their light that the night-sky would be unusually still – certainly stiller than he had ever seen it, and perhaps stiller than it had ever been before.

'Well,' said Abdalkuri, when the two of them had mounted up and come into formation side-by-side. 'It will be a strange night in which to die, and a far stranger morn if either of us should live to see it. Are you ready?'

'Yes I am,' Dathan said. 'I did not think I would be, but I think I am. I am a man and a warrior, not a boy.'

'I have been more than a man for as long as I can remember,' the thrall-wizard said, bleakly, 'and cannot now remember that I ever was a boy, but I wish I were a little less ready than I am. I would wish you well, child-become-man, were I capable of such a wish.'

'And I would thank you, if you were,' Dathan answered solemnly, although he was not entirely sure what he meant by it.

Then the line of cavalry moved forward, all as one, although Dathan had not seen the signal given. This time, his mount was quick to change its paces, first to a trot, then a canter, and finally a gallop.

The gallop seemed to go on for an unconscionably long time as the gloom of dusk gathered and the stars came out in full force. They were steady, silent and proud. Dathan, still suffering the after-effects of Gavalon's inquisitive stare, thought that he had slipped out of time altogether, and although the massive hooves of his multicoloured mount were drumming thunderously upon the coarse and desiccated ground he felt as if he were almost floating, keeping closer company with the stars than with the earth.

He fetched his rifle from its lodging-place and held it up in his right hand, lifting it high above his head as if to display it to his companions – but they were going too fast now to pay any heed to him, and he could only catch fleeting glimpses of them as they levelled their lances and began to unfurl their banners.

He thought that the banners must be a wonderful sight to behold, even though the uncommonly bright and uncommonly white light of the stars could not do full justice to the riot of reds and purples, blues and pinks, golds and violets, but he could not bear witness to that glory himself while he was part of its headlong rush.

Then he saw the enemy, and understood how close to death he was.

The steady stars, which could not do justice to the flamboyance of his own side, were mere echoes of the blazing white lights that the enemy had now turned upon them – but the enemy's searchlights were not there to enhance appreciation of the banners' many colours; they were there to find targets.

Dathan had met the enemy before, and had subconsciously allowed those two tiny contingents to formulate and constrain his notion of what the battle would be like. Now he understood his error. The headlamps of the trucks by the pool had been mere candles compared with this array of searchlights, and the trucks themselves mere toys by comparison with the arms and armour drawn up before him now.

There were trucks there, to be sure – trucks enough, it seemed, to fill the horizon – but there were bigger machines too, and stranger ones. And there were guns. Even before they opened up, Dathan realised how many guns there must be, and what a barrage they might lay down upon a charging enemy.

This is absurd! he suddenly thought, as his heart lurched. We are men, mounted on horses, most of us bearing nothing but lances. They are the Imperium!

For the first time, he had an inkling of what the Imperium was, and what it meant, and why it was such a fearsome enemy even for powerful men like Gavalon, who had been more than men since they were infants, and who carried such awesome weapons as the withering eye banner and the horn of agony.

Then the guns began firing, all at once, and the thunder blasted his eardrums. The dazzle of the searchlights was increased by multitudinous flashes, and the air was ripped by the shock- and heat-waves of countless explosive blasts. It seemed impossible that any man might ride through that tempest unscathed, and Dathan had no doubt that a great many of his companions had been killed on the instant, but he did ride through it, and he continued riding even as the lights rushed upon him and the storm reached out to swallow him up entire.

The first time Dathan fired from the saddle the recoil nearly knocked him off the horse, but he swayed back and then swayed forward again, and he fired and he fired and he fired.

He could not pick out human targets in the wells of shadow behind and between the lights, but he fired regardless, recklessly assuming that the enemy were so many that even random shots might strike home.

He did not catch a glimpse of Abdalkuri's standard, but he knew where Abdalkuri was – where he must be, if that first frightful volley had not blown him apart – and he felt the backwash of the hellfire it unleashed. His eyes, dazzled as they were, took note of the colour that suddenly infected the surrounding blaze of white, and his deafened ears still had reactivity enough to perceive the avid crackling of the air and the tortured screaming of the weapon's victims.

For his own part, Dathan continued firing the rifle he had liberated from his enemies, first this way and then that, while his horse wheeled and changed tack. The animal was no longer galloping now that they had reached their destination, but it had not paused; it was prancing and leaping, and the rhythm of its hoofbeats was dance-like. It was a deceptive creature, but it had to move in order to distort the perceptions of its enemies. It could not stand still – and Dathan was glad of that, for while death was all around him he could not bear the thought of stillness.

To be still, in such an inferno as this, would be to wait for death, to invite death, to accept death. Dathan was not ready to do that, for his first purpose was to kill, and to make the cost of his eventual death higher than the enemy could stand to pay.

If Dathan had already slipped, subjectively, out of time, he now seemed to be slipping out of space as well. He had lost touch with any sense of place, and might have been anywhere in the vast confusion of the battle, although he could not possibly have penetrated deep into the enemy's lines. He was no longer sure whether he was tiny or vast, or whether the lights that formed an infinite cage around him were fireflies or suns. It was astonishingly easy to visualise himself, in his mind's secret cycloptic eye, as a winged giant soaring high above the battle, glorying in all that wondrous fire and fury, soaking up the souls of the dead as if they were intoxicating liquor, aflame with the heady alcohol of sacrifice.

It was astonishingly simple, now that the stars were standing still in the sky, for Dathan to forget the nothing that he had become, or the quantity not merely negative but strange, and see instead the not-self that was greater by far than he could ever have been: the not-self whose tiniest finger had more cleverness, when severed, than any human fool; the not-self that had only needed to lay its ear upon his shoulder to infect him with a corrosion that would eat his soul; the not-self that was still only part-way to the Great Metamorphosis, which had lain in embryo within the heart of the world, not for two hundred years but for two thousand, and now was grown into its mayfly firefly dragonfly maturity, to burn for just a moment but to burn so brightly, so very, very brightly...

He emptied his rifle and reloaded, and suddenly found the ability to see human figures within the shadows: human figures that could not see him, or even the coloured blur that hid him, and should not have been ready targets for a creature such as he.

He fired and shot a man in the mouth, blasting his jaw to shreds.

He fired again, and saw his bullet tear into a man's thigh, ploughing through the fat and flesh to rip the femoral artery apart.

He fired again, and saw his bullet ricochet from the plate of steel to strike a sniper in the very eye that he was pressing to his gunsight.

He fired again, and saw a man hurl away his laspistol in order to clutch his navel, as if by holding his intestines in he could stem the rapid ebb of his life-force.

He fired again, and saw...

He saw the shadow of incredible wings fall precipitously across the battlefield, and understood that Sathorael had indeed arrived, not to help Gavalon's army but to feed upon its reckless sacrifice, and to feed upon its fallen foes, and to feed and feed and feed...

And Dathan understood, then, what Gavalon had meant – although he certainly had not known it – when he had said that the one certain thing in a mist of confusion was that Sathorael would come and that Gavalon's victory would be the daemon's victory.

Then his horse was shot from under him, and he fell – far more roughly this time than he had during the skirmish at the farmhouse. He fell into the shadow of those awful wings, into a darkness that almost let him see again, into air so deftly muffled that he could almost hear again.

He would have liked to lie still for a moment or two, to collect himself, but he did not have time to pause. There were lesser shadows all around him: men who would certainly kill him if he could not kill them first. He had to use his rifle as a mere staff to parry a sword-thrust, and then as a brute club in order to strike back, and he knew that the fight would go on and on and on until he fell, and that he would likely never rise again.

He wondered what had become of Gavalon, and all the magic the sorcerer had hoarded so carefully for this evil day: the withering eye banner, the horn of agony, and so much more.

He parried another sword-thrust, then struck back again. He felt the force of an impact, and knew that he must have hurt someone, but the killing power he had wielded with such brief efficiency was gone now; he was alone and earthbound, outnumbered and overwhelmed. There were too many enemies, and he had too little strength.

He lashed out again, and again, hitting nothing.

Then he was struck in the back, and he fell.

For a moment he remained kneeling, his arms reflexively outstretched as if they were wings that might somehow lift him up into the sky and out of the pit of death – but they were not, and he pitched forward.

His face descended into a pool of mud. Dathan knew that the mud was compounded out of soil and blood, not soil and water, because there had been no rain hereabouts for many days.

I wonder what Hycilla is doing now, he thought. *I pray to every god there is that she is safe.*

TWENTY-FOUR

HYCILLA CREPT CAREFULLY towards the wreckage of the flying machine.

It had come down at such a shallow angle that it might have been able to land safely if the ground had been better. Whoever had been in control – or not quite out of control – had managed to steer it away from the densest clumps of plants, but almost as soon as its landing-wheels had touched the ground their tyres had burst. One of them was torn away, dropping the left-hand wing on to the baked earth. That had sent the body of the machine into a spin, until the dragging wing had shattered. After that, the body had begun to fracture and come apart, different sections skidding in three different directions.

At first, Hycilla could not believe that anyone inside the machine could possibly have survived the crash – but when the roar of the impact finally died down she heard a few muffled voices. Some were merely coughing – the crash had stirred up a great deal of dust – but others were complaining or calling for help.

She did not doubt that Sathorael had told her to watch the sky for a purpose, and that this was it, but considering that the

253

daemon had been so unexpectedly loquacious while she was perched on its shoulder, she found it surprising that it had given her no indication of what she ought to do when the watched-for event occurred.

The machine was obviously Imperial in origin, so the men injured in the crash were presumably soldiers. It seemed highly improbable, therefore, that she had been posted here to render assistance. Had she, then, been set here to make sure that the crash survivors did not survive for long?

That seemed the likeliest possibility, for the moment – and it certainly accorded with her own inclinations, so she held her blade at the ready while she moved toward the first of the broken sections.

This had been the mid-section of the aircraft's body, from which both the front and rear end had been separated. She could only hear one man's voice emanating from within it, and the voice was calling intermittently for help – intermittently because it had to break off repeatedly in fits of racking coughs.

As she peered round the ragged edge of the hull, whose alloy had been sheared as easily as poorly-woven cloth, she saw not one man but two, both spreadeagled on what had been the side of the compartment but was now its floor. Neither man was dead, but neither seemed able to rise; they had broken limbs or badly bruised backs.

Hycilla moved quickly, hardly pausing to note that only one of the two wore military uniform, the other wearing what might have been a priestly robe. She slit their throats swiftly and easily, hoping that anyone who might be listening would take no warning from the abrupt cessation of the imploring voice.

She remained within the tubular section while she attempted to figure out where the other survivors might be. Logically, the controls of the flying machine should have been located at the front, with at least one man in charge of them. When the craft had begun its descent to the ground, others might well have run forward to see what was happening. They might easily have been crushed, but some might have survived. It seemed to Hycilla it would be more sensible to go to the rear section first.

Having made this decision, she was quick to act upon it.

Keeping her head down, she scampered across the bare ground towards the tail-section of the machine's hull, dodging several pieces of jagged wreckage. She had heard a voice coming from this section before entering the other, but it had fallen silent now, so she approached very cautiously.

Because the open end was turned away from the brightest moon the interior was shadowed, and there was a considerable amount of dust swirling about the interior. Even so, it only took her a few seconds to decide that there was only one living person within: the second body, of a burly man in what was presumably civilian dress, lay so crookedly that it was obvious that the man's spine had been snapped.

The living man, on the other hand, seemed relatively unhurt. He must have been bruised, but his limbs were sound enough to have let him scramble to his companion's side and kneel over him.

Hycilla made every effort to be quiet, but it seemed that she must have made a sound of some sort, for the survivor turned to look at her while she was still five or six paces away. He was unarmed, and if she had moved quickly enough she might have been able to stab him in the throat or breast before he had time to take any effective defensive action – but something made her hesitate.

She did not know what it was that had made her pause until she saw the expression flaring up in his eyes: a kind of recognition, not merely of what she was but actually of who she was – not merely of who she had recently become but of who she had always been.

The man was a wise-dreamer. He had seen her before, in his dreams.

And she, she now realised, had seen him. The fact had slipped her mind, but the sight of him brought it back.

Hycilla had not suspected until now that the Imperium might have wise-dreamers of its own, and even though the suspicion surfaced now, she could not quite believe it. She had been told that the Kalazendrans hated everything that the people of Gulzacandra were, especially their traffic with the worlds beyond the world.

Her first assumption, therefore, was that this must be a captive: a prisoner, transported against his will.

Was this, she wondered, why Sathorael had sent her here? Was she here to accomplish a rescue rather than a massacre?

'Who are you?' she asked, in a voice as low as it was taut.

Instead of replying, the man stared at her with increasing horror. 'Witch!' he eventually said, in a voice far tenser than her own. 'Hellspawn! Monster!'

Hycilla saw immediately that her deductions must have been at fault. Obviously, the Imperium did have wise-dreamers, who probably considered their Gulzacandran counterparts to be evil – but there was still an atom of doubt. He had recognised her, and she had recognised him. They had seen one another in their dreams, and their fates were bound together. Surely he understood that, just as she did. Or did he?

Hycilla knew how much she had changed since she had first been touched by Sathorael's vessel, and she knew that the villagers among whom she had grown up would have been horrified to see her so grotesquely mutated. They too might have called her monster – though not witch or hellspawn, which were presumably Kalazendran terms of abuse. For this reason, she continued to hesitate over what to do next. It still seemed to her that this dreamer – this particular dreamer, above all others – might be useful to Sathorael's cause, and therefore worth preserving.

In any case, he was unarmed, and he had made no move to retrieve the weapon carried by the man with the broken back.

'What's your name?' she asked. There was power in names, she knew. If he would only tell her that, she thought that she might be able to exert some form of control over him, as a sorcerer to a thrall-wizard. Perhaps that was the manner in which their fates were entwined.

But the other had no intention of telling her – and she had lingered too long.

She felt something cold and metallic against the back of her neck. A voice that was far too close to her ear hissed; 'Drop the knife!'

She thought about whirling around, trying to knock away the hand holding the gun and plunging the knife into her adversary's guts, but she knew that he would certainly blast her head off if she did not do as she was told.

She dropped the knife, but she remained tense and alert, ready to pick it up again if the opportunity presented itself.

She turned to face the man who had trapped her. Like the wise-dreamer and his companion he was not wearing military uniform. Nor was the second man who stood behind him, mopping blood from a cut to the side of his head.

The man who was covering her with a pistol was dressed in what seemed to her an unusually austere style, which should have indicated that he was a man of discipline and a true champion of order. There was, however, a glint in his eye that Hycilla immediately recognised as a flicker of kindred spirit. Somehow, presumably in spite of himself, this man had been touched, if not by Sathorael then something similar. There had been a chink in his spiritual armour: some kind of obsession that had created space for the wiles of her own god to work upon him like a worm in the bud.

She knew, though, that this would not make him any less dangerous. Quite the opposite, in fact.

'Shoot it!' the bleeding man urged. 'I don't know what it is, but for the Emperor's sake, Ragan, kill the thing! My guards are all dead or disabled – Moberg and the vox operator too. We can't take any risks. Kill it!'

'It's a she,' the man with the pistol replied, pensively. 'She's a mutant, but she's young in spite of her height – hardly more than a girl.'

'Whatever it is, it's dangerous. If you and your crazy psyker didn't bring the plane down, she probably did. Kill it!'

'We don't know that she's hostile,' the man named Ragan countered, with the ghost of an odd smile playing about his lips. 'Even if she is, she might be useful. Can you talk, hellspawn? Do you understand my language.'

'Of course I can talk,' Hycilla replied contemptuously. 'What other language would I use?'

'Is Governor Melcarth right?' the man with the pistol had the temerity to ask. 'Did you bring the aircraft down? Should I shoot you, before you blast us all with sorcery?'

Hycilla was briefly tempted to claim credit for the crash, but she decided that the wiser course was to try to appear harmless in spite of her alarming appearance. The man with the pistol would have been more than a foot taller than her two days ago, but she had an equal advantage now. She was slender, of course, but so was he. He was hesitating for a reason. He really did think she might be useful to him. Was it possible, given

that she hadn't caused the flying-machine to crash, that he
might have done so, as his friend appeared to suspect? If so,
was he too a pawn – presumably an unsuspecting one – of
Sathorael?

'I came to see what I could do to help,' she said, hoping that
they had not seen what she had done to the wounded men in
the mid-section of the hull.

'Nonsense,' said the man addressed as governor. 'You can see
that she's a mutant, Ragan. It's an inquisitor's job to purge the
world of such as her.'

At least, Hycilla thought, he had stopped referring to her as
'it'.

'Why did you ask his name?' the inquisitor asked.

'She's a witch,' repeated the man who was now behind her.
'The governor's right, sir. She's dangerous. A psyker, far more
powerful than me.'

'A psyker,' echoed the man with the gun, as if that were the
heart of the matter. 'That's what I thought.' Hycilla realised
that the man who held the pistol was no less afraid of her, and
no less horrified by her, than his two dread-stricken companions – perhaps even more so – but that something else was
getting in the way of his fear.

That something was not courage, if her judgment of such
alien creatures could be trusted, but desperation.

'Shoot her,' the governor said, again. 'Why won't you shoot
her?'

'Look at the sky, Orloc Melcarth,' the inquisitor said. 'Two
moons are up and bright as they've ever been, but the stars are
out in all their profusion. Tell me, excellency: what do you
see?'

The man to whom he had spoken did not respond, but the
other man hurried past her into the open air, where he threw
back his head in order to look up towards the zenith.

'They're standing still!' the Imperial dreamer said. 'The
warpstorm has died! I can do it now – I'm sure I can. I can get
through to the Fleet!'

'I dare say that you could,' the man with the pistol said. 'We
must certainly try – and perhaps they will reply to your cry for
help. I cannot help but wonder, though, if they would pay
more attention, and take the matter more seriously, if there
were more than one silent voice to be heard.'

'Don't be ridiculous, Ragan,' the governor said. 'That thing isn't going to help you! She's a mutant, more likely to summon sorcerers and daemons.'

'Who will not come, given that there is a more immediate enemy to face in Fulbra. Of course she will not help, sire – not willingly. But how much control does she have over her own powers, when she is in the grip of the drug? And how much control could she keep, if she were overdosed? Psykers acting in concert usually become confused, even if they are twin souls so far as their loyalty to the Inquisition and the Emperor is concerned – but even confusion may be productive. If we can get a cry for help to the Fleet, all well and good – but if we can let loose a cry of rage and agony too, might we not be better able to communicate the urgency of our situation?'

'You're mad,' said Orloc Melcarth.

Hycilla had never expected to find herself in agreement with an Imperial governor, but she thought it a sound judgment.

'No,' said the Imperial dreamer. 'Please sir, no! You don't understand. It would destroy me. Sir, she'd tear my mind apart as easily as the plane was torn. You can't. Kill her, sir. Kill her, please!'

Hycilla suddenly realised, almost as if she were belatedly remembering a trivial fact that had somehow slipped her mind, exactly why Sathorael had set her to watch the sky, and exactly what she was now supposed to do.

The man the governor called Ragan had now relaxed sufficiently to let her dodge any bullet he fired, had she cared to do so, and she was certain that she could have picked up the knife and gutted him before he fired a second time. Inquisitor or not, the man had not the slightest idea what he was dealing with. The terror and the horror that should have told him what to do had been snared in a net of confusion. She, not he, was in control here – or, more precisely, it was Sathorael that was in command, operating through the flesh that bore his stigmata.

'He's right,' Hycilla said, mildly. 'If you set us to dream together. I won't need to know his name to enter into his nightmare and tear him apart. It will not matter whether his dying scream reaches the spaceships or not; they will not come. But if you let me walk away, you have a chance to live out your lives – in Kalazendra, if you can find a way to return.'

'We can get back easily enough,' the governor was quick to say. 'Fulbra's forces cannot be far away, and when the battle is joined in earnest they will win it in a matter of hours. We can still return as part of a victorious army, albeit more slowly than I had planned. Shoot her, Ragan. Just shoot her.'

'Please,' said the dreamer, weakly.

'All you've ever wanted, Orloc Melcarth,' said the man named Ragan, 'was to be governor of Sigmatus. You've never cared how well the war against Chaos went, and you'd rather the Fleet never made contact again than share your power with those who are worthy to wield it. But the hour of the Imperium is come – not the faded shadow that is your Imperium, but the true Imperium: the Imperium of All Mankind. That greater Imperium shall know what is happening here, and what has happened during these last two hundred years. The masters of the ships will know what has been done and what has not, and what must now be done, and what must not. I was never more certain of myself than I am now. All praise to the Emperor Magnificent!'

This speech, although oddly stirring in its way, had given Orloc Melcarth time to make plans of his own. He knelt down as if to inspect the leather of his boots, but he had a holster strapped to his leg and there was a gun in the holster. The pistol was not nearly as large as the one the inquisitor was holding, but at this close range the difference hardly mattered.

As Melcarth drew his stubgun, though, the man he had called Ragan swivelled and shot him.

There was plenty of time then for Hycilla to pick up her knife, and she could have killed the dreamer as well as the inquisitor, but she made no move at all.

Orloc Melcarth had time to look down, in utter astonishment, at the hole in his lower abdomen before the momentum of the impact bowled him over. He crumpled slowly to a sitting position, and looked for a moment or two as if he might hold on to that position long enough to fire his own weapon – but the wound, though by no means instantly mortal, was too painful.

Tiny as it was, the weight of the stubgun dragged his hand down, and the governor sagged on to his side. Some reflex made him draw his knees up towards his chest, so that he lay in a quasi-foetal position. His left hand clutched at his wound as if to stem the flow of blood, while the right remained out-stretched, the little gun still stubbornly clenched in its fist.

'Now,' said the inquisitor, doubtless imagining that he actually possessed the authority that he had just exerted. 'Let's see what can be done about rectifying the disastrous situation of this sad, mad and tainted world. Even if it proves to be an invitation to Exterminatus, at least we shall have done our duty to the Emperor, and to Mankind!'

TWENTY-FIVE

DATHAN FOUND, somewhat to his surprise, that he was no longer face down in the mud. He thought for a moment or two that he must have drowned.

Once, when he had been very small, his mother had insisted on placing him neck-deep in a tub of water in order to make him clean. An entire tub of water was a rare thing in the village, where it rarely rained enough even in the winter to keep the water-tower and the collecting-butts half-full, but such was the waywardness of the weather that every fifth or sixth summer would bring a very violent storm, when a whole month's rain would fall in a matter of hours, creating a temporary glut. Although such storms could be disastrous for the crops in the field – and even more so if the lightning associated with a storm happened to strike a thatched roof or the water-tower – the village had its age-old customs for dealing with the liquid surplus, one of which was 'bathing the children'.

At first, the young Dathan had deeply resented the discomfort of this ritual, but when he had tired of crying he began to find that the experience had its interesting features. Because he was so very small and the tub so capacious, he could actually lift his feet from the bottom for a moment or

two while flailing his arms to keep his head above the surface
– and when he did that, he seemed to become weightless. It
was a peculiarly pleasant sensation, but he had been tempted
to over-indulgence, and on one occasion he had missed his
footing when he had attempted to regain a standing position.
His feet had slipped, his head had gone under the water, and
he had completely lost his bearings. He had flailed his arms
more desperately, but instead of bringing his head back to the
surface the hectic movements had actually seemed to hold him
under – and when he opened his mouth to scream it was
instantly filled with soapy, scummy water.

His mother had pulled him out, of course, and had held him
upside-down until he coughed the water out of his lungs – and
when the next opportunity to bathe the children came around
he was so big that he could hardly fit in the tub at all – but
there had been an instant in between his fall and his salvation
when time had seemed to stop and his apparent weightlessness
had been translated into something more profound: a buoy-
ancy that was of the soul as well as of the body. When his
mother had told him afterwards that he had nearly drowned,
he had immediately connected the unfamiliar word with that
moment out of time and that all-encompassing sensation of
being buoyant and adrift, not merely in a bathtub but within
the great sea of existence.

Now, having let the mud of blood and soil into his unwary
mouth, and having sucked it down into his avid lungs in spite
of his every reflex, Dathan felt that he was drowning again –
but now that he was a man and not an infant, he knew that
drowning was a kind of dying.

He was not afraid of dying. He had already fallen once on
a field of battle, thinking himself dead, so he knew – or
thought he knew – that dying was a great deal easier than
some people claimed. But his first experience of not-quite-
drowning and his more recent experience of not-quite-dying
turned out to be more relevant to his present circumstances
than he imagined. He figured out after ten or twenty seconds
had elapsed that he was neither drowned nor dead, because
something else had stepped into the role his mother had
played when he was a very little child, and had plucked him
out of the suffocating mud and shaken the stifling liquid
from his lungs.

That something held him tightly clasped within an enormous claw, whose talons were curled around his shoulders and his thighs. It was as if he were a mouse snatched from the ground by the claw of an owl or an eagle – but not as prey.

Not, at any rate, as any ordinary prey.

Breathing was a great deal more painful than drowning, for a while, just as living was a great deal more painful than any kind of dying he had yet come near to, but he was grateful nevertheless. In any case, he had never expected to be able to fly, and the fact that he was flying now seemed to be one more privilege to add to his life, one more blessing to count before the axe of destiny finally fell upon his scrawny neck.

He could not see what it was that had snatched him up from the battlefield, because its starshadow was too vast, but he knew what it was, and the only question it occurred to him to ask was: *Why?*

Why not? was the only answer he received – or thought he had received. He had no talent, and could not connect his consciousness to Sathorael, but he had been touched by the daemon, and there was a secret part of him that was connected more securely than he could imagine.

Without Gavalon to channel the daemon's nascent intelligence into speech there was no way Dathan could hear Sathorael's words, but the part of its sensations that was beyond and beneath words overflowed directly into that part of Dathan's inner being which was compounded out of the basest instincts and emotions.

With this advantage, Dathan knew well enough where he was and what he was becoming, even though the conscious part of himself – the part that he thought of as his essential self – remained distinct: a mere spectator.

That spectator watched the battle from on high. Although he was lost in shadow he could still see much of what was happening on the ground, albeit fitfully. He saw it by the light of those searchlights that still shone, the lightning-flashes of Imperial weapons, and the eerie illumination that had activated the banners and standards that were his own side's most powerful weapons. He saw much that he had been unable to see while he rode to the battle on his coloured steed. He saw the stolen trucks used as battering-rams, smashing suicidally into Imperial tanks. He saw cloaked assassins worming their

way through the dark ranks of the Imperial vehicles, evading
the attention of the massed troops. He saw the scavengers moving in to seize the weapons dropped by Imperial victims of
brutal magic, then carrying them back to supply Gavalon's
reserves. He saw the surviving horses using their horns as
weapons to lacerate the faces of enemy soldiers or to disem-
bowel fallen men.

He saw confusion: a vast and hectic vortex of violence and
hatred, which would have been pure unadulterated chaos had
it not been for the discipline and order of the Imperial army –
which now seemed not merely a possessor of machines but a
machine in its own right: a megamachine of wheels within
wheels within wheels, whose invisible cogs and levers were the
produce of organization and the strict divisions of labour and
authority.

The magicians against which that megamachine was arrayed
were infinitely more colourful, but from the height at which
Dathan was now able to observe they were like maggots
swarming in a carcase, randomly and self-obsessively, moved
by a blind determination to survive: mere atoms of greed.

Now, Dathan was able to see Gavalon the Great for what he
really was, at the full extension of a sorcerer's capabilities. He
could see the blasts of the withering eye as they shrivelled the
flesh on the bones of Gavalon's attackers, sweeping in majestic
arcs across one forefront after another. He could see the effects
of the horn of agony too – although he could not hear the note
it sounded – far more clearly than he had had the opportunity
to do at the farmhouse. He saw the way in which it reduced
men to pain-racked puppets, usurping control of the nerves
which transmitted signals from their brains to their limbs and
flooding those nerves with blasts of pure hell.

With weapons like these at his disposal, Gavalon might have
been reckoned invincible, but Dathan saw that the matter was
not so simple. The great majority of men, he felt sure, would
have been petrified by horror and fear at the prospect of facing
such devices. Whole armies, thus threatened, might have turned
tail and run in panic – but the Imperial army, no matter how
many generations removed it was from its authentic original,
was the inheritor of traditions that informed and convinced its
individual soldiers that this kind of hectic destruction must be
opposed at all costs, checked and obliterated.

The Imperial soldiers were well trained, but there was something more than mere training in their refusal to be intimidated and their refusal to be panic-stricken. These were men who knew what kind of weakness panic was, and who were determined not to give in to it. Men died in droves trying to reach Gavalon, who seemed for a while to be untouchable by any fire they dispatched in his direction, but those who came behind the men who died did not stop trying, and they did not stop firing.

Dathan understood, while he watched the Imperial forces lay siege to Gavalon's position, what the sorcerer had meant – or, to be more precise, what the daemon using Gavalon's voice had meant – when it had said that the Imperial soldiers were the true heroes. They were heroes because they could maintain discipline even in the face of the forces of Chaos; they were heroes because they would go to any lengths to hold back those forces. They did not choose to do it, because they did not choose; they did what they did out of necessity. And in the end, their necessity was enough to put a stay to all Gavalon's wit and trickery and raw formless power.

Dathan saw Gavalon hit by bullets, again and again. He saw the sorcerer racing this way and that, hacking with his massive blade, using all his powers of deception to avoid reprisal. Dathan could not count the number of men Gavalon killed by means of his various alloys of magic and brute strength, but he could and did measure the phases of Gavalon's gradual exhaustion as the sorcerer used up his resources...

And his enemies kept coming at him.

Dathan realised, eventually, that the reason he could see all this so clearly was that the daemon was interested – because their partly-magical perceptions were shared even though their thoughts and conscious responses were not. The daemon was interested in Gavalon – but the daemon did not intend to help him. The daemon and its maker had always intended that Gavalon should die. Sathorael and its maker did not intend that the defender of Gulzacandra should die easily, but it had no interest at all in the possibility of his salvation.

The only person Sathorael had plucked from the battlefield was Dathan. It had not done so, Dathan presumed, in order to save him, but merely as a matter of reflex: a casual result of their chance connection. Doubtless there had been something

of that in the way his mother had snatched him from the bathtub so many years before, but his mother had acted in order to
save him, because his mother loved him.

For Sathorael, love was not an issue.

Dathan had been close enough to Gavalon and Gavalon's
thrall-wizards, albeit briefly, to have a good idea of what
Gavalon had expected of the daemon for whose advent he had
so carefully prepared the way. Gavalon had expected the daemon to deliver Gulzacandra from the Imperial threat and to
save the worshippers of Gulzacandra's god from annihilation
by the empire. Gavalon had expected help in his own struggle,
his own war against adversity. Perhaps he had always known
that the god whose favour he sought was not a motherly god –
not a loving god, perhaps not even an honest god – but he had
believed nevertheless that he was entitled to ask for help in his
hour of need, and that he had some right to expect that help
would come.

Dathan understood now that this expectation had been an
utter illusion. Sathorael was here about its own business. It had
come to cast its vast shadow over the battlefield not to render
assistance but to obtain it. The slaughter on the ground was
helping to empower Sathorael, and to aid its further metamorphosis, far more effectively than all the bizarre foodstuffs that
Nimian had consumed.

From the viewpoint of Sathorael – the viewpoint Dathan
now shared, although he had never asked for any such favour
– all the deaths that were suffered down below were sacrifices,
and it did not matter in the least within the scheme of which
Sathorael was a part, which side the dying men were on.

'Sacrifices will come,' Nimian had said, while he was still more
vessel than possessor. 'Sacrifices will come. I will bring ships.'

Gavalon had wanted to be Gavalon the Great. He had dared
to aspire to a kind of daemonhood himself. He had chosen to
become a champion of Chaos – but all that the god he worshipped had wanted of him was sacrifice: the sacrifice of his
own flesh; and of his own life; and, in the process, the sacrifice
of thousands of other lives.

That Gavalon's god had proved to be a treacherous god
would not have surprised Gavalon, so it did not surprise
Dathan – but what did surprise Dathan was the sheer hunger
of Gavalon's god for fervent destruction.

This was what Sathorael was, he realised: an instrument of destruction. Any distinction it made between its own creator's worshippers and their implacable enemies was purely tactical. Gavalon's god had such a powerful appetite for destruction that even worlds were of merely tactical significance. Gavalon's god had a hunger that would not be appeased even if the whole universe were to be consumed.

And the only thing that stood in the way of that consumption was the Imperium of Mankind.

Dathan saw Gavalon die, and understood the meaning of his death. He saw and understood it because the daemon of which he had unwittingly become a part was interested in both the fact and the significance of Gavalon's death – not because that particular death was of any unique importance, but merely because the daemon, in becoming incarnate in the material world, had acquired the ability to be interested, and had been delighted to occupy some tiny fraction of itself in the exercise of that ability.

In dying, Gavalon the Great became merely Gavalon the Hideous. With all his sorcerous power exhausted, the bullets embedded in his transformed flesh began to take their toll. He must have been bleeding internally and externally from a dozen different wounds, but still he kept himself erect and still he slashed to the right and left with his awesome blade. Now, though, his thrusts were cleaving empty air, unable to find targets that had somehow usurped his talent for evasion.

His horrible eyes were aflame with rage and hate, but there was no longer anything withering in his gaze. If anything, the opposite was true: the sight of his monstrous face, now agonized in its own turn, gave heart to his attackers and made them all the more determined to shoot or cut him down.

In the end, it actually came to cutting. The Imperial soldier who killed him had run out of ammunition for his rifle, but that had not forced him to fall back or quail before apparently superior strength – and the cry of triumph that he let out as he slammed his own blade deep into Gavalon's breast, skewering the sorcerer's heart, told everyone within earshot that he knew exactly what he had done.

But still the shadow of the daemon lay upon them both, accounting the sacrifices that might make the soldier's little victory worse than irrelevant.

Dathan had already reconciled himself, so far as he could, to the knowledge that he would be unlikely to survive the clash of Imperial and Gulzacandran forces. His mother was probably dead already, his village effectively destroyed, his life comprehensively blighted. He owed his own continued survival entirely to the whim of fate that had introduced him to the Vessel of Sathorael. He knew that Hycilla had been right to judge that every moment of life they enjoyed after their capture at the pool was profit. Now, though, he began to doubt that reconciliation and recalculate that profit.

If the world is only what I see, Dathan thought, then it dies with me. I need not care about what happens to it when I am gone. If it has already lost everything I care about, that is all the more reason for disregarding its fate. Even Hycilla is no longer the person I once loved; she is a part of the daemon now, more intimately bound to it than I. But a human being is not merely his own life. He is the product of his family, his village, his world and the entire history of the human race. He is heir to all that legacy, and if he is to count himself truly human he must accept a responsibility to all the heirs that are yet to come. If a man is really a man, he cannot take the view that it does not matter what happens after he is dead. He cannot cease to care, merely because he is doomed.

I am within the daemon and the daemon is within me, and I would be dead were that not the case, but if I am a man my concern is mankind, not the daemon – and I am a man. I am not an infant in danger of drowning, nor a boy excluded from the secrets of his people. I am a man. All the men who are dying down below are heirs to the heritage that made me a man, and their sacrifice is my sacrifice, no matter what unconscious impulse made the shadow snatch me into itself. The daemon's hunger is not my hunger, and never should be any man's hunger, because it is a hunger intent on devouring humanity itself, which every man who is a man is bound to resist.

It was a fine speech, Dathan thought, even if it had to be issued silently, with not a human ear to hear it. But what did it matter, given that it could have no consequence or sequel?

What was it but so much wasted thought, so much wasted anguish?

What, given his paradoxical nature and situation, could he possibly do?

TWENTY-SIX

EVEN THOUGH IT would be a grave tactical mistake for the enemy to attack the positions he had chosen to hold until Melcarth's aircraft arrived, Ierius Fulbra had taken every rational precaution against the possibility of being taken by surprise. When the enemy did come at him, his men were adequately fore-warned and they took up their positions without delay. As the enemy force swept forward, therefore, they ran into a veritable hurricane of gunfire: gunfire far more devastating than any-thing the members of Gavalon's ragged army could ever have imagined, let alone experienced.

At first, when Fulbra took up his own position in the belly of a tall-turreted tank, he assumed that the charge was a grave tac-tical mistake, born of a failure of imagination. He was able to observe the attack through a periscope, which he had only to move through thirty degrees in either direction in order to obtain a panoramic scan of the entire front. By the searchlights of his first defensive line of armoured vehicles he could see the effects that his initial barrages had on the enemy, and found them most satisfactory.

The enemy's absurd cavalry proved a surprisingly mercurial target, riding through the blizzard of shells with astonishing luck, but the infantrymen following in their wake absorbed a full measure of shock and shrapnel. They dropped like flies, and the first two hundred yards of ground they crossed after the guns opened up cost them casualties so heavy that Fulbra almost came to believe that victory would be his within minutes. It was not until his line of sight was blocked by his own heavy metal, as the remaining attackers came close enough to be eclipsed by the ranks of armour drawn up before them like a wall, that the balance of the battle began to tilt.

The three radio operators manning the vox apparatus at the front of the narrow cabin were silent to begin with, having neither new orders to transmit nor urgent reports to receive, but as soon as the pre-set defensive plan was stretched to its limit reports of casualties began to trickle in – and it did not take long for the trickle to become a flood.

Fulbra's two colonels-in-chief had a rough-and-ready sketch-map of the Imperial positions. It had been made purely as a matter of routine, but the fact that the attack had begun was ample proof that the insistence of routine was a very valuable asset.

Fulbra tapped the map three times, saying: 'Their cavalry seems to be split into three main contingents. These will be the stress-points if their luck continues to hold. Strengthen the second lines at all three positions, and be sure that we can plug the gaps twice over if any develop.'

Hamera and Diambor had no experience of large-scale defensive manoeuvres; all of their relatively vast experience was of attacks, sieges and chases, with nothing more by way of reprisal than hasty and ineffective ambushes. They had, however, carried out many exercises, in the field as well as on the gaming table, and they knew how to put their learning into practice. The vox operators began chattering away to the field commanders, concentrating the Imperium's forces in support of the positions that seemed most vulnerable. It was now that information began to come back about casualties inflicted by enemy sorcery.

'They have some kind of fire-generating apparatus,' Diambor's operator said, 'and there's something that can dry the flesh on a man's bones, sucking all the moisture and life out of him.'

'How are they generating the effects?' Fulbra wanted to know.

'It's something to do with illuminated flags,' Hamera's man said. 'Maybe the flags are just signals or markers, but they seem to be closely associated with the sources of destruction.'

'Order the snipers to take out the banner-carriers,' Hamera said, instantly. 'Get flame-throwers trained on the banners themselves. I've seen such devices used in Zendamora, though never more than one at a time. They're limited in range.'

Fulbra had been briefed on the banners, not merely by his own men and those who had gone into the field before them but by Ragan Balberith's drug-assisted psykers. He knew that the banners could be countered – but the last message that had been received from the party sent out to search for relics of Operation Probe had not mentioned banners at all.

'They have other devices,' he was quick to say. 'Don't let the gunners concentrate too closely – we need to respond to the unexpected as and when it arises.'

'The heaviest casualties seem to be in the centre, here,' said Diambor's radio man.

Fulbra returned immediately to his periscope, directing it to the place Diambor had indicated. For a moment, he caught sight of two banners himself, one carrying an image of a great taloned hand with an eye in its palm, the other bearing only the image of a vast and furious eye. The brightly-embroidered cloth of each banner shone with an eerie light, and each of the eyes seemed to be emitting a ray sharper than any searchlight.

The lenses of the periscope, over which many prayers had been said while they were being polished, should have protected Fulbra from the effects of such magic, given that the glimpse he caught was so brief, but he felt a strange shockwave move through his mind, threatening the fabric of his being with laceration or breakage. Discipline came to his aid, though: discipline and faith in the necessity of his cause. Fulbra could see well enough that the soldiers who looked directly upon the banner – especially those who were closest to it – were quite unable to put up the same resistance.

Some of them stood stock still, as if immobilised by horror, while others collapsed gibbering, as if in the grip of irresistible terror. None, the general thought, were actually struck dead, but he was not certain that very many would recover sufficient composure to take up their weapons again – and while the harlequinade of magical cavalry still swirled around them like smoke, the helpless victims were being cut and slashed.

The gunfire in that sector of the front was the most intense of all, and it seemed impossible that the banners were still raised, or that the horned horses should still be prancing around them, but Fulbra could see that their ranks were now being swelled by those infantrymen who had contrived to make their way across the field of death. Only a few had guns, and most of the guns they had were common rifles, but even those who only had blades were close enough to do considerable damage now, and they were moving between and behind the armoured vehicles that formed the first line of the Imperial defence.

'Strengthen the centre,' Fulbra ordered. 'They can't possibly have men enough to be trying to outflank us, but keep reserves to either side in case they have held anything back.'

Afterwards he had to step away from the instrument, slightly dizzied by his first encounter with Gulzacandran magic. Like Hamera, he had served in Zendamora and had encountered magic there, but only in small-scale encounters, and never with so much at stake.

'Have you looked at the sky, sir?' Diambor asked.

The one thing the periscope could not look at was the sky, and Fulbra was tempted to issue an irritably abrupt reply – but Diambor was not Hamera, and if Diambor wanted to draw his attention to something, there had to be a reason. The hatch at the top of the turret had been thrown back in order to let a little fresh air into the belly of the machine, and there was a circular patch of sky visible through it. No more than a dozen stars were visible to the naked eye, but a dozen were enough to let Fulbra know what Diambor meant.

The stars were not moving, and their light was white.

'Balberith was right,' he murmured. 'The warpstorm has abated – but for how long?'

'That may be why they attacked, sir,' Diambor said. 'They must dread the stillness of the sky as much as we dread its turmoil. Even if they know nothing of warpstorms they must know that the stars stood still when the Imperium first came to Kalazendra. To them, it must be a terrible ill omen.'

At that moment, the dozen stars were abruptly eclipsed. They were obscured for several seconds. It was impossible to judge the shape and size of the eclipsing object from this narrow vantage, but the duration of the event convinced Fulbra that the entity must be very large – and could not, therefore, be the aircraft whose arrival he had expected, and which seemed to have been delayed some time after making contact. But if it was not an aircraft, what could it possibly be?

'There's something above the battlefield,' he said to his vox operator. 'Ask the men in the rearmost position to try to catch a glimpse of it, and tell me what it looks like.'

The vox operator passed on the order, and waited. 'They can't tell, sir,' he reported back, eventually. 'Some think it's shaped like a bird, others like a flying spider – but it's damn big. Even if it's only a few hundred feet up, it's bigger than anything that could possibly get airborne using wings. If it's further away – some of the men think it's out among the stars, although that seems implausible.'

'Could it be a ship?' Fulbra demanded, urgently. 'Could it be an Imperial starship?' He knew, even as he asked, that it couldn't possibly be a ship like those whose empty shells were still proudly displayed in Sostenuto. It would have to be a ship of a very different kind. But who here on Sigmatus, knew how many kinds of starships there were within the Imperial Fleet?

Any elation to be obtained from that thought, Fulbra realised, had to be countered with the doubt that sprung from another: who, on Sigmatus knew how many kinds of starships there were in fleets other than the Imperial one? The lore handed down through the last two centuries spoke of the eldar, and of tyranid Hive Fleets, but no man now alive on Sigmatus had any clear idea as to what those names might actually signify, or how many similar names might have been forgotten.

At any rate, there had to be a possibility that the shadow was the shadow of an enemy.

'Is it firing down at us?' Fulbra wanted to know. 'Or is its presence having any magical effect?' The possibility occurred to him then that it might be the vastest and most powerful banner of them all, needing only the glare of Imperial searchlights to expose its awful malignity.

'Not so far as they can tell, sir,' the vox operator reported. 'It's just circling the battlefield... as if it were interested... except that...'

'Except that what?'

'The tech-priests have reported that their psykers are getting very agitated.'

'Of course they are – we're in the middle of the biggest battle against the heretic forces of Chaos this world has ever seen. More magic has been unleashed against us in the past half hour than the previous half-century. I'm surprised they aren't having fits.'

'Oh, they are, sir – but the tech-priests can't make any sense of what they're trying to say. No sense at all. They think something's wrong.'

'They're tech-priests!' Hamera broke in excitedly. 'Of course they think something's wrong. It is wrong – but we're winning. All praise to the Emperor Magnificent, we're *winning!*'

Fulbra returned to the periscope, while Diambor offered sober support to Hamera's judgment. There was no sign of either of the two banners with the eye motifs, nor of the exotic cavalry that had enjoyed such astonishing good fortune in reaching its first target. He could still see enemies standing, but each was alone and each was surrounded. One by one, they were being cut down.

They were fighting back, of course – he could still see his own soldiers falling back here and there, some wounded and some dead – but no ground was being given up, and for every man that fell another pressed forward. The line had held, and was solid again. The enemy forces had wasted their entire strength in a whirlwind attack, but the whirlwind had blown itself out, and there was nothing left of the gale now but a few near-exhausted gusts.

'It's almost over, sir,' Diambor said. 'They committed suicide.'

From Hamera it would have been a figure of speech, but Fulbra knew that Diambor meant it literally. The attack had been suicidal: to charge against so much armour, so carefully arrayed, had been an act of total folly. It would have made far more sense, tactically and strategically, for the enemy to fight a campaign of attrition, tempting fragmentary contingents of the Imperial forces on to ground of their choosing, striking swiftly and fading away into the alien forests.

Had Gavalon the allegedly Great elected to fight a guerilla war, he might have extended the business of conquest and suppression for years. In the end, of course, he could not have won – once supply-routes were established, the Imperial strike force could be reinforced, and increased by degrees to impregnability – but he could have made things far more difficult.

Instead, he had committed suicide.

Why?

For a moment or two, Fulbra wondered whether it even made sense to ask questions like why when dealing with sorcerers, but that was too easy a dismissal. There must be a sense, however twisted, in which what Gavalon had done had been worthwhile. Why had he acted so recklessly – almost as if there were no tomorrow to worry about?

Fulbra had no alternative but to return to the hypothesis that it was because the stars had stood still in the sky. Whatever the shape above the battlefield might be, the way was clear for the Imperial Fleet to come to the aid of the little Imperium of Sigmatus – and if the way was clear, Balberith's psyker must have got through.

How delighted the Imperial commander will be, when he finds out what I have done this day, Fulbra thought. That vain fool Melcarth fancies himself the future ruler of a world, but when the Imperium returns, they will not be interested in him. I shall most surely be the one to reap the best rewards of recontact. Even Balberith has only shown his loyalty in petty ways, but I have won a victory of exactly the kind that the Imperium loves best. I might yet have the opportunity to serve as a general on a stage of stars!

The sound of gunfire was beginning to die away now, fading gradually into silence.

'Suicide,' Diambor repeated. 'What a debt we owe them, in spite of all the casualties we have sustained. We might have lost three or five times as many men had they made us work harder for their annihilation.'

'Their foolishness has always been our greatest strength,' Hamera observed. 'They do not have our discipline, our faith, or our purity of purpose.'

'Is the shadow still visible in the sky?' Fulbra asked his vox operator. He was looking up at the circular patch of frail starlight, but he knew that the sky was a much vaster expanse than that.

'No, sir,' the other replied. 'It seems to have gone.'

'Good,' said Fulbra.

Immediately, the dozen stars visible through the hatchway were eclipsed again. Fulbra could hardly help thinking that the shadow had returned, or that the observers who had declared it gone must be fools, but he had military reflexes, which were already responding to his danger before he was consciously aware of it.

As the Gulzacandran assassin dropped through the turret, poised to land on his slippered feet, with his blade ready to strike out at any target within arm's reach, Fulbra's right hand snatched the pistol from the holster at his belt.

As the assassin landed, Fulbra fired.

The man-shaped shadow crumpled and fell, as if it were indeed no more than a wisp of darkness strayed from the infinite dark beyond the sun. The knife clattered harmlessly to the floor.

I am a hero! Fulbra thought.

There was, of course, a sense in which he had been a hero before, to whom the credit for an epoch-making victory was due, but there was something about a direct kill so cleanly executed which had a special heroism of its own – something, he felt sure, that even men who commanded starships and fought whole worlds would understand.

'Well,' he said, with pretentious calmness, 'we have plenty of work to do before dawn. We'd better make ready to move on as soon as that damned aircraft arrives, before the stink of the dead makes our positions unbearable. Soon, the real business of extermination will begin.'

TWENTY-SEVEN

WHEN THE BATTLE was effectively over and the forces of Gulzacandra had been all but annihilated, the shadow that had lain upon the battlefield passed on, with Dathan still clutched in its claw. Sathorael's wings were now so vast that a single beat was all that was necessary to send its huge form soaring high into the sky. Dathan felt himself growing colder. The air that he sucked into his lungs seemed as weak and unfulfilling as it was sharp and chilly – but the stars grew no larger; they were too far away.

No sooner had it soared away from the battlefield than Sathorael wheeled about, and began a long gliding descent.

Dathan could hear the rush of air in the daemon's huge feathered wings, and knew that his sensation of weightlessness was mere illusion. Sathorael was far from weightless; its mass was tremendous. Had it fallen from the zenith it had briefly attained it would have hit the ground like a meteor, blasting an enormous crater. While it had wings, though, it was a graceful creature, and Dathan's eyes had adjusted well enough to the starlight to let him see the gleam of its brazen plumage and the glint of its yellow eyes.

Sathorael might have been beautiful but for its huge bald head and its monstrous beak, but the gleam in its eye made it seem limitlessly cruel and infinitely arrogant. There was nothing of its Vessel left now; Nimian had been utterly devoured, body and soul alike.

The dive became steeper for a little while. There were no lights below them now to indicate the lie of the land, so it seemed to Dathan that they were diving into a vast well of darkness – but as Sathorael's course began to level out again Dathan caught a glimpse of a light on the horizon, faint and flickering but undoubtedly man-made.

It was a group of fires, and as Sathorael homed in on it, seeming now to be skimming the ground, Dathan was able to count them. There were five in number.

Dathan realised belatedly that Sathorael intended to set him down, in order that he might carry out some small task on the daemon's behalf. He could not flatter himself with the illusion that this was the reason why Sathorael had snatched him up from the battlefield. The daemon certainly did not need him in order to complete this part of its plan, but since it had him, it condescended to use him, for reasons of simplicity and aesthetic elegance.

You love her, the daemon whispered, without needing to pronounce the words aloud. *I give her to you, for a moment. She is yours to save and savour.*

But the daemon knew perfectly well that Dathan understood that Hycilla was no longer the person he had loved, and that whatever he did he would do for other reasons.

Dathan knew this because it was only the subconscious part of his mind that had fused with the daemon, leaving the conscious part free. Because of this, he had the power to disobey if he were so minded. He was still the commander of his own limbs, still the master of his own movements – but he had no intention of asserting his individuality now. Whether or not she was still the person he had loved, Hycilla was Hycilla. If she needed him, he had to go to her. If she needed to be saved, and he had been granted the chance, then he would do it.

He was even prepared to be grateful for the opportunity, knowing that Sathorael could have done as much itself, with casual and contemptuous ease.

I am still a man, Dathan reminded himself. I am still
Dathan, son of Ora, pupil of Pater Saltana and friend of
Hycilla. I am a man and I have my pride.

He did not even stumble when Sathorael set him down,
although he had to run full tilt for a dozen strides before he
could begin to slow himself down. He managed to avoid running into a thorny thicket, and had the presence of mind to
skirt it very carefully, using its bulk to shield him from the
makeshift arena marked out by the five fires.

When he was able to compose himself and creep closer, he
obtained further cover from the wreckage of some kind of big
machine, which was scattered all around.

There were four people within the pentagram described by
the fires, but one of them was badly hurt. He had a gunshot
wound in his belly.

Dathan had never seen any kind of mortal wound until the
skirmish at the farmhouse, but he had been told blood-curdling stories which alleged that belly-wounds were the worst
of all, because they caused a slow and agonising death. The
wounded man seemed to be of much the same opinion;
although he had been propped up in a sitting position, with
his back to a squat cactus, he did not seem to be taking any
notice of his three companions. His eyes were closed, and he
seemed utterly lost in the depths of his own predicament.
Dathan could see that the white-faced man did not want to
die, and was utterly determined to cling to what life he had
left but Dathan understood – perhaps because Sathorael
understood – that he knew full well how dear the cost of his
obstinacy would be.

It was hardly surprising that the wounded man had not
noticed the shadow of Sathorael or felt the wind of its wings
upon his fevered face, but Dathan was astonished that the
other two men did not seem to understand what had passed
them by.

One of these other two men was clearly the orchestrator of
whatever ritual was being enacted. He was tall and spare, and
he carried a gun in a manner which suggested that he was
more than ready to use it. He was pacing back and forth impatiently, keeping a close watch on all three of his companions.
He must have looked up when Sathorael passed, and must
have felt the downdraft of the mighty wings, but he had

already put puzzlement behind him in order to focus on the private matter in hand: the matter of his own intention, his own ambition and his own obsession.

It did not seem to Dathan that Hycilla and the third man required watching any more than the wounded man did. They too were sitting down, back to back, apparently quite meekly. They did not appear to be injured, but they did seem weak and distant. Their arms hung loosely by their sides, and their eyes were half-closed and inattentive. If they had been drugged – and Dathan was certain that they had, presumably because Sathorael was certain – they had consented to their condition. Both of them had been aware of Sathorael's passage, but neither had reacted visibly or audibly, one out of paralysing terror and one out of satisfied relief.

They too were waiting – and Dathan had hardly taken up his final hiding place, some twelve or fifteen paces away, than the first signs that their waiting was nearly at an end became obvious.

The five fires had been burning steadily, their flames cosily yellow, but now they began to change colour. The one which remained yellow became more sulphurous and vivid; the others glowed red, blue, green and violet. Their flames crackled and danced, as if their dry fuel were being vigorously stirred and excited by invisible bellows.

The night had been tolerably warm, but a sudden cold descended like a blanket; it was almost as if the entire scene had been plucked up into that thinner air which Sathorael had briefly tasted before bringing Dathan down to this peculiar rendezvous. There was a sound of shattering glass, although Dathan could not see what it was that had been broken.

'Now!' said the man with the gun. 'The moment is at hand at last. Share her power, Deir. Draw it into you. The dose I gave her will numb her brain and kill her within the hour, but while she lives her power is yours for the stealing. Take it! Use it! Bend the power of evil to the cause of good! The Fleet is there; you have only to cry out to be heard. Cry out, Deir! Send forth a shout that will be heard across the light-years. Bring the ships, Deir! Bring them at all possible speed. Tell them that we have dire need of their power of destruction: that there is corruption here that needs rooting out.'

As he finished this speech, the tall man knelt down by the man with the belly-wound, and struck him sharply across the face. The blow was a slap intended to force the other to pay attention, but the stricken man only screwed his eyes more tightly shut. The man with the gun struck him again, just as insistently.

'Don't be afraid, Orloc,' the tall man hissed. 'Everything will come out right. Everything. Fulbra will win his battle, and Deir Ajao will summon the Fleet to capitalise on his victory. The Chief Inquisitor of Sigmatus will never again have to run the risk of being struck down by an assassin's bullet. All is well – praise be to the Emperor Magnificent! Everything is in place, including that lump of lead shot in your intestines.

'I know why you suddenly decided to come here, Orloc. You came to claim the victory for yourself, to establish yourself in the eyes of all your anxious followers as a man of power, a man of authority, a man of destiny. And I know why you gave me a place on the aircraft: because you intended to have me killed, far from my friends in Kalazendra. And you intended that Deir should die too, to make sure that you would never have to surrender the power you had won to any higher authority. But everything has come out right. Everything.

'You may close your eyes, Orloc Melcarth, if you will, but you cannot shut out the knowledge of what is happening here. Can you not feel it in the air? Can you not feel the edge: the power to cleave through the awful density of space and time? Can you not hear the voice of the infant world screaming for its protective parent? Can you not see, even within the darkness of your own mind, the ruination of all your dreams and ambitions – all your corrupted dreams and ambitions? I know that you can, Orloc. I know that you can.'

While the tall man was raving in this manner Dathan fixed his own eyes on the two wise-dreamers – for he did not need the subtle influence of Sathorael's intelligence to know that the man with whom Hycilla sat back to back must be one of the Imperium's wise-dreamers.

Hycilla still seemed stupefied, but quite relaxed. The man, by contrast, was as straight as a ramrod now, and his arms were no longer hanging loose by his sides. Instead, they were possessed by what must have been a painful rigidity – and the rack-intensified tautness that had taken possession of his body was obviously internal as well as external, because his nose had begun to bleed and his face was aglow with a light so violet as almost to constitute a new colour normally invisible to human eyes. His eyes, which glowed brightest of all, had begun to curdle; they were all white now, having lost every vestige of iris and pupil. Dathan had to suppose that the Imperial dreamer – Deir Ajao, as the ranting man had named him – must have gone blind, and would never see again.

When the blind dreamer began to mutter, the tall man immediately broke off his taunting and scuttled back to place his ear close to the other man's lips.

'The way is clear,' the blind man was saying. 'The way is clear and the need is great. Here is a world that cries out for redemption. Here is a world that requires reunion with the community of mankind. Here is a world in need of Imperial weaponry and Imperial discipline. Here is a world of souls in need of salvation, a world of souls which yearn to serve the Emperor in every way possible and in every way conceivable, a world of souls which pleads for succour in the face of a terrible threat, a world which cries mayday, mayday, mayday, mayd...'

Presumably, the world for which Deir Ajao dared to speak would have continued crying out the same unfamiliar word for some time longer had not something invisible clutched at the wise-dreamer's throat, choking back the syllables and causing his eyes to bulge out of his head. Foam flecked the corners of his mouth.

The tall man put the stubgun to Hycilla's head, saying: 'Don't fight him, witch! He's about the Emperor's business. Let him leech your power, and don't even try to subvert his cry for help, or I'll blow your brains out now. There's nothing you can do. The message is through, and the ships will come. There's nothing you can do.'

Dathan knew that the tall man was badly mistaken. He knew what was really happening here. He had seen more of the game than anyone else – more even than Sathorael, for all that Sathorael had the power to eavesdrop on the thoughts of any man or woman in the world.

Dathan had seen more because he had lived, and Sathorael had not. Dathan had not had the power of thought thrust upon him, as a brief and fascinating gift; he had grown into thought as its natural heir. No matter what powers of intelligence Sathorael might have, the daemon had nothing to guide them but momentary whim and casual reflex. Dathan knew how ignorant he was by comparison with this Imperial madman, and how limited his powers of reasoning were, but he was a man, and he understood the enduring reality of mind – of hope, of endurance, of desire, of commitment, of fury, of tranquillity, of self-sustenance and self-fulfilment – far better than any daemon ever could.

For this reason, it was Dathan, not the sharer in his more primitive being, who understood the way in which the game was now being played – and what was at stake.

Dathan also understood that the tall man was very likely to carry out his threat, and blow Hycilla's brains out, before she could collect herself and make use of the gift that he had unwittingly offered her. Dathan was prepared to assume that Hycilla might no longer be human enough to be destroyed by the calculated overdose of the drug that she had been fed, but he knew that she was still human enough to be killed by a bullet in the brain.

Dathan had no weapon, but he had the advantage of surprise.

When Dathan sprinted forward, the man with the gun neither saw nor heard him. Surprisingly, the wounded man did – indeed, he opened his eyes as if on cue, focusing them immediately on the running figure – but Orloc Melcarth never even considered the possibility of calling out a warning to the ranting man. He was perfectly content to watch.

Dathan cannoned into the tall man with all the momentum he could muster, meeting him shoulder to shoulder. His opponent was far taller than he, and considerably heavier in spite of his leanness but the crucial factor was that his opponent was unready and off-balance. The impact sent him sprawling, and the stubgun flew out of his hand, skidding away in the loose dust; it did not come to halt until it was five or six yards away, nearer to the wounded man's extended foot than his own convulsively clenching fist.

What the tall man should have done was to dive for the gun immediately, while Dathan was still reeling from the after-effects of the impact. He could not have reached it unchallenged, but he had by far the longer reach and he might have held Dathan at bay for a few precious seconds while he picked up the weapon. What he did instead, betrayed by his reflexes or his bad judgment, was to hurl himself at Dathan, confident that a man as strong as he could master and over-power any mere boy.

The ranting man could not help but think of Dathan as a mere boy, in spite of all that had happened in the last two days. He could not know what strength Dathan now had – but Dathan only needed one more backward step and a half-turn to balance himself again and make himself ready for a war of fists and feet. When the tall man tried to smash him down with a blow to the head he ducked under it, and he rammed his own fist into the other man's midriff with all the power that wrath could give him.

Dathan did not have mass enough in his arm and shoulder to put his opponent down, but he certainly hurt him and put him direly ill at ease. Although the tall man promptly lashed out again, his blow was wild and easily avoided – but when Dathan launched his foot into the tall man's groin the kick was perfectly measured.

Dathan had regretted two missed opportunities to replace his crude boots with loot of Imperial quality, but he did not regret in the least that it was the village cobbler's work which ripped the tall man's frame with pure agony, and laid him helpless on the ground. Nor did he regret that it was the same poor man's craftsmanship that stamped its crude authority on the tall man's face, breaking his nose and bruis-ing his eyes.

There was plenty of time after that for Dathan to walk to the place where the gun had fallen and pick it up.

The wounded man was still watching him.

'Who are you?' Dathan asked the wounded man.

'I'm Orloc Melcarth,' the other replied, his voice exceedingly ragged. 'Planetary Governor. Emperor of this world.' It must have cost him a tremendous effort to add the final phrase, but he did it. He did it with the air of a man who was determined to say the words aloud, even if they were the last words he ever spoke – and even if they were utterly, absurdly false.

'You gave the orders, then,' Dathan said, colourlessly. 'You ordered the destruction of the village.'

He could read the other man's mind, perhaps because Sathorael could, and he understood immediately that the answer was both 'yes' and 'no'.

No, Orloc Melcarth had never given a direct order to Ierius Fulbra to the effect that he should send men across the Amber Waste to attack the village he called Odienne. If any one person were ultimately responsible for that decision, the blame might more obviously be attached to Ragan Balberith the ranting man or Deir Ajao the unwise-dreamer, both of whom were here, available to justice.

But yes, Orloc Melcarth was indeed the governor of this tiny fragment of the Imperium of Mankind that had gone astray, without knowing or realising quite how far it had gone astray, and there was a sense in which all the orders in the world were Orloc Melcarth's orders to give or withhold, to sanction or revoke.

Dathan shot Orloc Melcarth between the eyes, knowing as he did it that it might be reckoned as a mercy killing by anyone but Orloc Melcarth himself.

Then he shot Deir Ajao in the head, knowing as he did it that the blind man might well have reckoned it a mercy killing, had he been in any condition to reckon anything at all.

Then he went to shoot the tall man.

'It's too late,' the tall man mumbled, although the effort of speaking seemed to cost him as much as the similar effort had cost Melcarth. 'The message got through, and the stars are standing still in the sky. The ships are coming, and they'll scour... this planet clean of your kind, heretic filth. You've lost... and I've won.'

He did not ask Dathan's name, because he did not care who Dathan was. He did not care about the name of anyone in Gulzacandra; to him, all men other than his own narrow kind were mere vermin, who had no need of names. He had a very different opinion as to the necessity of his own name, which was Ragan Balberith.

The shot that killed Ragan Balberith, when Dathan fired it, was as clean as the others: an efficient and perfunctory completion of the business of murder. First, however, he took the time to tell him: 'It's a trick, you poor fool. It always was a trick. The trap was laid long before you were born, before

your ancestors first set foot in Kalazendra. Now it's set, and
you have set it. The daemon is waiting, your ships are
doomed, and you did it, Ragan Balberith. You did it all.'

He wished that the other had the power to read his mind,
so that he might know beyond a shadow of a doubt that it
was all true, but the ranting man was as deaf to his thoughts
as to his name.

Finally, Dathan went to help Hycilla. That, after all, was
what he had come to do.

TWENTY-EIGHT

To begin with, when the wise-dream unfolded like a sun-loving flower in the furnace of her inner being, Hycilla concentrated on making herself seem small.

She knew, of course, that she was lending Ragan Balberith's not-very-wise-dreamer the power he needed to blast his message across space to the Imperial Fleet, but she did not want to run the risk that the psykers receiving the message might realise that its sender was not in control. She knew that they might be able to detect the influence of the native drug with which his master had dosed him, but she dared to hope that the fact might work to her advantage in helping to obscure the real peculiarity of Deir Ajao's cry for help.

So she had to make herself seem small. She had grown as large in her inner being as she had in the flesh since the touch of Sathorael had infected her with greatness, but she still had the power to seem small, and the skill to use it.

While Ajao did manage to establish a telepathic link with the Fleet's psykers, therefore, Hycilla made a cunning effort to remain perfectly passive, allowing the awareness she shared to flow through her without response. That was not easy, for much of what she learned during her brief communion was

291

startling, but she did it – and it was the human part of her, rather than the daemonic part, that had provided the necessary practice. The human part of her had always known how to make herself seem small. Although she had been an apprentice wise-dreamer, she had been a girl for far longer.

In the games she had played as a child, the boys had always made the decisions, and the rules. She had learned to accept those decisions, and those rules, and to work within them invisibly, to her own ends. Subtlety had been second nature to her long before she had begun to dream in a particular way, long before her initiation had begun into what Pater Saltana had called the Wisdom of the Dreamers. The daemon part of her could never have attained such subtlety as that, even though it was as intrinsically deceptive as well as intrinsically destructive. It was the human in her that was able to let Deir Ajao claim and accept full credit for the contact he made with the Imperial Fleet. And it was the human in her that marvelled at what she learned while she remained passive, burning no less hot for burning so very meekly.

Hycilla had long known, as a matter of mere fact, that the Imperium had arrived on her world in spaceships, and that those ships had been part of a Fleet maintained by a great star-spanning empire, but until she was party to Deir Ajao's communication with other ships of that same Fleet she had not had the slightest idea of the implications behind the fact.

She had always imagined the ships of the Imperium crossing space in much the same way that she had imagined wooden ships crossing the ocean that separated Gulzacandra from Kalazendra, but now she realised that the analogy was a bad one. In much the same way that the flying machine that had brought Ragan Balberith and Deir Ajao to her had simply hopped over the ocean through the empty air – which had no apparent means of supporting any machine – so the ships of the Imperial Fleet were capable of hopping outside space itself, into a timeless dimension where distance was immaterial. It seemed even less likely that such a dimension could support human-made machines than that the empty air could support the thing that had crashed, but it could and it did.

Ordinary humans, Hycilla realised, could not guide ships through the strange wilderness outside space. Only mutants touched by the wilderness could do that, and in order to do it they needed a beacon lit and sustained by an army of people like herself: what she had always called wise-dreamers, although the Imperium called them psykers. But the Navigators who steered the starships of the Imperium and the psykers who maintained the Astronomican always had to operate in opposition to the innate tendencies of the timeless dimension they called 'the warp'. The warp was afflicted by dangerous storms, which sometimes disturbed the interface between the dimensions and spilled their energies into space, as did the one that caused the stars to swim in the sky.

The warp was also inhabited by its own native entities: minds quite like – and yet quite unlike – human minds in their possession of intelligence, imagination and purpose. Some such mind, she realised, was the god of Gulzacandra: the god of Gavalon the Great and the creator of Sathorael. Sathorael, she realised, was like the storm that stirred the stars: an irruption of the warp into the space that framed her world and her life, immensely powerful but inherently unstable, only capable of maintaining its fragile integrity and purpose for a very short time.

Transmitting telepathic messages through the warp, Hycilla understood, was a difficult business – as difficult, in its own way, as steering ships through it. Briefly united with Deir Ajao, she understood the near-impossibility of what Ragan Balberith had been trying to do. The astropaths of the real Imperium, she realised, had to undergo many years of rigorous training – far more rigorous, she supposed, than the training she would have undergone as a wise-dreamer – and had then to bind their souls to the Emperor of Mankind, who had once been human but had now passed beyond mere mortality to a higher state of being.

As a wise-dreamer, she too would ultimately have bound herself in time to another power, either to a sorcerer like Gavalon or – if she were especially privileged – directly to the god that Gavalon had served, but that process had been dramatically shortened by the arrival of Sathorael. She understood, however, that there was a significant difference between her own soulbinding and that of the Emperor's instruments.

The Emperor of Mankind was unique because the Emperor of Mankind was a champion of Order in a universe of Chaos, the sole potent force interrupting and delaying the inexorable processes of universal decay.

Although Ragan Balberith had thought of himself as an authentic inquisitor and his associate priests as genuinely learned men, and moreover had fervently desired that his psykers might become true astropaths, two hundred years of isolation by the warpstorm had made it impossible to complete Deir Ajao's training, let alone bind his soul to that of the Emperor. Deir Ajao was a flawed instrument, who had needed the amplification of his powers by native drugs to allow him to catch the merest glimpses of Imperial ships in his dreams. He could never have made himself heard by the Fleet's astropaths by that means alone, because the drug was too wayward, too fundamentally chaotic – but Deir Ajao did not know that.

Nor did Ragan Balberith.

Nor, it seemed, did the astropaths who received his cry for help.

The only way that Deir Ajao had been able to get a message through to the Imperial Fleet was to borrow the power of someone whose soul was very firmly bound – but not necessarily to the Emperor. Even now, Ragan Balberith thought that he had found and provided that last advantage, but he was quite wrong. Even Gavalon the Great's part had been very minor. What was happening now was the culmination of a game whose first moves had been made centuries before.

This was its final flourish, its key deception. And the deception, it seemed, had worked. The ships were coming. They were responding to Ragan Balberith's plea.

Or were they?

Deir Ajao's link was to the astropaths of the Fleet, not to the captains of the individual ships or the ultimate commander. Hycilla saw the situation as the Imperial psykers saw it – but they too were essentially passive, mere instruments of communication.

Perhaps the ships were coming to lend material assistance to Kalazendra's cause: to refresh the echo of the Imperium that persisted here in spite of all adversity, and to welcome it back into the greater Imperial fold. And perhaps not.

Perhaps their commander could not tolerate the least risk of being cut off as his luckless predecessors had been, and thought those predecessors such fools that their descendants could not be worth saving. Perhaps their priests and ministers had decided that whatever fragment of Imperial force and purpose remained on the world was already too degenerate to be worth the effort of redemption.

Perhaps, in fact, the ships were coming to scour the planet clean of life of any kind.

Sathorael, Hycilla realised, would not care either way. The only thing that mattered to the daemon was that the ships should come, because the daemon's one overriding purpose was to be a destroyer of Imperial ships.

The daemon would not be here – 'here' meaning not merely the world but also the universe of space and time – for more than a moment, and it did not care at all what became of the world, or of the entire universe of space and time. It was interested in such matters, to be sure, even fascinated by them, but its interest was a mere aesthetic whim, whose ends would be as well served by annihilation as by preservation, and perhaps all the better served, given that Sathorael itself had been made for annihilation and not for preservation.

What fate, Hycilla wondered, had the god of Gulzacandra planned for her world? Had the god even bothered to figure the world into any further calculations he – or it – might have made?

She did not know.

No matter how tightly her soul was bound, she did not know.

And that was why, when Dathan shot Deir Ajao in the head, abruptly cutting her line of communication to the Imperial Fleet, Hycilla did not know whether to rejoice or mourn. She felt the heat of Dathan's anger – and also felt, in spite of its lesser intensity, the residual warmth of his love – but she did not know whether to be grateful for his furious arrival or not. She knew, when Dathan had completed his methodical vengeance, that when he came to help her he was also acting, as a true hero had to act, on behalf of Gulzacandra, and on behalf of the world of which Gulzacandra was a tiny fragment. But she did not know whether he had wrought salvation or disaster. Had she been able to speak coherently, she would not have known what to say to him. Had she had time to tell him the story of what she had learned, she would not have known whether to tell it as epic, tragedy or farce.

She kept silent, in the end, because she did not want to scream, but she felt utterly and terribly alone with the burden of her new knowledge, and with the margin of ignorance that still remained.

Bound as she was to Sathorael the Destroyer, she could not help but share its purpose and its destiny, but there was enough of the human left in Hycilla to wonder what would happen after that purpose had been fulfilled and that destiny conclusively met – and not merely to wonder, but to *care*.

TWENTY-NINE

WHEN DATHAN TURNED back to Hycilla she was still sitting bolt upright, back-to-back with the equally rigid corpse of Deir Ajao. He went to stand in front of her, but she did not seem to be capable of reacting to his presence. Although her eyes still had vivid green irises and pinpoint pupils he was anxious that they might be as sightless as Ajao's. He knelt down and took both her hands in his, hoping that the contact would reassure her.

The actual effect was the opposite of what he had intended. Instead of reassuring Hycilla, the contact immediately unsettled him, and the disturbance was profound.

He had been moving like an automaton while he shot the three representatives of the Imperium, his mind seemingly clear and his thoughts seemingly in perfect order – but that had been a brief illusion. The moment he touched Hycilla's mutating flesh the strength of his connection to the daemon became obvious again. It was still a matter of feeling and not of intellect, but the raw power of aroused emotion made the authority of his conscious reason seem very weak indeed.

Had the flood of emotion been entirely his own Dathan might soon have regained a measure of equilibrium, but he and Hycilla were too intimately involved with Sathorael for his feelings to be self-contained. His most elementary impulses and appetites merged with hers, and its, and became confused – and the dream in which Hycilla was lost burst into his mind like a cataract.

Dathan knew that his body was still on the surface of his world, released by the claw in which Sathorael had previously borne him up into the sky, but the dream he shared with Hycilla and the daemon took some less tangible part of him far higher than before.

Sathorael was moving upwards at an astonishing speed. Dathan saw the world whose surface he inhabited become tiny, contracting into a miniscule half-disc no bigger than the discs that its moons displayed as they careered through the night sky.

He knew that it was the shadow of night that obscured the remainder of the circle. He knew, too, that he was somewhere in that shadowed part, hidden from his own supernatural sight.

He saw the sun fade into a mere star and fall into a background that had thousands – perhaps hundreds of thousands – more stars in it than he had ever been able to see from the surface of his own world.

Dathan had never imagined that the sky could be so glorious, or so full of sublime light.

For a moment, the image was clear, but then it began to blur and smear. The austere whiteness of the pinpoint stars was stained with colour, and their light flowed and merged – in exactly the same manner, he thought, that his inner being and Hycilla's had flowed and merged.

He and she and it, Dathan felt, should have been distinct points of intelligence and enlightenment, clear and white, but they were not. They had become something very different: something blurred and tinted, smeared and unsteady... and the cause of that was exactly the same as the cause of the stars' uncertainty.

Two dimensions of reality, which should have been distinct, were overlapping and interfering with one another...

And the confusion was the turbulence stirred up by the beating of daemonic wings.

Sathorael was too large now to be visible, and perhaps too attenuated to be tangible, but it was there. What had begun as a seed within a human Vessel was reaching the climax of its brief existence, and the product of its final metamorphosis was now obvious.

The grub that had begun as Nimian and had transformed itself by reckless consumption into a Lord of Change was now in the process of becoming a warpstorm: a warpstorm that would form a monstrous net in which to ensnare a fleet of Imperial starships.

Dathan still had consciousness enough to count the starships, a feat of which even Hycilla had been incapable.

There were twelve.

Dathan did not have consciousness enough to count the stars into whose bed the sun that lit his world had fallen, but he knew that there must be thousands of millions, perhaps hundreds of thousands of millions.

If the Imperium of Mankind spanned the whole of that starfield, he thought, how many starships must the Imperium have? Of what real significance could twelve ships possibly be?

Once, when Dathan was very young, his mother had scolded him for being wasteful because he had broken one of the nails that she had given him to repair the wooden fence of their chicken run.

'It's only a nail,' he had said. 'The smith has a bucket full of them.'

'Aye,' Ora had replied. 'And now we shall need another, and he will have one less. Our extra nail might have secured a horse's hoof, for lack of which the horse might cast his shoe, and strand its rider in the wasteland. And were that man to be lost, his children might go hungry, and all the children that they might have fathered and mothered might not come into existence at all – including the one that might have become the wisest dreamer Gulzacandra ever produced, the liberator of his people, and the scourge of Kalazendra.'

What his mother had been trying to explain was that everything great and wonderful that happened in the world depended for its fulfilment on a host of prior events, each of them part of a complex pattern of causes and effects, and that there was no way of knowing whether a tiny loss here and now might eventually be magnified into a far greater loss elsewhere and elsewhen.

Where had those twelve ships been going, when they were interrupted by Deir Ajao's telepathic cries for help? What difference would it make if they never arrived? Perhaps none, or very little – but perhaps not. For lack of one ship, a battle might be lost, or a world. For lack of twelve... Who could possibly know what was at stake here? Not Dathan, not Hycilla, not Sathorael – but perhaps the devious Chaos god that had made Sathorael knew, and cared.

The twelve ships were steering a course through warp-space for Dathan's world. Their Navigators had the sacred Astronomican to guide them. Dathan knew this because Hycilla knew it, and understood it to the extent that she understood it.

As soon as the ships re-entered what their commanders expected to be normal space they would be caught up in a warpstorm. Their final transition would, in effect, be sufficiently complicated and confused to make it impossible for them to reclaim their proper relationship with space and time. They would be destroyed – not merely ripped apart, in the way that the aircraft that had brought Deir Ajao to Sathorael had been ripped apart on landing, but turned inside out and subjected to even more peculiar contortions.

Dathan knew this not so much because Sathorael knew it – because Sathorael's capacity for knowing was rapidly dissolving – but rather because Sathorael was the warpstorm that would wreak such exotic havoc, and because a substantial part of him would also become the warpstorm, as would an even greater part of Hycilla.

Dathan and Hycilla and Sathorael would be torn apart along with the ships – but of the three, only Dathan would be able to reserve enough of himself to think about what was happening to them. Hycilla, like Sathorael, would be content to feel it.

But content was the wrong word, Dathan realised. She and the daemon would be far more than content. They would be ebullient, exultant and ecstatic. For them, the feeling would be everything: not merely the culmination of their existence but its justification and its glory. The fire of their lives would burn hotter and brighter than any other life – human or daemon – could ever achieve, and the two of them really would experience that blast as the ultimate bliss, as if nothing else could ever matter to any being except the manner of its burning.

But I am a man, Dathan thought, and I cannot do that. I am a man, and must ask myself what will come after me. I am a man, and must care about the answer. I am a man, and must serve the cause of mankind, no matter how many individual men have been my enemies and would-be murderers. The Imperium is my enemy now as it has always been, but because I am a man I must ask the more difficult question of whether it is also the enemy of another and even greater enemy – and, if so, which of those enemies I ought to hate the more.

The Imperium had destroyed everything Dathan held dear, except Hycilla. It deserved his hatred. But Dathan was a man, and he had to ask why. Had he only been a man, he could never have found the answer, but for the moment he was not, and he thought that he could see why. He thought that he could see the necessity of the Imperium. It was a bitter necessity, to be sure, but it was a necessity.

In a universe where peace was impossible, the cost of existence was war, and that was what the Imperium was: a war machine that spanned the stars, which dared to turn the weapons of the warp against the malign inhabitants of the warp.

The twelve ships attempted to come out of the warp then, in order to re-establish meaningful contact with space and time.

Instead, they were engulfed by the warpstorm that had been the daemon Sathorael.

Sathorael had found intelligence and imagination intriguing, and the business of thought quite fascinating, but it was no longer a being capable of calculation, vision or thought. Neither was Hycilla, whose subconscious self had been fully liberated by the power of the drug that made wise-dreaming possible.

'Wise' was the wrong word, Dathan realised. The drug helped psychically-gifted dreamers to see what they would never otherwise have been able to see, and to know what they would never otherwise have been able to know, but it was wrong to reckon that arcane insight as a species of wisdom. Wisdom was another kind of intelligence, which had far more reason in it than sight and knowledge.

I am the wise one here, Dathan thought, because I am the only one who still has any capacity for thought. They are fire, and can only burn. I am a man, and I can plan.

In the meantime, the Imperial ships were being torn apart. One by one, as they fell into the net that had been Sathorael, they were turned inside out. It was a surprisingly slow process – but Dathan remembered that the warp was a timeless place, whose sly interference with the world of space and time was as likely to distort duration as it was to distort distance.

The people inside the ships were turned inside out too, so that they wore their lights on the outside and their skin on the inside. Their blood remained confined to their veins for a surprisingly long time, but their complex contours were stained and polluted by a stinking warpaint of foodstuffs in various stages of digestion.

Oddly enough, they hardly noticed their inversion. It was as if, from their own points of view, they seemed to be perfectly normal – except, perhaps, for being slightly more self-absorbed than usual. But that was while they were still intimately bound to their ships, and to the tiny life-bearing worlds that those ships had contained. One by one, the inverted ships exposed their crews to the hungry void of deep space: the furious vacuum which sucked the blood from its fragile vessels, curdled their brains and burst their eyes like so many trodden grapes.

Had the soldiers on the starships not been wearing such restrictive armour they might have been more comfortable in their everyday work, but they did not seem to Dathan to be the kind of men who placed a high value on comfort. Their minds were entirely given over to discipline and calculation, to reverence and faith, to duty and purpose. The soldiers hardly knew what was happening to them as they were peeled and pulped, shredded and scathed. They died as bravely and as sanctimoniously as they had lived, praising their God-Emperor.

Their Navigators, on the other hand, realised quickly enough what was happening to them, because their inversion had wrenched their particular connection with the Astronomican out of true. They knew immediately that they were steering a new course, and that its destination was damnation – but they could not say so. Any words they might have spoken, like any screams they might have loosed, were lost and crushed inside themselves.

And the inversion was, of course, only the beginning.

Already, Dathan saw, the newly-metamorphosed beings were beginning to change again, to lose what little integrity they had left. They were becoming blurred, turning into smears of colour on the gaudy face of eternity.

This, Dathan understood, was when the real torment would begin. This was not a quick way to die, given the warpstorm's lascivious play with duration, and it was a bad one. The storm that had been Sathorael was sucking them in and digesting them, making nutrient of these new sacrifices just as it had made nutrient of the more ordinary deaths that had paved its stairway to the stars.

Dathan had no idea whether or not he could stop the process, but he knew that he had to try. He did not have to forgive his lifelong enemy the Imperium of Mankind, but he did have to deal with it as a human being, and not as some creature of the warp for whom thought was a disposable luxury and appetite was everything.

I am the only conscious mind that the storm has, he thought. I never surrendered my consciousness to Sathorael, nor could the daemon take it from me while it was so dull and fireless. I am the only conscious mind here, and I need only exert that consciousness to take control of what the storm has in place of limbs.

Alas, it wasn't that easy.

Dathan did reach out, mustering all his willpower, and he did indeed discover that he had the ability to influence the storm – but he was only a man, and the storm was not only bigger than a world but bigger than a solar system.

For a moment or two, Dathan felt that he might as well have been a tiny worm, almost invisible to the naked eye, which had burrowed into the brain of a giant, entertaining ridiculous delusions of grandeur as to the possibility of replacing the giant's own guiding intelligence. In truth, though, he was no mere invading parasite. The daemon had used him, and made him a part of its fast-evolving self. He did have power, if only he had will enough to use it and fortitude enough to bear the consequences of its use.

When he tried to hold back the storm, he felt the fury of the storm, and he felt it as fire.

It might have been preferable, he thought, to have been turned inside out. He felt the fire course through him, burning him alive – except that it did not consume him by turning him to smoke and ashes. It burned him and it continued to burn him, as if it might yet burn him for all eternity.

He felt his skin catch fire; he felt his heart and lungs roast; he felt the blood in his veins boil; he felt his brain melt – but all of this was mere feeling, and could not become actual unless he let it. All he had to do to prevent his body from burning in actuality was to cling stubbornly to consciousness, to refuse to become a mere bundle of emotions.

That was far more easily thought than done, but the mere fact that it could be thought was proof enough that it could also be done.

So Dathan burned while he fought the storm, and lived with the agony. He would not surrender the privilege of being a thinking being. No threat was adequate to make him do that, and no temptation. He was a man, and he had the power of choice, and he knew where his duty lay in the exercise of that choice.

Dathan understood now what a petty fool he had been to think himself a hero merely because he had shot a man with a stolen rifle. He understood now what a real hero was, and why the Imperium really did have heroes while their enemies had only victims of casual choice and corrupting temptation.

He could not quiet the storm, of course, or make it into anything other than it was, but he could disrupt the process by which it was tearing the Imperial ships apart, and everything within them. He could not even do that for long, but he did not have to.

He only had to win time for a few of the ships to make their escape.

Winning time from timelessness was difficult, but binding time was one thing that human consciousness was good at, one thing on which the human mind had a reasonably secure grasp.

Dathan reached out with the hands that still clasped Hycilla's, and won time.

Men who had been turned inside out were turned outside in again, awakening with a start from their moments of dreamlike self-absorption. They leapt to work, knowing that they were on the edge of destruction but also knowing what to do about it.

They implemented the procedures in which they had been trained. They prayed.

They contrived order in the face of Chaos.

Three ships escaped the trap. Not everyone aboard them survived, but their casualties were relatively light.

The survivors had not the slightest idea, of course, that they had been saved, let alone that they had been saved by Dathan. Had anyone told them what he had done, they would not have believed it – but even if they had, it would have made no difference to what they did next.

The three surviving ships fell upon the world that they knew as Sigmatus, and as they fell they rained indiscriminate destruction upon its face.

They sowed their bombs in bright daylight first, devastating every city in Kalazendra. They reduced Sostenuto to blasted rubble and melted the empty hulls of the ships that had brought their cousins to Sigmatus. Then they moved to devastate Gulzacandra, which still lay hidden in the darkness – until the long lines of explosions tore highways of light across its languid deserts and patchwork fields.

The time that Dathan had won for the three ships was a prize their masters were avid to use – and could have used far better had the warpstorm not followed them to the surface.

Had Sathorael not been such a short-lived entity, it might have repaired the damage that Dathan had done to its scheme, but the storm was becoming increasingly tenuous with every moment that passed. Its remnant had the power to make the stars swim in the world's multicoloured sky, and to prevent the ships from rising out of the atmosphere, but it did not have the power to turn them inside out or to shatter them into so many glowing shards.

So the ships landed.

Having destroyed a lost fragment of the Imperium, they became a lost fragment of the Imperium. Having brought a climax to one perverse adventure, they became the prologue of another.

And so the world went on: battered, blighted, burned and bruised but by no means unfit for human habitation, of a relatively primitive but admirably ingenious sort.

And so the world went on, and on, and on.

Until the next time.

EPILOGUE

DATHAN WOKE UP, not having dreamed at all. He turned away from the cryptic stare of Hycilla's sightless eyes to watch a dawn the colour of blood.

The disc of the half-risen sun was crimson. In order to reach the surface of the planet its rays had to pass through the veil of the revitalised warpstorm as well as the curtain of smoke and ash that the Imperium's bombs had thrown up. These two translucent barriers had mingled and merged, like two happy children larking about together, and the games they played with the light surely should have been a wonder to behold. The whole sky was red and orange, pink and violet, streaked with exotic rainbows and host to dancing storms – but Dathan observed it dispassionately, without the least trace of wonder.

When Dathan saw what the trailing edge of the warpstorm Sathorael had done to the native vegetation he toyed with the question of whether it might not have been more interesting to wake up a little earlier, but he seemed to be quite incapable of remorse or regret – or, indeed, any other emotion. The question passed him by unanswered, as unengaging as any other whim of the imagination.

The vegetation of the wasteland had been bleak and ugly even before the aircraft had come down, bringing further ruination in its fiery train as it ripped through thickets and scattered hot shrapnel. The bushes had been dry and thorny, their randomly-twisted branches rigid. The bulbous cacti had been even drier and whitely hirsute. The leaves of every plant in sight had been thin and spiky or squat and lumpy. There had been purples and greys in abundance, ochreous yellows, dark reds and scabrous pinks, and only fugitive hints of emerald green. The soil in which they grew had been desiccated, coarse and lustreless.

Things were different now.

While Dathan slept, the entire landscape had undergone a profound metamorphosis. The soil on which he stood was a black and glutinous loam, over which slime-moulds stretched in astonishing profusion. There were flowers everywhere, all in glorious bloom. There were lemon yellows and creamy whites, bold scarlets and pale blues. The leaves on every bush were huge and palmate, tailored into all manner of strange templates. The bushes were twice as tall as their predecessors, explosions of straight but supple stems which stirred in the warm wind. The basal spheres of the cacti had budded dozens of smaller spheres, many of which bore eruptions of even smaller spheres, and the majority had sleek coloured fur instead of white hairs.

The broken sections of the aircraft were still scattered all around, but they had already been colonised by hectic vinous growths, their fabric pitted by all manner of purple lichens.

The dead bodies of Orloc Melcarth, Ragan Balberith and Deir Ajao had lost every vestige of flesh, although the yellowed bones remained. Their skulls and rib-cages provided frames for lesser vines, whose pale flowers projected from the eye-holes and lodged between the front ribs.

Hycilla was still there, quite dead but also quite untouched by the processes of decay and reclamation. She was the last physical relic of the storm: the last repository of its energy and its power. Thus far, her body had retained its integrity, but she was dead flesh nevertheless, and in time she too would melt and fade into the new landscape, dispersing her body and her soul into the wilderness.

Dathan looked back, at last, into Hycilla's dead eyes, expecting to meet the ghost of her gaze. He had not yet released his grip on her cold hands.

She was dead, but she spoke to him nevertheless.

'Thank you, Dathan,' she said.

'For what?' he asked. It shouldn't have been easy to meet the accusing stare of those dead eyes, but Dathan didn't have to look away. He wasn't in the least intimidated.

'For betraying me.'

'Who's "me"? And how could anyone give thanks for a betrayal? It doesn't make sense.'

'You know who I am, Dathan,' Hycilla replied – although he noticed now that her lips weren't moving. 'Who else could give thanks for a betrayal? Who else could entertain such a paradoxical need?'

'I didn't do anything for you,' Dathan said, figuring that it didn't really matter who 'you' might be. 'I did what I did for my own reasons, because I am a man.'

'So you were,' Hycilla replied, placing no particular stress on that last word. 'But ask yourself, Dathan: how do you feel? And then: what will you become?'

'I don't feel anything,' Dathan said. It was true. He didn't feel anything at all. It was as though the feeling part of him had been stolen: cut out, ripped up and thrown away.

It was, of course, the feeling part of him that had been bound to Sathorael, merging with the daemon of the storm. What had remained unbound, separate and capable of independent action had been his conscious mind – but without the emotional part of him, his conscious mind could never have done what he did, because it would have had no motive force to drive it: no fear and no ambition; no pride and no lust; no sense of duty to the vast star-strewn family of humankind.

So what was he now – and what might he become?'

'I'll get it all back,' Dathan said, uncertain as to how he knew. 'I'll live, and the practice of living will bring back desire, and hope, and anxiety, and–'

'You might become a great sorcerer,' said dead Hycilla, 'with the right guidance.'

'I never had an atom of talent,' Dathan reminded her. 'That's why I'm still alive, and you're not.' He should have said, and Hycilla isn't, but he couldn't care about such niceties.

'There are exceptions to every rule,' dead Hycilla said. 'I adore exceptions – and you could learn to love them too, with just a little more practice. You don't have to be bound by rules if you don't want to be, Dathan. Think about that, when you become capable of wanting again. Ask yourself what a wise-dreamer might sensibly want, in a world such as this. You'll never know another.'

'I'll never serve your cause,' Dathan said. 'Never. I'll always betray you, because I'm a man. Mankind is all that stands between things like you and the ultimate annihilation of everything.'

'Nothing stands in the way of the ultimate annihilation of everything,' the god of Gulzacandra told him through Hycilla. 'In the end, everything possessed of life returns to air and ash and dust, and everything possessed of energy returns to listlessness. All that matters is how things burn. Not how quickly, but how. How could one delight in taking the side of Chaos, in being Chaos, if there were no Order to make a game of it? Where is the spice in easy victory? Where is the pride, the joy, the sense of achievement, the triumph? I need enemies, Dathan, even more than I need allies. There is nothing quite so precious to me as a traitor. But it doesn't work the other way around. Remember that, Dathan, when you begin to feel again. Order cannot tolerate traitors, or weaklings, or maladjustment, or creativity. Order needs nothing but order, and calm of mind. You can have that if that's what you decide to want, when you become capable of wanting anything at all, but you might do better to choose otherwise. If you choose wisely, you might become a greater sorcerer than Gavalon.'

'Never,' Dathan said. 'That's not what I am. I am a man, no matter what I might have lost in the defence of my kind. I can't and shan't become anything other than a man – and if I can't feel, then at least I'm free from all temptation. I am no longer corruptible.'

'That's good, very good,' the being that was not Hycilla said. 'The only thing more valuable to the Ruinous Powers than a corruptible soul is an incorruptible one. I would wish you long life if you were capable of it, and good luck if there were any such thing. However, I do believe you'll find that you stand a better chance of survival if you start walking westwards.'

Dathan let go of Hycilla's soft and leprous hands, and she toppled sideways.

No sooner had her body hit the ground than the flesh began to melt from her bones, flowing into the rich dark soil as if it were avid to fertilise the renewed world, eager to take part in its forthcoming adventure in evolution.

Dathan knew that he had not been dreaming. It would take time, he thought, to learn to dream again – and when he did, there would be not an atom of so-called wisdom in his dreams.

He raised himself to his feet, and lifted his face so that the warm red wind could stroke his feverless cheeks. The sun was arterially scarlet now that it had climbed a little higher in the blood-stained sky, and it was not in the least inviting.

Even so, when Dathan set out in search of a place to be, he headed eastwards rather than westwards, because he knew now that only a fool would take the word of a god. If he had been capable of wanting anything, he reasoned, he would surely have wanted to discover exactly what had become of the home that he had shared with his mother – who might, if fate had been unusually generous, be still alive.

There, if anywhere, would be the logical place to start his life over, in an orderly way.

ABOUT THE AUTHOR

When asked why he dresses entirely in black, Brian Craig claims to be in mourning for H.P. Lovecraft, but the real reason is too dreadful to reveal. The rumour that he joined the British Antarctic Survey in 1993 'to get away from it all' is false; he failed the medical and had to join the French Foreign Legion under a pseudonym instead. He is not allowed to discuss the reasons for his dishonourable discharge therefrom in 1999, but he is glad that he will now have more time to write and play cricket.

Brian Craig is the author of *The Wine of Dreams*, and also *Zaragoz, Plague Daemon* and *Storm Warriors* in an earlier range of Warhammer novels, and has contributed short stories to a range of anthologies, including *The Dedalus Book of Femmes Fatales*, edited by the infamous Brian Stableford. He is 28 and only looks older because his troubles have aged him.

More Brian Craig from the Black Library

THE WINE OF DREAMS

A Warhammer novel by Brian Craig

THE SWORD FLEW from Reinmar's hand and he just had time to think, as he was taken off his feet, that when he landed – flat on his back – he would be wide open to attack by a plunging dagger or flashing teeth. As the beastman leapt, Sigurd's arm lashed out in a great horizontal arc, the palm of his hand held flat. As it impacted with the beastman's neck Reinmar heard the snap that broke the creature's spine.

As soon as that, it was over. But it was not a victory. Now there was no possible room for doubt that there were monsters abroad in the hills.

DEEP WITHIN the shadowy foothills of the Grey Mountains, a dark and deadly plot is uncovered by an innocent young merchant. A mysterious stranger leads young Reinmar Weiland to stumble upon the secrets of a sinister underworld hidden beneath the very feet of the unsuspecting Empire – and learn of a legendary elixir, the mysterious and forbidden Wine of Dreams.

More Warhammer 40,000 from the Black Library

13th LEGION
A Last Chancers novel
by Gav Thorpe

GLANCING OVER my shoulder I see that we're at the steps to the command tower now. You can follow the trail of our retreat, five dead Last Chancers lie among more than two dozen alien bodies and a swathe of shotgun cases and bolt pistol cartridges litters the floor. A few eldar manage to dart through our fusillade, almost naked except for a few pieces of bladed red armour strapped across vital body parts. Almost skipping with light steps, they duck left and right with unnatural speed. In their hands they hold vicious-looking whips and two-bladed daggers that drip with some kind of venom that smokes as it drops to the metal decking. Their fierce grins show exquisitely white teeth as they close for the kill, their bright oval eyes burning with unholy passion.

ACROSS A HUNDRED blasted war-zones, upon a dozen bloody worlds, the convict soldiers of the 13th Penal Legion fight a desperate battle for redemption in the eyes of the immortal Emperor. In this endless war against savage orks, merciless eldar and the insidious threat of Chaos, Lieutenant Kage and the Last Chancers must fight, not to win, but merely to survive!

More Warhammer 40,000 from the Black Library

FIRST & ONLY
A Gaunt's Ghosts novel
by Dan Abnett

'THE TANITH ARE strong fighters, general, so I have heard.' The scar tissue of his cheek pinched and twitched slightly, as it often did when he was tense. 'Gaunt is said to be a resourceful leader.'

'You know him?' The general looked up, questioningly.

'I know *of* him, sir. In the main by reputation.'

GAUNT GOT TO his feet, wet with blood and Chaos pus. His Ghosts were moving up the ramp to secure the position. Above them, at the top of the elevator shaft, were over a million Shriven, secure in their bunker batteries. Gaunt's expeditionary force was inside, right at the heart of the enemy stronghold. Commissar Ibram Gaunt smiled.

IT IS THE nightmare future of Warhammer 40,000, and mankind teeters on the brink of extinction. The galaxy-spanning Imperium is riven with dangers, and in the Chaos-infested Sabbat system, Imperial Commissar Gaunt must lead his men through as much in-fighting amongst rival regiments as against the forces of Chaos. FIRST AND ONLY is an epic saga of planetary conquest, grand ambition, treachery and honour.

More Warhammer 40,000 from the Black Library

GHOSTMAKER
A Gaunt's Ghosts novel
by Dan Abnett

THEY WERE A good two hours into the dark, black-trunked forests, tracks churning the filthy ooze and the roar of their engines resonating from the sickly canopy of leaves above, when Colonel Ortiz saw death.

It wore red, and stood in the trees to the right of the track, in plain sight, unmoving, watching his column of Basilisks as they passed along the trackway. It was the lack of movement that chilled Ortiz.

Almost twice a man's height, frighteningly broad, armour the colour of rusty blood, crested by recurve brass antlers. The face was a graven death's head. Daemon. Chaos Warrior. *World Eater!*

IN THE NIGHTMARE future of Warhammer 40,000, mankind teeters on the brink of extinction. The Imperial Guard are humanity's first line of defence against the remorseless assaults of the enemy. For the men of the Tanith First-and-Only and their fearless commander, Commissar Ibram Gaunt, it is a war in which they must be prepared to lay down, not just their bodies, but their very souls.

More Warhammer 40,000 from the Black Library

NECROPOLIS
A Gaunt's Ghosts novel
by Dan Abnett

GAUNT WAS SHAKING, and breathing hard. He'd lost his cap somewhere, his jacket was torn and he was splattered with blood. Something flickered behind him and he wheeled, his blade flashing as it made contact. A tall, black figure lurched backwards. It was thin but powerful, and much taller than him, dressed in glossy black armour and a hooded cape. The visage under the hood was feral and non-human, like the snarling skull of a great wolfhound with the skin scraped off. It clutched a sabre-bladed power sword in its gloved hands. The cold blue energies of his own powersword clashed against the sparking, blood red fires of the Darkwatcher's weapon.

ON THE SHATTERED world of Verghast, Gaunt and his Ghosts find themselves embroiled within an ancient and deadly civil war as a mighty hive-city is besieged by an unrelenting foe. When treachery from within brings the city's defences crashing down, rivalry and corruption threaten to bring the Tanith Ghosts to the brink of defeat. Imperial Commissar Ibram Gaunt must find new allies and new Ghosts if he is to save Vervunhive from the deadliest threat of all – the dread legions of Chaos.